Indecent Proposals

Quills®

First Published 2009
First Australian Paperback Edition 2010
ISBN 978 0 733 59911 8

First Published 2009
First Australian Paperback Edition 2010
ISBN 978 0 733 59911 8

THE RAKES DEFIANT MISTRESS
© 2009 by Mary Brendan
Philippine Copyright 2009
Australian Copyright 2009
New Zealand Copyright 2009

THE MAJOR AND THE COUNTRY MISS
© 2009 by Dorothy Elbury
Philippine Copyright 2009
Australian Copyright 2009
New Zealand Copyright 2009

Published by
Harlequin Mills & Boon™
Level 5
15 Help Street
CHATSWOOD NSW 2067
AUSTRALIA

® and ™ are trademarks owned and used by the trademark owner and/or its licensee. Trademarks marked with ® are registered in Australia and in other countries.

Cover art used by arrangement with Harlequin Books S.A.. All rights reserved.

Printed and bound in Australia by
McPherson's Printing Group

CONTENTS

The Rake's Defiant Mistress

MARY BRENDAN

Mary Brendan was born in North London, but now lives in rural Suffolk. She has always had a fascination with bygone days, and enjoys the research involved in writing historical fiction. When not at her word processor, she can be found trying to bring order to a large overgrown garden, or browsing local fairs and junk shops for that elusive bargain.

Author Note

The path of true love never runs smooth, so the old saying goes, and I have written a duet of novels with those wise words in mind. In the first book, THE VIRTUOUS COURTESAN, it was certainly a fitting adage! The heroine, Sarah Marchant, had suffered a traumatic childhood. When her future was cruelly bound to that of Gavin Stone—something neither of them wanted—it seemed matters must only get worse...or would they?

This second story, THE RAKE'S DEFIANT MISTRESS, features Ruth Hayden as the heroine. Widowed when very young, she has also endured a great deal of heartache in her early years. Then Sir Clayton Powell arrives. He's a man she wants to refuse, but a scandal results in their engagement. Can a marriage without love survive?

May you enjoy them both to the full.

Chapter One

'I think I must ask you to leave, sir.'

The lady received no response to her firm request. The gentleman she had attempted to eject from her small sitting room continued to pace across the rug, stamping a deeper trench into its tired pile.

'Doctor Bryant!' Ruth Hayden's suffocated plea held a hint of irritation. 'I beg I will not have to again ask you to go.'

The fellow halted, exasperatedly planting his hands on to his hips. 'I cannot believe you will not hear me out, Mrs Hayden.' A grimace stressed his bewilderment. 'Why will you not at least let me fully explain to you the benefits—?'

'I need no full explanation, sir,' Ruth Hayden interrupted him briskly. 'I have the gist of your proposal and it is enough for me to want to spare you…spare us both…the embarrassment of any further mention of it. I am conscious of the honour you do me, but I cannot marry you. Now I must bid you good day.' Ruth walked swiftly to the sitting-room door and pointedly opened it.

As he realised he was being summarily dismissed, the look of surprise quit Dr Ian Bryant's features to be replaced by one of anger.

In the rural town of Willowdene he was an eminent member of society and not used to receiving such a set down. The woman delivering the snub was barely tolerated in company hereabouts and that made her attitude to his proposal the more unexpected. As his wife she would once more be welcomed into the fold.

He was a ruggedly good-looking man in his middle thirties with nothing exceptional or objectionable in his demeanour. He was moderately broad of shoulder and quite tall. Now he drew himself even higher in his shoes before stalking towards the exit.

'Had you not once given me reason to hope that you would welcome my attentions, madam, I would not be here at all.' His lips curled in satisfaction as he noticed how that barb unsettled her.

High spots of colour burned on Ruth's slanting cheekbones as she recalled the incident to which he referred. But she tilted her head to a proud angle and squarely met his eyes. 'I think on that occasion too, sir, you presumed too much,' she rejoined coolly. 'I was in need of a little comfort when my father died suddenly. I again thank you for giving it to me. Now there is no more to be said.' She opened the door a mite wider, but still he seemed reluctant to go. Eyes that were unwavering settled on her face as Dr Bryant relentlessly studied the object of his desire.

Ruth Hayden was beautiful rather than fashionably pretty. She was not blessed with delicate features and her complexion was not fair enough for what was considered nice in a genteel lady. Her thick dark brown hair had resisted sleek confinement in the pleat at her nape and glossy locks wisped untidily against her cheeks. Beneath defined brows were large chocolate-coloured eyes that were far too direct and steady for a modest female of gentle birth. The womanly trait he normally found alluring, flirtatiousness, was absent from her character. Today she might have blushed and lowered her eyelashes before him, but that was due to her being disconcerted, not playful. Yet in mocking contrast to her straitlaced attitude was the curvaceous body he had once—far too briefly—felt moulding to his. His eyes were drawn to it now: full high breasts and rounded hips that were separated by a divinely tiny waist he ached to girdle with his hands.

Her unequivocal rejection had astonished him as well as dented his pride. A woman in her unenviable position ought to have jumped at the chance to improve her status and prospects. But she had thwarted not only his desire to bed her, but to have her mother his infant son. Ian was abruptly jolted from his brooding thoughts by a polite reminder that he was outstaying his welcome.

'I have much to do, sir; I must insist you leave and again bid you good day.'

Without another word Ian strode out. Within a moment Ruth closed her eyes in relief as she heard the bolts being slid home. Her maid appeared on the threshold to the sitting room. 'Shall I put on the kettle, Mrs Hayden?' the girl asked in concern.

Ruth gave Cissie a small smile and a grateful nod. So Cissie knew she was in need of a little comfort! She did not believe Cissie to be an intentional eavesdropper. Her maid had sensed rather than heard the delicate nature of the conversation that had taken place moments ago between her and Dr Bryant. Cissie would have deduced from the doctor's grim expression that she'd declined his proposal. Now the girl was curious to know her reasons for turning down an offer of marriage from an eligible gentleman.

One only needed to glance about the sitting room to realise that Mrs Hayden lived frugally. The fresh herby atmosphere that wafted throughout the spotless cottage could not improve furniture that was shabby or furnishings that had seen far better days. If one were to venture into the kitchen and investigate the larders, similar proof of want would be found. The obvious conclusion to be drawn was that this widow's lot in life would improve dramatically were she to marry a rich widower.

And Dr Bryant was such a fellow—so everyone hereabouts thought. He had a fine home and income and had increased his wealth on marriage. Therefore it was reasoned that his worthy profession was a philanthropic vocation rather than necessary toil.

As Cissie went off to prepare the tea Ruth sank into a chair. She turned her head to frown over the bright budding gardens and wondered why she had, with so little thought given to the certain benefits she was rejecting, turned down Dr Bryant. She might have asked him for a little time to mull over becoming his wife. It was an accepted response by a lady startled by a marriage proposal.

When she'd been a gauche eighteen-year-old, Paul Hayden had taken her by surprise and asked her to marry him. In her tender innocence she had guessed it might be deemed vulgar, after so short an acquaintance, to seem too keen too soon, so had given him a blurted prevarication. A private smile curved her mouth at the sweet memory of it. But by the time he had reached the door and turned to take his leave, her overwhelming happiness had prompted her to fly to him and insist that she'd like nothing better than to be his wife. She had loved him too much to make him unnecessarily suffer her indecision.

Doctor Bryant did not stir any such passionate longing in her. But she had thought him to be her friend until the day he had ruined it all by asking her to become his mistress. Now he had lost his wife in childbed, he had improved his offer to her.

Was she simply a silly fool to yearn to fall in love with a man before she'd consider the advantages to be had in matrimony?

'You're becoming tiresomely repetitive, my dear,' the gentleman told the pouting brunette who was lounging, naked, amid rumpled silk sheets.

Undeterred by her lover's softly spoken reprimand, Lady Loretta Vane smoothed the sulky expression from her pretty face and rolled on to her belly in a flash of lissom white limbs. Satisfied with her seductive pose, she raised long dusky lashes to reveal limpid blue eyes. Triumphantly she noticed his flinty gaze drop to her lush breasts alluringly presented on an artfully plumped pillow.

Sir Clayton Powell stopped buttoning his shirt and sauntered back towards the four-poster where his mistress excitedly awaited his approach. As soon as he came within reach Loretta stretched out elegant fingers to curve on his thigh, her hard oval nails pressing indents in the material covering solid muscle.

'Come back to bed,' she invited huskily. 'Perhaps I might change your mind and show you what you will soon be missing if you don't make an honest woman of me.'

Clayton leaned towards her, planted a hand on the mattress either side of her slender figure. Sinuously she flipped on to her back and coiled her arms about his neck, dragging him close.

'Think what beautiful children we would have,' she whispered urgently against his mouth. 'A little girl with blonde hair like you and a boy…your heir…dark like me.'

Clayton smiled against her lips. 'And what does your fiancé think to bigamy and bastards?'

Loretta threw back her head and chuckled, deliberately tempting his lips to an alluring column of milky skin. She wriggled delightedly as a moist caress moved on her smooth white throat. 'He would be most put out...but it does not signify. You know I would drop Pomfrey tomorrow and take you in his stead.'

'Yes...I know you would,' Clayton said and lifted his head to look at her with slate-grey eyes. He touched his mouth to hers in an oddly passionless salute.

Just a short while ago the bed had been the scene of torrid lovemaking. Now his response to Loretta Vane's seductive teasing had cooled considerably. His change of attitude was not simply caused by his irritation at her constant marriage proposals. He'd no quarrel with the Honourable Ralph Pomfrey and had no intention of becoming embroiled in one because Loretta had now pinned her ambitions to net a wealthy husband on him.

It had recently come to light, when Pomfrey unwisely approached Claude Potts—a known blabbermouth—for a loan, that he might not be quite as flush as was generally thought. In fact, it was rumoured that Loretta's bank balance might be healthier than was Pomfrey's following a disastrous run of luck he'd had backing nags.

Thus, it had become more obvious why this pleasant fellow of impeccable lineage would propose marriage to a woman who, although a lady by name, was a courtesan by nature.

Loretta had been left a tidy sum by her late husband, Lord John Vane. She had already frittered away a good portion of it. Doubtless she was now fretting that, far from improving her prospects by marrying the Earl of Elkington's youngest son, she might put in jeopardy what remained of her little nest egg. It was surely no coincidence that her enthusiasm for the match had waned with Pomfrey's luck.

Worried by her lover's lack of response, Loretta tugged at Clayton's shirt front and slid her tongue on his lips to tempt him to kiss her properly.

'Pomfrey is your fiancé,' Clayton reminded her lightly, holding her by the wrists away from him. 'You will make a good couple. He is the right husband for you.' He released her as he said that and, collecting his jacket from the velvet *chaise longue*, pushed his arms into the sleeves.

'You are the right husband for me!' Loretta fiercely objected. Realising he was about to go before giving a satisfactory answer, she sprang upright and swung two shapely legs off the bed. Her honed features were no longer softened by sensuality, but set in determined lines that set aslant her full mouth and dark brows.

'I'm not the right husband for any woman…trust me on that,' Clayton returned with a wry smile as he negligently stuffed his cravat into a pocket. 'Do you want to go to the opera tomorrow evening?' he asked idly, his hand on the doorknob.

'Marry me!' Loretta demanded. 'It's *you* I want. It's always been you I want. *We* make a good couple. I swear if you do not, Clayton…if you do not…' she repeated, playing for time to rally enough courage to issue the ultimatum.

'If I do not?' Clayton prompted. He leaned back against the door to watch her, while shooting two pristine shirt cuffs out of his jacket. A steady dark gaze was levelled on her flushing face. 'Come, tell me what you plan to do to punish me.'

'I will finish it between us,' she stated in a brittle tone and tilted her chin to an obstinate angle. 'I will go ahead and marry Ralph Pomfrey as soon as maybe and once I am his wife I will not cuckold him. I will sleep with only my husband.'

A spontaneous laugh broke in Clayton's throat. 'I'm impressed. You're going to be a faithful spouse. That's most unusual for the *ton* and most certainly novel for you, my dear. I'm sure your late departed husband would be miffed to know you've reformed rather too late for him to gain any benefit. I hope Pomfrey appreciates your sacrifice.'

Ralph Pomfrey was aware—as was the whole of the *ton*—that he'd proposed marriage to the woman who had been Clayton Powell's mistress for over six months. The knowledge that his betrothed was continuing to sleep with another man seemed not to trouble Pomfrey. Naturally, it was assumed that once the nuptials were imminent the liaison would end, at least until Loretta had done her duty and provided her husband with a legitimate son and heir.

'You won't find it all so amusing when I turn you away,' Loretta said with a choke of annoyance. She had used her ace and had it immediately trumped. Now she wished she had saved it for another time, but could not withdraw it. 'You won't find another woman to please you as well as I do.'

In Clayton's view, that petulant afterthought *was* her ace and it kept him loitering by the door while he gave both it and her his attention. Without doubt Loretta Vane was an enthusiastic and uninhibited bed partner.

A slow appraisal roamed over the naked young woman provocatively posing on the edge of the bed. Her figure was undeniably lush and perfectly proportioned. But it wasn't just Loretta's physical charms that made men keen to win her favours. She'd gained a reputation as a wanton with an appetite she'd been previously unashamed to sate in adulterous affairs during her first marriage. If she'd meant what she said about staying true to Pomfrey once they were wed, it would indeed be an odd union. Polite society was, for the most part, composed of people untroubled by discreet promiscuity within marriage, once the nursery was full.

Clayton tilted Loretta a wry smile that hinted at his capitulation. He approached her, noticing sultry triumph glittering in her eyes as she rose gracefully from the bed to sway towards him.

'How do you know you please me very well?' he asked and pressed a kiss to the pulse bobbing beneath the porcelain skin of her throat. 'I've never told you so.'

'You don't need to say. I know I do,' she said huskily. An ardent gleam was darkening her blue eyes as she peeped up at him. 'Shall I make you say it?'

'Do you think you can?'

'I *know* I can,' she promised and flicked her small tongue to curl on his ear.

'Well…in that case I suppose it would be rude to decline the challenge,' Clayton said before his lips hardened on hers, parting her mouth wide so he could immediately plunge inside. He gasped a laugh as her nimble fingers immediately opened the buttons covering the magnificent bulge straining the material at his groin. They slipped inside to slide with skilful rhythm until he growled at her to cease. She did so and instead lithely dropped to her knees in front of him.

With blood pounding through his veins, Clayton curved long fingers over the dark head rocking efficiently in front of his hips. With a groaning oath he tensed and drew her up. Swinging Loretta in to his arms, he carried her back to bed.

At six in the morning Clayton again shrugged in to his coat and approached the door of Loretta's boudoir. As she softly called his name he turned to smile at the dishevelled sight of her. Her half-open eyes were glazed in torpor.

'I know I pleased you,' she purred. 'Deny it if you can…'

'You pleased me. Without doubt you make an excellent paramour.'

Sensual languor was still drugging her mind, but Loretta frowned at the amusement in his tone. 'I'll make a far better wife than mistress. I meant what I said, Clayton,' she whispered throatily.

He shot her a grin. 'So did I,' he said and went out, quietly shutting the door.

A nebulous March morning was moistening the cobbles as Clayton emerged into the street. He turned in the direction of Belgravia Place, a leafy square hemmed by elegant town houses, the largest of which was his home.

John Vane had left his young widow her own apartment conveniently situated in the heart of town. Thus it was just a short time later, and with a weak dawn light at his back, that Clayton was taking the stone steps to his mansion two at a time.

On entering the hallway he was surprised to see Hughes, his butler, striding towards him as though anticipating his arrival. The elderly servant had been in the army in his heyday and, being sprightly for his years, still strutted about as though on parade.

'An urgent post arrived, Sir Clayton,' he told his master and held out the tray on which reposed a parchment. If he deemed it odd to see his master arrive home at daybreak with his cravat trailing from a pocket and the remainder of his clothes in a state likely to give his valet an attack, he gave no outward sign.

Clayton took the letter while issuing an order. 'Arrange for hot water for a bath, please, and coffee and toast.'

'At once, sir,' Hughes said with a crisp nod and marched off.

Clayton took a proper look at the writing on the note he held. A grin split his face. He recognised the hand as that of his good friend Viscount Tremayne. He guessed that, as the post was urgent, Gavin was already on his way to Mayfair from his estate in Surrey. Clayton dropped into his chair in his study and read the very welcome news that Gavin Stone was due in town today.

Chapter Two

'Oh! You have not brought him for me to cuddle!'

'You may cuddle me instead!' Viscountess Tremayne teasingly replied and proceeded to give Ruth a warm hug. 'I have missed you,' she said fiercely.

'And I have missed you,' Ruth said simply, tightening her arms about her best friend. 'I am longing to hear more wonderful news about Surrey. But first tell me—where is that darling baby boy?'

'He has been snuffling a little bit and I thought it best to leave him in the warm with his nurse as the weather has turned so bitter cold.' Sarah gave Ruth an expressive look. 'James is teething and I fret that he might take a chill.' A soft maternal smile preceded, 'He is a darling little chap, the image of his papa, and at times I feel I will die for love of him.'

Ruth linked arms with Sarah and led the way to the sitting room. Once her visitor had shed her hat and gloves, they sat in comfortable fireside chairs. Logs were crackling valiantly in the grate, keeping at bay the draughts. Outside was weak spring sunlight, but the March winds were strong enough to infiltrate the casements and stir the curtains.

Ruth poured tea from the prepared tray that sat on a table

close to the hearth. Once they had sipped at the warming brew their conversation was resumed with a fluency that mocked the long months and miles that had separated them. To an observer they might have been dear sisters, so affectionate and natural were they as they chatted and warmed their palms on the china cups.

'How long will you stay at Willowdene Manor?'

'Until Michaelmas…if I have my way,' Sarah said with a grin.

Ruth cocked an eyebrow at her friend. 'And I imagine you have a tendency to get your own way.' She sighed in *faux* sympathy. 'Poor Gavin!'

'Poor Gavin, indeed!' Sarah mocked, but her expression softened as she named her beloved husband. 'He likes it very well when I get my own way, I assure you he does,' she added saucily.

'Hussy!' Ruth chided and clucked her tongue.

'Indeed I am,' Sarah agreed with an impish look from beneath her lashes. 'And ever was…as you know…'

An amicable quiet settled on the room for a moment while they dwelled on the events Sarah had alluded to and how, subsequently, her life had improved so wonderfully.

Just a year ago Lady Tremayne had been Sarah Marchant, a kept woman, shunned by the locals as a brazen harlot. Following her lover's untimely death, she had been living frugally in the rural town of Willowdene when she met and fell in love with Gavin Stone, new master of Willowdene Manor. A few months after their wedding in the chapel at the Manor, Sarah had moved with her husband to his magnificent estate in Surrey to take up her new life as Viscountess Tremayne.

Now Sarah was a fine lady, with an adorable baby son. Once the two women had been united in living quietly, ostracised by the townsfolk. Now a chasm had opened between

their positions. Sarah's status as the wife of a distinguished
peer of the realm meant her company was highly sought by
everyone, especially the hypocritical. But far from resenting
her friend's astonishing good fortune, Ruth was glad that
Sarah had been so blessed.

'You're very happy,' Ruth stated with quiet contentment.
'I knew you would be. Gavin is a fine gentleman and all that
gossip about his roguish ways was piffle.'

'Not quite…' Sarah demurred. 'Besides, roguish ways
have their benefits,' she said archly. 'Gavin says he now has
too many responsibilities to rake around town. He leaves that
to his friend, Sir Clayton Powell, who, by all accounts, still
does it very well.'

Ruth lowered her teacup and cocked her head to one side.
'I remember him. He came to Willowdene and stayed for a
short while when Gavin was here chasing after you.'

'He did, indeed.'

'Would it worry you if soon you saw Sir Clayton again?'
Sarah recalled that Ruth had been rather wary of her
husband's best friend. 'One of the reasons we are back in
Willowdene—apart from to see you, of course—is to make
arrangements to have James christened at the Manor's
chapel.' She placed down her cup to continue. 'I so wanted
to have the ceremony here where we were married and where
my best friend is. I can't deny that the chapel at Tremayne
Park is much finer than the one at Willowdene Manor, but it
won't do.' She paused. 'And we very much want you to agree
to be James's godmother. Please say you will.'

'I would be most happy to accept,' Ruth said huskily.
Spontaneous tears glossed her eyes at the great honour and
privilege being bestowed upon her.

'That is good!' Sarah exclaimed in delight. 'Clayton is to
be godfather. Gavin says he must be asked, for beneath the

heart of a scoundrel beats one of pure gold.' She gestured in emphasis. 'Gavin says he takes his responsibilities most seriously. His heir—his nephew that is, for there were no children from his own marriage—is being educated at Clayton's vast expense.'

'He is married?' Ruth spluttered, faintly amused. 'And still he rakes around town as if a bachelor?'

'Oh, he *was* married.' Sarah inclined her head to impart, 'Apparently it was a long time ago and a very great *mésalliance* that lasted barely a year. His wife, Priscilla, led him a merry dance, then defected with a foreign count! I do not know all the ins and outs, but I know the marriage was annulled and Clayton was, from Gavin's report, very bitter over it all at the time.' A sigh stressed her sadness. 'Clayton has vowed never again to wed and that is why he is grooming his nephew to take the role his own son ought to have occupied.'

'Perhaps I need not have worried that he might have dug into my past and found skeletons.' Ruth raised her dark brows. 'It seems he has a scandal of his own to keep buried. So to answer your question: I do not mind if I meet him again.'

'You needn't worry over him asking impertinent questions. I've come to know him a little, and to like him a lot. He is most charming and mannerly.' After a brief pause Sarah said firmly, 'You must agree to dine with us both this evening. It is all arranged,' she insisted as she glimpsed her friend preparing to object from good manners and the fear of playing gooseberry. 'Gavin is not yet home. He had to break his journey in the City as he had business to attend to. But he is due to arrive by six and in time to dine. We both said how nice it would be for you to join us this evening and celebrate our return to the Manor. And of course you will see baby James.' That last was added in a cajoling tone that made Ruth smile as she guessed its purpose.

'In that case, I would be delighted to join you both.' Ruth accepted with a dip of her dark head.

Sarah grasped Ruth's hands and gave them an affectionate squeeze. 'Good,' she breathed. 'Now, tell me what I have been missing in Willowdene? I thought I might die laughing when you wrote to me about Rosamund Pratt's fall from grace! And with an ostler at the Red Lion, too!' Sarah chuckled as heartily as she had on first learning that the respectable matron who had been particularly mean to them both had been caught rolling in hay with a tavern groom young enough to be her son. 'I want all the latest tattle, you know!'

Ruth, too, had been savouring the memory of Mrs Pratt's come-uppance, but now her amusement faded. 'Well, you have arrived at the right time to be the first to know some gossip. I imagine by the end of the week the rumour mill will be grinding in Willowdene.'

That information was delivered in such an odd tone that Sarah immediately begged to know more.

'I have recently received a marriage proposal from Dr Bryant. I turned him down.'

Sarah's eyes grew round and her lips parted in astonishment. She knew that the doctor had propositioned Ruth over a year ago. She knew, too, from a letter she'd received from Ruth, that later that year Ian Bryant's wife had tragically died in childbed. 'How did he take it?' she eventually blurted.

'Not very well, I'm afraid. He seemed astounded by my answer. I had to ask him more than once to leave. Eventually he did go, wearing a thunderous expression.'

'He assumed you would accept.' Sarah sat back in her chair.

'He assumed I would be very grateful.' Ruth's small teeth worried at her lower lip. 'He did not say so, but I could tell from his attitude.' A humourless little laugh preceded, 'Of course, the whole of Willowdene will join him in thinking me a fool to reject him.' She shot a frown at Sarah. 'He turned up without warning and I would never have guessed what had prompted his visit. But why did I turn him down with so little consideration given the benefits attached to what he offered?'

'Because you don't love him?' Sarah gently advanced.

'No, I don't love him...but is that reason enough to decline a nice home and financial security?'

'I can't answer that for you,' Sarah replied. 'But instinctively you thought it was. You adored Paul and I can understand why you would again want to have a husband to love.'

'It is rather vexing to have been indulged in a love match,' Ruth wryly complained. 'It is equally irksome to have a friend who is blissfully happy with her rich, handsome lord.' Ruth gave Sarah a mock-stern look. 'Now I constantly berate fate for not being equally kind to me.'

'If it is of help, I too would often pray fate might be kind to me, just a little bit.' Sarah clasped Ruth's hands in comfort. 'And eventually it was.'

'How long must I wait for that little bit?' Ruth asked with wry gravity. 'After nine years as a widow perhaps it is time I was sensible and stopped pining for heroes on white chargers to happen by.' She gave a sigh. 'I have to admit that if I were to be given a list of all the available gentlemen hereabouts and told I must pick from it a husband, Dr Bryant would probably be the most appealing to me.'

'Yet instinctively you refused him,' Sarah gently reminded Ruth. 'So we must widen your circle of gentlemen acquaintances forthwith. If you were to socialise in London, you would attract suitors like bees to a honeypot.'

'I doubt that an impecunious widow of twenty-eight years...soon to be twenty-nine...who has forgotten how to dance and flirt will seem very sweet to our drones,' Ruth said ruefully.

'I can teach you how to dance and how to flirt,' Sarah offered impishly. 'Not that I think you will need much reminding on the latter once the right gentleman comes along.'

Ruth rested back into the sofa and gave her friend a tranquil smile. 'You always cheer me up. Thank you. I now feel much less sorry for myself. Things are not so drear. I have this cottage and a few investments Papa left to help me get by. I think I will settle on waiting in Willowdene for my knight in shining armour. After all, there are far worse places to be—Almack's wallflower corner for a start!' She gave an exaggerated shudder on mentioning the renowned matchmaking venue in London. As a débutante of seventeen she had been there regularly and danced with young bucks in the market for a suitable wife. In the event she had met her future husband, Paul Hayden, at her aunt's house. But she could quite clearly recall the alcove in Almack's ballroom where the more mature single ladies—who acted as chaperons and companions to the débutantes—would congregate. The thought of ever joining their number was as depressing now as it had been then.

'Come, I shall wait while you get ready and we will return to the Manor together in the landau. There is still time to cuddle James before he is put to bed. And there is so much more I want to tell you about Tremayne Park. When we return to Surrey you must come too.'

'I imagine your husband might want to take you on honeymoon now you are well enough to travel,' Ruth protested laughingly. She got to her feet to get ready to go out. The thought of a very pleasant evening spent with her friends, and her first sight of their darling baby boy, cheered her enormously.

* * *

'I've always liked the silver-grey silk, but the plum satin is pretty too.'

'The silver-grey it is,' Ruth said and put the other gown away.

'Do you think Dr Bryant is sufficiently rebuffed or might he return to try again?' Sarah asked as Ruth went about her *toilette* quite unconcerned by her friend's observation or her uninvited assistance in closing buttons or pinning curls that were hard to reach.

'I think he is too indignant to be persistent,' Ruth answered. She stood up from the stool, pleased with her appearance. She had collected her warm coat and hat before she concluded, 'I think I have heard the last from him on that score. When he left he looked as though his pride had taken a hefty dent.'

'You've dented her pride and a woman scorned is best avoided for as long as possible.'

'Amen to that,' Clayton agreed, scowling at his friend's wry philosophy. His black humour didn't subdue Viscount Tremayne's amusement. As his friend chuckled beneath his breath, Clayton leaned back into the sumptuous squabs of the splendid travelling coach that bore the crest of the Tremayne clan and was presently heading, at breakneck speed in the hope of outrunning the snow clouds, towards Willowdene Manor.

Clayton was glad to be spending time with his good friend and glad to be away from the metropolis for a while. Yet niggling at his conscience was a feeling that he was fleeing from an unpleasant situation and he never usually did that. Beneath his breath he cursed Loretta Vane for having managed to spoil his long-awaited reunion with Gavin and his family.

Shortly after Gavin had arrived at Clayton's home that afternoon a letter from his mistress had been delivered. It had conveyed the outrageous news that Loretta expected him to arrange for their betrothal to be immediately gazetted. In anticipation of his submitting to that action, she had written to Pomfrey to warn him of his jilting. Loretta had also found the gall to infer that she'd dropped Pomfrey at Clayton's behest…as though Clayton had browbeaten her into it.

After Clayton had spent an incredulous few moments rereading the unsubtle blackmail, he had been vacillating between laughing out loud and swearing at the ceiling. Seething anger had triumphed and he had screwed the perfumed paper in a fist and hurled it as far as he could while fighting down the need to storm straight to her house and shake some sense into the scheming minx.

He knew he would never allow himself to be coerced into marrying her, no matter how devious her strategies. A curt, unequivocal note had been despatched to tell her that. It had also made it clear that their relationship was at an end and that shortly his lawyer would contact her regarding a settlement.

Aware of his friend's steady gaze on him, Clayton turned his head aside to stare at the dusky passing landscape. The first fat flakes of snow drifted past the carriage window, but still Clayton's simmering fury at Loretta's scheming preoccupied his mind. 'The vixen is intent on stirring up trouble between Pomfrey and me,' he remarked, almost to himself.

'Don't rise to the bait.'

'I've no intention of doing so. But Pomfrey might. He won't want to be made a laughing stock over this. He might feel obliged to act on it simply to protect his family's good name.'

'You think he might call for pistols at dawn?' Gavin asked with a sardonic smile. He knew very well—as did the whole of the *ton*—that his friend was an excellent shot and unlikely to be challenged by a sane man to a duel. 'Pomfrey has his pockets to let, not his attic. He won't allow her to pull his strings any more than will you.'

'She is extremely adept at pulling the strings of gentlemen.'

'I'm sure,' Gavin said on a dry chuckle. 'Let's hope Pomfrey is able to resist her persuasion as well as you can.'

Clayton stretched out his long legs comfortably in front of him and a slow grin softened his features. 'You'd best tell the driver to slow down. The bad weather's caught up with us.'

Gavin whipped his head about to frown at the falling snow. The urgent need to be reunited with his beloved wife and baby son made him reluctant to issue the order. With a sigh he realised he risked never seeing them again if they continued to drive at reckless speed on roads that would soon be treacherous. Having taken Clayton's good advice and instructed the driver to rein in and take extreme care negotiating the road, he settled back into the seat and turned his mind again to his friend's unfortunate plight.

'It could all be a bluff, in any case,' Gavin reasoned. 'Lady Vane might not have sent Pomfrey a letter yet. She might be hedging her bets. I'll warrant she won't drop Pomfrey until she accepts it's all over with you.'

'I'm inclined to agree on that,' Clayton said reflectively. 'If she doesn't understand plain English, as soon as I get back to town I'll make sure she knows that I mean what I say.'

'There is one certain way to make her accept you mean what you say and that you'll never have her as your wife.'

'And that is…?' Clayton asked with lazy interest.

'Marry someone else,' Gavin said.

Chapter Three

'I do hope Gavin has put up for the night somewhere. It would be foolhardy to travel on in such dreadful weather.'

Ruth gently settled baby James in his crib before turning her attention to the boy's mother. Sarah had spoken in a voice sharpened by anxiety and with her melancholy gaze directed through the nursery window.

Inside the Manor all was cosy and warm, but sloping away from the house the lawns, that this afternoon had been murky green, appeared icy white. It was after eight o'clock in the evening and more than two hours since the time of Gavin's expected arrival. The snow had stopped falling and the sky had become the darkest shade of blue, threatening a night of perilous frost lay ahead. A pale, hard moon had escaped from a scrap of cloud and beneath its faint light the snow scintillated back at the stars.

'It is possible Gavin has not yet set out at all,' Ruth soothingly reminded. 'I expect he has sensibly remained in London if the snow has come from that direction.' It was a valid reassurance, given more than once since the snow started, yet it did little to erase the look of strain from the Viscountess's features. Sarah's small teeth continued to nip ferociously at her lower lip. Forlornly she peered at the long driveway that led to the house as though willing her husband's carriage to hove into view.

When they had travelled together from the hamlet of Fernlea, where Ruth lived, the air had held a cruel effervescence. But the breeze had kindly whipped the heavy clouds before it, giving them no chance to hover and shed their load. Within an hour of their arrival at the Manor the elements had turned against them. The wind had dropped, leaving the heavens concealed behind an unmoving blanket of sullen grey. The first gentle flurries had seemed harmless, but inexorably the dainty flakes had thickened and settled on the ground. Sarah and Ruth had taken turns at the window to report on the creeping progress of the frosting on the grass. Now the two women stood side by side, silently surveying the treacherous white landscape that stretched as far as the eye could see.

'There is the tavern at Woodville.' Ruth quickly attempted to comfort her friend. Sarah's countenance had become as still and pale as the scenery they gazed upon. 'If Gavin was close to home when the weather took a turn for the worse, I expect he instructed his coachman to pull in there.' Again the suggestion was valid: Woodville was a small town situated about seventeen miles south of Willowdene and the King's Head was a well-known stopping point for travellers going to and from London.

'Yes, I'm sure he would have done that.' Sarah managed a constrained little smile. 'Gavin would not be foolish enough to carry on regardless simply to get home to us…would he?'

'Of course not,' Ruth reassured fraudulently and drew her friend away from the window and back into the room. 'Little James is a contented soul. His nurse must dote on him,' she said, trying to divert Sarah's attention to something pleasant as they sat down by the cot.

A moment after they had settled into their chairs to watch James peacefully dozing, Sarah suddenly cocked her head, then leaped to her feet. In a trice she had flown back to the window and was craning her neck to peer out. 'He is here!' she sobbed out at the glass. She whirled about to gulp at Ruth, 'The carriage is here.'

Quickly Ruth joined her at the window and was instantly enveloped in Sarah's hug. 'Oh, thank Heavens! He is safely home.' Sarah snuffled back tears of blessed joy, her eyes glistening with the strength of her relief.

'You must go and welcome him.' Ruth was well aware that Sarah yearned to do so. 'I shall be quite happy to stay here with this darling boy if I may.'

'Gavin will think me quite a nincompoop to get in such a state.' Sarah knuckled away the wet that dewed her lashes. But she was soon at the door, leaving Ruth to gaze down, soft-eyed, at the infant left in her care. James was sleeping soundly, his cherubic face turned away from her. Carefully, so as not to disturb him, Ruth drew the covers closer about him, then stroked a tiny curled palm. Reflexively the baby clutched at her finger. Ruth felt her chest constrict and an ache surged up her throat at the memory of another baby—one whose delicate fingers had remained cold and unresponsive to her loving touch.

Ruth went to sit close by the fire. She eased back gratefully into the comfy chair, realising that she was quite enervated. In truth she, too, had begun to feel extremely concerned for Gavin's safety as nightfall came with no sign of a thaw or the arrival of the master of the house. Feeling now relaxed and quite cosy, she allowed her weary eyelids to fall.

The baby's whimpering woke her. Immediately Ruth

looked at the fire; it had burned low in the grate. She then glanced at the clock on the mantel. It was approaching nine o'clock. Jumping to her feet, she quickly went to peer in the cot. From his scrunched, angry face and drawn-up knees, and from female intuition, Ruth guessed that colic was the culprit.

Having lifted the fretful baby to her shoulder, she began murmuring soothingly to him. Rhythmically she rubbed at his back in the hope of easing his cramps while walking towards the door. The corridor was deserted. The baby's nurse had earlier been dismissed for the afternoon so Sarah and Ruth could chat and enjoy each other's company in private. With no idea where she might find James's nurse, and guessing Sarah and Gavin might be in the small salon, Ruth headed off in that direction.

'Mrs Hayden?'

Ruth had traversed many yards of quiet, carpeted corridor and was close to the top of the majestic staircase when she heard her name called in a cultured baritone voice.

Turning about, she stared, astonished, at a tall blond gentleman who was strolling towards her. She recognised him at once and that was odd, she obliquely realised, for after their brief introduction—which could not have lasted more than a few minutes—she had never again seen Sir Clayton Powell. It was equally odd that he should remember her after that meeting in Willowdene over a year ago. Or perhaps Sarah or Gavin had informed him she was a guest this evening.

'I had no idea you were staying at Willowdene Manor,' he said pleasantly as he came closer and executed a polite bow. 'Our hosts made no mention of it.'

'I had no idea you would be here either, sir,' Ruth said quickly. So her presence had not been mentioned, yet he *had* recognised her. 'And I am not staying here. I received an invitation to dine this evening with the Viscount and Viscountess.'

'Do you live close by?' Clayton asked with a frown. 'The roads are now virtually impassable. I doubt you will get home tonight.'

That thought had already occurred to Ruth. She had guessed that Sarah would kindly offer her a bed for the night. And Ruth would have accepted, despite having no night things with her. She would never contemplate putting at risk a coach and driver by insisting on going home through miles of lanes blocked by snow. A short while ago the thought of staying a day or two while they waited for a thaw had not presented a problem. Now, for some odd reason, the thought of sleeping beneath the same roof as this gentleman made her feel awkward.

'You have both arrived safely, if a little tardy,' Ruth pointed out rather lamely.

'Gavin would have moved heaven and earth to do so.'

'I imagined he would,' Ruth replied wryly. 'And so did Sarah. It worried her half to death that he would take risks to get here.'

'The power of love,' Clayton muttered exceedingly drily, but he cast a fond look at the baby boy fidgeting on Ruth's shoulder. 'Should he not be abed?'

'I think he should,' Ruth answered politely, yet rather indignant on hearing him sound so cynical. He might have been embittered by a bad marriage, but he had no right to scoff at her dear friends' wedded bliss. 'His nurse was given the afternoon off and I'm just on my way to find Sarah,' Ruth informed him briskly and took a step towards the head of the stairs. 'I think he might have a pain…or perhaps it has passed,' she said as quite an embarrassing noise and unpleasant smell issued from the little boy's rump.

Clayton grinned. 'I imagine young James is feeling much better now.'

An involuntary giggle escaped Ruth, despite her cheeks having turned pink. 'Still, I shall look for Sarah and hand him over. We were in the nursery when she heard the coach arrive and she rushed off to greet Gavin. I was on my way to the small salon. They might have gone there. I expect they have much news to catch up on.'

'Indeed,' Clayton drawled, amusement far back in his slate-grey eyes. 'But I doubt you'll find them in there yet.' He paused as though mentally phrasing his next words. 'I believe Gavin went to his chamber to freshen up after the journey. Sarah accompanied him.'

'Oh…I see,' Ruth said and averted her face to hide her blushing confusion. She felt quite silly for not having guessed that the two lovebirds would find an opportunity to have some time alone on being safely reunited.

While Ruth composed herself by fussing over the baby, Clayton began to subtly study her with a very male eye. He'd been attracted to her when they had briefly met in Willowdene town despite the fact she had been garbed head to toe in mourning clothes. She'd been capably driving a little pony and trap through the High Street and, from their short conversation that day, he'd learned that she wore weeds because her father had recently died. He'd also learned that she was related by marriage to one of his commanding officers, Colonel Hayden. It was a while later that he'd learned from Gavin that Ruth Hayden had been a widow for many years.

Clayton's roving appraisal continued and he knew he'd been right in instinctively sensing that beneath the dreary bombazine that had been shrouding her body on that occasion, and the dark bonnet brim that had made sallow her complexion, was a woman of rare beauty.

On first glance Ruth Hayden's features might appear rather severe, yet on finer appraisal were undoubtedly exquisite. Her deep brown eyes were fringed by lengthy black lashes and topped by delicate brows that looked soft as sable. Her nose was thin, her mouth asymmetrical with a lower lip that was fuller than the curving cupid's bow on top. She was petite, her smooth peachy cheek barely reached his shoulder, and fragile wrist bones were in his line of vision as she cuddled James close to her. But her figure was generously curvaceous in all the right places. The weight of the baby pressing on her chest had accentuated a satiny ivory cleavage swelling above her bodice. His hooded eyes lingered a moment too long on silver silk straining enticingly across her bosom.

Feeling once more adequately self-possessed, Ruth looked up and immediately her cheeks regained a vivid bloom as she noticed Sir Clayton eyeing her breasts. On the previous occasion when they had conversed she had sensed he found her interesting, and not just because he'd discovered he was acquainted with her in-laws. At the time she'd dismissed the idea he was attracted to her as fanciful and scoffed at her conceit. Yet there was no denying that she'd just caught him regarding her lustfully. Knowing that he found her desirable caused a peculiar mixture of uneasiness and excitement to tumble her insides.

It might have been many years since she had lain with her husband, or even been kissed, but she could recognise the signs that a man wanted her. She had seen the same smouldering intensity at the back of Ian Bryant's eyes just a couple of days ago when he proposed to her. She had known for a year or more that Ian wanted to bed her. But the doctor didn't possess skill enough to neutralise a tense situation, or his passion, as it seemed this man could.

Sir Clayton didn't look in the least disconcerted at being caught out. He raised a long finger, stroked the baby's soft cheek and lightly remarked, 'There's a young maid hovering at the end of the corridor.' He gave Ruth a nonchalant smile. 'Perhaps she has come to see to James.'

Ruth slowly expelled her pent-up breath. She pivoted about, grateful for the distraction, and gave young Rosie a beseeching look. At the signal the nursemaid immediately hastened to them and dipped a curtsy.

'Beggin' your pardon, ma'am…sir…' she began in her lilting Irish way, 'but the mistress did tell me to come to settle the little lad down sooner. When I said to her that I'd found you was asleep and so was little James, she said to leave it for a while and not to disturb you at all.'

Ruth gave the nervous girl a smile. She could tell that Rosie was in awe of the handsome gentleman by the way she kept sliding glances at Sir Clayton, then blushing and shuffling on the spot.

Ruth handed over her precious burden. 'I think he might need some urgent attention,' she told the girl and gently patted at the baby's bottom.

Rosie took the baby carefully and with natural fondness immediately smoothed the fair down on his head. 'Come on then, me little lad,' she crooned against his warm cheek. 'Let's get you seen to.'

Once the maid had disappeared with her charge, and Ruth and Clayton were left alone at the top of the stairs, they both attempted to immediately breach the quiet with conversation.

'I thought we had left this behind us…'

'Are you staying long in Willowdene…?'

They had spoken simultaneously and fell silent at the same time too.

'Please do finish what you were saying, sir,' Ruth blurted.

'It was nothing important, just a remark about the unseasonal weather. I thought we had left the snow behind us in the winter months. Only last week we were enjoying fine spring sunshine in town.'

'Indeed, it was glorious in the countryside too,' Ruth responded quickly. The weather was always an easy topic to discuss and she eagerly picked up the thread he'd dangled. 'But it is not so unusual to have snow at this time of the year,' Ruth spun out the dialogue. 'I recall my mother telling me that it was snowing in March in the year of my birth. The doctor had quite a journey through the blizzard and was almost late for my arrival.'

'So…you've had a birthday recently, Mrs Hayden,' Clayton observed with a smile.

'No…not yet…it is my birthday next week,' Ruth admitted, suddenly wishing she had kept that particular anecdote private. Into the expectant pause she said with a hint of defensiveness, 'I shall be nine and twenty on the twenty-fifth of March.'

'Will you indeed?' Clayton said, gently amused, but genuinely surprised. She certainly did not appear to be so close to thirty. 'You're still a youngster, then,' he added charmingly. 'In November of this year I shall turn thirty-five.'

A small smile from Ruth rewarded him for his gallantry. 'Then you must be either born under the sign of Scorpio or Sagittarius,' she remarked, gladly turning the focus on to him.

'Very possibly,' he admitted on a chuckle, 'but I have little interest in stargazing or what it all means.'

'I find the study of the heavens quite pleasing,' Ruth said.

'Whereas I prefer to concentrate on earthly pleasures.'

Ruth felt herself blush, but shot back rather acidly, 'Sagittarians are often hedonistic. I would hazard a guess that your birthday falls at the end of the month of November.'

He gave her a smile, but no further information. Instead he said easily, 'I interrupted you earlier. I believe you were enquiring how long I intended to stay in Willowdene.'

'I…yes…I did…' Ruth admitted, while hoping he did not think she cared if he was soon to leave.

'You asked from courtesy rather than curiosity, I take it,' Clayton remarked.

The note of mockery in his voice made Ruth bristle and tilt her chin. 'Indeed, and I expect we might need to find some more polite topics of conversation while we wait for our hosts.'

Clayton's slow smile turned to a chuckle. 'I expect we shall; and probably quite a few of them. I wouldn't be surprised if the fond couple are occupied…catching up on news…for some while yet.'

This time Ruth refused to turn away in embarrassment despite sensing heat fizzing beneath her cheeks. Her earthy dark eyes clashed with his in a way that deepened his smile.

'Shall we go to the library?' Clayton extended an elegant arm. 'When I arrived there was a good fire in there and plenty of weighty tomes to peruse, in the event that we run out of polite chitchat while we wait for our supper to be served.'

After a barely discernible pause Ruth extended a hand to hover on his arm. As they descended the stairs together she was again impressed by the way he could dissolve tension between them. He looked down at her with engaging grin. 'I'm feeling ravenous, actually. I hope a good dinner is waiting for us. And plenty of it.'

'Sarah is a very competent hostess,' Ruth championed her friend. 'And the last time I dined here—just before they left for Surrey—there were fourteen courses.'

'Ah! That should just about fill me up,' he said contentedly. 'It is a shame you missed their marriage,' Clayton remarked as they gained the hallway and turned towards the library.

Ruth nodded her shiny dark head and sent him a glancing smile. 'Yes, it was,' she softly agreed, recalling her sadness at having turned down Sarah's invitation to be her matron of honour. 'But at that time my papa had only recently been buried and, much as I would have loved to be part of the celebrations, it would not have been appropriate. Etiquette must be observed,' she said ruefully.

'Etiquette can be a damnable nuisance,' Clayton returned and slid her a look. 'I had hoped to see you that day.'

That blunt admission surprised Ruth to such a degree that for a moment she was unable to tear her gaze from his. 'Well…I think our dinner will be worth waiting for,' she blurted and swung her face towards the green baize door that led to the kitchens. 'Something smells exceedingly good.'

Clayton sniffed at air that was thick with a tantalising savoury aroma. 'Beef and horseradish,' he guessed.

'I would say chicken…or perhaps goose.' Ruth was sure she could discern the tang of sage-and-onion stuffing wafting in the atmosphere.

'A wager?' Clayton carelessly challenged.

'Of course,' she accepted with a gay laugh. 'And I know exactly what I claim as my prize. If I am right, I must insist you demand we play cards later when Sarah suggests I entertain the company by playing the pianoforte. She will have it that I can sing in key. I assure you that I cannot and you won't want to listen to me prove it.'

Clayton chuckled. 'Agreed. But what if I win…?'

Ruth tossed him a smile. 'Oh, if you win, I shall allow you to beat me just the once at piquet. I'm very good, you know.'

'Are you, indeed?' Clayton murmured. 'Most of the ladies I know are very bad…'

Ruth turned her head, the knot of excitement within tightening. He was a practised flirt, she told herself—a man with a reputation as a womaniser. Nevertheless she felt quite elated that, after an inauspicious start, they seemed to have established a fragile rapport.

Chapter Four

'Would you like something to drink?' Clayton asked, having escorted Ruth to a chair close to the fire.

A console table was dotted with sparkling crystal and he picked up each decanter then, following a brief inspection, knowledgeably identified its contents for her to choose which she would like.

'A small sherry would be nice, thank you,' Ruth said quickly on noticing Clayton was still awaiting her answer.

Clayton approached to hand over her drink and then took the chair opposite. Ruth watched surreptitiously as he stretched out his long legs in front of him and turned his head towards the mesmerising dance in the fire.

His lean profile was softened by the warm glow, his blond hair burnished to an autumn sheen. In his long fingers a brandy balloon gently oscillated. Far from being interested in continuing to flirt with her, or to engage in a little more light-hearted banter, he seemed to Ruth to have forgotten she existed and to have plunged deep into his own thoughts. Perhaps he thought to pay her back for her preoccupation moments ago. Thus, confident she was unobserved, she deemed it safe to slowly study him.

Ruth knew that a good deal of the gentlemen of the *ton* favoured bright colours and all manner of fobs and trinkets as personal adornments. This man was no dandified peacock. He was elegantly rather than fashionably clothed in a dark tailcoat and trousers and his person seemed devoid of jewellery. Then she noticed a heavy gold signet ring as it winked on a finger of the hand that was swinging the glass. Her eyes slipped on and a glint of gold could be seen where a watch reposed low in a waistcoat pocket.

She lifted her eyes from his lap and immediately her face flooded with blood. Unwisely she took a swift gulp of her sherry, then tried to quell the burning in her throat with fingers that flew to press her mouth. How long had he been watching her look him over in so vulgar a fashion?

'Would you like another?' Clayton asked with soft mockery and a deliberate glance at her depleted glass.

'No…no, thank you. I was looking…that is, you seem rather melancholy, sir. I didn't mean to stare.'

'I'm sure you didn't…or rather, you didn't mean me to see you at it.'

Ruth's dark eyes flashed dangerously at him. 'As you didn't mean to be caught eyeing me earlier?'

Just before Clayton despatched his cognac in a single swallow he said, 'I've no objection at all in you knowing I think you attractive.'

For a long moment Ruth simply sat quite still, her eyes on the fire. Would it be best to thank him briefly for the compliment? Or should she ignore what he'd said as simple flattery from a notorious philanderer? Just a short while ago she'd learned from Sarah that Sir Clayton Powell was an incorrigible rake.

'Perhaps we should think of something else to talk about,' Ruth suggested calmly. 'You know a little about my family history—would you tell me a little about yours?'

A humourless noise issued from Clayton's throat. 'I take it you would like to discover why I'm no longer married?'

Astonishment kept Ruth momentarily speechless, her eyes captured by his, her soft lips quivering and slightly parted. Sir Clayton Powell was certainly a bluff individual! Or perhaps he reserved such shocking candour for women he deemed to be too inquisitive? She had not wanted to pry into his personal life. She'd hoped, as he knew she had lost her father, they might have an innocent chat about his parents or his siblings. A slow anger burned in Ruth, boosting her determination to regain her composure and give him the answer he deserved.

'On the contrary, sir, I have no interest in your marital status,' she snapped icily.

'Have you not?' he enquired. 'Well, you must be the only female of my acquaintance under fifty who has not.'

'And you must be the only gentleman of my acquaintance who has the arrogance to suppose I might care to know whether or not he has a wife.' That fierce declamation came after quite a pause and in a voice suffocated with indignation. How quickly he could change from charming companion to cynical churl.

'So you didn't know that I'm divorced?' Clayton challenged softly, his eyes fixed pitilessly on her face.

A betraying flush began to creep under Ruth's skin. She *did* know. Just today she had discovered from Sarah that Clayton had once been married. She wished she could honestly say she was ignorant of his *mésalliance* with Priscilla and had no interest in knowing of it. But, in truth, while quietly sitting with him, she *had* pondered on why a handsome and wealthy aristocrat would make a disastrous match. And, had Sarah not already told her, she could have easily deduced from his attitude that his divorce had left him extremely bitter.

Clayton watched Ruth fidget and blush beneath his gaze and his lips slanted in a hard smile. It seemed he'd touched on a nerve. He had agreed to journey to Willowdene on the spur of the moment after Gavin suggested he distance himself from Loretta and her pathetic scheming. Perhaps his invitation to spend a little time in the country with the Tremaynes hadn't been as impromptu or philanthropic as it had seemed. Had Sarah given Gavin instructions to persuade him to come because she had an ulterior motive?

He liked Sarah very much. He envied Gavin for having such a lovely wife. But that didn't alter the fact that every society hostess of his acquaintance had made it her business at least once to try to pair him off with a nubile friend or relative.

'Did the Viscountess tell you I would be invited to dine here this evening?' he asked bluntly.

Finally, Ruth understood what was prompting his sardonic questions. He was not so much bothered that she knew he had lost his wife as that she might have designs on replacing her. Her lips tightened as a ferocious anger bubbled inside. The nerve of the man! He seriously believed she might have collaborated with Sarah to trap him! No doubt he also believed she'd schemed at having this time alone with him. 'I believe I've already said I didn't know you would be coming from London with the Viscount,' Ruth reminded him in a frigid tone. 'And when I mentioned your family it was not with the intention of discovering if you were a husband or a father. You know my father died because we briefly spoke about it when last you were in Willowdene. I was simply making a polite enquiry as to the health of your kin.' With no table close to hand, Ruth put down her empty glass on the hearthstone and stood up. 'I had hoped our hosts' unexpected absence might not become an ordeal for either of us. Unfortunately, it has…'

The thought of staying here, alone, with this conceited swine was now unbearable to Ruth. She didn't want to upset Sarah by leaving, but if the snow had cleared—even just a little bit—she would go home. In truth, she wished she'd not agreed to come at all. And that angered her, for her longed-for reunion with Sarah had been spoiled through no fault of her own.

Swiftly she went to the long window that looked out on to the grounds of the Manor. She twitched back the heavy velvet curtain, then folded back the shutter just enough to peep at the night. The whiteness glistened back at her; lifting her eyes to the heavens, she saw small sparkling droplets defiantly descending. With heavy heart and a soundless sigh of regret she turned back in to the library.

Clayton had also left his chair and was refilling his glass from the decanter. He tossed back the brandy and his blond head remained tilted towards the ceiling for some time before he addressed Ruth.

'I'm sorry,' he said quietly. 'I don't know why I said what I did.' His hands plunged into his pockets, withdrew almost immediately. 'Well, perhaps I do, but, whatever my mood, I had no right to make my problems yours. I behaved with unforgivable rudeness just now. Unfortunately, my manners seem to be sadly lacking this evening.'

'It's heartening to know that you believe you possess some,' Ruth responded coolly, only a little mollified by his apology.

A small noise issued from Clayton's throat that could have been a mirthless laugh. 'I take it from your disappointed expression that the snow hasn't melted enough for you to flee my boorish company and allow you to go home.'

'You're very perceptive, sir,' Ruth replied and slid a book from a shelf to peruse the cover.

'Come…sit down again, please,' Clayton invited. 'It's impossible for either of us to make our escape and I wouldn't want a bad atmosphere to ruin our evening with our friends.'

'No more would I,' Ruth answered with some asperity, yet she didn't give him the courtesy of a glance. Busily she turned the pages of the book, though she saw not a single word or picture on the fluttering pages.

'Come back to the fire,' Clayton urged gently. 'It looks to be quite draughty over there.'

Immediately Ruth ceased rubbing absently at an arm to warm it. But she wouldn't give him the satisfaction of knowing he was correct or that he could make her do his bidding.

'Gavin and Sarah will join us soon,' Clayton said persuasively. 'I promise you I shall be returning to town tomorrow, whatever the weather.'

'There is no need for you to risk such a journey,' Ruth said briskly and deposited the book back on the shelf. 'I haven't so far to go. I shall go home in the morning.' Ruth prayed inwardly that she might be able to do just that. From what she had seen through the window a moment ago, it seemed unlikely that the conditions would improve overnight. The snow had started to fall again, very lightly, but if it settled the condition of the roads might be yet more hazardous.

'Well, let's not squabble over who insists on leaving first,' Clayton said with a return to rueful humour. 'It's enough that we've both seen fit to offer to do so.'

Inwardly Clayton was cursing himself to the devil. He had been enjoying Ruth's company. There was a quiet grace about her that he found as enchanting as her physical beauty. Yet, despite his fascination with his lovely companion, he couldn't quite block from his mind the memory of his minx of a mistress.

Loretta's plotting had prompted him to take up Gavin's offer of a sojourn in the country. Even at a distance she was constantly infiltrating his mind as he pondered on whether he ought to have stayed in Mayfair and sorted out the mischief she seemed determined to concoct. He had no reason to apologise to Pomfrey. He'd done nothing wrong. His relationship with Loretta had been established when Pomfrey asked her to marry him. And now it was over. Yet he felt as though he ought to make contact with the man and reassure him that, whatever Loretta said, he didn't want her as his wife, now or ever.

'Ah! There you are, Ruth. I'm sorry I abandoned you,' Sarah happily chirped, entering the room in a shimmy of pretty lemon silk. 'When Rosie said you were taking a nap it seemed wrong to wake you.' Her sparkling eyes settled on Clayton. 'Good! You have had Sir Clayton to keep you company. Have you been having a nice chat?' Sarah sent a winsome smile to her husband, a few paces behind, to include him in her chatter.

A protracted pause was breached by Clayton saying lazily, 'Mrs Hayden has been diverting company. She told me you appreciate listening to her sing and play the piano.'

A look of startled disbelief froze Ruth's features. An expressive glance demanded he say no more on the subject. He returned her an easy smile that promised nothing.

'Ruth *is* very accomplished,' Sarah said with a proud look at her friend. 'And she is far too modest. It takes a lot of persuasion to get her to perform even one song.'

Gavin appeared rather more perceptive to the frost in the atmosphere than did his vivacious spouse. He sent his friend a penetrating look that terminated in a slight, quizzical elevation of dark brows.

'I'm famished and I expect our guests must be too.' Gavin took his wife's dainty fingers and placed them on his arm. 'Come, we can talk at the table. Let us go in to dine.'

'Oh, you must stay here tonight, Ruth. I can lend you whatever you need. It's impossible to travel even a short distance in such atrocious weather.' Sarah gaily sent that instruction back over an elegant shoulder as she allowed her husband to steer her towards their dinner.

With elaborate courtesy Clayton extended a hand to Ruth. After giving him a sharp glance, she lifted five stiff fingers on to his sleeve. She wanted to berate him for bringing musical entertainment to Sarah's attention. She guessed that was what he wanted her to do, so she swallowed the reprimand. In silence they followed their friends towards the dining room.

After several courses of fine food and several glasses of mellow ruby wine, Ruth had relaxed enough to overcome her annoyance and allow her eyes to meet Clayton's. Throughout the meal so far she'd often sensed him looking at her. On the few occasions he'd addressed her directly there had been no hint of challenge or mockery in his polite conversation and she imagined he had consciously made an effort to leave behind in the library his conceit and irascibility.

Their hosts were indeed fine company and there had been no lapse in genial chatter. They had discussed the start of the Season in London and, more lengthily, matters closer to home. Clayton had been interested to know how the unexpected snowfall might affect people in the villages obtaining necessary supplies and going about their business. His own country estate lay far to the south-west of the country, he'd explained to Ruth, where such bad weather was uncommon. He had added that he rarely visited it—being too fond of town living—so had thus far never been inconvenienced by the vagaries of the seasons. What a boon and a curse could be the weather! It had provided an ample source of neutral conversation, yet it also had trapped her here!

'Do you spend time in London during the Season, Mrs Hayden?'

Ruth placed down her spoon and gave Clayton a rather startled glance. She hadn't been expecting such a leading question. 'I don't, sir. I haven't been to London since I lived there as a child.'

'And whereabouts did you live?'

'Close to Chelsea, in Willoughby Street,' Ruth supplied and gave her attention to her pudding, taking a dainty mouthful of syllabub.

'Ah…I know it,' Clayton said pleasantly, undeterred by her hint that the subject was closed. 'A friend of mine, Keith Storey, lived there with his parents until he took a wife.'

Ruth gave a spontaneous smile at being reminded of the family. 'I knew them; my parents were friendly with Mr. and Mrs Storey.'

'And did you move to the country while still young?'

'No, sir.' Ruth again placed down her spoon, feeling a little miffed. He had no hesitation in interrogating her over her past, yet had become unpleasant at the first mention of discussing his. 'My parents moved to Fernlea after my marriage. I moved here to live with my father nine years ago; he was by then a widower.' Ruth turned quickly to her right and said to Sarah the first thing that came into her head. 'Little James had a pain earlier. I think the poor mite had colic.'

'He does suffer with it,' Sarah answered, well aware of her friend's wish to curtail a conversation with Clayton that must lead eventually to her late husband and perhaps the manner of his death. 'Mrs Plover,' she named the housekeeper, 'has a remedy for it. Just a small spoonful of the stuff seems to put him to rights. She's quite a marvel with her pills and potions. And she's of enormous help with planning extravagant menus and so on.'

'On which note, I must thank you for a delicious dinner,' Ruth said graciously, indicating she'd eaten her fill.

A polite murmur of assent came from Clayton as he too laid aside his cutlery.

'Well…shall we leave the gentlemen to their port?' Sarah suggested.

Ruth gave her a grateful smile. She could always rely on Sarah to sense her mood. Her friend knew very well she was keen to escape any further of Clayton's probing questions.

'If James is abed, we can bid him goodnight even if he is asleep.'

As the door closed on the two strikingly attractive ladies— one very fair, one very dark—Gavin gave his friend a wry glance and a measure of port he'd dispensed from the decanter. 'I take it you're glad you came.'

'What makes you say that?'

'I'd need to be a blind man not to notice you're smitten by Mrs Hayden.'

'And I'd need to be a cynic to think that perhaps you're glad of that. As we both know, I'm a cynic.'

Gavin grimaced bemusement. 'I'm not good with riddles. What's that supposed to mean?'

'Did you know that Mrs Hayden would be here when you asked me to come home with you?'

'Of course I did,' Gavin said and lounged contentedly back in to his chair. 'Sarah was keen to see her best friend straight away. I still don't see…' A look of amused enlightenment crossed his rugged features. 'Ah, you think Sarah has some maggot in her head about matchmaking the two of you.'

'It wouldn't be the first, or the hundredth, time a lady had arranged a dinner party for just that purpose. So, am I correct?'

'No,' Gavin said bluntly and sipped at his port. 'You might have designs on Ruth, but, not to put too fine a point on it, my friend, I doubt she has any interest in you.' Gavin gave Clayton a cautionary look. 'She's no man's mistress…not even yours, no matter how generous you're feeling. Take my word on it.'

Clayton sat back in his chair and fondled the stem of his glass with long fingers. His slate-grey eyes watched the crystal as it performed a balletic twirl. 'Is she spoken for?'

'Sarah told me earlier this evening that Ruth's recently received a proposal of marriage.' Gavin refilled his glass and pushed the decanter towards Clayton. 'Her suitor is by all accounts a pillar of society here in Willowdene. Don't ask more,' he said ruefully. 'I've been indiscreet as it is. Sarah adores Ruth, and with good reason. Ruth was a loyal friend and a support when Sarah was very much alone and in need of help,' he explained gruffly. 'I'd hate Ruth to think I'd spoken out of turn.'

Clayton nodded acceptance of that. 'He's a lucky chap, whoever he is.'

'Indeed,' Gavin murmured. He sent a subtle look at his brooding friend and amusement tipped his lips upwards.

He knew, of course, that Clayton was a hardened cynic where women were concerned. Clayton's wife had made a complete fool of him by acting like a seasoned trollop throughout their short marriage. Since his divorce ambitious women had constantly thrown themselves at him, hoping to take her place. He was mercilessly hounded by every mama with aspirations of marrying her débutante daughter to a man of great wealth and lineage—when Clayton's octogenarian grandfather died he would take a clutch of titles to add to the baronetcy he already had.

It seemed the longer Sir Clayton Powell remained stubbornly single, the more of a challenge the hostesses seemed to find him. Gavin knew that wagers had been laid amongst the *ton*'s *grandes dames* as to which of them might finally snare him for a favoured niece or goddaughter.

Clayton knew of their scheming too, and their ulterior motives. He knew he was wanted at their balls for what he had rather than himself. The more desperate they became to have him attend their functions, the more reluctant he became to turn up. The fact that his friend would choose to spend his evenings at the theatre with a demi-rep, or gambling with male friends, rather than socialise with women of his own class, spoke volumes about his friend's attitude to courtship and marriage. In fact, Gavin mused, he would not be at all surprised to learn that Clayton had badly misjudged the situation tonight and treated Ruth as though she were some mercenary temptress with an eye on his wallet. It would certainly explain the frost he'd sensed in the atmosphere when he and Sarah had joined them in the library.

A soundless laugh tickled Gavin's throat. He imagined from Clayton's rather mystified expression that he was still wondering why Mrs Hayden had refused to flutter her eyelashes and gaze adoringly at him, as did every other single woman of his acquaintance. He could have told his friend that, in fact, Mrs Hayden had turned down the doctor's proposal, but for some reason he had not. And it was not just because in another respect he'd told Clayton the truth.

Ruth would undoubtedly be better off financially as a rich man's paramour, but in Gavin's opinion she would hold out for a man to love, and to love her, before she slept with him.

Chapter Five

'No! Please don't say anything,' Ruth begged. 'Sir Clayton has apologised and been charm personified since his odd outburst.'

'And so he ought to improve his behaviour!' Sarah responded pithily.

After they had settled down into chairs beside the crib to chat and listen to James's gentle snores, Ruth had quite naturally told Sarah she had clashed with her gentleman guest. They had long been kindred spirits and didn't have secrets. But Sarah's reaction to knowing that her husband's friend had been rather insulting to *her* friend had been stronger than Ruth had anticipated. She'd immediately said that she'd tell Gavin to speak to Clayton about his manners.

'How dare he suppose we might plot to get him to marry you!' Sarah hissed beneath her breath so as not to wake her son.

'Now I think on it,' Ruth commented ruefully, 'I'm not sure marriage entered his mind.' The more indignant Sarah became, the more her own annoyance receded and she saw a farcical side to it all. 'I'm a widow, unattached, of limited means,' she listed out her fair-game status. 'It's possible he believed I harboured no such high aspirations and was angling for a less formal arrangement with him.' On seeing

Sarah's anger re-igniting, she made a small dismissive gesture. 'No doubt he is used to women fawning over him. He is handsome…rich too, I expect.'

'Oh, yes!' Sarah stressed, nodding her head vigorously and setting her blonde ringlets dancing. 'He's chased mercilessly by the débutantes, and equally enthusiastically by ladies of a different class,' she added as she recalled she'd once seen him at the theatre with several demi-reps in one evening. 'And he must have an enormous fortune, for Gavin jokes that he makes him feel like a pauper. But none of that excuses his rudeness to you.'

'Well, we must make allowances for such a popular fellow. It is not worth making a fuss.' Ruth shook her friend's arm gently to emphasise she meant what she'd said. 'I imagine Sir Clayton is now feeling awkward too. There's just this evening for us to get through, then tomorrow I shall go home and that will be an end to it. When we go back to the drawing room, shall we suggest a game of cards until bedtime?'

'I was going to ask you to play and sing for us, but after what you've told me he doesn't deserve to listen to your fine voice.'

Ruth clucked her tongue and raised her eyes heavenwards. 'You will have it I can hold a tune. I cannot, Sarah. Honestly, I cannot.'

'Of course you can!' Sarah contradicted. 'Compared to my musical efforts, you are talented enough to perform at Drury Lane.'

'That's true,' Ruth said, mock solemn. Sarah's description of her attempt to warble soprano sounding like a cat having its tail trodden on, was, alas, correct.

'Well, really! I was hoping you might fib and flatter me just a little bit,' Sarah reproved with a twinkling smile. 'Come, let's join the gentlemen. I won't say anything to Gavin about Clayton's behaviour, but I'm not sure I'll let him off too lightly either. If the rogue thinks me capable of meddling, I might feel inclined to prove him right.'

'Ah…we were just saying, my dear, that if horse riding is out of the question in the morning Clayton and I might take a different sort of constitutional and have a snowball fight.'

'What a good idea!' Sarah chirped gaily as she and Ruth, in a cloud of freshly sprayed French perfume, joined the gentlemen in the drawing room. 'Perhaps we might join you. I doubt Ruth would be averse to throwing missiles at Clayton.'

Ruth inwardly winced. Sarah had not after all been able to refrain from a little barbed remark about what had occurred between her guests.

'What is your answer, Mrs Hayden?' Clayton asked mildly, apparently unperturbed to discover that she'd told tales about him. 'Shall we draw battle lines and bombard each other?'

'I'm not sure it would be a fair fight,' Ruth responded lightly. 'You have an unfair advantage, sir, having been in the army.'

'Did I tell you that?' Clayton inquired in surprise.

'Um…yes,' Ruth answered quietly and quickly looked away. Why on earth had she mentioned the army? Obviously he'd forgotten that when they'd met in Willowdene last year he'd commented that he was acquainted with her father-in-law, Colonel Walter Hayden, from his army days. Now she'd idiotically paved the way for the conversation to once more turn to her marriage and perhaps her late husband, Captain Paul Hayden. And she certainly had no desire for that.

'We could make a snowman,' Sarah blurted, once more coming to her friend's rescue. She knew very well how loath Ruth was to talk about Paul, for invariably questions would be asked about his untimely demise. 'If there's no sign of a thaw tomorrow, I think we should do that. Of course, we wouldn't want to sculpt the fellow, then see him too soon melt away before our eyes.'

Ruth rewarded her friend with a subtle smile for valiantly attempting to divert the conversation away from a sensitive subject. 'But let's hope for a thaw,' she commented lightly. 'Then Sir Clayton can ride to his heart's content.'

'Towards London?' Clayton ventured in a drawl, with a steady look at Ruth.

'If you wish, sir,' she responded and held his eyes.

'And what do you wish, Mrs Hayden?'

'Shall we play cards?' Sarah interjected hastily and gave her husband a meaningful frown. Gavin seemed privately amused by the verbal battle between their guests. 'I know Ruth is good at piquet and so am I. We shall play together and beat you two gentlemen,' she declared. 'And the losers must…well, we'll decide that later,' she said, rather flustered by the sultry look her husband bestowed on her.

The following morning Ruth arose early, despite being reluctant to quit her bed as it was wonderfully warm and comfy. Her cold toes sought the satin slippers Sarah had lent her. Drawing about her the warm dressing gown that was also being loaned by her friend, she padded to the window.

She drew back the heavy velvet curtains and gazed out, rather blearily, at a stunning sight. Small clouds were scantily placed on a high azure sky. The sun was blindingly bright and beneath its rays the ground was a sheet of twinkling white. The trees, shrubs, hedges gracefully bore their sugar coating, only rarely shedding granules as the breeze stirred branches to life. Despite being disappointedly aware that the conditions were still too perilous for even a short journey through back lanes, Ruth marvelled at the natural beauty she gazed upon. It made her wish that she had an ability to paint or draw and capture the pristine scene.

Turning into the room, she approached the dresser and tested the water in the pitcher. It was cold, but not unbearably so. Logs had burned in the grate all night and were only now disintegrating into flaky grey ash. Quickly she filled the bowl and used the scented washing things Sarah had thoughtfully provided for her.

Having freshened up, she quickly donned her clothes without waiting for a maid to appear. She knew that Sarah would send someone to attend on her, but not yet, it was far too early. She would not be expected to rise till after ten at the earliest. Now she looked down at her silver silk dress with a frown. It was not suitable daywear, but would have to suffice for just this morning. This afternoon she hoped to be in her own home.

Now ready to face the day, she none the less lingered in her chamber. She sat upon the bed and wondered if it was too early to go downstairs. Not that she was expected to stand on ceremony when enjoying the Tremaynes' hospitality—she was treated as one of the family. But she'd guessed that Sarah and Gavin might enjoy a lie in while their other guest might be up and about as early as she was. She'd no intention of again finding herself alone with Clayton, desperately seeking to engage him in some innocuous conversation till their hosts appeared.

When she'd bid Clayton a goodnight yesterday evening at close to midnight, and had received a similar cordiality from him, they had seemed to part on fair terms. It would be wise to keep it that way for the short time they remained penned together in close proximity.

After they had played piquet together and each team had won a game, Gavin and Sarah had opted to play dominoes. Ruth and Clayton had persevered with the pack of cards.

Ruth had then won two hands of piquet, playing solo. She'd had a suspicion that Clayton had allowed her to do so and had been initially rather miffed in case he was attempting to patronise her. Then she'd mused that his intentions could be philanthropic. He might have been seeking to compensate for his boorish behaviour earlier and so she'd graciously accepted her victory. But it had been impossible not to bring to his notice their wager. She'd been correct in guessing they would dine on poultry with stuffing. She'd also beaten him at cards, yet he'd cheated her of her prize in bringing a musical evening to Sarah's notice. He'd affected to look chastened and had offered to make amends by fetching for her another small sherry. But when he'd handed it over he'd again raised her hackles by giving the softly scornful advice that it might be advisable to sip at this one slowly.

Thus had the evening progressed in an atmosphere of gentle joviality till bedtime. Yet she knew that, for all his sophisticated charm and easy smiles when their eyes had held for a second more than necessary or their fingers had inadvertently brushed together, an undeniable tension had strained between them.

With that thought in her mind, Ruth lingered by the dressing table and again picked up the hairbrush. She drew it slowly through her thick dusky hair and, raising her eyes to the mirror, gave her reflection a wistful smile. At least her unexpected meeting with Clayton had helped her forget the other gentleman unsettling her. She'd given Ian Bryant very little thought since she'd again made Clayton's acquaintance. Nevertheless, she must soon return to Fernlea and the gossip that would spread about her rejecting the doctor's proposal.

A noise from outside her window was slowly penetrating Ruth's introspection. She approached the glass to peer out. A groom was by the stables and she craned her neck to see more of what was going on. It was a bright sunny day, but surely the conditions were still too perilous for the gentlemen to ride? The stable lad had a black horse by the bridle and it skittered in his grasp, prancing and pulling as though to gain its freedom. The boy seemed to gratefully relinquish the steam-snorting beast to someone just emerging from the stalls. With lithe ease Clayton swung himself into the saddle and gave the boy a nod of thanks.

He cut a dashing figure in his long leather riding coat and with the sun burnishing his pale hair. He appeared to be an impressive horseman, too—the stallion seemed calmer beneath his mastery despite Ruth not seeing him do much to bring it about. But then she knew very little about equestrian matters, having only ridden infrequently. But she could drive a pony and trap very well, she reminded herself with a little smile. Her humour faded as she became aware that he was looking up at her window and it was too late to duck from sight. She stood quite still, solemnly returning his gaze although every fibre of her being urged her to slip aside. With acute embarrassment she saw him smile slowly as though he guessed her predicament. With exaggerated politeness he tipped his hat before he turned the horse's head and was galloping away over virgin snow.

For a moment longer Ruth stood where she was, her cheeks flaming. She put a cool hand to her hot cheek to ease the burn. Little wonder the man thought she had an interest in him! That was the second time he'd caught her gawping at him like an infatuated schoolgirl.

Annoyed with herself, she flung the silver-backed brush on to the bed and made for the door. At least he'd taken himself off and left the coast clear for her to venture downstairs and find some breakfast. Then, if the weather stayed fine and the sun continued to shine and melt the snow, she hoped she might escape to her own home before the infernal man reappeared.

And come back he would, she was sure of it. He hadn't looked set for a long journey. No doubt when he set off back to London he would take a carriage and luggage with him.

'Did you sleep well?'

'Indeed I did, thank you. I slept like a log in that comfy bed.' Ruth smiled at Sarah as she swept into the small salon with baby James cradled in her arms.

'Good, I hoped you would be cosy. I told the servants to warm the bed with a pan and build you up a good fire. Did it last the night through?'

'It did,' Ruth reassured her. 'I was warm as toast. I think the sherry helped, too,' she said with a little laugh. She rarely drank alcohol and had indeed felt quite flushed and tipsy by the end of the evening. The glasses of sherry that Clayton had brought to her, added to the wine that had been taken with dinner, had been rather too much for a novice imbiber.

Without ceremony or permission Sarah took her son to Ruth and handed him over. 'I'm quite famished,' she announced and went to the sideboard laden with silver dishes that contained a breakfast selection. Sarah removed the covers and peered within. Taking a plate, she began to ladle food on to it.

Ruth had already breakfasted abstemiously, being still rather full from the delicious dinner she'd eaten the previous evening. Now she looked on in amazement as Sarah sat down at the table and tucked heartily in to scrambled eggs, bacon, kidneys and toast.

'You *are* hungry.' Ruth choked a laugh. 'I shall refrain from inquiring how you got such an appetite.'

Sarah slid her friend a wicked smile and continued to eat. 'I miss him so when we're apart.'

'And I can tell he misses you, too,' Ruth said. 'I'm surprised you're yet out of bed. Are you not exhausted? It was past midnight when we all retired.'

'I shall have a nap this afternoon by the fire in the library. Gavin's gone to check outside. He wants to see if the ground is too slippery to take a horse or carriage out. He intends going in to Willowdene on business, weather permitting.'

'Thankfully, it looks like a thaw might set in,' Ruth said. 'It is a glorious day.' With the baby in her arms, she rose from the chair and went to the window. She gazed again with rapt wonderment at the quiet white landscape. 'If the sun continues to shine, I expect the snow will quickly disappear.'

Sarah sighed. 'So I suppose you will then go home.'

'I will,' Ruth said. 'I must,' she said with smiling emphasis for her downcast friend. 'I haven't told Cissie that I will be staying away. She will come as usual to do her chores if the track is passable and worry herself half to death on finding me not at home.'

'You could send her a message.'

'No. I must go home,' Ruth insisted and handed over James as Sarah came to take him.

'If Clayton were not a guest, too, you would stay, wouldn't you?'

Ruth made a dismissive gesture. 'It's not just that the two of us don't get on…I've much on my mind.'

'Another vexing gentleman, you mean?' Sarah guessed that Dr Bryant's proposal was still preying on Ruth's mind. Her friend's immediate nod proved her right. 'At least the doctor won't venture out to Fernlea in this weather to see you. You have a while to plan your response in case he comes to propose again.'

'I hadn't thought of that.' A rueful smile from Ruth

rewarded Sarah's wisdom. 'Now I don't know if I want the wretched weather to improve or worsen.'

'Well, I would have it worsen, simply so you must stay here with me.'

'I'm not sure your other guest would agree with you on that. During our spat I said I'd definitely go home today. I expect Sir Clayton will return later hoping to find me gone.'

'Have you seen him this morning?' Sarah inquired while cooing against her son's soft pink cheek to make him give her a gummy smile.

'I saw him from my window. He went out riding on a lively black horse quite early.'

'He took Storm out?' Sarah raised her eyebrows, her tawny eyes widening. 'That stallion has a wild temperament. He's not the sort of animal to ride for the first time in hazardous conditions. I hope he knows what he's doing.' Sarah frowned in concern. 'Gavin's an excellent rider, yet sometimes he opts to leave Storm in his stall if he seems agitated.'

'Sir Clayton looked quite competent in the saddle,' Ruth reassured Sarah. And indeed he had, casually giving her that mocking salute. Yet what Sarah had said about the beast was undoubtedly valid. The horse had seemed highly strung. Oddly, she felt a quiver of anxiety pass through her. She might not like the man, she might think him arrogant and conceited, yet she hoped no harm came to him. Had he gone off specifically to avoid her and give her time to return home as she'd said she would? That thought made her feel guilty and even more concerned that he should return safely from his ride.

Chapter Six

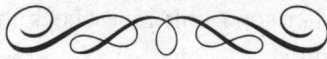

'The snow on the eaves and gutters is melting so fast that puddles have formed everywhere.'

Gavin strode in, brushing water droplets from his elegant dark riding jacket. 'If the temperature drops later, the ground will be fit to skate on.' Having given his weather forecast, he gave Ruth a welcoming smile and pecked his wife modestly on the cheek. Rubbing his palms together to warm them, he went to the breakfast selection and, obviously as in need of energy as his wife, doled a good amount of food on to a plate.

'We were just saying,' Sarah began, 'is it wise for Clayton to ride Storm when the conditions are so unpredictable?'

'Is he?' Gavin asked, mildly surprised. He waved a fork dismissively. 'Clayton can ride practically anything you sit him on,' he praised his friend's skill. 'An ass…an Arabian…he'll bring them all soon under control.' Gavin seemed unperturbed to know his friend was even now negotiating snow-covered ditches on the most tempestuous beast in his stables.

'Yet he spends little time at his estate in Devon,' Sarah commented. 'One would think that a man who loves to ride would be there often. It's a good hunting estate, is it not?'

'It is,' Gavin confirmed. 'I expect it's overrun with game, too, as he hunts there so infrequently. I must persuade him to hold a rout.'

'That would be excellent!' Sarah exclaimed. 'The estate is close to the sea, isn't it? I should like to see the coast again. I was a child on a visit with my parents the last time I visited Lyme Regis.'

'Have you been to the coast, Ruth?' Gavin asked pleasantly while enthusiastically tucking in to his breakfast.

'No...I have not,' she admitted rather wistfully. 'I've spent all my life in town and country.'

'It's high time you went there, then,' Gavin said from behind a linen napkin.

A neutral smile met that declaration before Ruth blurted, 'If the thaw continues, I should be home by mid-afternoon.' For a moment she had feared Gavin might suggest speaking to Clayton, on his return, about planning a visit to his country estate, specifically so she might have her first sight of the sea. Gavin might see no harm in it, but his friend was sure to think the reason she was wangling for an invitation was inspired by her hankering to peer at him rather than at the beach. The very thought that Sir Clayton Powell might look at her again with hard mockery in his eyes because he believed she'd taken a fancy to him made her determined to be on her way today. 'Might I have use of one of your carriages to take me home? I think perhaps by three o'clock the sun will have done its work.'

'Of course,' Gavin said, pushing away his empty plate. 'If you want to go, and the roads are passable, you are welcome to a ride. But I'm not so sure the bad weather is yet over.'

A short while later Gavin's prediction that the weather might take a turn for the worse was proved correct. The sun was eclipsed by woolly cloud and darkness hung over the horizon.

The air felt colder, too, and the servants started to scurry to and fro, making sure that all the fires were heartily ablaze and that apple-scented logs were stacked high on the hearths.

Ruth knew that it was unlikely she would now journey the few miles to Fernlea today. In truth, if she'd not clashed with Clayton, she'd have happily spent more time with the Tremaynes in the cosy confines of Willowdene Manor. It was a rare treat for her to be a houseguest in such splendid surroundings. When she went home she would enter a stone-cold cottage housing larders ready for replenishment.

With a sigh Ruth turned from the dispiriting sight outside the library window and again sought the warmth of the fire. She sat down and gazed across at her friend with an indulgent smile curving her lips.

Shortly after his papa went to his study to deal with his papers, baby James, protesting loudly, had been carried off by his nursemaid to be put to bed for a nap. The little chap had become fractious and Sarah's attempts to soothe him had come to nought. It was his teeth troubling him, she'd said, and had summoned Mrs Plover to find something soothing for his inflamed gums. After that little drama had passed, the boy's mama had gratefully nestled in to a fireside chair in the library. Before Sarah had finally succumbed to the soporific warmth cocooning her, she'd urged Ruth to take a snooze too.

Now as Ruth listened to Sarah's gentle snuffles and sighs she wished she could catnap for a while. But she didn't feel tired; she'd slept soundly last night, no doubt helped into slumber by the sherry she'd drunk. But primarily her mind was too alert to allow her to relax.

Spending time with her friends was a wonderful interlude in her humdrum life and she wished to squeeze from it every drop of enjoyment. But she must go home and face reality.

Would Ian Bryant come to see her again? And if he did, what would be her answer now she'd had time to reflect on what he'd offered? He'd been civil to her, if unable to conceal his disappointment at her rejection. She felt rather ashamed that she'd so gracelessly sent him packing.

Still, she baulked at the idea of spending all her days…and nights…with him, providing him with all the comforts a good wife should ungrudgingly supply. Mentally she chided herself for desiring romance when harmony would do. Yearning for handsome heroes to love was all very well for dreams at bedtime. What she needed was a husband to help her get through the day. The little pot of investments her papa had left to her was dwindling too fast.

Quietly she got up and took a slow promenade of the room's perimeter simply to stretch her legs. She wandered to the door and on impulse went out into the corridor. Finding it quite draughty out there, she decided it was a too rigorous constitutional and turned back towards the library. As she passed the window she peered up at the murky heavens. It was snowing again.

An icy draught stirring her skirts first alerted Ruth to the fact that the huge double doors, situated many yards away, had been opened. She'd moved into the window embrasure and now peeked around stone to see the butler helping Clayton remove his coat. A hum of male voices reached Ruth's ears as the servant busily shook snow from the coat's capes, then took Clayton's hat and gloves. His duties done, the elderly servant ambled away towards the cloakroom with the garments. Suddenly conscious that she was still craning her neck to spy on the scene in a most unladylike fashion, Ruth stepped back briskly into the deep recess, her heart pounding.

She didn't want Clayton to see her loitering about in the

hallway. He'd already made it clear he believed she was attracted to him...or perhaps he thought his fortune was tempting to her. A man of his conceit might readily jump to the conclusion that she'd been patrolling the vestibule to intercept his return. If she attempted to dart back to the library door and disappear within, she was sure to be spotted. Beneath her breath she cursed that she had, for no good reason, left that warm sanctuary. She decided to stay where she was while hoping he would head straight to his chamber. If he went to the stairs, there would be no need for him to pass this spot, thus he would remain oblivious to her presence.

Huddled against the stone window ledge, she listened as rapid footsteps cracked smartly over marble. She pivoted about to look through glass just in case he came her way...

'Are you hiding from someone?'

Ruth spun about, her complexion turning a violent pink. 'Oh...Sir Clayton...no, of course I am not hiding,' she fibbed while feigning surprise at seeing him. There was no need for him to utter a word for Ruth to inwardly wince at his reaction. The expression in his eyes was concealed with long dark lashes, but his mouth formed a half-smile. She had the impression he'd known of her whereabouts all along. An awful thought assailed her that he might have glimpsed her peeping around the corner at him.

'I'm surprised to find you still here,' Clayton said. 'I imagined you would make use of the thaw and go home.'

'I intended to, sir,' Ruth returned sharply. 'Unfortunately, the sunshine didn't last quite long enough for me to take advantage of it.'

Clayton came a little closer to her and looked out of the window. 'The road to Willowdene was just about passable earlier and will remain so if this fresh fall doesn't settle.'

Ruth felt more disturbed by his closeness than by his inference that she could have gone home had she really wanted to do so.

'I don't travel on that road, sir,' she replied tartly while stepping back from him. She dismissed the *frisson* that raced through her as being caused by the crisp winter air that clung to his clothes. Close to, she could see that his lean complexion looked taut and chilled. 'My home is in the village of Fernlea and the track to it isn't nearly so wide or even as the road to Willowdene.'

'Do you still want to go home?'

'Of course,' Ruth confirmed after a small pause. 'But I have no intention of putting at risk a coach and driver to take me there.'

'If you want to go, I'll take you home,' Clayton said. 'It's the least I can do as it's my presence here that is making you uneasy.'

Ruth gazed at him, her soft lips slightly parted in surprise. Sir Clayton Powell had no qualms over being blunt, that much was obvious. It was also obvious that his arrogance had in no way diminished. 'You overestimate your importance in the matter, sir.' Her flashing dark eyes clashed on his. 'I have pressing affairs to attend to at home. Nevertheless, I think the Manor is roomy enough to accommodate us both. It should be possible for us to avoid one another for a short while longer.'

'And if the weather tomorrow is no better...perhaps worse?'

'Then I shall go home regardless,' she said, vexed by his persistence in pursuing the matter. 'Unless you withdraw your offer to risk the journey, I shall spare the Manor's coachman and allow you to take me there.'

'And I shall be very happy to oblige you on that,' Clayton drawled with a glimmer of a sultry smile. He raised a hand to brace it on the stone, casually, as though he was unaware he'd trapped her between his body and the window, or that he'd brought a heightened bloom to her cheeks with his suggestive tone. 'So what were you doing out here in this draughty hallway when you might have instead been curled up by the fire? Cursing to the devil the weather? Or were you anxious that some harm might have befallen me while gallantly I removed my odious person from your vicinity for the best part of the day?'

'Perhaps if I believed that to be true, I might have given a thought to your safety,' Ruth retorted sourly.

'It's the truth,' he said mildly. His storm-grey eyes slid immediately to watch the movement of her tongue tip as it circled moisture to her soft red lips.

'In that case, sir, you overestimate *my* importance in the matter. There's no need for you to risk life and limb on my account.'

Clayton continued to study the bristling beauty beside him. Her eyes were lustrous and dark as bitter chocolate, her cheekbones flushed with a mix of embarrassment and annoyance.

'I've risked my health for less worthy individuals.'

'I'm sure…' Ruth purred and made a move to pass him. But he seemed unwilling to budge and she was reluctant to attempt to push at the muscular arm that imprisoned her. She wouldn't risk an undignified tussle with him.

As though he had read her thoughts, Clayton dropped his arm and gave her a lopsided smile when she didn't immediately rush off. He wanted her to stay and talk to him, but he wasn't sure why. She'd made it clear that she thought him rude and arrogant. Considering his behaviour yesterday, it wasn't surprising she'd drawn that conclusion about him. But he'd apologised at length at the time and to do so again now would be pointless.

He sensed she remained where she was because she found

him as intriguing as he found her. But she didn't like him. Unfortunately, he knew he liked her rather too much. Just being this close to her put a throb in his loins. He had a nagging urge to trap her against the wall and kiss her despite knowing she was, or was soon to be, betrothed to a fellow described as a pillar of Willowdene society. The thought of another man having her annoyed Clayton and that made him ashamed of his selfishness.

Despite Gavin's suggestions that a wife would protect him from the likes of Loretta, he had no intention of ever again offering marriage to a woman. Yet he envied the rustic dignitary who had Ruth Hayden as his future bride. In no small part his resentment sprang from knowing that he'd arrived here in Willowdene only fractionally too late to proposition her. And he would have generously offered her *carte blanche* as his mistress despite Gavin's caution that she wasn't that sort of woman. In Clayton's vast and varied experience, every woman had her price.

'I know we both want to enjoy the unexpected extra time we have to spend with our friends,' Ruth blurted, making an emphatic little hand movement. She felt flustered by his brooding silence, and his broad, muscular body just inches from hers…warming her. 'It's surely not too difficult for us to tolerate one another's company for a further day?'

A dry chuckle rolled in Clayton's throat. 'It's no hardship at all on my part, Mrs Hayden.'

For a moment longer Ruth hesitated, then, with a slight nod, she slipped swiftly past him. She hastened to the library door, well aware that his eyes were following her.

As the door to the library closed Clayton turned towards the stairs, his expression a study of ironic amusement. Could he tolerate her company? she'd pleaded to know in that calm yet appealingly breathy way she had. A corner of his mouth pulled upwards. Given the opportunity, he'd slowly savour her company. He greatly desired seeing much more of her and in the early hours of the morning had almost succumbed to that wild need.

At half past midnight he'd been sitting by the fire in his bedchamber still fully clothed and tapping his booted feet restlessly. At one o'clock he'd sprung up and quit his room with purposeful speed. In a moment of delirium—brought about by lustful images of Ruth sprawled, naked, beneath crumpled sheets—he'd set off towards her chamber specifically to seduce her. Thankfully a long walk through cool corridors had brought him to his senses and he'd continued, without faltering, past her door.

Downstairs in the drawing room he'd swirled to warmth by the fire, then downed, several cognacs. By three o'clock he'd been sufficiently relaxed by alcohol and tobacco to meander back to his bed and sleep fitfully till dawn. He'd risen early and put distance between them for his own benefit as much as for hers. He was awkwardly aware that he'd been acting like a horny youth stalking his first conquest, and, worse, Gavin had noticed him doing it.

Clayton accelerated his pace up the stairs, taking the final treads two at a time. Still he couldn't shake thoughts of Ruth from his mind. The memory of her peeking at him from behind stone brought a smile to hover on his lips. She'd tried to hide from him in the hall because she'd feared he'd suspect her of loitering with intent. With any other single female that cynical conclusion might have been valid. He'd lost count of the number of times he'd been ambushed by determined women concealing themselves behind pillars or in alcoves.

But it hadn't been the case on this occasion. Ruth had probably been pacing restlessly to while away the time. She had domestic affairs to see to, she'd said. So had he. They both had been prevented from leaving the Manor and going about their usual business by the heavy snowfall. But it gnawed at his consciousness that she might be pining to go home to see her lover whereas he had no desire to see Loretta…yet see her he must, if only to make sure she understood she was now out of his life for good.

Chapter Seven

'Good evening, sir.'

'Good evening to you, Mrs Hayden.'

Ruth's sepia gaze swept the dining room she had just entered but the only person within its quiet confines was Sir Clayton. It appeared that their hosts were late down to dine this evening just as they had been yesterday. But Ruth doubted they had this time been delayed for delightfully amorous reasons. As she had descended the stairs she had heard little James wailing. The poor mite was no doubt still suffering with teething pains. Ruth had guessed that Sarah might arrive late, choosing to stay in the nursery until the baby settled down to sleep. Gavin's absence indicated he too might be attempting to soothe his son, or his anxious wife.

It had been a full ten minutes after the gong had sounded that Ruth had left her room. She had loitered upstairs in the hope of avoiding again being stranded alone with this unsettling aristocrat. Inwardly she sighed; it seemed she must once more strive to calm the friction between them and ferret in her mind for something to talk about while they waited for their friends to join them.

Gracefully she proceeded into the room while a subtle

sliding glance took in his immaculate appearance. He'd stationed himself by the chimneypiece with a hand resting negligently on the marble mantel and the other thrust into a pocket. This evening he was dressed in a charcoal grey suit of clothes that looked to be of excellent cut and quality. An intricate knot had been formed in his cravat and in its centre winked a sapphire stone of considerable size.

Ruth's awkwardness was momentarily overcome by an unexpected burst of exuberance at having all to herself such a handsome and distinguished gentleman. Mercilessly she quashed it. She'd been made aware of an unpleasant side to his character yesterday evening, she reminded herself, and no amount of suave good looks or polished charm could alter it.

Unconsciously Ruth smoothed a hand over her grey dress, feeling rather shabby in the presence of such sartorial elegance. Earlier in the day she'd turned down Sarah's offer to choose something from her wardrobe to wear to dinner. Normally she might have enjoyed dressing up in one of her friend's glamorous gowns. They were about the same size, although Ruth's bust was a little fuller.

In the past she'd worn Sarah's cast-offs. Accepting charity was abhorrent to her, but it was different with her friend's gifts. Sarah had known what it was to be strapped for cash and donated useful clothes in a manner far removed from condescension. Ruth knew Sarah would never patronise her. But today she had declined her friend's kindness and now she knew her reason for doing so. She'd not wanted this man to suspect she might be primping in his honour.

'You rode quite a spirited mount earlier…'

'Will a servant tend to your pony?'

They both had started a conversation at the same time, as they had yesterday on meeting by the stairs and after suffering a protracted silence.

Ruth received an apologetic smile and returned him one of her own. A speaking gesture invited him to continue.

'I was inquiring after your pony. You were driving a pony and trap the first time I saw you in Willowdene. Will he be fed and watered while you are here?'

'I no longer have that little mare,' Ruth told him with a wistful smile. 'I let her go to a friend. But he's good enough to allow me to borrow her and the cart, too, when I need to go to town.'

'A friend?' Clayton echoed casually while strolling to the decanters on the sideboard. 'Would you like a sherry?' he asked while waiting to discover who her generous gentleman friend might be.

'I will not, thank you. I think I overindulged yesterday. I had quite a headache this morning,' she told him ruefully.

That admission drew a slow grin from Clayton, although he continued watching cognac flow into a glass. 'I imagine you're quite a stranger to overindulgence.'

Ruth bristled slightly. Was he inferring that she was a prude of some sort? 'It's true I rarely drink alcohol,' she confirmed, managing to keep her tone light.

'Or have many vices at all, I shouldn't wonder,' he said as he turned back to her and took a hefty swig from his glass.

He *was* inferring she was a prude. No ready retort sprang to mind to close the conversation, so Ruth sent him a tight smile and said nothing at all. As he'd left the cosy fireside vacant, she took up position there and warmed her palms by the glow.

'So…you were about to tell me which of your friends now has your pony and trap.'

A sharp dark look met that comment. She'd been about to do no such thing. And he knew it. But she wouldn't dispute the point. It seemed he had a love of trying to ruffle her and allowing him his mischievous way wasn't at all what she wanted. Besides, what did it matter if he knew to whom she'd sold her transport?

'Parson Greene bought them from me. He lives quite close by in the village.'

Clayton lifted his glass and gave her a thoughtful glance over its rim. Was Parson Greene her suitor? Her lover? It would explain why the fellow put his property at her disposal. It was hardly an extravagant gesture compared to what a mistress of his might expect him to provide to take her about town. Loretta had had the use of one of his new carriages and two pair of matching greys while his mistress. But then Ruth Hayden was not a woman much impressed by a gentleman's rank. She'd let him know that, in no uncertain terms, yesterday. And the parson might not be a man of wealth or position just because he was classed as a pillar of the community. The man's worth and importance hereabouts might be linked to what he did rather than what he had.

Clayton acknowledged that he knew nothing of Willowdene or its social hierarchies. He mused, too, that it might be time to rectify his ignorance. 'I expect you're friendly with the parson's wife as well,' he ventured innocently.

'Why do you think that?' Ruth returned.

'In London ladies usually have friends with whom they shop or take afternoon tea,' he smoothly explained. 'I imagine the women in rural communities socialise in much the same way.'

'The parson is a widower,' Ruth said and suspiciously narrowed her eyes on him. She sensed he was probing for information about the elderly parson for reasons unknown to her. Or perhaps he was just trying to spin out their dialogue in the hope their friends would soon arrive to rescue them. She decided to be charitable and settle on that theory. 'Parson Greene lost his wife several years ago. He has a daughter of about my age who lives with him.'

'Ah...so she is your friend.'

'An acquaintance,' Ruth supplied, turning away and briskly rubbing together her palms. She wasn't about to disclose to him that Verity Greene, along with the majority of the villagers, snubbed her because of the manner of her husband's death.

It was a long while since Paul had been court-martialled, then shot for desertion from the army, but, in her experience, small-minded people, with nothing better to do, liked to keep alive their prejudices. And tales of Captain Paul Hayden's cowardice—oh, how wrong they were about him!—were still resurrected and gossiped over in the absence of any fresh grist for the mill.

She was thankful that Parson Greene was more neighbourly towards her than was his daughter and the other local ladies. No sisterhood existed in these parts, as Sarah also had learned to her cost when she'd been a notorious, ostracised spinster. Attention and assistance were more likely to be forthcoming from those ladies' husbands and Ruth knew therein lay the crux of the problem.

She was a young widow of fine looks—such praise having been bestowed by her doting parents and her late beloved husband—therefore she was deemed a threat, despite never having harboured a romantic interest in any local fellow, even the extremely eligible Dr Ian Bryant. And perhaps, she reflected, she might soon rue that fact...

Swiftly she gathered her wayward thoughts and decided to make an effort to be pleasant to her extremely eligible companion.

'I was talking to Gavin and Sarah earlier about the black stallion...Storm, I believe is his name.' Ruth had spoken rapidly, hoping to prevent Clayton interrogating her further over her neighbours. 'That horse is, by all accounts, a very spirited beast. Did you know he was a difficult ride before you decided to take him out?'

'Were you concerned for my safety?'

'No more than I would have been for any person who unwisely decided to mount such an animal in perilous conditions,' Ruth said. His smile deepened, infuriatingly, prompting her to continue briskly, 'Such a foolhardy action might make the perpetrator appear cocksure about his prowess, don't you think?'

Clayton came closer, stood by her side by the fire and let out a regretful sigh. 'And I know you deem it possible I might possess that deplorable character trait.'

Ruth tipped up her dark head, gave him a bold speaking look, her lips pressed together to contain a glimmer of a smile. At times he had quite an appealing way about him, even if his self-deprecation was, in itself, an irony. She imagined he could be very amusing company if he wished to be. 'And do *you* deem it possible you might possess that deplorable character trait?' she audaciously inquired with a tremor of suppressed laughter.

'At present I'm deeming it possible to curb every bad habit I possess in order to win your approval.' It was stated with a mock-solemn frown at the shadows cast upon the ceiling.

'And why would you seek my approval?' Ruth asked lightly. 'You need not strive to improve your character for my benefit. We inhabit different worlds, you and I, and will probably meet but rarely through our mutual friends.' She tilted him a mischievous smile. 'You may continue to be as bumptious as you please, sir. I shall never know.'

'Ah, but you will, and soon, so I have little time to make the required changes. James is to be christened in a few months' time. I hear from Gavin that you have agreed to be his godmother.'

'I have,' Ruth said, her eyes softening as she reflected on that honour. 'And very gladly do I undertake the role.' She had momentarily forgotten that she was to share the responsibility of godparent with this gentleman.

'Then, as I have agreed to be the boy's godfather, we have at least one future meeting already planned,' Clayton said with a steady look that made an odd sensation accelerate through Ruth's veins. 'And I'd very much like to secure your good opinion before then.' His tone became velvety. 'In truth, I'd like a little kindness from you far sooner.'

Swiftly Ruth tore her eyes from the overpowering pull of his smouldering grey gaze. The gentle banter between them had transformed into something far more deadly serious. She turned her head, frowned in confusion. He was flirting outrageously with her, making her think unsuitable thoughts, making her feel emotions she didn't want to feel…hadn't indulged since she'd revelled in Paul's loving words and intimate touches.

Foolishly she'd encouraged the attention of a notorious rake in the belief she could match his sophisticated skill in a trifling game. But she was at a loss to know what to say next to ease the heady atmosphere. The small space between them seemed to throb with tension. She sensed he was about to stretch a hand towards her, and she shot back a pace as speedily as she would have had a spark been spat out by the fire.

For an interminable moment she refused to meet his eyes while a riot of thoughts whirled in her head. She must cede him his victory in their verbal duel, but not let him know how greatly he'd unsettled her. She might be unworldly and wearing a tired-looking dress, but she'd not crumple beneath the sensual challenge he'd thrown down. She raised deep brown eyes to find he was watching her closely and with a lot less amusement in his eyes than she'd feared to see.

'Were you concerned for my safety, today?' he demanded to know in a gruff tone.

Ruth simply nodded, unable to lie or prevaricate or say anything at all.

'I chose that mount because I hoped riding him would focus my mind purely on the sport in hand and stop me thinking about a more dangerous distraction.'

'And did it work?' she whispered. His cryptic answer seemed to have some hidden significance that she instinctively knew applied to her.

Seductive grey eyes coupled with her shy earthy gaze, but the door opened and Clayton was prevented from telling her that despite the ice all around he'd burned hot as hell for her.

Gavin entered the dining room with a falsely cheerful smile that immediately dispersed the sultry atmosphere. It was obvious to both Ruth and Clayton that something was very wrong.

'Sarah shouldn't be too long. James is still coughing and spluttering, poor little lad, but once he's settled down we can dine.' Gavin had left the door ajar and the infant's loud wails could again be heard, causing him to turn and frown. But, ever the perfect host, he said, 'Of course, you both may dine now if you wish to. Dinner is ready to be served and there's no need to wait for us…'

His further offers and assurances were cut off as Clayton and Ruth simultaneously demurred at taking any such action.

'It is probably just the pain of cutting his teeth bothering him,' Gavin continued with a constrained smile. 'But Sarah wants to see James sleeping peacefully before she leaves the nursery.'

'Might I help in any way? Or keep Sarah company?' Ruth asked, a tremor of concern in her voice.

'I expect she might like that,' Gavin replied.

The immediate gratitude in Gavin's tone made anxiety

roll in the pit of Ruth's stomach. For all Gavin's composure, she feared the situation was worse than he was prepared to admit. She quickly went from the room.

'Why do I not know what to do?' Sarah put a frantic hand to worry her pale brow. 'He is my flesh and blood, my darling son, yet I can't comfort him and it's breaking my heart.'

Ruth enclosed her tearful friend in her arms and watched the nursemaid pacing to and fro, trying to calm the howling baby with little coos and clucks. James's tiny face was scarlet and scrunched up tight as he filled his lungs to recommence protesting against his discomfort.

'He is clean and dry, so that's not the trouble,' Sarah said. 'He cannot be hungry, for it's not yet the hour for his feed. Besides, I've tried to comfort him that way, but he won't suck,' she added with a frown. 'Cutting teeth surely can't be such an ordeal.'

Ruth murmured consoling words to her friend as she went to take a closer look at the baby. His distress was mounting and his cries had hoarsened as he wriggled this way and that in Rosie's arms.

'I was so foolish in not employing a nursemaid of experience and maturity. But I wanted to be a proper mother and do most for James myself. It was idiotic to take on a girl of such limited experience.'

If Rosie heard her mistress's comments and was offended she gave no sign and continued rocking the baby and crooning a lullaby.

'Perhaps he's taken a slight chill,' Ruth ventured on hearing the little mite start to cough with such force he shook in Rosie's arms.

'I fear his temperature is higher than it was this afternoon.' Sarah gave Ruth a look that appealed for reassurance. 'Is he ill, do you think? Or is it simply the teeth breaking through? Oh, why am I so ignorant of all this? Mothers should have an instinct about their infant's health, surely?'

Again Ruth drew her friend to her. 'I'm afraid that I don't know either what's wrong,' she admitted gently. 'You mustn't blame yourself for your lack of experience. James is your first-born. Rearing babies is, I imagine, something only learned through practice.'

'I don't know if I am being too silly over it all…but it is better to be safe than sorry. I want Gavin to fetch the doctor; it's the only way to ease my mind. Would it be awkward for you to see Dr Bryant so soon after having rejected his proposal?'

'Of course you must send for him!' Ruth said emphatically. 'If you think he might help James in any small way, he must be fetched directly.'

'I shall go and tell Gavin to ride to Willowdene at once,' Sarah blurted on a sob of determination and was immediately hurrying towards the door.

After listening for a few moments to the baby's plaintive cries, Ruth relieved Rosie of her squirming burden. The poor little lad might be suffering, but he certainly had energy and strength left. Ruth rocked him in her arms to no avail—his clenched fists continued to wave at her. She then attempted to settle him against her shoulder. But he seemed all elbows and knees and refused to be comforted or calmed by strokes and pats or whispered words.

She laid a cool hand against his hot little brow, curved it over his downy pate. He certainly did feel very feverish.

'Is there some water to cool him?' she asked Rosie.

Immediately the girl sped to the water pitcher and returned with a cold damp cloth. 'The mistress tried bathing him earlier, but it made no difference,' she told Ruth with a worried frown. 'He's been crying too long; he needs something to drink is what I reckon. He must be thirsty for sure, but he's too exhausted to suckle.'

'Ask cook to have some water set to boil. When it's cool enough he might take a little of it from a spoon.' Ruth thought Rosie's advice sensible.

As Rosie went out on her errand Ruth patted very gently at James's blotchy complexion with the cool cloth and was greatly relieved when, for a moment, it seemed to soothe him. Gently she wiped the damp compress against his scarlet cheeks. But soon he again began to cough and rattle and then high-pitched heartrending cries broke from him. Ruth felt panic needle her skin at the force of his distress. At that moment she was far from wishing Ian Bryant away from her. Indeed, she longed to see him very, very soon.

Chapter Eight

It was close to ten o'clock when Clayton arrived back at the Manor with Ian Bryant. He'd insisted on taking the mission, sensing that Gavin would sooner stay with his distraught wife than travel to Willowdene to fetch the doctor. Gavin knew his friend was as competent tooling the ribbons as he was in the saddle and had gratefully succumbed to Clayton's arguments. If anyone could get the doctor to the Manor in good time, over bad ground, Clayton could. Just an hour after quitting the Manor he was back with Ian, proving Gavin's trust in him to be well placed.

Following concise words in the vestibule as to the infant's symptoms, Ian was soon swiftly taking the stairs with the worried father. Seconds later the gentlemen entered an ominously hushed nursery.

Ruth and Sarah were still within the warm room, both stationed close to the crib where the little boy silently lay. James now appeared lethargic rather than restful. He'd taken a few spoonfuls of warm water, but it hadn't seemed to either worsen or improve his condition. Neither had he wanted his mama's milk when she cuddled him close to her breast and tried again to feed him.

Only very briefly did the doctor's professional manner slip when he spied Ruth. His eyes fixed on her for several long moments, his surprise, and something else—pleasure, perhaps, at seeing her—apparent in his intense gaze. Then once more he was briskly attending to James. He began to unclothe the boy to examine him.

Feeling now superfluous and, in any case, keen to be gone lest her presence again distract Ian from his vital work, Ruth murmured a few words to Sarah, then withdrew.

Clayton was pacing the vestibule as Ruth descended the stairs. When he saw her, he strode to the banisters and waited for her to come closer before issuing an inevitable question. 'How is he?' he urgently demanded to know as she reached the bottom step.

'A little calmer, but I'm not sure that's a good thing.' An anxious frown accompanied her shake of the head. 'The poor mite was coughing fit to burst his lungs.' Tears needled her eyes at the memory of it. 'I can understand why Sarah is so distraught. He looks and sounds a very sorry little chap.'

Instinctively Clayton took one of her pale trembling hands into his to comfort her, for he'd noted the distress in her voice. 'The doctor is here now.' His fingers stroked quite naturally to soothe her. 'All that can be done will be done. He seems a good enough fellow and needed no persuading to come out on such a treacherous night.'

Clayton drew Ruth down from the step she stood upon and linked her arm in his. Immediately Ruth turned to gaze at whence she'd just come, reluctant to move away in case she might again be of some small assistance upstairs.

'You're cold and there's nothing for us to do to help,' Clayton urged, moving her again about. 'Come into the library and warm yourself by the fire. We shall know soon enough how James fares.'

Ruth nodded absently and went with him. She sat in the chair to which he led her and accepted, without demur, the glass of warming sherry he pressed firmly into her chilly hand.

'When one has no children of one's own, it's hard to imagine the heartache a parent must endure watching a child suffering,' Clayton quietly mused, his solemn gaze contemplating flames leaping from the grate. 'The threat of illness and loss must be a constant torment.' He slanted a grave look at Ruth, probably anticipating her murmur of agreement.

But she simply gazed back at him, her eyes slowly filling with brine until some spilled on to her cheeks.

Clayton frowned, then a dawning realisation tautened his features. With a silent oath he closed his eyes, passed a hand over his jaw. He made a small gesture, croaked a gruff apology, although she'd said not one word to confirm his awful suspicions.

Without understanding why she did so, Ruth confided quietly to a man she barely knew the bare bones of her greatest heartache. 'A daughter…stillborn…she would now have been eight years old.'

Clayton cast again a long sideways look at her, watching her lower her beautiful soulful eyes beneath his steady, sorry scrutiny. By the time he'd thought of something that he prayed might be right to say, the door had opened and the doctor and the boy's parents entered the room.

Ruth jumped to her feet as Sarah sped across the room to her.

'He seems a little better,' Sarah breathlessly told Ruth. 'Doctor Bryant has given James a draught to help him sleep. He seems cooler and able to breathe more easily.'

Having listened to the good news intently, then asked for it to be repeated, so welcome was it, Ruth hugged her friend happily to her. Over Sarah's shoulder she saw that Ian was watching the scene. She sent him a small smile that she hoped conveyed her very great gratitude for his prompt arrival. For a moment she thought he might remain impassive, but eventually he returned her a similar salute. She was glad he appeared to harbour no resentment towards her. She didn't want them to be enemies, she knew that for definite, even if all else regarding the outcome of their relationship was uncertain.

'Please stay and take a drink before you venture back into this awful night,' Gavin urged the doctor. He proffered a glass and, at a murmur of acceptance from Ian, poured a generous measure of cognac into it.

Ruth and Sarah joined the group of gentlemen and contributed a few words to the general dialogue about the severe weather. Inevitably the talk turned to the evening's horrible drama.

'That was an experience I hope never will be repeated,' Gavin declared vehemently as he drew his wife close to his side and comforted her with a subtle little caress. Sarah was still trembling despite her relieved smiles and constant burbling chatter.

'I'm afraid I anticipate it will be repeated,' Ian disabused them bluntly. 'These early maladies are quite common, but you must take heart from the fact that even very young children are surprising in their resilience.' His eyes again strayed to Ruth, lingered just a little too long before moving on to the boy's mother. 'He is obviously a well-nourished and healthy little chap. You are caring very well for him and will find in the morning that James is much better after a good night's rest.'

'And the mixture for his gums and tummy ache?' Sarah asked anxiously. 'Are we wrong to try and ease his discomfort with it?'

'It's a mild herbal remedy and quite frequently used. I've

not known it to cause any problems. But at present it's best to give him nothing other than a little boiled water if he seems thirsty or colicky between feeds. His digestion might be delicate and the mixture not efficacious.'

Sarah nodded, then turned to Clayton, who had been standing a little aside from the group, observing the proceedings and the two couples from beneath closely drawn brows.

'You, sir, have proved to be an invaluable friend tonight, fetching Dr Bryant so quickly to us through the snow.'

Sarah's praise drew a quiet simple response from Clayton. 'I would have undertaken far more than I did to ensure James's health and comfort.'

'You haven't seen your future godson today,' Sarah said in a choked little voice. 'Would you like to see how peacefully he is now sleeping?'

'Indeed I would,' Clayton said gently and, at Sarah's beckoning, he accompanied her to the door.

Shortly after his wife and friend departed the room, Gavin swung a discreet glance between the doctor and Ruth. Having drawn the conclusion that the atmosphere was thick enough to slice, and thus supposing they might appreciate a little time alone, he excused himself with the perfectly credible comment that the kitchen staff must be eager to know whether to continue to keep warm their dinner. At the door Gavin turned and frowned an apology at his lack of manners in not issuing the invitation sooner. 'Will you stay and dine with us, Dr Bryant?'

Ruth's startled gaze flew to Ian's face, causing his top lip to lightly curl. He understood her silent demand as to what response he must give. 'I thank you, but no,' he politely declined. 'I have a young son of my own asleep in his bed and would like to return directly to him.'

'How old is he?' Gavin asked.

'Joseph has just had his first birthday.'

Gavin nodded and smiled wryly. But he said nothing more as he opened the door.

Once Gavin had quit the room, Ruth attempted to set a neutral tone between them. 'The poor cook must be praying that her hard work is not in vain, and the food is still presentable. But I'm sure all the servants will be greatly relieved to know how James is improved. They dote on him—'

'I didn't realise you were so well acquainted with the Tremaynes.' If Ian had perceived her desire to avoid personal questions, he'd blatantly ignored it.

A little frown from Ruth met that blunt interruption, but she gave thanks that at least he'd not referred to their last meeting. 'Sarah...Lady Tremayne...and I are good friends,' she mildly replied. 'We became close when Sarah lived in Willowdene, before her marriage to the Viscount.'

'I recall she lived alone at Elm Lodge.' A significant pause preceded Ian adding acidly, 'A great triumph it was, too, for Miss Sarah Marchant to catch an aristocrat and move from an estate cottage to the manor house, especially when one considers her previous...*unfortunate*...circumstances.'

Ruth's eyes flared in astonishment at his quite obvious disdain for her friend. Of course, everybody hereabouts knew that Sarah once had been a scandal-wrecked woman, but most accepted that her reputation had been repaired when she married. 'I know the Viscount deems himself to be the lucky one to have secured such a wonderful woman for his wife.' Ruth's voice remained calm, but a steely inflection stressed her great disapproval for what he'd said. She moved away from Ian in a way that displayed her disgust at his attitude more clearly than any words might have done.

'So...you believe that baby James is not afflicted with any dreadful complaint,' she said before he could add to his impertinent opinions about her friends. 'Is it often the case that babies cut their teeth with such worrying symptoms?'

Just for a moment Ian continued gazing at her as though deciding whether to this time bow to her unspoken demand that their conversation be limited to the circumstances requiring his presence here this evening. Abruptly he swallowed what was left of his cognac and carelessly replenished his glass from the Viscount's decanter. 'The pain of teething causes great discomfort,' he shortly explained. 'Distress is a self-perpetuating malady and can result in such symptoms as exhaustion and thirst. Once assuaged, the patient usually recuperates and gains strength enough to once more display distress at whatever ails them. And so the cycle continues until the pain abates or is controlled.'

'Well, we are greatly relieved and thankful that you came here this evening, put an end to James's suffering and allowed him some restful sleep. We must hope that tomorrow the tooth appears.'

A curt nod was all the agreement she received to her heartfelt wish. A silence developed and Ruth prayed that someone…anyone…would soon return to disperse the stifling atmosphere. She knew that Ian's taciturnity indicated he was brooding on presenting her with another awkward question. It wasn't long in coming.

'And are you also friendly with Sir Clayton Powell?'

'Why…no…I hardly know him at all,' Ruth returned truthfully. Briskly she approached the window to peer at the night. 'I hope your journey home will be as safe and speedy as the one that brought you here,' she said over a shoulder. 'It's atrocious weather for this time of the year.'

'If I return with Sir Clayton driving me, no doubt I'll be within doors in no time at all.' The inference that she hoped him soon gone from the Manor had not been lost on Ian.

'He is a very good horseman, so I've been told.'

'He is a very great scoundrel, so I've been told,' Ian returned scathingly.

'Perhaps he is, but tonight we must cast him very credibly in the role of hero,' Ruth shot back. 'Sir Clayton insisted on being the one to brave the elements and fetch you despite the Viscount's protests that the duty was his.'

'Ah…I think I can guess the reason why you praise him so prettily.' Ian barked a low laugh. 'Is the notorious Lothario close to making another conquest? You would be well advised, madam, to give him a wide berth. I have a town residence and know a little of London society and the debauchery that goes on in his vicinity.'

'But you can know very little of me, sir,' Ruth smartly cut him off, 'or you wouldn't hint at my behaving so ridiculously. And I hope you aren't about to be very indiscreet, and repeat vulgar town tattle that might have reached your ears.'

That fluent rebuke caused Ian's cheeks to mottle, but he forced a smile to twist his lips. 'I take it you already know of his rakish reputation and yet have no objection to remaining in his company. I think that ridiculous, madam.'

Ruth's eyes flashed a warning at him and she took a pace or two closer. If he added just a little more to his insolent opinions, she'd give him a piece of her mind. How dare Ian Bryant sermonise about philandering gentlemen when he had propositioned her to be his mistress while his wife was alive and well! How dare he imagine she'd act the simpering flirt with any gentleman! He certainly couldn't be drawing on his own experience of her character. She'd smartly rebuffed his wooing on both the occasions it had been forthcoming. She was just in the right frame of mind to remind him of it.

It was at that moment that Clayton entered the room and,

seeing Ian Bryant and Ruth Hayden so close, their eyes locked together, the atmosphere solid with tension, confirmed the suspicions he'd had earlier. He'd now met the gentleman who'd proposed to Ruth Hayden. They were lovers...or soon to be...

A corner of Clayton's mouth moved, but scant humour warmed his eyes. On realising they were no longer alone, Ruth had guiltily skittered back and put a decent distance between her and the doctor. Clayton sauntered to the sideboard and snatched the decanter, allowing the startled couple time to compose themselves.

He also needed to compose himself, he realised as the fist that held the fragile neck of the bottle began tightening perilously on the glass. A rush of ferocious jealousy had stormed his veins at having his suspicions about the pair confirmed and it was a novel and unpleasant experience. He felt a fool, too, for having just hours ago considered that this beautiful, principled woman might be involved romantically with an elderly man of the cloth who loaned her a horse and cart. She deserved far better. Grudgingly he accepted that if Dr Ian Bryant was about to become her husband, he looked to be a fitting partner for her.

He guessed the doctor to be about his own age, in his middle thirties. He was of good height, well built and seemed personable enough in character. Having visited his Willowdene residence, Clayton knew he possessed a very presentable house staffed by neatly attired servants. Clayton uncharitably wished to see the damnable fellow return there without delay.

With a tumbler in his hand and a smile on his lips, Clayton pivoted about to face the couple. 'James looks very peaceful now. I think he'll sleep the night through.' It was pleasantly observed; not a trace of his mood showed in his face or speech.

'Good…that's good,' Ruth blurted. 'Is Sarah staying with him in the nursery for a while longer?' She wished that her friend would arrive and take the focus of attention. For all Clayton's easy words and smiles, she sensed he too was brooding on something other than the drama surrounding the little boy upstairs. She noted his piercing grey gaze was on Ian, and little welcome was in his eyes. Ruth felt her stomach lurch as it occurred to her that Clayton might have overheard the slanderous remarks that Ian had made about his character and reputation. She didn't believe Clayton would intentionally eavesdrop, but he might have also over-heard Ian disparage Sarah. By association he'd criticised Clayton's best friend on his choice of wife.

'I believe Lady Tremayne went to speak to the servants about dinner.' Clayton gave Ruth a charming smile that served only to unsettle her further.

'Gavin has gone to do so, too,' Ruth replied to fill the ensuing quiet. 'Why is it that disasters always strike when one is least able to promptly deal with them?' she continued, chattering aimlessly. 'It would be a miracle indeed if just once such an emergency were to occur during daylight in fine weather.'

Her eyes flitted between the two gentlemen, imploring for a contribution of bland dialogue from one of them.

Clayton removed his pitiless gaze from the doctor, who had become a mite uneasy beneath it. He looked at Ruth and immediately his eyes warmed as he noted her strained features. She looked anxious that he might say or do something to upset her lover. And much as he wanted to—for purely selfish reasons—he decided not to invite the fellow to drink up so he could get him back to his own home. 'I imagine Dr Bryant would know about fate's contrariness, Mrs Hayden. I expect he has such a tale to quote.'

If either Clayton or Ruth expected the fellow might regale

them with a few interesting anecdotes, while they waited for the Tremaynes to appear, they were to be disappointed.

Ian continued moodily brooding and simply muttered an agreement to the hypothesis that this wasn't the first time he'd been called out at dead of night in foul weather to attend the sick or needy. He abruptly took a gulp of brandy.

'Another?' Clayton held out the decanter indicatively towards Ian, a ghost of a smile acknowledging that he was rather contented to know that the worthy pillar of Willowdene Society could act unpleasantly sullen.

Clayton's glimmer of private amusement was not lost on Ruth. She'd recently been subjected to that sardonic look and knew what lay behind it. And indeed Ian was acting in a most idiotic way. 'I hope the road has not worsened,' she said in a desperately small voice.

'Indeed, so do I,' Ian gritted drily. 'Or I might be forced to remain here the night.'

'Oh, you won't,' Clayton promised silkily. 'Whatever the weather, I'll get you home. You've no fears on that score.'

The two men exchanged a combatant stare before Ian turned away.

Ruth glowered at Ian. The doctor seemed determined to make a show of his bad humour rather than act courteously until the viscount and viscountess returned and he might properly take his leave. In answer to Ruth's prayers, Gavin and Sarah appeared, arm in arm.

'Um…dinner is still quite presentable,' Gavin announced, having sensed at once that the crackle in the atmosphere hadn't dispersed in his absence. When the doctor made no move to take his leave at that hint and remained looking dour, Gavin added, 'Are you sure you won't stay and dine with us, Dr Bryant?'

'I thank you, but no,' Ian retorted. His eyes quit Ruth and

returned to the glass that rocked in his palm. He swiftly despatched what remained in it and put down the empty vessel.

Clayton mirrored the movement, returning his own glass to the sideboard. 'I'll have the carriage brought round,' he said.

Having firmly quashed Gavin's protests that it was his turn to go out, Clayton opened the door, allowing the doctor to go before him into the hallway. 'Don't wait longer for dinner on my account. I can get something to eat at the Red Lion tonight, and a bed too,' he said. 'I insist, Sarah,' he stated softly to his hostess, for she looked appalled at the very idea of him taking bed and board in a tavern. 'The roads might be yet worse to travel on. In any case, it will be well past midnight by the time I reach Willowdene and into the wee small hours before I again reached the Manor.'

Sarah nodded a reluctant acceptance of his logic. She prayed that they would safely reach town; it was silly to expect Clayton to turn about and return in the dark over treacherous terrain.

Clayton's eyes slid to Ruth, tangled with her solemn sepia gaze. 'I bid you a goodnight, Mrs Hayden.'

Ruth moistened her lips. She knew very well she wouldn't see him in the morning. He wanted it that way. 'Goodbye, sir,' she replied quietly.

Chapter Nine

'I suppose you will go home, then.'

'You know I must,' Ruth told Sarah with a husky chuckle as she tied her bonnet strings beneath her chin. Her disappointed friend was given a hug as her mouth drooped. 'As soon as the puddles have gone you must come and visit me again.'

They were stationed just outside the great double doors of the Manor, on the top step of a wide flight that flowed gracefully to the gravel drive. Golden warmth played over Ruth's complexion, urging her to turn and squint at the waterlogged landscape. 'I hope there is no bad flooding.' Her earthy eyes soared to the azure heavens. 'But it is a glorious day and I'm sure there will be more fine weather on the way to dry the fields.'

'I thought Clayton might have returned by now,' Sarah said, peering into the distance. 'He knew you would leave today if the conditions improved. I'm surprised he is not here to bid you farewell. I hope he is not planning to abandon us and return home too.'

'I'm sure you and Gavin will find some occupation,' Ruth blurted, unaware of the *double entendre* in her comment. She was simply keen to change the subject, for just a mention of

Clayton's name was enough to make her stomach lurch and a wistfulness assail her.

'I suppose we might.' Sarah's saucy smile brightened her countenance. 'Do you think Dr Bryant will visit you soon? Did he hint he might propose again?' she probed earnestly. 'I didn't have a chance to speak to you about it yesterday evening. Despite the crisis with James, I recall thinking I'd never seen a man look so smouldering and smitten. He hardly took his eyes from you and seemed marvellously Byronic in your company.'

'I know,' Ruth said flatly. 'Although I'm not sure I was impressed by his sulking.'

'I can't find fault with him,' Sarah said simply. 'However odd his attitude, he gave James expert treatment. The little love is greatly improved this morning.'

Ruth smiled her agreement. She couldn't deny that Ian was a conscientious doctor. He'd done his professional duty before he allowed his personal feelings to spoil his humour. 'I hope he will *not* arrive today,' she said with quiet vehemence, 'for I am still at a loss as to what to say if he proposes to me again. It's no love match on either side, but I suppose he has proved his worth despite his scowls.' A small sigh escaped Ruth before she continued to voice her uncertainties. 'Of course, he needs a mother for his infant son and perhaps wants one quite soon, before the boy gets much older…'

Sarah took Ruth's hands and gave them a comforting squeeze. Her friend's predicament was an unenviable one, but the conclusion she drew to it must be hers alone. 'I can't help you make up your mind,' she said gently. 'Yet I wish I could, for you were a very great help and a dear friend to me last night.'

Sarah's oblique reference to her baby prompted Ruth to smile. 'And you must give that darling boy a cuddle for me when he wakes.'

'I shall,' Sarah said, then looked past Ruth's shoulder and waved. 'Here is Gavin. He said he'd return from his ride in time to bid you farewell.'

Once the viscount and viscountess were lost to sight and she could no longer wave at them through the carriage window, Ruth settled in to the comfy vehicle and closed her eyes. In her mind reeled unwanted thoughts, the most persistent of which was that she'd wished, since she'd risen that morning and seen the snow had gone and the sun was shining, that the dawn had been kinder and brought with it just one more icy blast to strand her at the Manor.

Clayton wouldn't have reneged on his promise to take her home whatever the weather. He would have come back to carry out the duty. But in the event he'd not needed to return. The day was fine, the roads passable. The viscount's coachmen risked no more personal injury than splashes of mud to their smart uniforms in returning her to Fernlea this afternoon.

Clayton had purposely stayed where he was, in Willowdene's Red Lion tavern, avoiding her…removing his presence from her vicinity…she imagined he might say.

It was a test for her and her pride would not allow her to fail it. He knew, as did she, that if she chose to stay on, she did so because of him, because she wanted to see him again. On almost every occasion that they'd been alone he'd told her he found her attractive, then watched for her reaction and ultimately been amused by her blushes or protests. Yesterday evening, before the drama unfolded, she'd been sure he was about to reach for her to kiss her. At the time she'd felt agitated by his cool audacity; now she felt cheated that they hadn't gained just a few more private minutes together.

There was no longer an available barrier behind which she might conceal and indulge her fascination for him. The way was clear for her to go home, and if she did not, he would think he'd been right about her all along. He'd think she was finally ceding the game, signalling her interest in him and that she was his for the taking.

Ruth lowered her eyes, clasping tight her hands to steel against a tremor of warring emotions that burned her to the core. Despite knowing all of it, and feeling the greatest hussy alive, she was sorely tempted to tell the driver to turn about and take her back.

'Are you to dine with us tonight?'

Having just spent a tedious yet necessary hour with his lawyer in Willowdene, Gavin gratefully slouched in to the battered old armchair in the Red Lion's private parlour. Opposite him sat Clayton, idly flicking over the pages of a newspaper while occasionally prodding the smouldering logs with the toe of a boot.

Clayton folded the paper and let it drop to the rug in the space between them. Gavin picked it up and perused the headlines. Finding nothing worth commenting upon, he discarded it and gazed idly about. Realising his question remained unanswered, he looked at his vacant-eyed friend. Clayton's hands were clasped at the back of his flaxen head and he was gazing into space.

'Did you hear what I said?' Gavin asked, rather miffed that his hospitality was being ignored.

'Sorry…' Clayton murmured and frowned an apology. 'What did you say?'

'You're not still fretting over that silly jade Loretta and her mischief making, are you?' Gavin said derisively.

Clayton grunted a mirthless laugh and, folding forwards, plunged his elbows on his knees and examined his knuckles. He'd forgotten about Loretta and her scheming until Gavin just again brought it to mind. 'No, I'm not thinking about any of that. But I should return to London.'

'Whatever for?' Gavin said. 'There's nothing there that won't wait a few more days. Why not stay in Willowdene a while longer? It's obvious to me you enjoy Ruth's company…'

'And it's obvious to me Mrs Hayden would sooner be in Bryant's company,' Clayton gritted out as he surged to his feet. 'Had you not already told me she'd received a proposal of marriage, I'd have seen the evidence for myself last night when I watched the two of them together. She's not wearing a ring. Is she engaged to him yet?'

That fluent and forthright piece of dialogue brought a surprised smile to Gavin's lips. So…indeed, his friend had not been fretting on Loretta. A different woman entirely was occupying his thoughts.

'I wonder that you didn't ask the doctor outright when you drove him home. You're not usually shy and you've obviously been brooding on it.' At Clayton's scowl, Gavin continued, 'Did Ruth say she was soon to be married?'

'No…but then she wouldn't confide in me anything so private. I'm not sure she trusts me.' It was a spontaneous response and it was a moment or two before Clayton realised it might be untrue. She'd confided something terribly private: that she'd lost a daughter in childbirth. It was hardly something you'd say to a person you didn't trust. But perhaps it had been an aberration due to the drama and emotion of the moment when they were united in acute anxiety over James. No doubt she now considered having mentioned the tragedy at all an embarrassing and regrettable weakness.

'What sort of fellow is he?' Clayton abruptly asked.

'I hardly know him,' Gavin answered truthfully. 'I've spent little time in these parts. Sarah knows Ian Bryant better than I do, for she lived here for several years. I've heard nothing bad, and, if I were to judge him on the way he treated James I'd have to say the doctor's a top fellow.'

Clayton grasped the mantelpiece with long fingers and averted his face from his friend's astute gaze. 'Good…glad to hear it,' he said in a strange voice as he watched smoke curl from the logs. 'She deserves to have such a husband.'

'Indeed she does. But she won't have him.'

'What?' Clayton's face whipped up, revealing eyes that were narrowed and stormy.

'She turned him down,' Gavin explained. 'If you were watching them together I'm surprised you hadn't deduced that for yourself. The atmosphere between them was thick enough to carve up.' Gavin picked up the newspaper again and flicked it open. 'Let's pretend that you did guess about that. I've already told you that I very much like Ruth and I'd hate her to think I've spoken out of turn.' Gavin shot his friend a penetrating look. 'The rest is up to you. It's as much as I'm going to tell you.'

Clayton's face swung back to the fire. 'Thanks…I appreciate knowing it,' he muttered hoarsely.

'But I meant what I said when you first arrived: she's no man's mistress.'

'I thought you weren't going to say anything else on the subject,' Clayton reminded him sarcastically.

'Wouldn't like to see you wasting your time…or your money. Don't bother trying to blind her with expensive trinkets before you leave,' Gavin said smoothly and shook the paper to remove a crease from an amusing article. He drew the paper closer to his face. 'A plain gold band might do it…'

'God's teeth!' Clayton exploded. 'How many times do I have to tell you that I'm not marrying anyone ever again!'

'Why not?' Gavin asked from behind the newsprint.

'Have you forgotten that I once had a wife who made my life hell?' Clayton thundered.

'No, I haven't forgotten,' Gavin returned quietly, 'and unfortunately neither have you.' He returned the paper to the floor and looked Clayton directly in the eye. 'Marrying Priscilla was a grave mistake, I'll grant you. But it's the sort of mistake any man in love might have made. She had the face of an angel, the body of a goddess and aristocratic breeding. How were you to know she had the nature of a harlot?'

'I should've known,' Clayton sneered with savage self-mockery. 'God knows I've had enough dealings with them.'

'And plenty more to come, I suppose,' Gavin suggested. 'As you're so determined not to settle down with a decent woman.'

'I've never said I don't want a decent woman,' Clayton protested.

'I know, but there we have the problem as I see it—if you want a proper lady to act indecently for you, you'll have to marry her.'

'Not necessarily,' Clayton returned mordantly. 'I can think of plenty of reputable ladies who've very much enjoyed my company.'

'And your money,' Gavin reminded him acidly.

'That's perfectly acceptable,' Clayton said with a grin. 'I'm glad when we understand each other too.'

Gavin stared lengthily at him before saying, 'Believe me, you're wasting your time with Ruth. She would never understand you in a million years.'

'All women understand the offer of unlimited luxury and security.'

'I never thought I'd say this, but…at times you can be a callous bastard, my friend.'

'And I never thought I'd say this,' Clayton returned through his teeth, 'but you've turned in to a pious prick since you got married.'

'I'll take it as a compliment,' Gavin replied coolly. 'For

God knows if I hadn't married I might have ended up like you—a bitter man who's allowed a disastrous alliance that lasted not even one year to ruin his prospect of having a happy family life.'

'Well, what are you waiting for?' Clayton asked in a deadly soft sneer. 'Why don't you quit my loathsome company and return to your happy family life?'

Gavin pushed himself out of the armchair and stood for a moment facing Clayton. The space between them crackled dangerously with belligerence. 'And what are you going to do?' Gavin jeered. 'Return to London and Loretta?'

'Not yet,' Clayton bit out grimly. 'I'm going to test your theory that not every woman's a harlot at heart.' With that he turned on his heel and, on quitting the room, crashed the door shut behind him.

'What is it, Cissie?' Ruth asked, looking up from the linen she'd been hemming. She'd been home some hours and, while Cissie had flown to and fro from hearth to hearth trying to bring some warmth to the cottage's stone-cold rooms, Ruth had taken on the mending basket that was her servant's usual mid-week task.

Cissie wiped coal dust from her palms on to her crumpled pinafore. 'A gentleman caller, ma'am, and he says not to announce him.' Cissie's voice was low and her eyes slid sideways, indicating that the gentleman was probably within earshot in the hallway.

Ruth looked startled and the colour in her cheeks ebbed away. The conversation she'd had with Sarah earlier came back to haunt her. She'd not heard a knock at the door and she had been primed to listen for it. But surely Ian had not come so soon! It was bad manners indeed not to have allowed her even one day to settle back home before he visited. Yet she had sensed as soon as they met at the Tremaynes' that he wanted to approach her again and would quite quickly do so.

Reading her mistress's confusion in her puckered features, Cissie hissed, 'You wouldn't have heard him arrive, ma'am. He didn't have to knock 'cos the door was open where I was lugging in the scuttle to the front sitting room.'

Ruth nodded her understanding of the situation and stuffed the needles and cottons quickly back in to the workbox on the table. She stood and brushed down her dress, for small, snipped threads littered her plain dark skirt.

So engaged, and conscious of the proximity of her visitor, she instructed in an underbreath, 'Show him in, please, Cissie. And you may go. Thank you for staying on. I know it is well past the hour you usually return home.'

'I don't mind staying on a bit longer, ma'am…' Cissie began.

Ruth was ruefully sure Cissie meant what she'd said. Cissie was a good girl, but no doubt as eager as the other villagers to discover the likely outcome of the negotiations between the widow and the doctor.

When she'd arrived home earlier that day she'd barely stepped a foot outside the Tremaynes' carriage before having proof that the rumour mill had been grinding in her absence. Two of the village matrons had materialised from nowhere, huddled into their warm woolly shawls. Already aware of Mrs Hayden's acquaintance with the local gentry, they'd given short shrift to the splendid carriage. What had brought Mrs Stern and Mrs Brewer out in the cold was a great desire to know, as they'd not seen her for a while, whether Mrs Hayden had lately been keeping well. Or had she been in need of the doctor…? they'd slyly enquired.

'Are the fires lit? And the cooking range?' Ruth asked in a hushed tone.

Cissie nodded. 'All of 'em got going,' she confirmed. 'I'll fetch him in and be off, then.'

Ruth nodded. As her servant disappeared, she closed her eyes and drew in a deep calming breath. No amount of stitching and thinking this afternoon had brought her to any definite conclusion on what she must now say. Advantages and disadvantages had refused to stay still for her to weigh them. Her concentration had been hijacked at every turn by memories of another gentleman. Drat the charming rogue!

As she heard the door click shut, she twisted about and what little blood remained in her cheeks fled before returning with a vengeance. The charming rogue she'd been silently cursing was before her in all his sartorial elegance and with a very disturbing glint in his eye.

'Sir Clayton…I…I was not expecting to see *you*…' She lapsed into silence and her small white teeth attacked her lower lip. Her rattled comment had sounded very unwelcoming, the more so because it had been ejected so spontaneously.

'But you were expecting another gentleman to visit?' Clayton suggested in that dry tone of his.

It was obvious he'd guessed the identity of the person to whom he alluded, but Ruth had no intention of confirming his suspicions. 'My maid didn't give the caller's name. She said he wanted it that way.' Inwardly Ruth chided herself for not having prised such a vital fact from Cissie. She'd not done so because she'd immediately jumped to a wrong conclusion—that the caller was Ian Bryant and he'd wanted to remain incognito because he feared being turned away after their run- in yesterday.

'I didn't give her my name,' Clayton said simply as he proceeded further into the room. 'Don't tell her off; she did ask for it.'

'Did you want me to think you were someone else?' Ruth asked, confused.

'No; I thought if you knew it was me you might decide to feel indisposed,' Clayton answered with a quiet truthfulness.

Having digested that, Ruth said, 'I know we've had our differences, sir, but I thought we parted on reasonable terms.' She clasped her hands behind her back, out of sight, for they were visibly quivering. 'Am I to deduce that you've come to say something you believe might give offence?'

'As you say, we parted harmoniously yesterday,' he replied, smoothly sidestepping her question. 'Nevertheless, I'm not certain that you've forgiven me for my brutish behaviour at the Manor.'

'And have you come to repeat such behaviour?' Ruth asked quietly, determined to have her answer. Her earthy brown eyes clung to his in mute appeal as she awaited his response. It was a long time in coming.

A silence had developed between them that seemed heavy with sensual tension. He'd not come closer to touch her; the aura of cold air and cologne that clung to his clothes was only faintly scenting the room. Yet Ruth felt so acutely conscious of his presence that her limbs had weakened and her lips lightly parted in anticipation of him soon plunging his mouth on to hers. As the seconds passed, Ruth finally tore her gaze from his and grew pale.

'I've said before that I want your good opinion. Why would I want to hurt you?' Clayton said gently. Even as he uttered the words he felt the callous bastard that Gavin had named him.

She knew what he wanted. Ruth Hayden was bright as well as beautiful. She was aware that he was here to proposition her and he'd read her reaction to it in her face. Yet she'd allowed him to stay. Not that he'd imagined for one moment that he wouldn't eventually get his way. She'd turn him down, perhaps once or twice. But she'd succumb in the end.

She'd changed out of her silk dress and now was garbed in a plain and serviceable day dress. The room was spartan and cold. She had one servant—a young maid who had hurried off home, leaving her quite alone. She was shabby genteel, eking out a small inheritance that barely covered necessities, and too proud to accept financial aid from her friends. And he knew Gavin, or perhaps Sarah, would have offered it.

He'd had dealings with a lot of widows in just such frugal circumstances...not one of them had blenched and avoided his eye on guessing his purpose in visiting them. Some had turned him down to test his generosity. Ruth would turn him down to test his leniency, and when she found it lacking she'd turn him down again. And then when the enormity of what he was offering her was too great a temptation to resist, she'd acquiesce...unless she decided to settle for Bryant instead. But for some reason Clayton no longer considered the doctor a serious rival.

Once he'd learned that Ruth had rejected the doctor's proposal, the reason for the fellow's sullen disposition had become clearer. Clayton had imagined that a lovers' tiff had been the cause of the tension between them last night. Now he knew that the fellow was unhappy because the attraction between them was one-sided.

Whereas Clayton knew that, wary and disapproving of him as she was, Ruth Hayden found him as fascinating as he found her, and it would take no more than a kiss to know for sure...

Chapter Ten

'Would you like a drink, sir?' Ruth's offer of hospitality sounded stilted to her own ears, thus she strove to be more affable, adding, 'There is a bottle of port in the front sitting room.'

'Do you prefer port to sherry?'

A corner of Ruth's lips twitched and a cluck of her tongue denied any such thing. 'I keep it for visitors, sir.'

'Doctor Bryant?'

'Have you something you wish to ask me about Dr Bryant?' she demanded, faintly annoyed by his indolent hints.

'I've no need to ask about him. I think he proposed and you rejected him. Am I right?'

So…indeed he did not need to ask about her dealings with the doctor. Ruth felt indignation grip her chest. 'Did he tell you that when you took him home yesterday?' she choked out, appalled to think they might have discussed her.

'We shared little conversation on that return trip. Bryant said nothing about you. And neither did I.'

'I don't believe that Sarah would have mentioned I'd received a marriage proposal from him.'

Despite his clash with his friend, Clayton's loyalty to

Gavin remained resolute. Besides, Gavin had not betrayed the identity of Ruth's suitor. He'd easily deduced that for himself.

'It wasn't difficult to guess the nature of your relationship. I needed only to watch the two of you together yesterday to form an opinion on it.'

It wasn't the first time this man had rendered Ruth at a loss for a reply. 'How perceptive you are,' she resorted to murmuring.

'And am I right in thinking that you expect Bryant to return to try again?'

'I can't fault your perception, sir, but I think your manners are still lacking,' Ruth breathed. 'What business is it of yours, pray?'

'None, of course,' Clayton said quite impenitently as their eyes held in the muted light. 'Will you accept him next time?'

Ruth made an exasperated little movement. But eventually his silent persistence beat her defences and she gave him a stuttered answer. 'I…I don't know…'

'Why not?'

'Please, sir…' Ruth begged through an ache in her throat.

'Why not?' Clayton persisted in a treacherously appealing way. 'Are you unsure because you know you don't love him?'

'I doubt he loves me either,' Ruth spontaneously returned. Now the admission was out, it seemed she was obliged to say more. 'There is more to it than that,' she carefully explained as her brunette brows drew together in concentration. 'Doctor Bryant is a widower. He has an infant son and wants a mother for his child. But he might choose a woman to fill the role too soon and deprive the boy of parents who feel affection for one another. Ian might yet find someone to love, who loves him. And that would be best,' she ended gruffly. To indicate the matter was most definitely closed she said, 'I shall fetch the port.'

She started for the door, her step faltering when she realised that her rash decision to gain a little respite from his overpowering presence would bring her very close to him. Every fateful pace was taken with her eyes screened behind long dark lashes and as she came within his reach they softly…naturally…fell closed.

One of his hands curved on her arm, turning her so the other might also assist in bringing her against him. Ruth felt honeyed warmth steal into her veins in response to his hard masculine body pressed to the softness of her curves. She was not expecting words from him and he gave none. His face lowered as hers angled up, their mouths meeting in a perfect blend of size and shape.

Clayton felt the pressure of small fingers on his forearms vary in strength as though inwardly she battled between pulling him closer or pushing him away. To help her decide, he kept the kiss sweet and courteous.

In rogue daydreams—that previously had been impatiently ejected from her mind—Ruth had imagined that an infamous womaniser would quite selfishly and swiftly seduce. Sir Clayton Powell was such a man, nobody denied that…not even him. But he was kissing her as though he had endless time to mould her mouth to his and give her innocent pleasure. Ruth had not expected brutality from him, but neither had she anticipated a touch so exquisitely tender that it began to melt her bones. Gently he coaxed her lips apart so his tongue could caress their silky inner plumpness while long fingers splayed beneath the soft curls at her nape to stroke and support.

Ruth's hands crept to his shoulders and anchored there, curving over solid muscles that almost defeated the span of her delicate grip.

With that tacit permission Clayton deepened the kiss, tantalising her tongue with his. He heard her little moan and sensed her opening explicitly for him. His tongue plunged and retreated in slow erotic rhythm and a hand stroked from her back to her front to enclose a voluptuous breast and graze a nipple into rigidity.

Linking her fingers behind Clayton's neck, Ruth dragged his mouth to bruise hers while her back sensually bowed. The words might have refused to quit her throat, but Clayton understood her desire to have more of his touch.

It wasn't an invitation Clayton was able to resist. With his mouth fused to hers, swiftly, expertly, his fingers worked loose tiny buttons, then slipped inside her bodice. Above her camisole her lush breasts began rising to firmly fill his palms. As his thumbs circled skilfully, he felt her pelvis graze on his and, as he shifted position, her thighs instinctively parted, sweetly accommodating him. Having exposed milky silken skin on a slender shoulder, he slid his mouth to pay homage to it. He felt her become tense with excitement as his lips sought sensitive places and she swayed her head to better enjoy the bliss. Momentarily Clayton stopped the seduction to observe the rapturous expression tautening her features. Her head was back a little, her eyes closed and her mouth visibly pulsing, swollen and scarlet from his assault and still parted in willingness for more.

Yet despite the tormenting thud in his groin and the ache to see naked the superb figure he could feel heating beneath the cambric, a small part of his mind was urging him to let her go.

His courtly strategy had worked better than he'd expected, but instead of being satisfied Clayton felt ashamed. Ruth wanted him as much as he wanted her, he'd proved that to them both. He could take foreplay to a natural conclusion now if he wanted, and there would be no quibbling over whether or not she might agree to be his mistress. The deed would be done and only the delicate issue of money to be broached.

The fact that his powers of calculated seduction hadn't deserted him out in the sticks didn't make Ruth any less fine a person. It made him more egotistical and cruel than he cared to know.

A boast, made in anger, that he could prove Ruth no better, no worse, than any other woman with whom he kept company was troubling him. He could bed her…right now if he chose…his throbbing loins furiously taunted his conscience. But it wouldn't validate his cynicism, remonstrated a niggling voice of reason.

Ruth was the antithesis of the vain, self-centred woman that Loretta and her ilk represented and deserved so much more than he wanted to give her. She deserved what the doctor had offered—a lifetime of respectability and support from a circle of relatives and friends. She'd lost several loved ones in her twenty-eight years, including her baby daughter. She'd known much heartache, yet seemed devoid of self-pity. She was more concerned that a motherless child should feel secure in his parents' love than grasp at security for herself. She was all a woman…a wife…should be. She deserved that happy family life that Gavin had taunted him over.

Through a daze of warm lassitude Ruth sensed he might be withdrawing from her. But she dismissed disappointment, for a vital part of him was irresistibly hot and hard against her yielding belly. A vague sigh escaped her as, far back in her mind, she subdued pride and conscience simply by wallowing in the promise of more wonderful loving from him. A lonely moment later her weighty lids lifted and their eyes merged in sultry passion.

Clayton's gaze roved her rosy face and, as he saw confusion steal to stifle the fire in her eyes, he managed a slight smile. 'I should go,' he said gruffly, while feeling a wretched fool. Women were supposed to tease men and withdraw at a crucial moment, not the other way around. Gently he drew together her bodice and did up a button. He got no further than the first one.

With a stumble in her step, Ruth jerked and spun away from him, her trembling fingers flying over fasteners. 'I shall not fetch the port, then, sir, as you are leaving,' she said in a voice that was shrill, yet cold as ice. 'I know you are able to show yourself out as easily as you found your way in.'

'Ruth…listen to me…' Clayton began, his tense visage pale with guilt and regret. He took a step towards her ramrod-straight back. 'Would you truly have wanted me to continue?'

Ruth swished to face him, then backed up when she saw how close he'd again come to her. 'You were correct, sir, in saying you should go,' she snapped in a voice that sounded suffocated. 'You were correct about something else too—I *am* expecting the doctor to soon call. I shouldn't want him to arrive and find you here. Please leave.'

An involuntary laugh escaped Clàyton, but his eyes were as mirthless as the sound. His head tilted back and a grimace of indecision distorted his handsome features.

'It isn't over between us, Ruth.'

It was issued as a soft vibrant promise that sent a tremor to shimmy through Ruth. A tongue flick soothed her swollen lips. 'I must contradict you on that, sir. It is.' A gulp of air and she continued, 'My neighbours are very alert to strangers arriving in the village. Your visit to me will have been noticed. I live alone and should not want to be the butt of salacious gossip, so please don't come here again.'

A fierce defiant stare made Ruth turn her head, then her body away from him. A moment later he turned on his heel. By the door he halted, casting a sideways look at her stiff form. 'I wish you a happy birthday for next week.'

Jolted from her humiliation by the unexpected felicitation, she spun to look at him, but he had gone.

When Ruth heard the front door close, the power in her tight little muscles seemed to ebb away. She crumpled forwards while forcing her hips against the wall for support. Tiny silent sobs jerked her as she fumbled her way to the armchair and fell into its familiar old embrace.

What a fool she'd been! From the moment at Willowdene Manor when Sir Clayton Powell had arrogantly inferred she had an interest in him, she'd vowed never to be a victim to his philandering. Henceforth she'd known that a challenge simmered between them. She'd sensed, too, that he wasn't a man to take defeat well. Deep down she'd known he wouldn't return home before he'd attempted to soothe his masculine conceit and claim victory in their battle of wills. And what an easy triumph it had been! She had possessed no defences, showed no resistance to his subtle assault.

In the most calculated and callous way he had just impressed on her how weak she was. And how unscrupulous! She'd implied she might accept Ian's proposal. Yet the prospect of becoming another man's wife hadn't curbed her wantonness. Her small palms flew to soothe the burn in her cheeks, for she felt utterly ashamed of her behaviour, and of having made Dr Bryant seem ridiculous.

Ruth had guessed that Clayton hadn't warmed to the doctor. And Ian had made it quite apparent that he considered Sir Clayton Powell a reprobate. Had their animosity spurred Clayton to act the predator? Had he gained some perverse satisfaction in discovering that he was able to take what the doctor wanted?

He'd had his answer. She'd revelled in his mesmerising virility. For those few witless minutes that she'd clung slavishly to him, and he had lavished on her his artful lovemaking, she'd felt more vital and attractive than she had in very many years.

What had he felt? Aroused by her female body? Certainly. Bored by the ease with which he'd secured the conquest? The distressing possibility pierced her heart, trapped a little painful noise in her throat. Her small hands scrubbed anew over her scalding cheeks. Swine! she whispered through her teeth before the epithet was ejected too vociferously.

A loud knock at the door brought Ruth immediately to her feet. In an odd way she hoped it was him come back again, because she had much straight in her mind now and she was ready to give vent to it.

'Is anything amiss, Mrs Hayden?' Mrs Brewer asked while Mrs Stern attempted to peer over Ruth's shoulder into the interior of her house.

'All is well, thank you.' Ruth quickly had subdued her dismay at seeing the women and had uttered the reassurance levelly.

Mrs Brewer accepted that with a twitch of a smile. 'It's just that we…' she indicated her friend with a tip of her cap '…believed we heard you shout out and thought, as we'd seen Cissie go off, that somebody else was with you and up-setting you. We came to make sure that you are not in need of anything.'

'I need nothing. Thank you for your concern,' Ruth said and, with a nod, withdrew and shut the door. She leaned back against the wooden panels and stuffed a fist to her mouth, stifling a hysterical giggle from her vigilant neighbours' acute faculties. The women must have been loitering in the lane to pounce as soon as an opportunity presented itself to quiz her over her imposing visitor. The arrival of a gentle-man such as Sir Clayton Powell, with his handsome looks and distinct air of affluence, was sure to stir avid curiosity in a backwater such as Fernlea.

Ruth gained no cheer from having had the proof that she'd used a valid excuse to make Clayton go. She'd certainly given the gossips something to tattle about.

She heard the gate click shut and straightened, stood quite still for a moment as the events of the afternoon ebbed and flowed in her mind. The one that rushed in and stayed to make her eyes prickle once more was that he'd remembered something that she had forgot: next week she had a birthday.

The following day Clayton was up and about early. He'd enjoyed little sleep overnight, having been plagued by various frustrating discomforts. His unfinished business with Ruth was undoubtedly the most potent of them. But the revelry that had gone on into the small hours, in the private parlour below his chamber, had also kept him restless the night through.

On his return to the Red Lion yesterday the landlady, Mrs Rolley, had immediately accosted him, with much bowing and scraping. Would m'lord be obliging enough to give up the back parlour for one evening so an impromptu wedding party might take place? she'd begged to know. How could he refuse when the young bridegroom had gazed at him with solemn appeal in his bright boy's eyes? That inducement, together with signs of a very distended belly beneath his child-like wife's pretty dress, had disposed Clayton to be charitable.

His weary generosity had extended to the handing over of a banknote to the scrawny youth to wish them both well. Now he had his private domain back, and as he looked about the spick-and-span surfaces, he realised that Mrs Rolley and her maids must have toiled hard and fast to clean it up for him this morning. He took out his watch. It was just after eight o'clock and he had no idea what had prompted him to get up so early, unrefreshed, when a little peace might finally be had in his bedchamber. Now he would have to kick his heels for at least a couple of hours before collecting his belongings from the Manor and setting off back to London. He wanted to be on his way immediately, but it was an ungodly hour to make his farewells. It was equally unthinkable to collect his things and head for London without first thanking Gavin and Sarah for their hospitality.

'Will you be wanting your usual…or somethin' different?'

Clayton turned from contemplation of the cloudless sky to see Molly. She was an impish girl, and this morning her sly saucy comment served only to further irritate him. But he gave the serving maid a half-smile that made her blush. 'Just coffee and toast.'

'What of eggs 'n' bacon 'n' beefsteak 'n' ale?' Molly protested. She knew this fine fellow had eaten his fill of all of that just yesterday breakfast time.

'I'm going out,' Clayton said and turned his head to indicate he was in no mood for banter. In fact, he had enough time to while away to eat a very hearty meal, but had no appetite to do so.

Once Molly had gone, Clayton stood up and strolled to the window. He braced an arm on the timber frame and rested his forehead on it as he watched the ostlers going busily about their work. A few of the wedding guests who had taken rooms were preparing to leave. One of the women turned and waved up at a window just as she was about to clamber aboard her ride. Clayton slanted an idle look in that direction and saw the young bride returning the salute until her husband drew her back from the window and the curtain dropped.

Clayton's mouth tilted wryly. The romantic little tableau reminded him there'd been another reason why he'd got no sleep. The newlyweds had taken the room next to his and the wretched bed squeaked.

Thrusting his hands into his pockets he turned, leaned the back of his head against glass. Finally he allowed his mind to dwell on the real reason for his irascibility. He'd acted the moral martyr yesterday and now regretted it.

He should have ignored his conscience and stayed with Ruth last night. She was a widow approaching her third decade, not a virginal miss just out of the schoolroom. What in damnation did he think he was doing trying to save her from herself…or from him?

She'd rebuffed Bryant's proposal before he'd quit London. He'd not turned up to seduce her and take away her chance of happiness with the doctor. There was nothing for him to feel guilty about on that score.

After his bizarre behaviour yesterday, what did she think of him now? Did she believe he was playing a careless game and had no proper interest in her? He'd never been more deadly serious about bringing a woman under his protection. He wanted to see her wearing velvets and jewels that complemented the rich cocoa colour of her hair and eyes. He wanted her by his side, partnering him at salons and parties. Wryly he acknowledged that, despite that being quite true, his greatest desire was to see her naked next to him in bed.

So what was he to do? Go back and visit her in Fernlea despite her edict that he must never again darken her door? They were the same people; if she allowed him to get close enough to touch her, he could again seduce her.

Clayton's brooding was abruptly curtailed as the door opened and Molly sashayed in with a tray that held a silver coffee pot and a cup and saucer. 'Toast is coming,' she chirruped, as she poured. As she was leaving the room, her exit was blocked by a gentleman about to enter the parlour. 'Shall

I fetch another cup?' she asked cheerily on recognising Sir Clayton's friend. A nod from Viscount Tremayne sent the girl on her way.

''Struth! What are you doing here at this time of the morning?'

'Being a good friend...which is more than you deserve,' Gavin grumbled in response. It was his oblique way of clearing the air between them after their heated exchange yesterday.

A bashful grimace and a gruff mutter from Clayton was his acknowledgement that he'd behaved badly. He also gave up the first cup of coffee from the pot.

Gavin fumbled in a pocket of his coat and drew out a letter. 'This arrived for you early this morning. It came express so I guessed it must be urgent and came to find you.'

Clayton took the proffered parchment and looked at it. His name and direction had been written in an unknown hand. Certainly it was not from Loretta. But somebody had taken the trouble to find out from his staff in Belgravia Place where he'd gone when he quit London. He broke the seal and quickly scanned the two paragraphs.

Gavin noticed his friend's expression altering from mild curiosity to contained wrath.

'Bad news?' Gavin ventured quietly.

Clayton wordlessly handed him the letter to read.

'The man's a fool. He can't hit a barn door at five paces.' Gavin gave back the letter and watched Clayton once more frown fiercely at the note from Ralph Pomfrey challenging him to a duel.

'He's an enthusiastic amateur out for my blood and that makes him dangerous,' Clayton said grimly.

Chapter Eleven

'You are off *where*?'

'To town, sweetheart,' Gavin told his stunned wife. 'I shouldn't be gone more than a week.' He pivoted with one boot still planted on the first stair. 'Would you like to come too?'

'No, I would not,' Sarah said crossly. 'This is too bad of you, Gavin. I thought we were to make plans for James's christening. You have not long arrived from London and now you say you want to go back?'

Gavin strode across the hall to cradle his wife's vexed countenance between his palms. 'I must go…I didn't want to worry you with the ins and outs, but…' he sighed in resignation '…Clayton has a bit of a problem to sort out.'

Sarah's jaw dropped and, unmollified, she flicked free of his touch. 'You are not about to tell me that you think Sir Clayton Powell unable to sort out his own problems?' she scoffed.

'He said much the same thing to me when I insisted on going with him.' Gavin's expression sobered. 'He's left for town already and you know I would not go after him unless it were a serious matter.'

'Now you are worrying me, Gavin.' Sarah's brows knitted together. She quickly came close to him and her small fingers gripped his forearm to hurry his answer. 'Has something happened to one of his houses or servants in his absence?'

Gavin drew his wife towards the library; once they were within the room he turned to gaze at her. He didn't relish telling Sarah that Clayton's mistress had stirred up such trouble behind his back that, if not skilfully defused, it might end in blood and crime.

If Pomfrey refused to listen to reason from Clayton or himself, then his friend would be obliged by honour to keep the dawn appointment. And Gavin would stand second for him. In truth, Gavin felt rather guilty for having dismissed Loretta's scheming as unimportant, and for having encouraged Clayton to view it in a similar vein. She'd obviously known exactly how to incite Pomfrey to suicidal recklessness. The note that Clayton had received challenging him to return to town and turn up at the appointed hour had been venomously concise.

If, despite efforts at conciliation, Loretta had done her work too well and the duel went ahead, the protagonists could end in a courtroom. And that was assuming one or other of them survived. The outcome looked cut and dried—if pistols were used, Pomfrey should miss his target, allowing Clayton to delope. If swords were chosen, Clayton should be able to disarm Pomfrey within minutes. But fate was impossible to predict and accidents happened. A nick from a rapier or a graze from a bullet could be deadlier than it at first seemed if infection set in. There were instances to cite of nice fellows who had allowed a petty grievance to put a premature end to their otherwise healthy and blameless lives.

An impatient sigh from Sarah cut into Gavin's troubled brooding. An anxious, entreating look from her settled the matter. Clayton was a close friend, but Sarah was his wife and no secrets were allowed between them. He told her everything.

'Trollop!' Sarah fumed.

'I know,' Gavin concurred. 'But he will keep company with such people.'

Sarah's eyes narrowed on her husband at the self-mockery in his tone. A few years ago, before they'd met, her beloved husband had kept company with just such people.

'How stupid you gentlemen can be at times! The hussy is not worth taking a small scratch for! Go at once! Clayton might be stabbed or shot to death.'

'Unlikely…unless Pomfrey's employed an assassin to impersonate him.' Gavin hoped his light tone might reassure Sarah, for she looked close to tears. He thrust his hands into his pockets and strode away a few paces. 'Pomfrey, the blasted fool, can't use a gun or a sword, whereas Clayton… can,' he concluded with masterly understatement. He thought it unnecessary to add that his friend's military background had furnished him with quite deadly and awe-inspiring combat skills.

'You must start to pack…' Sarah insisted and started urgently towards the exit.

'Will you come and join me later in the week?' Gavin caught at her arm to arrest her mid-flight and gently draw her close. 'Bring whoever you want with you to Lansdowne Crescent. Let's make the most of a bad situation. We haven't spent much time in town during a Season. James is much better, is he not, and up to the journey?'

Sarah nodded while frowning. 'I had wanted to spend some time here with Ruth. I haven't seen her for so long.'

'Why not ask her to accompany you?' Gavin suggested innocently. 'I'm sure she would like a change of scenery and to put a little distance between herself and the doctor.' He added wryly, 'The poor chap looks distinctly lovelorn around her. And she looks a little embarrassed by it.'

'She hasn't completely dismissed the idea of becoming his wife, you know,' Sarah said. 'She simply needs time to weigh it all up. Marrying somebody when no love is present is a decision of great import.'

'Absence, they say, makes the heart grow fonder. If Ian Bryant is right for Ruth, she should know it by the time she returns.' Gavin opened the door for his wife and, arm in arm, they proceeded towards the stairs discussing the good sense in entering matrimony only after much inner debate.

'But *we* didn't,' Sarah pointed out, turning to her husband with a hand on the banisters.

He grinned and touched a kiss to the ivory knuckles he'd brought to his lips. 'Ah…but that was different. I knew straight away we were made for each other…and persuading you of it gave me great pleasure.'

'Well, if you won't come, then I won't go.'

'Don't be silly, Sarah,' Ruth chided as she bobbed little James on her lap. She was rewarded with a grin that displayed two tiny pearls embedded in the baby's bottom gum. Having planted a little kiss on James's silken crown, she said, 'Of course you must go. You will enjoy yourself in town. There is so much to do at this time of the year. The Season is just under way…'

'I shan't go without you,' Sarah declared adamantly. 'I came to Willowdene to spend time with you and I shall. I doubt Gavin will be gone long in any case if I refuse to join him in Lansdowne Crescent.'

Ruth sighed. 'You are doing a fine job of making me feel guilty.'

'Am I?' Sarah enquired brightly before looking chagrined. 'Sorry. It would never have occurred to me to go, but once Gavin had infuriatingly planted the idea in my head, I came to think it a very good suggestion.' She looked appealingly at Ruth. 'I think it would be very good for us both. You might benefit from having a little time away from here in order to think what you must do.'

Ruth continued to thread her fingers through little James's soft locks. She could not deny what Sarah had latterly said was true.

'Have you seen Ian since the night James was ill?'

Ruth shook her head and glanced at Sarah. 'I'm not sure if I am relieved or indignant at his absence.' Her lips slanted ruefully. 'It is simple vanity. I know he ought to transfer his attention to a more appreciative lady…but perhaps not too soon.'

'He will be back,' Sarah declared confidently. 'And it would be as well if you had your reply ready.'

'Indeed it would,' Ruth concurred.

'So it's best to put distance between the two of you till you have quite clear in your mind what you must say,' Sarah said triumphantly.

Ruth chuckled at her friend's tactics. 'I should like to visit London and think it all through while spending more time with you, but it is not practical.'

'Do you mean money?' Sarah asked bluntly.

'In part,' Ruth owned up. 'But it is not just that. It is a long time since I socialised amid the *ton*. I have become quite provincial. Sometimes I think I will end up talking with a pronounced country burr.'

'But mainly you are concerned about stylish dresses and bonnets and all those things we ladies must have if we are not to appear ridiculous out in polite society.'

'Yes,' Ruth said simply. It was crystallised truth. It did prick at her pride that she might be considered some quaint yokel visiting the metropolis with her fashionable friends. 'Why has Gavin gone so suddenly?' Ruth asked, for she sensed Sarah was about to offer to provide her with everything she might need for a sojourn in Mayfair. 'Why did you not travel together?'

'Oh, Clayton has a crisis in his life and has gone already back to London. Gavin insists he must also go to be of assistance.'

'Crisis?' Ruth echoed faintly, the blood seeping from her complexion. It was the first time Clayton's name had cropped up in their conversation, although thoughts and images of him were constantly infiltrating her mind. 'Has a calamity occurred? Is he ill?'

'No…it's a drama of his own making, for if he hadn't got involved with such a woman in the first place…but I shan't bore you with the sordid details.' Sarah abruptly decided to change the subject.

Before he set on the road Gavin had suggested it might be as well to keep Clayton's woes from Ruth. It would solve nothing, he'd said, to worry her with it. If Ruth found out Clayton might soon be embroiled in a great scandal, it was sure to deter her from taking a trip to town. And why should she miss out on the benefits to be had in escaping from Fernlea for a short while?

In fact the opposite was true. Having been quite sure she would remain where she was, Ruth felt a sudden strong compulsion to insist she must accompany Sarah to London.

'Is his wife causing him problems?' Ruth finally asked, her features puckered with tension as she awaited an answer.

'No…not his wife, his mistress,' Sarah admitted on a sigh. Despite Gavin's sensible cautions to keep mum, she would not lie to Ruth when asked a direct question. 'Gavin did not elaborate, but I gather that the hussy has been plotting outrageously to trap Clayton into marrying her while she is still betrothed to another chap. Loretta Vane has put it about that Clayton has browbeaten her into accepting his offer instead.' Sarah grimaced her disgust. 'Her fiancé,

Ralph Pomfrey, naturally feels gravely insulted. He's taken it into his head to call Clayton out rather than taking the lying minx to task.'

Ruth shot to her feet, making little James, clasped in her arms, catch his breath. Swiftly she handed Sarah her son. 'Clayton is to fight a duel?'

'Quite possibly.' Sarah frowned at Ruth's increased pallor and agitated dance on the spot. 'I admit I was fretting too when I first found out. But Gavin assures me that Pomfrey can't shoot straight and is probably hoping the gauntlet won't be picked up. He's a jilted fiancé with ruffled feathers and keener, I'll warrant, to protect his good name than his marriage prospects to such a woman.'

If he'd been unsure how much of Loretta's pernicious mischief had become common knowledge, it took just a couple of seconds to find out. Momentarily Clayton remained standing on the threshold of the Palm House gambling den. A hush rippled away into the room as conversation ceased and gentlemen began turning their faces his way.

Clayton started to stroll into an atmosphere murky with the odour of alcohol and tobacco smoke. He returned greetings from those fellows who offered one. With great ruefulness he noticed that a few acquaintances pretended not to notice him in order to avoid his eye.

A knot of Pomfrey's chums had congregated about a dice table and Clayton started in that direction despite being conscious of their hard stares designed to deter him.

'Is he due here this evening?' Clayton asked bluntly. He'd called at Pomfrey's house and been informed by the man's butler that he was out. In fact, he'd made the trip back and forth to Caledon Street several times over the past days since he'd arrived in town, and always received the same answer from his manservant. Any probing inquiries as to where his master might be found had been met with tight-lipped silence and a shake of the fellow's ancient head.

So far Clayton had kept away from places such as this, knowing that his presence was likely to evoke just such an atmosphere of morbid speculation. The only gentleman with whom he presently wanted to have a conversation on the confounded matter of the looming duel was Pomfrey. And, damn the man, he was nowhere to be found.

He looked from one to the other of the few men grouped by the dice table. Christopher Perkins and his younger brother John shuffled their feet before striking up an urgent whispered conversation about a sick relative.

Claude Potts was not a good friend of Pomfrey's. He was not a good friend of anybody's. He was the sort of preening dandy who flitted about on the fringes of various circles, but who invariably managed to wriggle into view when a drama was unfolding in order to strut in the limelight.

'You'll see Pomfrey soon enough,' Potts stated loudly while keeping an eye on his audience. Many gentlemen seemed fascinated enough by the proceedings to have come closer. 'I'll wager a tidy sum it'll be a meeting at dawn light.'

'If you'd kept your mouth shut about the size of the loan you'd made him, it might not have come to this.' Clayton's remark transformed the smirk on Claude's face to ruddy embarrassment. Clayton immediately turned his back on the crushed fellow.

'You've gone too far this time, Powell,' Claude spat. He was furiously aware that the looks directed his way were now derisive. 'You think you can take whatever you want. Loretta Vane might be your mistress, but she was Pomfrey's future wife…'

'And still is, as far as I'm concerned.' Clayton continued to scan the area by the door for new arrivals.

'You're backing down?' Claude barked a jeering laugh and cast about glances that invited support. 'Are you saying you haven't tried to steal her for yourself?'

'Don't need to steal what's freely available,' a gentleman called from the back of the crowd and started in motion a roll of amusement among fellow spectators.

'Freely available?' another wag chipped in mournfully. 'I think not. The lady cost me a small fortune.'

'And went on her way when you were on your uppers,' was added by another fellow with comical sympathy in his voice.

'And now Pomfrey knows all about how that feels…' a different voice added mockingly. The general air of jollity faded a little. The gentlemen present were again aware that this was no laughing matter; it could be deadly serious.

Clayton started towards the door. He had no reason to protect Loretta's reputation; she'd blatantly lied and schemed in trying to trap him into marrying her. But he was a gentleman and as such not about to be drawn into contributing to the attack on her character, much as he might have liked to do so. Ruefully he realised that his reticence wasn't all noble in cause; he was cast in no better light than were the other gentlemen here who'd fallen foul of her grasping, mendacious nature. He'd known Lady Loretta Vane's reputation when he took her on, yet had succumbed to her seduction and kept her in style for the basest of reasons.

'Everybody knows Loretta's lying.' Clayton's friend, Keith Storey, had moved from the Palm House and into the street with him. They stopped beneath a gas lamp. 'I suspect Pomfrey does too, in his heart. Nobody has seen him for days. I'll wager he's already regretting his action.'

Clayton gave Keith a faint smile in appreciation of his support.

'He's been put in a damned awkward situation,' Keith continued. 'Trouble is, I don't feel much sympathy for Pomfrey and nor does anybody else. The blockhead should never have proposed to the golddigger in the first place. It was obvious her sights were still set on you.' Keith blew out his lips, shook his head in dismay. 'As soon as it got around his pockets were to let, it was obvious it would end badly.'

Clayton grimaced agreement.

'You know I'll stand second for you if it comes to that.' Keith gripped Clayton's arm to reinforce his sincerity.

'I'm hoping it won't come to that,' Clayton returned quietly and, having clasped Keith by the shoulder to show his appreciation of the fellow's offer, turned and strode towards his carriage. About to climb in, he turned back. Keith was where he'd left him at the entrance to the Palm House.

A few slow steps brought Clayton back towards him. Even with the duel imminent, he couldn't quite banish Ruth from his thoughts.

'I believe you know Mrs Hayden. I made her acquaintance through the Tremaynes. She tells me she used to live with her parents in Willoughby Street and you and your family were neighbours.'

Keith frowned, tested the name in a murmur.

'Ruth Hayden…' Clayton said to jog his memory.

'Ah…Ruth Hayden, *née* Sanderson…' Keith's face split into a grin. 'Lovely girl. If that Hayden chap hadn't got to her first, I might have proposed to her myself.'

'Do you know she's now widowed?'

Keith nodded, his face grim. 'Poor little Ruth couldn't have been more than nineteen when her husband was shot. It broke her parents, you know, the scandal. By then they'd moved away from Willoughby Street and gone to live in the country.'

'Scandal?' Clayton echoed. 'He was killed in the war, surely?'

Keith nodded. 'He was shot during the war right enough, but not by the enemy. I knew Paul Hayden and a fellow less like a coward I can't imagine.'

'He was court-martialled?' Clayton sounded incredulous.

'I suppose it won't hurt to repeat the tale. It was a long time ago and the subject of gossip for a while. Captain Paul Hayden was executed for desertion from the army. It was in Belgium…1815. Ruth was there with him and heavily pregnant. He was named a coward for absconding to see her when she was gravely ill in childbed and expected to die with the baby inside her. She survived, but their baby was lost.' Keith shook his head. 'In my opinion, Paul had no choice but to do what he did. She was close by…too close perhaps. Had she been safe in England perhaps he'd still be alive. But as far as I see it, he had no choice but to go to her. It might have been the last opportunity he'd have to see his wife alive. I know what decision I'd have made in those circumstances.'

Clayton's shock kept him momentarily speechless. 'What of her husband's family? Did they not help her?' Clayton already knew the answer to that question. Colonel Hayden had not been rich, but when Clayton knew him he'd lived comfortably. It seemed none of that comfort was bestowed on his daughter-in-law. Ruth looked to be struggling to make ends meet.

'Disgraceful behaviour, in my opinion,' Keith muttered. 'The Haydens blamed her. They thought she'd sent a message to Paul demanding he come to her on the eve of battle. They continued to believe it even after one of Ruth's servants owned up to contacting Paul behind Ruth's back.'

'The Haydens will have nothing to do with her?' Clayton asked quietly.

'Nothing! The family disowned her…banished her as though she'd perished along with their son and grandchild. Disgraceful behaviour…' Keith repeated with quiet vehemence.

Chapter Twelve

On arriving back at Belgravia Place at close to ten o'clock in the evening, Clayton was informed sternly by Hughes that his best friend had called this afternoon three times in three hours. He learned too that the viscount had again come and gone just a short while since and on this occasion left a note. The disapproving droop to Hughes's clamped lips once they'd imparted the news caused Clayton to comprehend that his old retainer was feeling far from pleased at repeatedly having to tell Gavin that he was out and no message was to be had.

Clayton knew that over the past couple of days Gavin had called on him a total of nine times. He'd been actively avoiding his friend, and quite successfully, as he'd been out from dawn till dusk seeking somebody with the same zeal that Gavin was pursuing him. Clayton was quite relieved that no chance meeting had taken place between him and Gavin at one of their clubs.

Under normal circumstances Clayton would have been pleased to see his friend and would have paid Gavin an immediate return call. But circumstances were far from normal. Gavin sought to urgently confront him about the confounded mess in which he was now mired in order to insist he take

up his offer of support. Knowing he had such a loyal and te-
nacious friend made Clayton feel humble…and guilty. But
still he had no plans to go to Gavin's town house in Lansdowne Crescent and make his apologies for having been
oddly aloof. The next time he saw Gavin, he intended to confidently declare his friend's assistance to be unnecessary. In
short, Clayton wanted to resolve the problem between him
and Pomfrey as soon as possible and without Gavin having
been involved in it.

Gavin Stone was no longer a carefree bachelor. He was
newly a peer of the realm and a doting husband and father.
He had commitments and responsibilities that were too
precious to be risked on the paltry altar of Loretta Vane's
spite…or his regrettable lechery. For, no doubt about it,
Clayton knew that he was partly to blame for the sorry situation in which he found himself.

Aware that Hughes was still waiting for him to take the
letter from the silver salver, Clayton obligingly picked it up
and broke the seal. He scanned the parchment and his mouth
formed a soundless laugh at the few sarcastic sentences that
expressed—between expletives—Gavin's resentment at
being ignored.

Having handed Hughes his coat, he gave the servant a
conciliatory look before striding on towards his study.

Hughes was not mollified by half a smile. 'What shall I
tell the viscount when he comes tomorrow, Sir Clayton?' he
peevishly insisted on knowing.

'Tell him I'll soon go and see him,' Clayton sent back over
a shoulder as he continued to cover the marble in long strides.

Once inside his cosy den, he headed towards the fire and
warmed his palms on the yellow glow. He placed Gavin's
note on the mantelpiece, then lifted his eyes to the huge gilt-
framed mirror that soared above it. Solemnly he scrutinised

his reflection until his lashes lowered, shielding eyes darkened by self-disgust.

He found the decanter and glass on the desk and poured a measure while trying to concentrate on places to go tomorrow in his search for Pomfrey. When that didn't work and his mind stubbornly strayed, he considered the thankless sacrifice Gavin had made in leaving his wife and son—a baby who had been so recently ill—to make the journey back to town to stand by his side. But pondering on the Tremaynes inevitably led him to reminisce on his recent stay in Willowdene and in turn that brought his thoughts circling back to Ruth. And try as he might, he could not find the energy to again wrestle free of the gentle memory of her.

What he had learned from Keith Storey about her husband's tragic execution, and her unfair ostracism by his family, had only served to make his present predicament seem yet more squalid and contemptible. Captain Paul Hayden had died for love of his wife and unborn child. Clayton could think of no more honourable death for a gentleman. Soon…this very week perhaps…he might risk his life…or take a life…and for what? The answer caused a nauseating sense of shame to sour his stomach. He'd become bewitched by Loretta's artful tricks. He'd known before he took her on that she was rumoured to be a sly wanton. As soon as she became his paramour, he knew it to be true and had mixed feelings about her. Her sensuality he encouraged, her lies repelled him. What Loretta had failed to grasp was that he gave little heed to her overspent allowance or her dalliances with gallants. He had money enough to be generous; he didn't care enough to be jealous. She'd had no need to constantly dissemble.

What he'd failed to grasp was that her deceit might very soon outweigh her allure. And he should have known it straight away. Her calculating nature should have prevented him getting involved with her at all. Lord knew he'd had experience of such a woman. He'd fought a duel over a mendacious harlot before. On that occasion she'd just happened to be his wife. Priscilla Winslow had been Loretta's equal in perfidiousness, if superior in looks and pedigree.

When he'd met Count Giovanni Montesso on Wimbledon Common the swordplay had been savage. He'd won, but not easily, and he had the physical scars as a lasting reminder of the ordeal that preceded his divorce. But he'd allowed the Italian to keep his life and his wife, much to Priscilla's indignation. The outcome of the fight and his unshakeable determination to divorce her had seemed to make him once again desirable in her eyes. But it was too late. After enduring ten months of pain and humiliation during which he had been constantly mocked by his wife and some of his peers as a cuckold, he felt nothing for her or her parade of lovers. When she left for the Continent with the count, he could not stir from apathy to even feel relief. It had been a wretched *mésalliance* from the start but, at a tender twenty-two years of age, he'd thought he was in love and ready to be a husband. No such tender emotion or honourable intent had been present in his liaison with Loretta. Now he pondered on it, he wasn't sure he had ever even liked her.

Clayton tipped back his head and sank what remained in his glass. There was no satisfaction in knowing that he seemed able to detach his heart and mind so easily from his nether regions.

Ruth's exquisite countenance flitted unbidden into his mind and a moment of quiet heart-stopping insight presented itself. With his breath wedged in his throat and a whisky tumbler in a fist frozen in mid-air, he finally understood why he'd let her go when every part of his being had been urging him to stay and properly make love to her. His eyes closed and his irritation melted as he revelled in the phantom feel of her mouth merging with his, of the instinctive response of her warm flesh filling his hands. He could sense the soft silky texture of her luxuriant hair passing through his fingers, see velvet brown eyes sultry with desire… wanting him.

A tortured oath tore from his lips and was sent flying at the ceiling. He thumped his empty glass down on his desk before wheeling away to the fire. Double-handed, he gripped at the mantelshelf and dropped his head between rigid arms. For some minutes he remained in that stance, corded muscle in his shoulders visibly bunched beneath the fine cloth of his jacket. His breathing was as laboured as that of a man who had sprinted some distance.

In his absence she might accept Bryant, she might give her word…and never would she break that pledge, no matter what was offered in exchange. She was a woman of pure integrity and what grotesque an irony it would be if he returned to Willowdene to tell her how he felt about her only to find he was too late. For he'd willingly fight to the bitter end for her if need be. He'd meet the doctor tomorrow and honour and principle be damned if it meant having the woman he loved.

With a vicious shove he sent himself away from the fire and to an upright position. His fiery eyes were raised to the mirror and he twisted an acrid little smile. 'Are you ready to risk taking on the role of lovestruck lapdog again? Are you?' he taunted his reflection.

'Did you see him this time?' That breathless query was launched at Gavin as he strode into the blue salon in Lansdowne Crescent. Sarah had jumped to her feet and rushed towards her husband. Moments before she and Ruth had been idly playing a game of cards while awaiting Gavin's return from Belgravia Place with, they'd hoped, some news of Clayton's predicament.

'He was from home...or so Hughes said.' Gavin's features displayed his displeasure. 'When I catch up with him, he'll have some explaining to do. I've left messages for him to contact me at the clubs, too. I missed bumping into him by mere minutes in St James's, so I was told. Keith Storey has spoken to him and knows he is after Pomfrey.'

'Is he *deliberately* avoiding you, do you think? Why would he do that?' Sarah had guessed what annoyed her husband and given voice to it. She turned her frowning countenance to Ruth to include her in this dialogue.

Ruth had been sitting listening earnestly to the exchange between husband and wife. Now she got to her feet and quickly approached. 'Has the duel gone ahead, do you think? Is Sir Clayton injured?' Her train of thought sped on into terrifying territory. 'If he is recovering at home, perhaps his butler has been instructed to keep secret his whereabouts as it is so grave and delicate a matter—'

'It hasn't yet gone ahead, you may rest easy on that score,' Gavin gently interrupted. He'd divined the agitation Ruth was striving to keep hidden behind a calm façade. He gained some contentment from knowing that Ruth appeared to be as captivated by Clayton as he was with her. There was obviously a bond between them, even if neither of them presently acknowledged its existence. Despite that small positive, his scowl had soon returned. He was not amused by Clayton's Scarlet Pimpernel act.

'Perhaps Clayton can't find Pomfrey because the man's come to his senses and is ashamed to show his face.' Sarah coupled an optimistic look with that observation.

'Perhaps,' Gavin agreed kindly. 'But now the matter is

common knowledge, both gentlemen have their good names to consider.'

'I wish Pomfrey would withdraw.' The vehement plea broke from Ruth unbidden. A faint bloom lit her complexion as she realised that the phrase that had been rotating furiously in her head had actually escaped her lips.

'And so do I wish it,' Sarah declared helpfully.

Ruth returned to her chair and sat down, allowing a conversation between husband and wife to continue. She was obliquely aware of the gist of what was being said, but actual words washed over her. She'd heard all she needed to. There was no news of Clayton and, despite Gavin's reassurance that the duel hadn't yet taken place, a sense of dread had constricted her chest. She could no longer ignore the reason for her distress or her abrupt change of mind about coming to town.

She cared for Clayton…deeply…and wanted desperately to know he was safe. The thought of him mortally injured, or hurt in any way, made her whole being shiver and ache. Even the memory of their final, frosty parting, of his rejection of her, couldn't prick her pride into subduing her anxiety for his health and safety.

Besides, she'd had time since that fateful afternoon to see the incident more clearly rather than viewed through a veil of excruciating humiliation.

Would you truly have wanted me to continue? he'd asked when putting her clinging, willing body away from his. Yes…she had almost cried…*please*…had teetered on her lips as they'd pulsated still from his passionate kisses. In her mortification she'd believed he'd stopped because he was cruelly toying with her. But had she too quickly thought ill of him?

He was an urbane gentleman, but no doubt conscious that people were the same in town and country and loved to gossip. Had he simply kept a firmer grasp on his self-control than she'd managed to exert over her own senses? Had he, far from being cruel, been kind in attempting to protect her reputation? He was a stranger—a gentleman of obvious wealth and position—and the reason for his lengthy visit would have been obvious had he been spotted emerging from her cottage some hours after dark.

I would have risked further ostracism for him...I wish I had made him stay...I might not see him again to tell him so... The wild thoughts spun crazily in her mind until she whipped up a cool hand to soothe a burning cheek.

'Perhaps Pomfrey is hiding beneath the skirts of the trollop who started this nonsense in the first place,' Sarah stated pithily, focusing Ruth's attention on her.

'I think we have spent enough time and emotion on this matter.' Gavin took one of his wife's expressive hands and gave it a calming pat. 'If Clayton prefers to deal alone with this affair, then so be it. If he wants me, he knows where I'm to be found.' He gave Sarah a smile. 'We said, did we not, that if you joined me in town—and how very glad I am that you did—that we would make the best of a bad situation. It is time we enjoyed ourselves. Keith Storey has invited us to his home. He and his wife are holding a *musicale*. I think we should go and perhaps accept one or two of the other invitations we've received.'

'I wondered when you'd turn up.'

The Honourable Ralph Pomfrey halted just inside his mother's back parlour with his jaw lengthening towards his chest. He had journeyed through the night to reach Elkington Tower's Dower House in Sussex and had hoped to delightfully surprise his mama with his unsolicited visit. 'You were expecting me, ma'am?' he said, a trifle crestfallen.

'Of course I was expecting you,' she returned rather testily.

'Your brother wrote me a note to let me know of the shenanigans you've started in town.' Yvonne Pomfrey, Dowager Countess of Elkington, cast her knitting into her lap and sent her youngest son a beady look. 'It's all a ruse, isn't it? How much did you have to pay him?'

Ralph trudged closer, stooping to give his mother's withered cheek a peck. As he straightened he said, perplexed, 'How much did I pay Gerald? Why, nothing at all. I know we don't get on, but if he's intending to bill me for sending a note maligning me to me own mother, he can whistle for the expense of it.'

A raucous cackle burst through the old lady's desiccated lips. 'He would try that, too, if he thought he might get away with it,' she agreed. 'Gerald never writes to me on his own account, only ever to damage you.' She frowned, scouring her muddled mind for the gist of their conversation before being diverted to comment on Gerald Pomfrey's malice and meanness. 'I didn't mean him. Talk of a duel's a bluff, isn't it? How much did you pay Sir Clayton Powell to take that vixen off your hands? Clever move, m'boy…I'm impressed.' She endorsed her praise with a gap-toothed grin. 'Didn't think you had it in you. 'Course, if you'd given heed to my good advice, you'd have got yourself unhooked from that Vane woman months ago.'

Ralph coloured slightly. 'You're quite wrong on that head, Mama. I'm most put out that the cad has seen fit to steal Loretta away from me.'

'Fiddlesticks!' the old lady snapped. 'You're nothing of the sort if the truth be known. It's plain as the nose on your face that she's concocted the whole thing so she can drop you now you've no money.'

Her son's pink complexion took on a more fiery hue. It was the first time he'd heard anyone actually put into words what the whole *ton* was thinking and whispering behind his back.

'No good looking so sorry for yourself, m'boy,' the dowager said. 'You've come here for some straight talking and that's what you'll get. Now you've sobered up, you expect me to tell you how you may wriggle your way out of the hole you're in.'

'I want no such thing,' Ralph spluttered, unconvincingly.

'But you *were* drunk or in her bed when you agreed to this lunacy of calling out Sir Clayton?'

Ralph choked and his mouth worked for a moment like a beached fish. He'd learned over the years to remain impassive when confronted by his mother's forthright ways. What disconcerted him was that she'd guessed correctly...on both counts...the origins of the challenge he'd stupidly issued. The note to Clayton had been composed in a haze of champagne while he lay propped up on Loretta's perfumed pillows. The lady herself had been stretched out naked beside him and, from time to time, giving him just the encouragement he needed to keep going when reason penetrated the fog in his brain.

'I see,' his mother said in a dry tone of voice that told him she did indeed see only too well. And hardly surprising, was it, that she knew what power an attractive woman could wield. In her heyday she'd been a beauty and a duke's mistress. But Yvonne had never lost sight of her duty to her husband, the Earl of Elkington. She picked up her knitting. 'What's brought you here, then? The cost of your funeral?'

Ralph swallowed audibly and the blood suffusing his face drained away. 'I've a fair chance of winning. I've been practising at the range,' he croaked.

The dowager snorted and then cursed as she dropped a stitch. She fumbled with wool and needles, picking and poking at the shapeless mass as she said, 'If you're lucky, Sir Clayton will wing you. If you're not and he's fired up enough over this to feel mean…' She cocked a dark eye up at her son. 'You'd better hope he's not…'

'I should have called him to account months ago, when our betrothal was announced,' Ralph blustered. 'The man's a scoundrel to carry on with another fellow's fiancée.'

'He was carrying on with her before you proposed, and you knew it,' the dowager returned. 'Were you drunk and in her bed that time too?'

This time the dowager took pity on her blushing, gulping offspring. She dragged her knitting from her lap to eye it grimly, then cast it on to the floor. 'Call Simmons, will you?' She pulled her shawl about her. 'Now you're here I suppose we ought to have some tea. Are you staying long?' The tone of her voice indicated she hoped to hear a negative. 'I suppose you will.' She sighed. 'No doubt you'll be under my feet until the day of the duel's come and gone. Your father would be most upset to know you've skulked away from a fight. But I understand. What else can you do if you've a mind to see thirty?'

'I shall turn up for it,' Pomfrey squeaked in a way that made his mother scowl.

'Bloodbath,' she spat. 'You could pay him to take her off your hands,' she suddenly said with a wag of a bony digit. 'I'd stump up the necessary for that.'

It was Ralph's turn to snort derisively. 'Have you no idea just how much the infernal Powell estate is worth?'

'Of course I have,' the dowager shot back. 'But he might be in need of betting chips. A million in the bank don't mean it's there to be used. Sir Clayton might be glad of a bit of blunt.'

Ralph cast a jaundiced eye on his mother, then at her faded surroundings. She meant it too. She might not have a million, but she had funds tied up in stocks and bonds and property and no intention of letting go of one halfpenny of it.

With her gnarled fingers on the chair arms, the old lady levered herself upright. She came towards her son in a slow swinging gait and, on passing, patted his arm. 'All I can say, m'boy, is you'd best contact Sir Clayton as soon as may be and make your excuses. After that, you'd best see that scheming trollop and do likewise.'

Clayton strode the length of the cold spartan hallway, then turned and retraced his steps. He felt inclined to rub together his palms so chilly was the atmosphere, yet outside the spring day was bright and sunny. The butler approached again. 'You may wait for the Earl in the small saloon, Sir Clayton,' he said solicitously. 'There is a small fire…'

'Thank you, but no,' Clayton returned. 'My business will not take long.'

The butler withdrew at the same moment Gerald Pomfrey, Earl of Elkington, hove into view. 'Did the old cove not offer you a warmer spot to kick your heels, Powell?' he inquired jovially.

Clayton gave the man a thin smile. He was aware, as was the whole of the *ton*, that the Earl was a miser. He doubted that there was a warm spot in the whole of the house. 'He was most attentive,' he said shortly. 'I cannot stop long and apologise for calling unexpectedly. I simply want to know if you are aware of your brother's whereabouts.' Clayton had not approached this man sooner for news of Pomfrey as he was aware, as was the whole *ton*, that the only connection between Gerald and Ralph Pomfrey was an enduring hatred. But time was fast disappearing and he was now scraping the barrel and desperate for some information as to where Ralph might be found.

Gerald snorted a laugh. 'He don't keep me informed of his movements. Haven't seen the snivelling wretch for six months. Haven't spoken to him for six years.'

Clayton gave a curt nod that incorporated his thanks and his farewell and turned for the exit.

The butler sprang with surprising agility from the shadows to the door.

'But I know where he's sure to be.'

Clayton swung back and frowned fiercely at the Earl's smug expression.

'He'll be where every blue-eyed boy is to be found when he's in bad trouble. He's sure to be in Sussex, hiding beneath his dear mama's skirts.'

Chapter Thirteen

'Mrs Hayden!'

On hearing that enthusiastic greeting Ruth turned about and her eyes flitted over unfamiliar faces before settling on one. A rush of recognition put a smile on her lips and a becoming blush in her cheeks.

A short while ago she had entered an elegant town house in Berkeley Square to enjoy Mr. and Mrs Storeys' *musicale*. Gavin, ever the perfect escort, had treated Ruth to the same solicitous courtesy as he did his wife. As soon as they'd alighted from his sleek dress coach he had tucked her hand on to his sleeve and, with Sarah similarly positioned on his other side, they'd ascended together the grand sweep of steps that led to their hosts' mansion.

Many eyes had followed the progress of the attractive trio. Ruth's rich dark beauty was in startling contrast to Sarah's fair loveliness and, of course, the distinguished gentleman between them had long set ladies swooning with his easy charm.

Once mingling with the other guests in the first-floor drawing room, Gavin and Sarah had been at subtle pains to introduce Ruth to some of their friends and include her in their conversations. Ruth had moments ago exchanged cordialities with the Earl and Countess of Morganston who had an estate close to Tremayne Park in Surrey. The Countess had a little girl who was about the same age as James and, as the conversation had turned to the wonder and worry of babies, Ruth had given the new mothers a fond smile and taken a step away to glance appreciatively at her opulent surroundings.

Now, having been spotted by her host and feeling quite overwhelmed by the genuine pleasure lighting Keith's eyes, Ruth gladly went to meet him. Oddly she'd recognised her childhood friend straight away despite the fact that almost a decade had passed since they'd last spoken. His chestnut hair was now shorter and neater than it had been when he was a gangly youth, but his hazel eyes and bluff friendliness were exactly as she remembered.

Keith Storey held out his hands and as Ruth's fingers touched his they were enclosed in a warm firm grasp. 'Mr. Storey indeed!' he gently mocked her formal address, then raised her small digits to his lips. 'It has been far too long since we had an opportunity to chat, but I would have recognised you anywhere. You look no different, you know, than you did at eighteen…just as captivating. And I recall clearly that you and I used the names Keith and Ruth in those days.' A chuckle burst from him as a fond memory surfaced in his mind. 'Do you recall what horrors we could be? I shall never forget the late summer afternoons we spent scrumping apples in the vicar's orchard. And that scoundrel of a cousin of yours would come with us sometimes. What was his name now…?' He frowned, private laughter still curving his mouth as he revelled in the reminiscence.

'Jake…' Ruth supplied with a faraway look as momentarily she wallowed in those carefree times. She bucked up to say, 'But hush, sir. No mention, please, of my hoydenish ways in such fine company. You will have your guests think me incorrigibly wayward.' Her humour faded. Of course, there was a far greater scandal in her past to be uncovered than her tomboy antics, and Ruth wondered who here might already know of it. She was sure Keith must be aware that her husband had been executed, leaving her stranded in the shadow of his undeserved disgrace. Her parents had recently resided in Willoughby Road at the time of the horrible episode and had been friendly with Keith's parents.

'I was so very sorry to hear about the death of your husband,' Keith said gently, correctly interpreting her slight withdrawal. 'And I believe your cousin, Jake, also did not come home from the war. I heard that your aunt and uncle moved to the Continent and now live close to where their son perished.'

Ruth gave a single nod, a ghost of a smile. 'It was a harsh unforgiving time...for so many people...for so many reasons... You have a very fine house.' She immediately launched into that gruff observation as emotion thickened her throat. 'You have done very nicely since you left Willoughby Road and got married...' Ruth frowned her regret. In her eagerness to talk about something more cheerful and less sensitive, she'd been very tactless and very insensitive. And she felt dreadfully churlish about that, considering Keith's kindness to her.

On the way to Berkeley Square this evening Gavin had told his wife and Ruth a little about the couple they were visiting. They'd learned that Keith Storey had married Susannah Vincent, an heiress who was also a baron's daughter. Keith had greatly prospered by the match, Gavin had said, and the couple were considered by polite society to be extremely popular people. It was from that recalled dialogue that her blurted reference to Keith's advantageous marriage had originated.

'That...that didn't sound as I meant it to...' Ruth stuttered apologetically and put a gloved hand to one of her tingling cheeks to shield her chagrin.

'I have indeed done very well for myself, Ruth.' Keith inclined a little towards her to add gently, 'And I'm always the first to admit it. Every day I give thanks for my good fortune…twice…because Susannah not only brought me great riches, but great happiness too. I shall not be a hypocrite and say we would be as blissful living in a hovel as we are in this fine mansion. Of course we would not. But my wife is the sweetest soul imaginable and I doubt I would have resisted her if she hadn't two ha'pennies to rub together. I love her dearly, you see.'

'Then you are, indeed, a very lucky gentleman,' Ruth said, adopting his wry tone.

'I should like to introduce you to Susannah. Might I steal you from your friends for a while? I believe Susannah is in the music room.

'I understand we have a mutual acquaintance,' Keith said as they strolled.

Ruth slanted up at him an enquiring look.

'Sir Clayton Powell,' Keith concisely informed her. 'I saw him recently. He told me he'd been staying with the Tremaynes and said he'd seen you.'

Ruth felt her stomach somersault at the mention of the gentleman who, even on a diverting occasion such as this, was continually disturbing her thoughts. 'I…yes…we both are very good friends of the Tremaynes and recently were their house guests at Willowdene Manor. I live close by, but the bad snowfall left us stranded at the Manor for some days.' With barely a pause Ruth asked, 'Do you know where he is?'

'Sir Clayton? I imagine he is still stalking Pomfrey in the hope of talking some sense into the chump.' Keith cleared his throat. It was not the done thing to talk to ladies—other than perhaps one's wife—about a delicate issue such as a duel, especially when a scheming trollop was the cause of the dispute. 'Ah…here she is,' Keith said quickly and with some relief as he spotted his spouse. He speedily introduced the ladies.

Susannah Storey was a petite redhead who warmly welcomed Ruth to her home and seemed genuinely engrossed when her husband launched again into an animated reminiscence about his and Ruth's escapades in Willoughby Road. Susannah's lively green eyes crinkled with genuine amusement as she heard about the plunder of the vicar's fruit.

'We had a huge old apple tree in York,' she interjected in to the conversation. 'Our head gardener made us a wonderful swing. As children we would have fine times and Mama says that it is as sturdy today as it was fifteen years ago…' Susannah's anecdote trailed away and a perplexed look creased her brow. A moment later her expression had hardened to encompass shock and annoyance.

Keith, disturbed by the change in his wife's mood, immediately cast a look in the same direction as Susannah was gazing. His subsequent consternation mirrored that of his wife.

'What in…!' The rest of the expletive was hastily muffled as Keith remembered where he was.

'I'm so sorry, Mrs Hayden.' Susannah gave Ruth an apologetic look. 'You must think us the rudest people to suddenly appear so out of humour. But…' Unable to contain her anger she ended in a suffocated voice, 'I cannot believe that Lord Graves has seen fit to bring that…that dreadful woman to my house after what she has done.'

'The lady was certainly not invited here on her own account,' Keith added grimly.

'Indeed she was not!' his wife endorsed in a forceful

mutter. 'Lady Vane has sneaked her way in on the arm of that silly old cove.'

'He meant no harm by it, Susannah,' Keith quietly soothed his vexed spouse. 'Graves's problem is that he sees no harm in anybody, and never has.'

Susannah gave her husband a brief smile and a little nod. She knew, as did everybody acquainted with the elderly widower, that he was kind hearted to a fault and apt to have advantage taken of him because of it.

Even before she'd heard the name of the unwelcome female guest, Ruth had had an inkling of who it could be. She turned her head just a little, not wanting to appear too eager to scrutinise Clayton's mistress, the woman who was trying to trap him into marriage and into fighting a duel over her.

Immediately Ruth noticed that she wasn't the only person taking peeks at the couple just entering the anteroom. Loretta Vane and her elderly escort were certainly arousing a great deal of inquisitiveness and scandalised looks. Once she'd located the object of her curiosity, Ruth found it difficult to tear away her gaze.

Lady Vane might be a shameless minx, but she was also exceedingly beautiful. Her raven hair was styled to one side so that it draped in ringlets to a milky shoulder. A low-cut bodice exposed more pale voluptuous flesh and beneath the diaphanous dress were visible long lissom limbs.

'I'll have a word with Graves.' Keith's features were set in a stony mask. 'The infernal woman could at least have found the manners to dress decently.'

Immediately Susannah put a restraining hand on her husband's arm. 'No…I have a feeling it is what the hussy wants—to cause a stir and be the centre of attention. I'll not allow her to spoil this evening. Just ignore her. Hopefully if she feels the frost in the air she might get him to take her elsewhere.'

As Loretta haughtily tilted her chin and set a contented slant to her rouged lips, Ruth comprehended that Susannah had given her husband wise advice. It seemed it was indeed the widow's intention to draw all eyes as she paraded into the room on the arm of her portly partner. As several of the other guests followed their hosts' suit and turned their backs on the couple, Ruth noticed a perceptible transformation in Loretta's demeanour. Indignation was starting to skew her pretty features.

Having decided on their course of action, Keith and Susannah clung fast to it. They went about the business of encouraging the invited company to be seated to enjoy the evening's entertainment. Solicitously Keith found Ruth a chair situated in a prime spot to enjoy the music.

'I shall reserve these two chairs beside you for the Tremaynes,' he told Ruth and was then off to politely attend to the comfort of others.

A moment or two later Sarah slipped on to the seat next to Ruth. 'Have you seen that baggage?' she hissed to Ruth in a low, scandalised tone. 'Everybody is talking about her. The nerve of the woman, to turn up uninvited knowing that the *ton* is scandalised by the mischief she's concocted.'

A small smile tilted Ruth's lips. 'She *is* very audacious…very pretty, too,' she added ruefully.

'Powder and paint!' Sarah dismissed with uncharacteristic cattishness. 'Whereas you,' she said to Ruth, 'are a most naturally beautiful brunette.'

'Thank you,' Ruth said.

'You're very welcome,' Sarah returned, adopting the same wry tone.

As the company quietened, and the first poignantly sombre notes of a viola trembled in the air, Ruth glanced down at her superb gown. She passed a hand lightly over the lavender-blue satin skirt. She did feel pleased with her appearance this evening and had seen genuine, if platonic, male admiration in Gavin's eyes when he first clapped eyes on her in his hallway earlier that evening.

When Sarah had initially tried to persuade her to accompany them to London, Ruth had felt uncomfortable with the thought of having all necessary garments for the trip donated to her by her friend. But once she'd learned of the severity of Clayton's troubles, any idea of standing on ceremony over it had dispersed. Clayton was in danger of being killed or injured and the thought of quibbling over sensibilities with a friend she loved as deeply as she might have loved a sister seemed ludicrously petty. She simply wanted to go immediately to London and be satisfied he was safe.

Thus Ruth had accepted Sarah's idly presented gifts and loans with muted appreciation so as not to offend, and had arrived in Lansdowne Crescent with several portmanteaux filled with all manner of stylish silk, satin and lace.

Ruth put up her head and listened to the soulful serenade before slanting a glance at Sarah's profile. A quietly fierce affection radiated from her and, as though Sarah felt it she momentarily covered one of Ruth's hands with a small soft palm before returning it to her own lap.

'This folly will do Bernard Graves no good at all. Does he not realise that he is likely to be blacklisted for the entire Season by all the hostesses?'

'And little wonder at it. I feel very sorry for Susannah. I certainly would not want the trollop under my roof.'

Ruth and Sarah exchanged a knowing look on overhearing a conversation between the Countess of Morganston and her sister, Joanna Peebles.

They'd just entered the ladies' withdrawing room. It was

a sanctuary set aside by their hosts so that female guests could rest and refresh themselves during the many hours of entertainment. Bright candle flame illuminated sofas and tables adorned with pot-pourri and bowls of daffodil trumpets that mingled their delicate fragrance with the ladies' French perfume.

The countess, on spotting the newcomers, beckoned them closer to whisper conspiratorially, 'We were just discussing whether that silly old fool Bernard Graves might rue succumbing to Loretta's charms.'

Sarah's expressive grimace indicated she thought it very possible. But she made no comment as she took a seat on the sofa next to Ruth. Both Ruth and Sarah began to idly tidy their coiffures while glancing at their reflections in the mirrors ranged along one wall.

'What do you say, Mrs Hayden?' the countess probed, obviously not yet done with the subject. 'I know you're also one of Sir Clayton's friends. Sarah said you've recently all been spending a nice time together. Are you aware that Lady Vane has gone to such wicked lengths to try to trap him into marrying her?'

Tucking a dark curl behind an ear, Ruth raised her eyes, meeting in the glass those of the countess. She'd no wish to become embroiled in any gossip over Clayton's mistress and she guessed that Sarah had held back her opinion for the same reason. Clayton was, after all, Gavin's closest friend and loyalty to him was paramount. Loretta Vane probably deserved every bad word that was said about her but, by association, Clayton must also be criticised for his poor choice of mistress. Worried as she was for his safety, Ruth realised she'd tell him so if the opportunity arose. He'd impertinently quizzed her over Ian Bryant and implied he didn't like the doctor. Why should she not return him her opinion on the dreadful woman with whom he was involved?

Aware of Ruth hesitating to comment on such an indelicate matter to people she'd just met, Sarah piped up, 'Ruth is too diplomatic to say what she thinks, so I shall do so. Gavin and I are to hold a party next month. We will invite Lord Graves, but stipulate on his card that he must bring Maude if he's to gain entry.'

A chorus of laughter from the sisters met that information. Everyone knew of Maude Graves. She was Bernard's spinster sister, a decade younger than her brother, and a committed puritan. It was doubtful she could be lured to take part in any such wicked self-indulgence and the countess and Joanna Peebles knew it.

'How very righteous you sound, Miss Marchant…oh, beg pardon, I forgot. You're now married to Sir Clayton's friend. It's most enterprising of you to have got Viscount Tremayne to make an honest woman of you. I'm impressed, and equally ambitious, you know.'

The four ladies, momentarily shocked into paralysis at what they'd just heard, finally turned, as one, to look at the entrance to the retiring room and see Loretta posing on the threshold.

Her piercing blue eyes darted belligerently over the assembled female company and she looked undaunted at being outranked by two members. If she noticed Sarah's complexion had turned chalk white at her cruel comment, it moved her not one jot. She relinquished her languid posture, one hand on her hip, one toying with an ebony ringlet, and swayed further in to the room. 'You're not so different to me, Lady Tremayne, although it's true I was not sixteen or a spinster when I became a kept woman. I've always had the status and protection of my late husband's name. But I promise I'll not shun you because of it.' Loretta gave a husky chuckle as Sarah jumped to her feet, then immediately sat down again as though her legs wouldn't support her. 'How nice it'll be when I am Sir Clayton's wife. We'll take tea together, dear Lady Tremayne, and our husbands will be so pleased that we get on.'

While listening to this outrageous and vicious attack on her friend, Ruth had blenched, too, but more in fury than in shock. She feared that this might not be the end of Loretta's spite. Perhaps the cat was simply sharpening her claws in readiness for another strike, and Sarah already looked to be close to tears.

Ruth calmly stood up. 'I think that you are deluded, Lady Vane.' Her voice was level, yet cold as ice. 'And I think you must apologise to the viscountess for your appalling insults.'

Loretta turned deliberately towards the exit, ignoring Ruth as though she were beneath her notice. Her smug expression displayed her contentment at the stupefaction she was leaving in her wake. The countess and Mrs Peebles had not altered position since she'd arrived. Both ladies were still drop-jawed and statue-like.

'Please don't ignore me or leave this room just yet or I'll have to ask my friend Mr. Storey to have you immediately ejected from his house.'

That did halt Loretta's triumphant retreat. She knew very well that the Storeys were itching to find an excuse to have her thrown out. She'd sooner go of her own accord than face the ignominy of being led away by a servant.

Loretta swished about and her eyes glittered in condescension at Ruth. 'And I think that you ought to mind your own business,' she snapped. 'Who are you and what, pray, has any of this to do with you?'

'I am Mrs Ruth Hayden,' Ruth introduced herself, although it took some effort to expel the words through her gritted teeth. Never had she condoned violence, but she presently felt sorely tempted to slap the smugness from Lady Vane's face. She desisted for one reason only: she sensed that Loretta would be glad to incite her to act in such a vulgar fashion. Instead, Ruth stooped to use another tactic that was normally foreign to her. She lied, and with convincing fluency. 'This matter is very much to do with me,' she said with admirable composure. 'I'm the viscountess's friend and I'm also Sir Clayton's fiancée. We're soon to be married and I must ask you to refrain from any further pathetic attempts to steal my future husband.'

Chapter Fourteen

'The harpy had no right to be so mean! I said not one bad word about her to the countess, despite being sorely tempted to do so!'

'Hush,' Ruth said and drew her agitated friend in to a comforting embrace. 'The vile woman has gone now. I expect she has quit the house of her own accord rather than be shown the door.'

'There will be mud raking about me…it will soil you, too…perhaps we should go home…'

'The mud raking here tonight will be about that spiteful cat, not you,' Ruth said. 'The countess and Mrs Peebles were shocked to the core by her disgraceful attack on you.'

Sarah hadn't received Loretta's apology, but she'd had the satisfaction of seeing her tormentor turn and flee from the withdrawing room with the smirk wiped from her face. When Loretta had made a dash for the exit, her complexion had looked as ashen as her victim's.

Lady Vane had been visibly shaken by what she'd heard. She'd not challenged Ruth's claim to be engaged to Clayton and Ruth knew why that was. No sane, genteel lady would disclose something so explosive in front of witnesses if it were untrue. The fact that Ruth had made her announcement while with the wife of Sir Clayton's best friend had polished its credibility. To top it all, it would be an act of social suicide to provoke the ire of Lady Morganston and Mrs Peebles—two of the *ton*'s foremost hostesses. The two women risked being made laughing stocks if they spread the tale she'd given them and it was later found to be false.

After breathlessly impressing on Sarah that she had their sympathy and support, the sisters had given Ruth startled smiles and breathy felicitations. Within a few moments they'd quit the retiring room hot on the heels of Loretta. Ruth guessed, with an awful pang, that only yards away chatter about her happy news was as lively as that about Loretta's atrocious behaviour. Within a very short while she feared talk about her engagement to Clayton would be spreading like wildfire throughout the *beau monde*.

Having supplied fresh succulent meat for the gossips to chew over, no real attention would be given to the facts of Sarah's past life as a fallen woman. It was already known that her father had been a cowardly embezzler who'd shot himself, leaving his children to fend for themselves. The general consensus of opinion, by all those people with a scrap of humanity, was that Sarah deserved sympathy for having stoically endured such a harrowing time. She'd been praised and admired for her intrepid, enterprising nature in protecting herself and her relatives and keeping them all from the poorhouse. When news of her marriage to Viscount Tremayne had been announced, even those ladies who'd harboured a yen for the rich aristocrat had admitted that Sarah Marchant deserved her good fortune.

'I must thank you for coming to my rescue. If I'd seen the attack coming, I'd have been ready for the strumpet.' A pugnacious glint fired Sarah's eyes. 'As it was, I was close to breaking down in front of her and I'd have hated that.' She pulled a handkerchief from her reticule and dabbed her nose and eyes. She gave a watery chuckle. 'It was priceless seeing her face when you announced you're to marry Clayton.'

'I know,' Ruth said and knuckled into submission a little hysterical giggle. 'I imagine watching Clayton's reaction when he hears about it will be less amusing.' A rueful expression slanted her soft mouth, but in no way reflected Ruth's inner turmoil. Her heart was battering painfully at her ribs and a quick glance in the mirror opposite alerted her to the fact that her guilt and apprehension showed in her appearance. Huge brown eyes stared back at her from a face that looked pale and peaky.

'I think Clayton's reaction might surprise us all.' It was Sarah's turn to offer comfort. Taking one of Ruth's lightly trembling hands, she gave it a squeeze.

'I'm certain he will be as furious as I am to know that you were subjected to such spite,' Ruth ventured optimistically. Whatever the present state of his relationship with his mistress Clayton must find abhorrent her meanness to Sarah. 'Thank Heavens he's at present keeping himself to himself,' Ruth mused and bucked up a little. 'At least while he's preoccupied with finding Pomfrey there's a little time to think of what to say to him…'

The last person Clayton had expected, or hoped, to see as he made to alight from his coach in Berkeley Square was Loretta. He knew that she wasn't friendly with Susannah Storey and unlikely to have secured an invitation to her home. As an elderly gentleman appeared in the open doorway to join her on the threshold, Clayton understood how she'd managed to gain entry to the *musicale*. Loretta had persuaded Lord Graves to act as her escort. As he watched her snatch at the elderly widower's arm and hurry him at a stumbling pace down the steps, her callous abuse of the nice old fellow deepened Clayton's disgust for her. It was due to him brooding on it that he omitted to think it odd that, having wangled her way in, Loretta had chosen to leave so early. Once the couple had crossed the road towards Lord Graves's vehicle, Clayton slammed shut his carriage door and strode towards the Storeys' house.

'So…you must have been privy to your good friend's happy news.' Lady Morganston's stage whisper was directed at Gavin's left ear. 'I know you've all recently been having a nice time in the country. Did Sir Clayton propose to Mrs Hayden while there? When is it to be made official?'

Gavin gave the woman a suave smile when she'd finished hissing at him. 'I'm sure you know I can't possibly comment on Sir Clayton's private affairs,' he answered disarmingly. 'You must ask him that question.'

'How annoying that he's taken himself off somewhere.' Lady Morganston frowned, for she was itching to know what had gone on to make the confirmed bachelor change his mind about once again becoming a husband. Everybody knew he'd vowed never to wed again thanks to the treachery of his first wife. His distinct disenchantment with the marital state had been one of the reasons that Loretta's scheme had always been doomed to stir scepticism.

The countess tried to catch Ruth's eye to no avail. She sighed. The lucky lady who'd hooked Sir Clayton and softened his hard heart was as tight-lipped as a clam on how she'd achieved it. Of course, the fact that Sarah and Ruth were close friends had probably helped the match succeed. The viscountess must be delighted to know her husband's best friend was marrying her friend. The countess was also dying to know whether Sir Clayton had yet given Mrs

Hayden a betrothal ring. No doubt it would be monstrously fine and she'd start to wear it once the announcement had been gazetted.

Having overheard Lady Morganston's dialogue, as of course it had been intended she should, Ruth inwardly squirmed beneath the countess's increasingly speculative looks. She knew that shortly there would be no escape. She took a glance about. Ladies were discreetly advancing on her from all sides. No one had rushed up to bombard her with impertinent questions when she and Sarah had, with an air of admirable insouciance, rejoined Gavin in the drawing room. Of course, the assembled company was far too well bred to do so. But slowly they were hemming her in. Inquisitive eyes were constantly on her and she sensed her looks, her attire, her manner and bearing were all under intense scrutiny. And soon…very soon…there would be subtle prying in to her past. She was a widow…who had been her late husband? What sort of a man had he been?

Up went Ruth's chin and she made a gay response to Gavin's comment on the fine concert they'd enjoyed earlier. Of course, he knew what stress she was now under and that she'd taken on that burden to defend his wife. In turn, he was doing his utmost to put her at her ease and keep the talk pleasantly neutral.

A movement at one side of her alerted Ruth to the fact that two middle-aged ladies sporting plumed turbans had manoeuvred themselves close enough to butt in to the conversation. No matter her outward calm, Ruth's heart was drumming erratically. She knew the newcomers were simply waiting for an opportunity to slide a question her way. She spied Sarah at a distance, close to the drawing-room doors, talking to their hostess.

'Mrs Hayden, is it not?' One of the matrons startled Ruth into attention as she made her opening gambit.

'Yes, I am Mrs Hayden…how do you do, ma'am,' Ruth replied. Before the lady could introduce a question, she pressed on mendaciously, 'Oh, if you will excuse me, I see that Viscountess Tremayne is beckoning me.' With an appealing glance Gavin's way, Ruth left the disappointed ladies to his patient courtesy. She began to head briskly towards the door of the drawing room. Briefly she stopped by Sarah and Susannah to exchange a few words with them. Despite her outward composure, her insides were painfully writhing and she knew she simply wanted to be alone with her turbulent thoughts to force them in to some sort of order.

What *had* she done! was the mantra that rotated in her head as she slipped out in to the quiet corridor, then kept going. She proceeded aimlessly, slid a palm over a pillar and felt it soothe her febrile skin. When she thought she'd put sufficient distance between herself and her would-be inquisitors, she came to a halt. Her forehead tipped forwards to sway soothingly against cool marble. But the refreshing sensation couldn't ease the torment in her mind. She knew very well what she'd done. She'd set dreadful trouble to brew.

You came to London because you were concerned about Clayton, but now you've caused more problems in his life. Loretta Vane tried to trap him into marriage. Now he'll think you are attempting to do so. He'll consider you to be no better than that scheming hussy. What on earth will you say to him? How can it all be remedied?

Her unsuspecting fiancé—when suspecting the worst— was sure to point out, in that sardonic way he had, that less extreme methods should have been used to send Loretta packing. The next thought to enter Ruth's mind was that it might be wise to immediately return to Fernlea while she pondered on it all and sheltered from Clayton's fury. She cringed on acknowledging how craven it would be to run away. Her friends might then suffer the brunt of the storm instead of her.

When they'd been at the Manor together, Clayton had initially, irascibly cast Sarah in the role of matchmaker. And if Ruth disappeared from town, it wouldn't prevent Sarah being bombarded with calling cards from *grandes dames* keen to discover more about Clayton's elusive future bride. No, Ruth decided she must stay and face the music. But that brave resolution couldn't prevent her eyes closing in sheer thankfulness that at least while Clayton was in blissful ignorance of it all she had a welcome reprieve…

As Clayton reached the top of the stairs, he turned right. He'd been friendly with Keith for many years and had been a frequent guest in this house. Even had he not known the layout of the property, a soft melody would have lured him in the right direction. But as he walked, he idly glanced across the void of the stairwell to the landing opposite. His pace slowed until he stopped and squinted through the wavering flames of a thousand candles shimmering amid crystal. His features displayed his astonishment before softening into an expression of pure pleasure. Retracing his steps, he reached the head of the stairs and proceeded along the other corridor.

'This is a most pleasant surprise.'

Ruth nearly started out of her skin at that husky greeting. She twisted about to face Clayton, the blood already gone from her complexion, for she'd immediately recognised those well-known ironic tones. How could she not when his anticipated reprimands sounded constantly in her head? She clutched behind at the pillar in support, for her legs felt suddenly boneless.

Clayton frowned. They might have parted in Fernlea on

bad terms, but he'd not expected when next they met Ruth would look anguished to see him.

'What's the matter? Did I startle you?'

Ruth swallowed, made to speak, but forcing words past the blockage in her throat was impossible. 'Yes…no…' she finally stuttered. 'Yes…you startled me,' she forced out through lips that felt frozen. 'Why are you here?' she softly wailed in a way that was distinctly unflattering.

'I received an invitation,' he returned drily as his eyes lowered to skim over the beautiful sight of her. He'd never seen her dressed so glamorously and his immediate urge was to take over where he'd left off in her little cottage. He wanted to reach for her, soothe her with a kiss, tell her there hadn't been an hour that'd passed since he'd left her on that day that he hadn't regretted his decision to go. He wanted to say that she'd been constantly in his thoughts despite the damnable business with Pomfrey. That she was here, in London, was an exquisite unexpected gift. He guessed that she'd accompanied Gavin and Sarah to town and, had he known about it, he would have returned Gavin's first call on him within the hour.

Clayton raised desire-darkened eyes from her face as a movement in the distance made his attention slew to the drawing-room doors. He noted with an indolent hike of one dark brow that they were being watched by a group of ladies who were congregating on the threshold. The consequence of being observed penetrated his mind and caused him to curse beneath his breath. The idea he'd had to slip with Ruth into one of the rooms close by was now dashed.

'It seems we're causing quite a stir. I suppose we should go in to stop rumours flying.'

'It's too late for that.' Her spontaneous response was followed by a sob of muffled hysteria and Ruth simply stared blindly at the hand he'd politely extended to her.

'Too late for what?' Clayton asked, returning his hand to his side. Ruth blinked at the marble pillar, her mind racing in an attempt to find an innocent answer. Of course there wasn't one and the rapidity of her breathing was straining tiny buttons fastened across her bosom. The lure was too great for Clayton to ignore. There'd been no release to the passion she'd aroused in him in Fernlea. During his lengthy search for Pomfrey he'd dissipated his frustration through mental and physical exertion and tiredness. But now he could smell the sweet scent of her skin, almost taste the shape of her mouth beneath his. The protracted pause between them was shattered as he repeated his question in a voice made harsh by unrelieved sensual tension, 'Too late for what, Ruth?'

Ruth recognised the sultry heat in his eyes and it caused her to feel a phantom touch of long fingers cupping her nude breasts. Her lips parted beneath the memory of a kiss bruising, then smoothing their softness. The blood that had fled her face returned with a vengeance and a small stifled noise rasped in her throat.

It was not a note of anguish this time; Clayton recognised its source only too well. With a soundless oath he realised her raw need equalled his own. One of his hands began to move as though to soothe the blush in her cheeks. He knew what memories she had. He had the same imagery in his mind and he would have given anything for a little privacy in order to prove to her how much he'd missed her. He glared at the drawing-room doors to see that one of the women had broken ranks and was on her way towards them.

'Please…don't go in there…not yet…please…' Ruth darted a beseeching gaze at him and inwardly cringed beneath a new shrewdness stifling the desire in his eyes.

A disturbing insight suddenly penetrated Clayton's passion-clouded mind. Ruth's anguish on seeing him had not been caused by their past clashes, but by something that had occurred here tonight. And then he remembered having seen Loretta leaving early and his expression became grimmer.

'Why should I not go in there?' he demanded quietly. 'Look at me, Ruth,' he added when she seemed unable to meet his eyes for even a second. 'What's the matter? And you'd best tell me straight away, because Lady Morganston is almost upon us.'

After a stunned second Ruth whipped about in a swish of lavender-blue silk to see that indeed the countess was just a few yards away. She raised frantic eyes to Clayton, a jumble of words cluttering on her tongue. She must tell him now…without delay. But how did one swiftly disclose to a gentleman who had vowed never again to take a wife that due to the terrible lie she'd told people expected him to soon again be a husband? Her husband…

'How clever of you to have persuaded Sir Clayton to attend this evening, Mrs Hayden.' Lady Morganston gave Ruth an arch look. 'He's devilish hard to secure as a guest, you know. But now, of course, we know how to make him come.'

Over the top of the countess's head, Clayton's eyes met Ruth's and a glimmer of suspicion made his grey gaze hold very thoughtfully still on her.

'I felt quite hot,' Ruth burbled. 'I came into the corridor for a little air. It is much cooler out here.' With that she took a step back towards the drawing room. 'Are the musicians making ready to again perform? Was it not a wonderful concert?'

For the entire time it took the three of them to stroll to the drawing room—probably mere minutes that seemed to Ruth to drag like an hour—Ruth kept up a constant chatter in order to prevent the countess hinting she knew of her companions' secret betrothal.

Of course, had Ruth lived longer in London and known but

a little more of *ton* etiquette, she would have realised that the countess was too polite to openly make mention to the prospective groom of an engagement that he'd not yet made official. But after the little romantic tableau in the hallway, witnessed by so many people, no doubting Thomas remained to challenge Mrs Hayden's claim to be the future Lady Powell.

That said, the countess, along with everybody here this evening, knew that Sir Clayton had yet to play his proper part and gazette the notice introducing Mrs Hayden as his future wife. Everyone knew too that, but for that minx Loretta acting outrageously and forcing Mrs Hayden's hand, it would all still be a secret. So the consensus of whispered opinion was that they must respect the confidence into which they'd been delightfully plunged!

Chapter Fifteen

'Where in damnation have you been?'

'And it's good to see you too.' Clayton had issued Gavin a naturally ironic greeting while his grey eyes continued scanning the assembled company.

'I've been trying to pin you down since I arrived in town.'

'I know…sorry,' Clayton muttered but still his attention was elsewhere. Almost as soon as he'd set a foot inside the Storeys' drawing room he'd sensed that conversations had dwindled on his arrival. It seemed people were now happier to peep his way than talk and that fostered Clayton's suspicion that something had taken place here this evening that should concern him. He rarely attended such functions and he accepted, with cynicism rather than conceit, that his appearance was likely to stir excitement amongst the débutantes and their mamas. He knew too that the business with Pomfrey and Loretta had notched up his notoriety. But that had nothing to do with Ruth and instinctively he knew she was also involved in a drama that was, as yet, unknown to him.

On reaching the drawing room, Ruth had seemed keen to urge the countess to go with her to mingle with Sarah's circle of friends. She'd slipped immediately from his side, but Clayton had noticed her eyes frequently darting back to him. A smile was fixed on her sweet lips for her friends' benefit, but it couldn't conceal from Clayton her nervousness. There was only one person Clayton could bring to mind who might have upset her, though how Loretta might have guessed he was falling in love and wanted Ruth as his mistress was beyond him. Nobody knew about it except Gavin, and it was ludicrous to suppose that his friend had spilled the beans. Of course, Ruth was certainly aware that he wanted her despite his proposition remaining unspoken. It was equally silly to suppose she would have taunted Loretta. But if some sort of catfight had taken place, it would explain why Loretta had left so early and why he and Ruth—and their interaction—seemed to be under constant surveillance.

'Has Loretta been stirring the pot in my absence?' Clayton asked Gavin. 'I caught sight of her outside with Bernard Graves. I imagine Susannah had her thrown out.'

Gavin drew Clayton towards an alcove where they might talk more privately. He'd watched Clayton inwardly weighing up hints and clues to the cause of the crackling atmosphere he could sense. During those few minutes of amicable quiet that had cocooned them, Gavin had been attempting to assess how much Ruth might have confessed to Clayton in the corridor. From Clayton's question, and Ruth's fawn-like stance, he now suspected that Ruth hadn't found the time or the temerity to tell him much at all. Inwardly he smiled. In Gavin's opinion, Ruth had no need to fret. Clayton was in love with her, and would eventually realise he wanted to marry her. His friend simply needed a little longer to believe in the miracle: Ruth was every bit as perfect as she seemed.

Clayton frowned on realising his question had gone unanswered. 'Has Loretta caused trouble tonight?' he repeated impatiently.

'Indeed she has.'

'What did she do?' Clayton demanded to know, his expression thunderous. 'Did she insult Ruth for some reason?'

'No, she insulted Sarah.'

'Insulted Sarah?' Clayton echoed in bewilderment. 'Why on earth would she do that?'

'Because she's a spiteful vixen, I suspect,' Gavin replied flatly.

Clayton gazed fiercely at Sarah as though searching for some sign of the hurt done to her.

'Oh…you needn't fret that Sarah is much bothered by it. She's far too strong to be bested by someone such as Loretta.'

Gavin wasn't as angry as people might have imagined him to be on hearing of his wife's ordeal. Gavin knew Sarah for an intrepid little fighter. If she could survive bearing the scars of a harrowing childhood, followed by several years of service as an innocent courtesan, a woman of Loretta's stamp would never bring her down. He had nothing but contempt for Loretta; nevertheless, he wasn't about to act the hypocrite and castigate Clayton over his choice of paramour. Before he'd met Sarah, Gavin had been a libertine too and had sometimes chosen a mistress simply for salacious reasons.

'Are you sure Sarah is all right?' Clayton asked in concern. 'Should I speak to her…apologise…?'

'There's no need,' Gavin said mildly. 'If you want to apologise to anyone, you should do so to Ruth.'

Clayton's eyes whipped back to his friend. 'To Ruth?' he echoed. 'Loretta insulted her as well?' He sounded incensed.

'I'm not sure; possibly she did. She seems to be indiscriminate with her malice.'

'God's teeth! What are you keeping back?' Clayton gritted out. 'Tell me what has gone on, dammit.'

Gavin overlooked his friend's churlishness. He recalled well enough that when he'd been pursuing Sarah he'd often acted cantankerously and Clayton had borne it with equanimity. 'Loretta raked up Sarah's past in front of Lady Morganston and her sister. Ruth jumped to Sarah's defence and put Loretta to flight.'

On knowing the fitting finale to Loretta's spite Clayton's strengthening smile deepened in to a chuckle. Admiration was smouldering in the look he was directing Ruth's way. 'Did she, now?' he murmured with throaty contentment.

'Indeed she did,' Gavin said. A rueful inflection in his voice betrayed that Gavin was also impressed by Ruth's heroics.

'Ruth always seems so calm and collected…well, not always…' Clayton added as an afterthought as though talking to himself and dwelling pleasurably on how wildly she'd responded to his lovemaking. Suddenly conscious of Gavin's repressed amusement, he stuck his hands in his pockets and examined his shoes. 'I'm surprised Loretta was sent packing. She can be quite thick-skinned.'

'Ruth used a very clever tactic.'

When no explanation was immediately forthcoming, Clayton prompted, 'And that was?'

'She said she was your fiancée.'

For a moment Clayton's countenance remained unaltered, his features still shaped by affection and humour. Slowly those emotions ebbed away, leaving his expression blank. He glanced up at Gavin. 'She said what?'

'She said you were to be married.'

After a silent moment Clayton turned again to look at Ruth.

* * *

Ruth knew the exact moment that Gavin told him. As soon as she'd seen the two men move to hug the wall, she'd watched with bated breath for it, dreading its cruel inevitability.

Beneath that pitiless stare directed her way she felt herself quake. Clayton's anger and astonishment might not be obvious to others, concealed as it was behind an impenetrable mask of suave civility, but she felt it like a physical blow. Could he divine the apology that was trembling, unspoken, on her tongue? She guessed not, for his unyielding stance hadn't altered one jot. The steady stare went on, no scrap of understanding or forgiveness apparent in it. And then he moved and she knew he was coming for her.

With no mind given to appearing craven, Ruth moved too. Following a murmured excuse to her companions about a visit to the withdrawing room, she headed hastily in that direction. A darted glance through milling people told her that he'd altered direction and was now walking parallel to her on the opposite side of the room. She knew she had nothing to match his long easy stride and at any time he could accelerate and traverse the crowd to cut off her escape route. But he was in no hurry; he was toying with her, allowing her to almost reach her sanctuary before surely denying it to her. She might have spontaneously tried to avoid him, but she wouldn't give him the satisfaction of intimidating her in to ungainly flight.

Valiantly she kept her chin up and forced her wobbly legs to keep to a steady pace. But the moment long fingers closed on her skin, forcing her inexorably to a halt just a yard from her target, she emitted a startled gasp.

'Let me go,' she squeaked in an underbreath, conscious of watching eyes.

'Only if you return the favour, sweetheart,' he shot back with deadly sarcasm. 'But you know that's not possible, don't you?'

'It is…*it is*,' Ruth stressed in a whisper as her complexion glowed with mortification at his damning words. 'I'm sorry…truly. But after a suitable time has elapsed we can call it all off…'

A low harsh laugh curtailed her desperate solution to the dilemma into which she'd driven them both.

'I'll let you apologise properly later,' he said silkily. 'Right now I think it's time I took my fiancée home.'

Ruth jerked her arm in an attempt to free it and this time her eyes clashed proudly on his. 'I shall leave in the same manner as I arrived—with Gavin and Sarah, in their coach.'

'You will leave with me now, willing or unwilling.'

The mutinous look she gave him told Clayton she'd opted for the latter.

'I'm sure I needn't tell you that if you leave here over my shoulder it's likely to deprive you of dignity and provide these fine ladies—those who don't swoon, that is—with yet more scandal to tattle over this evening.'

'You wouldn't dare,' Ruth said, her wide sepia eyes bright with shock.

He didn't answer for a moment, but his quiet, coarse laugh chilled her to the core. Finally he said gently, 'I expect you think I've never done it before.'

Ruth's eyes remained captured by his ruthless stare. Somehow she found that softly scoffing utterance more wounding than his righteous anger. Momentarily bravado deserted her; her voice quavered and her eyes glittered traitorously. 'I doubt you care about any woman's dignity. I believe you capable of it, and much more besides.'

'Good…that's settled, then,' he said dulcetly. 'Let's find our hosts and thank them for a wonderful evening.'

* * *

She had expected he might unleash his fury as soon as they were private in his coach, but she was mistaken. Having assisted her into the coach, he sprang aboard and threw himself down on the opposite seat in a way that displayed his bitter mood far more eloquently than any words could. After a leisurely piercing stare from beneath his brows, that sent her back into a corner, he kept his gaze through the window to one side of him and his lips thrust cynically aslant.

Ruth imagined his intention was to impress upon her how contemptible he found her. So contemptible, in fact, that he couldn't bear to look at her or speak to her. For some time she gazed at the starry night, too, while the carriage clattered through the dusky streets. But finally her insides had knotted so tightly that she felt quite ill. Unable to endure it longer, she burst out, 'I'm sorry. I know I've said and done a very reckless thing tonight. If I could undo it I would. But it will come right. Engagements end all the time…'

'Not mine,' he said, his eyes still on the stars.

She had expected he might snap off her head when he did speak, but he might have been commenting mildly on the weather. A little encouraged by his moderate tone, she ventured, 'What do you mean…not yours? Your marriage was brought to an end so why not—?'

'That's what I mean,' he interrupted her, still deceptively subdued. 'One failed marriage is enough.'

'We…we don't need to actually marry.'

'We're expected to. Every club in St. James's will be running a book on the date of the wedding by tomorrow morning. Every hostess in Mayfair will be debating with her friends how you'll suit ivory lace by tomorrow evening.' He shot a damning look at her. 'Some people are no doubt already wagering on whether it'll last.'

Ruth's small teeth worried at her lower lip. He'd sounded so poignantly bitter that she felt tempted to comfort him by saying she'd never be unfaithful or leave him. How dreadfully inappropriate that would have been! He didn't care about keeping her; he cared that he might not find a way to slip free of her clutches. And there was no denying the veracity of what he'd said about the *beau monde*'s fascination with this affair. 'Still, it can be put to rights.' It sounded more a hesitant question than the confident statement she'd intended.

Clayton brought his hard mocking eyes to hers and left them there till she squirmed and snapped, 'You are not without blame in this, you know, sir.'

'Is that right?'

'Yes, it most certainly is right!' Ruth spluttered. 'It was your…your *lady* friend who started it all. Had she not been so vile and mean as to almost make Sarah cry—when she'd done nothing to deserve it—none of this would have come about. I was goaded beyond endurance at seeing my best friend so upset.'

'So to ease your temper you declared to all and sundry that I had asked you to marry me. Did it make you feel better?'

'It certainly made Sarah feel better when the spiteful cat ran off.' It was a snappish rejoinder uttered while she twisted her hands in her lap. 'You were not there! You do not know what went on!'

That seemed to give him food for thought, for he remained quiet for several seconds, his shadowy features inscrutable.

'Why did you come to London?'

'What?' Ruth murmured, still gathering breath after her fluent outburst.

'Why did you come to London? Did you come to see me?'

'No,' Ruth whispered, but something in her stilted response caused a corner of his mouth to lift.

'Were you worried about me? Did you find out that I was to fight a duel?'

'Sarah asked me to accompany her to town,' Ruth quickly returned. Her cheeks had become quite hot and she was glad of the cool shadowy interior of the coach neutralising her blush.

'I don't think you would have quit your home without a pressing reason.'

'I had a pressing reason. I needed some time away from Willowdene to think about important decisions I must make.' It was a truthful prevarication, and she was pleased to have remembered it.

'Ah…the upstanding pillar of Willowdene society. Has the doctor proposed again?'

A glare met his drawled mockery. 'Ian might live in the countryside, but he is a mannerly gentleman. I doubt he would threaten to throw a woman over his shoulder and carry her out of a drawing room,' Ruth said sourly.

'I imagine you're right,' Clayton returned as though it were to the fellow's detriment. 'Perhaps with him you manage to curb your provocative nature. Whereas with me…you certainly don't,' he finished with soft insinuation.

Ruth knew what it was that he'd left unsaid, just as he intended she should. That he would wave her lapse into wantonness in her face at such a time made her choke out, 'If I'm provocative with you it's because you intentionally make me so.'

'It wasn't wholly a complaint, sweetheart,' Clayton said softly. 'But you know that, don't you?'

Ruth swung her face away and stared sightlessly at the sombre sky. A throb of tension was now between them and Ruth was as keenly aware of that as she was of him. The shadowy coach interior helped him conceal his expression, but she knew a glimmer of lust now mingled with the anger in his eyes. He might be repulsed by what he saw as her naked ambition to be his wife, but having her naked was still his ambition.

'If Bryant has proposed again, I take it you've no intention of accepting him just yet…not while your hopes are pinned on me.'

'How dare you!' Ruth swung her livid face towards him. In her heart she'd cherished a hope that he would never class her with the Loretta Vanes of the world. 'I'd far sooner marry the doctor than you. Just because I've told a lie to protect a friend doesn't mean I wanted to do so, but…'

'But you're glad you did,' Clayton jeered softly. 'Because you think you've got me hooked.'

That was enough! Ruth shot to the front of the seat, her small hands balled in to fists that looked primed and ready to strike. Her furious indignation prevented her noticing the glint of triumph that lurked behind Clayton's dropped lashes or the fact that a muscle in his clenched jaw had pulled his mouth aslant in a dangerous smile.

'You are the most abominably conceited man. I'm not surprised your wife left you and ran off with someone else!' Ruth fumed. 'I wouldn't marry you if my life depended upon it and tomorrow I shall make that very clear to anyone who cares to listen.'

'Methinks that the lady doth protest too much…'

The lazy goading spurred Ruth into immediate action. With a little cry she lunged a slap, then another, at his arrogant head.

A lazy hand deflected the blows, then imprisoned her arm before Ruth could snatch it back. With a light tug she was off balance and lay spreadeagled against a broad hard-muscled chest.

'I suppose I should make it clear that I expect my fiancée to act with decorum at all times. I'll let you know if I want you to play the wench for me. So…no more catfights over me, or with me for that matter.' Having delivered that in a sardonic tone, Clayton forked his hand over her chin and forced her evasive face up to his. 'Let's see if you can still provoke me in a way I like…'

Ruth became very still, her eyes huge and glossy with shock. Despite her indignation at his rough treatment, she could feel traitorous heat flowing in her veins simply because she anticipated his mouth soon on hers. Her breasts were heaving and every breath she gasped in rasped her taut nipples against his chest.

In the moment between his anger and his punishment Ruth was obliquely aware that the coach was rocking over ruts and bumping her body against him in a most erotic manner. And then his mouth swooped to take hers in a savage punishing kiss while a hand plunged into a mass of silky dark hair. Long fingers gripped her scalp, keeping her face hard against his.

Ruth struggled in earnest to be free of the strong arms around her and sit upright. But treacherous warmth had stirred immediately to life low in her belly as his mouth covered hers and was defeating her defences. Despite the aggression between them, her body had responded instinctively to his touch. Of its own volition her mouth was softening beneath the pressure of his probing tongue. She knew he had every right to be angry at what she'd done, but she didn't deserve this humiliation and she feared it was his plan to bring her down.

With that thought helping to subdue her languor, she continued to struggle for her dignity, quite ineffectually, and that was why she felt startled when suddenly Clayton changed tack. The bruising weight of his mouth was lifted from hers. Instead she felt a soft moist caress touch her cheek before it trailed tormentingly slowly to bury behind her ear. The hard grip on her scalp relaxed and his fingers slid to straddle her nape, moving with slow rhythm against the sensitive skin there while the play of his lips continued to tantalise her.

'Let me go,' Ruth gasped even as her eyes closed and she angled back against the soothing feel of his fingers.

Clayton's response was to bring his mouth back to hers. With gentle yet inexorable insistence his lips slid artfully against hers, persuading her to part her mouth. The stroking thumb continued working its sorcery on her nape, stoking the hunger in her to revel in the sweet sensuality he was offering. The clamped line of her lips was slackening, yet he didn't immediately take advantage. His kiss remained teasingly courteous, tempting her to crave more…invite more from him. And she did. Ruth kissed him back. Her bunched fists unfurled against his chest, clutched at his jacket for support as they pulled to his shoulders and anchored there. Her back arched instinctively as his hands girdled, massaged the slender bones below her thrusting breasts. Beneath this powerful onslaught the vehicle added its weight to her seduction, swaying her body seductively side to side as it negotiated bends and turns in the road. A gasp broke gutturally in her throat and, as though it was the signal Clayton had been waiting for, he deepened the kiss. His tongue plunged and withdrew with slow determined rhythm, coaxing her to widen for him. Ruth surrendered herself to abandonment. When his skilful fingers opened her bodice and cupped a breast, she sighed pleasure in to his mouth. When his thumb rotated over a turgid nipple, she thrust further towards his hand.

With a groan Clayton dragged his mouth from hers and

lowered his head. He tantalised the tight little nub with tongue and teeth until her squirming was invitation enough and he drew hungrily.

The pulse in Clayton's loins was a nagging agony and, in a reserved part of his mind that was crumbling to searing desire, he cursed himself for a fool. He'd wanted to punish her for what she'd done. God knew the shock of it was still reverberating in his mind. Ruth had resurrected all the hurt and humiliation he associated with marriage and having a wife. But Ruth wasn't Priscilla or Loretta. She was sweet, beautiful Ruth. He was falling in love with her. Was he going to insult her and tumble her quickly in a carriage because she'd rammed back into his mind the hell and emotional torment Priscilla had put him through? Ruth deserved night-long loving in luxurious surroundings and his deepest respect. She deserved affection and adoration and he knew he could give it…in time. He'd been so close to revitalising that withered part of his soul that he thought was for ever lost to him. But she'd forced his hand too soon, made him panic…and, coward that he was, he'd taken his revenge in the only way he knew how. It was the second time he'd started with Ruth something his conscience wouldn't allow him to finish. In a few more seconds he'd be lost in her passionate response to him and there'd be no way back. And how she'd hate him tomorrow for it!

Chapter Sixteen

With a little moan Ruth plunged her mouth up, desperately seeking Clayton's to demand he kiss her back. The slide of his artful hands on her feverish skin had kept at bay the memory of her dreadful lie and the hostility between them. Sweetly she strove to entice him with little nipping kisses and tongue touches until she sensed his lips form a smile against hers.

'Are you trying to seduce me, Mrs Hayden?'

His teasing was tender, but nevertheless embarrassment cluttered Ruth's throat. 'If I am, it seems I am unsuccessful,' she breathed in a suffocated voice.

'If only that were true,' Clayton returned on a sigh of self-mockery. He was tempted to kiss her to soothe her, but knew that if he did all his honourable intentions were doomed. Five fingers threaded though her long, soft hair to gently curve on her scalp. 'If things had been different…if I'd met you sooner…' He stopped and frowned. He'd spoken aloud his thoughts and didn't know now where next to take them.

A faint hope that had valiantly flickered in Ruth's breast extinguished as she listened to his gruff regrets. Now she accepted that the wounds he bore from his first marriage would never heal. He would never break free of the web of bitterness in which Priscilla had bound him. Her eyes closed and she garnered strength enough to swiftly sit upright and smoothly steal away. She settled opposite him again and clutched her silk cloak tightly about her open bodice rather than fumble with its fastenings. 'Surely we are nearly at Lansdowne Crescent?' she said in almost a normal tone. 'The journey seems endless…'

'Ruth…'

'Please don't say anything,' Ruth curtailed him in a brittle voice. Her eyes flew back to the window. She leaned towards it. 'Am I nearly home?'

'Yes.'

A nod of thankfulness met that confirmation, for she could not soon enough escape the leaden tension that once more had wedged them apart. A relieved sigh scraped her throat as the coach drew smoothly to a kerb. Immediately one of Ruth's hands darted to the handle. It was covered by one of Clayton's.

'I want you, but I don't want a wife,' he said hoarsely, apologetically.

'I don't want you as my husband,' she quickly countered and felt peaceful as soon as she'd found the truth in it. Heaven only knew she would sooner live out her life as a widow than be a wife to a reluctant, resentful man. 'I'm sorry I did such a senseless thing tonight,' Ruth blurted and slipped her fingers from beneath his. She was again composed and she met his eyes steadily. She would not crumble beneath his rejection or from knowing that a monstrous problem must be solved. Obviously he must now immediately contrive a plan to undo the mess she'd made and break their engagement.

Clayton shifted on the seat and leaned towards her. He planted his forearms on his knees and raised his eyes to lock his gaze with hers. 'A lengthy betrothal might have benefits for both of us.'

Ruth's tongue tip darted moisture to lips that still pulsed from his kisses. Eventually she asked, 'What benefits am I to have from such an arrangement, sir?'

'The protection of my name and my status. You may buy whatever you wish on my accounts and draw an unlimited cash allowance for anything else you want. You will be welcomed everywhere as my intended wife.'

'And yet I am not your intended wife and the whole affair is a sham.'

'Much of what goes on in polite society is not what it seems.'

'And what benefits are you to have?'

'I'll have the protection of your name and status,' he said softly, wry amusement glittering in his eyes. 'Your position as my betrothed will keep all the débutantes at arm's length.'

'I think you know that if you don't marry me within a reasonable time, people will presume I am your mistress.'

'People already presume that you are my mistress, Ruth.'

Ruth's eyes widened on him in astonishment but after a moment of frantic reflection she realised he'd probably spoken the truth. It was known that recently they'd both been guests at Willowdene Manor. They'd slept beneath the same roof in what was probably deemed to be a cosy arrangement with their friends, the Tremaynes. It was also obvious that she was a widow in her late twenties, not an innocent damsel. Now that she'd broadcast that a romantic attachment existed between them, of course sophisticated people would immediately think they were lovers.

'And what do you presume?' she asked huskily. 'That I will sleep with you in return for your money?'

'I assume that we will become lovers because it is what we both want,' Clayton differed very gently.

Ruth turned her face away. Was she about to act the hypocrite and say she didn't want that? She'd just again promised, in a way words could never equal, what a willing bed partner she would be. She couldn't deny she wanted his kisses and caresses. But what else did she want? Did she want to turn her back on the chance of meeting a man who would cherish her as his wife? How long would Clayton want her? Till her looks faded and her chance of marrying and having children were gone too? Perhaps in time he might fall in love again and manage to curb his contempt for the marital state. Perhaps he might change his rakish ways for his new wife's sake. What would become of her then? Did she want to risk conceiving and rearing children on her own? But most of all…did she want to love him, in and out of bed, knowing that he felt no such deep or enduring emotion for her?

Ruth looked back at him to see he was watching her intently. If she denied him, he would simply seduce her properly this time and she knew, to her shame, she wouldn't summon the will-power to stop him. 'I'm sorry I acted stupidly tonight. If needs be, I will admit I lied in order to help you end the dreadful farce of it. Goodnight.' She shook from her wrist the fingers that had immediately sprung to restrain her and, flinging open the door, stumbled out of the coach. She no longer cared that he saw her run from him and within seconds she was up the stone steps and rapping on the door of the Tremaynes' house in Lansdowne Crescent.

The following morning Ruth was started from a sound dreamless sleep by a knocking on her chamber door. A moment later Sarah had entered the room. Without ceremony, her friend settled on the edge of Ruth's bed.

'Did I wake you? Sorry…but I couldn't wait longer to find out what went on between you and Clayton.' Sarah's eyes were wide with a mingling of concern and curiosity. She pulled her wrap about her and, lifting her legs, curled them beneath her on the coverlet. 'I've been so worried that you and Clayton are now at dreadful loggerheads…and all because of me.'

Ruth pushed herself up on to her elbows and blinked at her friend. 'What time is it?' She gathered back a fistful of thick cocoa-coloured hair from where it flowed over her sleepy eyes.

'About nine o'clock. I'm glad you slept so well. I've barely shut my eyes for fretting. Did Clayton give you a dreadful roasting over it all?' Without waiting for a response, Sarah launched into, 'At first, I believed…oddly, I suppose…that he'd be quite glad you'd claimed to be engaged to him. It's obvious he has a deep fancy for you and I imagined he might need just such a nudge to stop him sulking over that harlot he married. Gavin has noticed, too, that he can't keep his eyes from you.' Sarah paused, nibbled at a lip, then a thumbnail. 'But then when you left the *musicale* early with him, he looked so furious and you looked so scared…'

'Was it obvious that I was scared?' Ruth interjected, jerked from her drowsy state by chagrin. She hated the idea that she might have appeared cowed by him.

'I know you both well and could tell you were apprehensive and Clayton was angry. But outwardly you both seemed remarkably composed. Clayton is always able to maintain a pleasant façade no matter what mood he is in.'

'Oh, yes…' Ruth agreed with quiet bitterness.

On hearing her friend's acrid tone Sarah's small teeth began to whittle her thumbnail again. Suddenly she clasped together her hands. 'It was so good of you to jump to my defence in the way you did. But I wish you had not. You've landed yourself in an awful pickle. He won't marry you, will he?'

'You cannot blame him, Sarah,' Ruth said. 'No gentleman would want to be forced to propose to a woman in such circumstances. When one considers his past misfortune with his first wife…'

'You've had past misfortune with your late husband,' Sarah interrupted. 'You've not allowed it to sour your view on marriage.'

Ruth managed a small smile and sat up properly in bed. As she moved, a luxuriant tumble of tresses settled about the shoulders of her crumpled white nightgown. 'I loved Paul and have fond memories as well as dark ones of being his wife.' Her slender fingers pleated the coverlet absently as she stared in to space. 'If Clayton gained nothing but deep unhappiness from once being a husband, then it is not surprising he refuses to take another wife.'

'I think you're too kind and understanding. He shouldn't make it so obvious he's smitten by you if he's not prepared to do the decent thing.'

'I don't want him to do the decent thing,' Ruth objected wryly. 'I have an equal aversion to being tolerated as a wife as he has to being forced in to the role of husband. In other words, I don't want to be married to him any more than he does to me.' Ruth put a hand on her dejected friend's arm and gave it a little squeeze. 'It will come right. It will be a scandal too for a while, I know. But I shall return to Fernlea once the truth is out. When I've gone away, the talk will dwindle, for there'll be no target for the gossips' scorn. Clayton will no doubt be showered with sympathy when it's generally known that another hussy lied to hook him. I suppose it's what he deserves.'

Sarah grimaced temporary defeat. She got up and paced to the window and looked at the bright sun behind the curtain she'd twitched aside. 'Gavin has said he'll take me for a drive in the park after breakfast. Will you come with us?'

Ruth shook her head, and, finding her slippers and dressing gown, she joined Sarah in gazing quietly at a bright new day.

'Do come,' Sarah said, turning from the light. 'I don't like to think of you here on your own, fretting on it all.'

'I shall like to be here on my own. I must pack and be ready to return home. I won't go, of course, until I know the matter with Clayton is settled. I've said I'll own up and do what I can to help him unravel the tangle if he wants me to.'

'I'll lend you one of my finest carriage dresses to wear if you'll come for a ride,' Sarah cajoled. In her eyes stood tears of frustration; there was nothing she could think of to do that might help Ruth out of the quandary she was in. And her friend was only in trouble for selflessly rushing to her aid!

'I *adore* the dresses you've already given me,' Ruth said softly. 'And I adore all the other lovely things you've been so very kind enough to donate to me for this trip.'

'You're my best friend, why would I not share with you?' Sarah said solemnly.

'I think, though, I must not share your husband...not all the time.'

'Oh, Gavin doesn't mind if you join us again on an outing,' Sarah said, snuffling on her sleeve.

'Of course he doesn't mind,' Ruth concurred. 'He's too much of a fine gentleman ever to be discourteous, even in thought.' Ruth smiled. 'But I mind. I mind that you both have had very little time to yourselves since we arrived in London. Shall we find some breakfast?' she suggested in the hope of bucking Sarah up despite the fact she felt too wretchedly queasy to enjoy a morsel.

'I can't eat anything. Take it away.'

With a dip of her mobcap the maid collected the breakfast tray and hastily obeyed her irritated mistress.

Loretta Vane picked up the note that had been delivered early that morning and her eyes again scanned the two concise paragraphs. Shock and disbelief were again shaping her features as she desperately tried to find some ambiguity in Ralph Pomfrey's prose.

But it was perfectly apparent that her official fiancé was eager to free her from their betrothal. He also no longer deemed it his duty to protect her honour by risking his life in a duel. She might marry whomsoever she pleased, he'd written as his parting shot before signing the parchment with a flourish.

Loretta let the paper drop to settle amid the debris of bottles and boxes on her dresser. She'd not seen Ralph for some while. Neither had she seen Clayton. She'd heard on the grapevine that Clayton was back in town and looking for Pomfrey to talk some sense in to him. Loretta had vainly believed she'd provided Pomfrey with adequate incentive to keep him hooked and hankering after her. It was galling to know Ralph had so soon been dissuaded from acting as her champion.

As soon as Loretta had learned of Clayton's arrival in Mayfair, she'd sent a note to his house, begging him to come and see her. He'd not even acknowledged the letter, but she'd drawn some meagre comfort from the fact that nobody else had seen or heard much of him either.

But Pomfrey had seen him. It was obvious to Loretta that the two gentlemen had settled the differences she'd engineered for them. She felt resentment tightening her chest. She'd been made to look a fool at the Storeys' last night. She'd made her audacious intrusion on Bernard Graves's arm in the hope of seeing Clayton there and persuading him to take her back. He'd not even been present. But his wretched fiancée had been there.

Clayton was to be married and now, when it leaked out that Pomfrey had rejected her too, she'd be a risible figure of fun. Loretta knew she could probably preserve a little dignity by

extracting a proposal from that old fool Bernard Graves…
but…a shiver of revulsion passed through her as she recalled
his ice-cold hands and the spittle that had flecked his bluish
lips as she'd drawn his face towards hers to tempt him to kiss
her.

'A visitor for you, madam.' The young maid managed to
keep amusement from curling her mouth at madam's excitement on learning that news. 'It is a lady…Mrs Beauvoir,' the
girl announced maliciously.

Loretta sighed disappointment. Obviously the woman was
the first of her few friends who'd be calling to feign com-
miserations on her humiliation yesterday evening. Christine
Beauvoir was more an ally than a confidante. Although
Loretta considered herself to be vastly superior in status,
having netted a title, the two women had remarkably similar
lives. Both had been widowed quite young and subsequently
lived as kept women. There were other similarities, too—
neither Christine nor Loretta were particularly well liked.
They were accepted by polite society under the mantle of
protection bestowed by a current lover. The higher the
fellow's rank and wealth, the better were their prospects.
Now, with no lover and no fiancé, and her bank balance
plummeting, Loretta had been left in a very vulnerable
position. And she didn't relish it one bit. The *ton* liked its
brazen temptresses to show humility in defeat. And that was
certainly not *her* way.

About to tell her maid to send the woman away, for she
felt in no mood to field Christine's barbs, Loretta suddenly
recollected something about her visitor that greatly buoyed
her mood. Momentarily lost in thought, she began to tap at
her lips with a long shapely fingernail. 'Ask Mrs Beauvoir
to wait in the Rose Salon; soon I will be down to receive her,'
she eventually directed her maid.

* * *

With a thin smile Christine Beauvoir accepted the news that her ladyship had agreed to see her. She flounced to a chair and sat down. After an impatient moment tapping her well-shod feet against timber, she was again standing. She moved to a window to scour the street scene. But she could not stay irritable for long, not when such delightful news continued to bubble away inside of her. And one person should be greatly indebted to her for kindly sharing her information. Christine would be sure to remind her ladyship of that fact when she needed taking down a peg or two.

'Did my maid not fetch you tea? I shall ring for some,' Loretta said on sweeping regally into the Rose Salon.

'Perhaps once we've had a little chat, you might call for something stronger. Champagne might suit…'

Immediately intrigued by her visitor's opening gambit, Loretta became alert to Christine's excitement. She indicated that her friend sit beside her on the sofa.

'Have you received news from that bumpkin town you used to live in? Willowdene, isn't it?' Loretta knew very well that Ruth Hayden and her friend Viscountess Tremayne came from that part of the country.

Christine pursed her lips, quite put out that Loretta was some way towards spoiling the effect of her revelation.

'As I recall,' Loretta pressed on, unwilling to wait for Christine to come out of her sulk and spill all the beans, 'you used to be on *intimate* terms with the brother of Viscount Tremayne.' Loretta leaned forwards to archly smile at her friend.

'I was indeed Eddie Stone's dear friend for many years until he died.' Christine twirled a chestnut curl with a finger. Her ambition had been to become Gavin Stone's dear friend after his brother died, but Gavin had quite brusquely declined her offer. The humiliation of it still rankled and was the main reason Christine felt she had a score of her own to settle with the viscount and his kith and kin. 'I still have contacts in the town and know all the gossip about what goes on there,' Christine resumed. 'Recently some gossip concerning Mrs Ruth Hayden reached my ears.'

Loretta's eyes sharpened to blue slits on hearing her rival's name linked to gossip. 'I take it you've heard that Sir Clayton is betrothed to her,' she said. 'The brazen hussy broadcast it last night despite the fact he has not yet made it official.'

'Talk is spreading already,' Christine said. 'I was in Williamson's drapery this morning when Joanna Peebles entered the shop with the Belmont sisters. They spoke of nothing else, I can tell you, but when the wedding will take place and how fine they imagine it all will be.' Christine's lips curved in a little spiteful smile as she saw the effect her words were having on Loretta. 'How dreadful for you to hear of Clayton's marriage in such a way.'

'What gossip have you heard about her?' Loretta demanded to know, her astute mind already turning over possibilities.

'She's very friendly with the viscountess. And of course you know Sarah's history, for I was the one who told you of it.'

Loretta wished now she'd not known of Sarah's history. She'd used that information in pique and had it backfire on her. 'Never mind about her,' she dismissed impatiently. 'What do you know about Ruth Hayden?'

'She lives close to Willowdene and is shunned by the townsfolk because of the manner of her late husband's death. He was court-martialled and executed for cowardice in the war.' Christine took a deep breath before delivering her *pièce de résistance*. 'As she is ostracised locally it was considered by most people to be extraordinary when a respectable and eligible gentleman proposed to her. Doctor Bryant is said to be smitten with the widow and the consensus of opinion is that he presumes she will agree to marry him.'

Loretta sat back, disappointed. What cared she for knowing that? The doctor might presume all he liked, but any sensible woman would snatch at the marriage proposal from a wealthy aristocrat rather than settle for the local leech.

Christine understood her friend's sour expression and added slyly, 'When Clayton was in Willowdene recently with his friends, he met the doctor. Ian Bryant went to the Manor and, rumour has it, was invited to dine with them all. If the fellow believed Ruth to be engaged to Clayton, why would he pursue her here to town to renew his proposal?'

'He is here?'

Christine nodded. 'He is not without connections and cash, you know. Ian Bryant's maternal grandfather was a baron and, although he couldn't pass on to Ian his title, he gave him a portion of his wealth and a town house in Connaught Street.'

'So…you think that Ruth Hayden is being a cruel tease to the doctor? Or is she trying to play them off against each other?'

'I doubt she has it in her,' Christine said flatly. 'I also heard the ladies in the drapery discussing Clayton's arrival and swift departure from the *musicale* last night.'

'He turned up?' Loretta spat in annoyance.

'He did, and he left almost straight away with Mrs Hayden. The ladies guessed that some sort of tiff between them might have occurred because she'd let the cat out of the bag about their betrothal.' Christine paused. 'In my opinion, there was no cat to let out of the bag. I know how very close Ruth and Sarah are. I know you were horrible to her friend and I know Ruth would act on impulse to protect Sarah.' After a deep breath she delivered her damning verdict. 'I think Mrs

Hayden told a wicked lie last night in saying she was Sir Clayton's fiancée and I doubt that Dr Bryant will be any more pleased than Clayton was on finding out about it.'

Chapter Seventeen

'Where did you eventually run Pomfrey to ground?'

Gavin had been on his way home from his attorney's when he'd spied Clayton strolling along St James's. His friend had looked to be deep in thought with his head down, shoulders hunched and hands thrust deep into his pockets. The elements had been whipping his flaxen locks to obscure his features, but the buffeting hadn't disturbed Clayton's air of preoccupation. Having rapped for his driver to halt, Gavin had sprung from his coach to accost Clayton and bark out his question.

Yesterday evening there'd been no opportunity for them to talk about the business with Pomfrey. The commotion between the ladies had precluded all other conversation. But Gavin had seen one of Pomfrey's friends in the park earlier when out driving with Sarah. Christopher Perkins had ridden over specifically to tell him, with courteous brevity as Sarah was with him, that the duel was off. Gavin therefore had gained no insight to the whys and wherefores and was now keen to get some.

With his eyebrows slanted to a quizzical angle, Clayton came to a halt outside White's. Gavin grimaced an apathetic acceptance to Clayton's wordless suggestion, and they entered the gentlemen's club.

'Brighton…he was staying with his mother,' Clayton eventually replied while dragging five neatening fingers through the knots in his hair.

'Was he in hiding?'

'He knows better than to go there for sanctuary.' Clayton grunted a laugh. 'The old lady had more of a mind to shoot him than me.' A signal at the steward requested drinks before he resumed the tale. 'She gave Ralph the choice of shaking hands with me, or wrestling away from her the keys to the gun cabinet. She looked peeved enough over it all to carry out the threat to put a bullet in him.'

'I remember she was always a game old bird.' Gavin chuckled. 'I doubt Loretta will be pleased to know that Ralph is further beneath his mother's thumb than hers.'

Clayton's eyes clouded with distaste at the mention of his erstwhile mistress. 'Ralph knows he's been a fool…' His voice trailed away but what he'd left unspoken was easily guessed.

'And he's not the only one,' Gavin supplied the words.

Clayton scowled and muttered about the steward's tardiness in bringing a bottle of cognac. He slumped into a chair at a table and immediately picked up a pack of cards. He thumbed them idly, then fanned them into a semi-circle on the baize.

'Are you going to take a guess at why I think you're an equal fool to Pomfrey? I'll give you a clue—on this occasion it has nothing to do with Loretta.'

'No,' Clayton said harshly and forcefully flipped the cards into a stack.

'Well, I'll tell you anyway. Yesterday Ruth acted with immense selflessness and courage and you—'

'I know,' Clayton whipped across Gavin's quiet lauding of Ruth. 'You don't have to say more. I know it's all my fault.' He stabbed a glance at his friend from beneath close brows. 'There's no need to worry. I'll take care of Ruth.'

'How?' Gavin demanded. But no matter what other probing looks and questions he used, his friend refused to disclose any more. They played a half-hearted game of rummy. When various acquaintances ambled over to grip Clayton by the shoulder and mutter gruff congratulations, Clayton remained stoically polite but uncommunicative. When Pomfrey turned up in White's and made a point of sauntering over to their table for a significant show of solidarity, Clayton barely quit brooding long enough to join in the charade. Just half an hour later he abruptly took his leave and Gavin knew better than to delay him and ask where he was going.

'A gentleman is here to see you, ma'am. He's waiting in the parlour.' Having delivered her message, the maidservant withdrew almost immediately from Ruth's bedchamber. Ruth quickly came to a sitting position on her bed. She'd been idly lounging there, flicking through a journal while awaiting Clayton's arrival. Not that she'd received word from him that he would call this afternoon. But she'd had an instinct that he'd come at some point during the day. In fact, so sure of it had she been that she'd turned down an invitation to take tea with Susannah Storey simply so she wouldn't miss his visit. Sarah had accepted the invitation and taken little James with her for Susannah to coo over.

But now the moment had finally arrived, Ruth sensed her chest constrict with a combination of exhilaration and dread. She wanted to see him despite knowing the atmosphere between them was sure to be thick with friction. Urgent and important matters needed to be resolved between them. What had he decided to do? What had *she* decided to do? Since waking that morning, whenever she'd attempted to calmly assess her predicament, a jumble of emotion had muddled her thoughts. All she knew for sure was that she loved him. But was that a good or a bad thing?

The maid had seemed a little apprehensive on announcing she had a visitor. From that Ruth had guessed that *the gentleman* did not look to be in the best of tempers. Her heart fluttered against her ribs, making her feel quite queasy. So Clayton was still angry. At least she had an indication of what lay in store for her. She *was* ready to admit she'd lied; it hadn't been an idle boast given last night to escape his dangerous virility. If he'd come to tell her that she must own up to her deceit, then so be it. With a last look at her reflection and with her stomach feeling as tight as a vice, she went downstairs.

'Doctor Bryant!'

Ruth had halted in astonishment on the threshold of the parlour. Recovering her composure, she quickly entered the room and closed the door. In a reversal of the incident that had occurred at her cottage in Fernlea, she'd today been sure her caller was Clayton. The other time she'd expected Dr Bryant's visit. On neither occasion had she taken the wise precaution of checking on the gentleman's identity.

'You are surprised to see me,' Ian stated in a voice that hinted at acrid humour.

'Why…yes…I own I am, sir. I had no idea you were coming to town,' Ruth returned in as pleasant a tone as her confusion would allow.

'And I had no idea that *you* were coming to town, Mrs Hayden,' Ian drawled her words back at her. 'Ignorant as I was of your plans to visit London, I'm no longer ignorant of the reasons for them.'

For a long moment Ruth remained quiet, a small frown marring her smooth brow. She sensed that beneath Ian's dialogue was a violent ire he was striving to subdue. 'If you're hoping to provoke me into demanding an explanation to a riddle, you're to be disappointed, sir,' Ruth answered levelly.

'I'm quite used to being disappointed by you, madam,' Ian retorted with heavy insinuation. 'Yet at one time you led me to believe that you'd more than satisfy all my expectations.'

Ruth sensed her spine stiffening and her hackles rising. She knew to what incident he'd referred just as he'd intended she should. But he wouldn't make her feel she'd done wrong in rushing into his embrace on the day her father died. She'd wanted platonic comfort from him. If he'd been too mean to allow her it, he should feel ashamed, not her. With a flash of insight Ruth realised what had prompted his resentment and his visit. She imagined that here before her was the proof that snippets of last night's brouhaha at the Storeys' *musicale* were already circulating.

'Have you been in town long, sir?' It was a leading question and she wasn't surprised when it drew from him a sour smile.

'Long enough to be apprised of some disturbing news concerning you.'

'Will you enlighten me further?' It was purely prevarication; Ruth was well aware of what talk he'd heard.

'I understand you are to be the rake's wife, not mine,' Ian spat out.

'I don't recall ever having hinted that I might become your wife.' Ruth elevated her chin to a proud angle. 'I do recall unequivocally turning down your proposal.'

Two angry strides brought Ian to Ruth's side and a grip on her upper arm jerked her close. His lips hovered an inch above her pale cheek. 'And I knew you regretted doing so. I knew eventually you would have me. And, by Christ, I would have you. You've been a fire in my blood since the day you pressed your body against mine, and you've known it.'

Ruth attempted to jerk free, but his fingers bit deeper into her soft flesh and he moved his mouth so his exasperation effectively steamed on her skin.

'Tell me now that you did not expect me to again propose to you.'

A flood of blood beneath Ruth's complexion answered that question.

'And, by God, you would have accepted me, would you not, but for Powell arriving on the scene?'

The flame in Ruth's face burnt yet brighter. She *had* expected the doctor to shortly renew his proposal and she *had* been giving consideration to the benefits of being his wife.

'You're so desperate to net Powell you've acted like a vulgar wanton. You've broadcast he'll marry you before he's made it official. What everybody's wondering is…has he any intention of ever making it official?'

Ruth shrank her face back from the bitterness blazing in his eyes. 'I had not taken you for a gentleman who'd listen to tattlers,' she whispered. 'You might have asked me to explain—'

'Explain?' he savagely curtailed her. 'Would you care to tell me if you were acting the whore for him under the Tremaynes' roof?' His fingers snaked tighter about her arm. 'No?' he jeered. 'I thought you might not. Then tell me instead why you chased after him to town when he'd done with you. Was it to pester him for a proposal?' Ian furiously demanded to know. 'Tell me…have you cornered the rake well enough to get him up the aisle or is he likely to slip your clutches?'

Ruth pushed violently at Ian's chest and momentarily gained liberation, but within seconds he'd renewed his grip on her arm and swung her back to face him.

'One of our neighbours from Willowdene paid me a visit earlier. Christine Beauvoir brought with her a friend. Lady

Vane's disappointment equals my own. It seems she anticipated becoming betrothed to Powell before you put paid to
her ambitions.'

'Did she also tell you that she's another man's fiancée?
Did she say she's caused untold problems pursuing her
ambition through outright lies?' Ruth could tell from Ian's
abruptly shuttered expression that he knew nothing of
Loretta's duplicity.

Beneath the onslaught of Ian's spite and censure Ruth felt
her whole being trembling. She knew his frustration was
powerful enough to make him act crazed. In turn she sensed
her disgust for him deepening with every passing second. If
soon he didn't let her go, she'd fight him with fists and fin-
gernails. Yet she felt a similar disgust for herself. She had contemplated marrying a man capable of violent jealousy
because of material benefits to be gained and without truly
knowing his character. And how could she condemn Loretta
Vane for falsely claiming to be Clayton's fiancée? She'd told
the exact same outright lie.

'Let me go and please leave at once.' Ruth strove to keep
a tremor from her voice. 'I don't want to create a scene in
the viscount's house. But if you make it necessary, I will.'

'Making a scene is something you seem to like to do,' Ian
mocked and brought his mouth menacingly close to hers. 'I'll
go and gladly, madam, now I know you for what you are.
You're nothing but a common tease. But before I leave I
think you owe me something—'

'At which point I believe it's my duty to say unhand my
fiancée or suffer the consequences,' drawled a lethal voice.

A startled silence fell on the grappling couple. Ruth
twisted her face from Ian's pursuing lips and looked up.
Clayton was standing with his back against the closed door,
as though moments ago he'd quietly entered the room.

Ian shot him a purely poisonous glare, but his need and his opportunity were too great to deny. With a tortured oath he jerked Ruth's face back to his and rammed his mouth home.

The ordeal lasted no more than a second or two. The next thing Ruth was aware of was Ian being dragged by his collar from the floor, where he'd been sprawled. She watched in a daze, one hand pressed against her bruised mouth, the other steadying herself against the sofa as Clayton shoved the doctor tottering back against the wall.

Ian fell spreadeagled against the paneling, a fist planted either side of him. Then one moved and pressed against his mouth. It came away bloodied and Ruth realised that Clayton had at some point swiftly and efficiently hit him.

'She's all yours,' Ian sneered. He looked at his blood, then at Clayton. 'I've taken as much as I want. I'm satisfied.'

'But I'm not,' Clayton said with perilous calm. 'Find yourself a second to stand for you. Your choice of weapons. Beech Common at dawn tomorrow. I'll arrange for a doctor to attend,' he added with a glimmer of mordant humour.

'As you wish,' Ian muttered hoarsely, but his complexion had turned pallid.

'No!' Ruth breathed so quietly that at first neither gentleman heard her heartfelt plea. 'No!' The word tore from her throat with greater volume this time. 'You can't. It doesn't matter...' She flew towards Clayton and was immediately caught and anchored to his side by a powerful arm.

'How touching...' Ian sneered. Without a farewell of any sort he straightened his dishevelled attire and strode from the room.

'Did he hurt you?' Clayton asked in a voice so controlled it sounded stilted.

Ruth shook her head and gazed up at him. The grey of his eyes was lost to black, so huge were his pupils. 'He didn't hurt me, I swear. You must go after him and tell him you didn't mean what you said about the duel.'

'I can't do that, Ruth,' Clayton said quietly.

'Yes…yes, you can,' she urged hysterically. 'I won't have you fight over something so…so trivial. Ian was consumed with bitterness because he's heard we're to be married.' Her briny eyes were raised to his. 'And it's not even true,' she finished in a whisper. 'Is a man to die for a lie?'

'I won't kill him,' Clayton promised gently. 'In any case, he might wound me,' he pointed out, his grim amusement barely perceptible.

Ruth shook her head frantically. 'You know he will not…cannot do so. He's not trained as you are in weaponry. And if either of you are wounded, there is a chance it might be a fatal injury. Please, Clayton…' her arms spontaneously hugged about his waist to stress that he must do as she wanted '…go after him and say you didn't mean to challenge him…'

Clayton's hands immediately sank into her soft hair to keep her close, but within a moment the soothing had stopped.

'Are you concerned because you care for him?' Clayton asked very quietly. He moved her back from him so he might see her expression. 'Look at me, Ruth,' he demanded. 'What did I interrupt just now? Was it a lover's tiff? Was it arranged that he would come to visit you in London?'

Ruth's glistening gaze shot upwards to merge with his. Her wet lashes were blinked rapidly as she strove to subdue her astonishment and answer him. 'Of course not,' she finally choked out. 'I was stunned to see him. He's enraged because your mistress and Mrs Beauvoir paid him a visit. I'm sure you can guess their motive for doing so,' Ruth finished sharply.

Two bluish lines bracketed Clayton's mouth as his lips compressed into a hard line. He wheeled away from her and went to the window to plant his fists against the frame. 'I can guess at something else too. Bryant came to London to look for you and renew his proposal.' He shot Ruth a fierce look. 'If nothing had happened last night, what would have been your answer?'

'Do you think I would consider marrying a man capable of such...such vile behaviour?' Ruth took a step towards him, her features crumpled by hurt.

'If nothing had happened last night, Bryant wouldn't have received a visit from two mischief-making women. He wouldn't have been provoked into showing his true colours. So, believing him an upstanding fellow, and a pillar of Willowdene society, what answer would you have given him, Ruth?' Clayton persisted.

Ruth made a hopeless gesture. 'I don't know,' she said, too truthful. 'I admit he has shocked me by behaving in such a way. I admit too that at one time...some years ago...I considered him to be a friend.'

'A friend?' Clayton echoed and slanted at her a trenchant stare.

'He was present when my father died. He offered me comfort and I took it,' Ruth said quietly. 'When I allowed him to hold me, he mistook my reasons and my feelings for him.'

'Ah...' Clayton murmured. 'And at the time you believed him too fine a gentleman to embrace a beautiful woman and later find an opportunity in it.'

Ruth snapped up her head, her temper beginning to simmer beneath his barbs. 'Perhaps you should not judge every gentleman by your own standards, sir.'

'Perhaps I should not,' Clayton concurred coolly. 'And at that time...when your father died...I take it the doctor was still married as he has an infant son.'

Ruth nodded and her eyes did not flinch from his, although she'd guessed his next words.

'He asked you to be his mistress.'

'Yes,' Ruth said hoarsely.

'And were you?'

'No,' Ruth breathed. 'I've said he mistook my feelings for him. Besides, I'm sure I need not point out to a sophisticate such as yourself that, had I acquiesced to an informal arrangement with the doctor, he probably wouldn't have bothered to improve upon it.'

A subtle smile touched Clayton's lips and lingered there. 'Indeed, you're coming to know me,' he murmured.

'And I do not like all I know,' Ruth returned in a whisper.

'Then I'm glad to have some qualities you find irresistible,' Clayton said and started back towards her. 'We'll always find common ground, Ruth. Perhaps we should settle for that…'

'Oh…um…sorry…'

Ruth shot a startled glance at the door to see that Gavin was hovering on the threshold.

'I was looking for Sarah,' he said apologetically. 'Never mind, I'll just see if she's…um…somewhere else…'

'Sarah went to Susannah's for tea,' Ruth informed him huskily. She darted a look at Clayton to see he was giving his friend a fearsome stare. Gavin responded with a barely perceptible gesture of regret.

On cue, Sarah's voice could be heard in the hallway. A moment later she appeared in the doorway with James in her arms. Her bright smile faded and her eyes immediately sought Ruth's with earnest enquiry.

'Sir Clayton has challenged Dr Bryant to a duel,' Ruth announced into the expectant quiet.

Chapter Eighteen

'What on earth has happened?' Sarah gasped.

Ruth sank into an armchair and her head dropped to rest in her quivering palms. For some minutes she seemed incapable of marshalling her thoughts well enough to answer Sarah's frantic question. Her friend knelt down beside her chair and hugged her, prompting salty tears to slide down Ruth's cheeks.

Shortly after Ruth had made her shocking announcement, Clayton had gone from the house with Gavin hot on his heels. But before Clayton had left he had quite tenderly drawn one of Ruth's hands to his lips in farewell. She'd feared he might be furious that her daze had caused her to spontaneously blurt out about the duel. A glimmer of exasperation had been at the backs of his eyes, but he had not reprimanded her by either harsh look or word.

Sarah rang for tea while Ruth, true to her word that in a moment she would be fine, dried her eyes and composed herself. A few minutes later, after Ruth had related all that had gone on, Sarah rattled her cup back on to its saucer. 'Hateful man!' she spat in disgust. 'And who would have thought it of him?'

'Not me, that's for sure,' Ruth said, smiling weakly.

'It is as well he is a capable doctor, for he certainly has no other commendable qualities,' Sarah returned pithily. She looked up urgently as her husband came back in to the room.

'He is in no mood to discuss the matter and has gone,' Gavin announced gloomily. 'I shall stand second for him. He can refuse me all he wants, it will make no difference. I shall be there.'

Sarah jumped to her feet. 'It is ridiculous!' she exploded. 'The meeting with Pomfrey has not been aborted for one whole day before Clayton gets involved in a different fight.'

'It's my fault,' Ruth said miserably.

'No, it is not!' A chorus of vehement denial issued from the couple.

'It is not, Ruth,' Gavin stressed softly. 'And if Clayton wanted me to know anything at all about what went on, it was that you are innocent of any blame.' Gavin came towards Ruth and took her hands in his in reassurance. 'He impressed that fact on me more than once and you must believe it.'

The idea of flouting etiquette to such a degree and visiting him at home would once have been beyond Ruth's scope of conduct. But with such damage to her reputation as had already been done, and might soon be added to, what did it matter? What value did a reputation have when set against a human life? There was an awful chance of a man being mortally wounded. Clayton and her friends wanted to shield her from the truth, but she knew she was the catalyst to an imminent tragedy. And her conscience could not bear it.

When she had told Gavin and Sarah that she wanted no dinner and must go out, she had noticed the bleak look that passed between them. But they had offered no demurral, although sweetly Sarah offered to accompany her. Ruth's insistence that she must go alone had then drawn a small sad smile and a nod of comprehension from her friend. When Gavin had quietly forced on her transport from his coach house, Ruth had accepted.

So, at seven o'clock in the evening she had set out for Belgravia Place in a sleek coach bearing the Tremayne crest. Sharing its luxurious comforts was one of Sarah's maids, seated opposite her. But now their journey was done.

Having told the young serving maid to wait where she was as she would not be long, Ruth now placed hesitant fingers on the door handle. She looked up at the imposing town house and fiercely quashed the temptation to tell the driver to set off back to Lansdowne Crescent. Nothing as paltry as faintheartedness was allowed to distract her from the vital task in front of her. She opened the door and got out.

'Ah, Mrs Hayden. Sir Clayton said you might come.'

Thoroughly unnerved by that polite yet very unexpected welcome, Ruth stared witlessly with huge dark eyes at the butler. 'Sir Clayton is expecting me?' she finally echoed faintly.

Hughes simply smiled and stepped aside, indicating that Ruth should come into the warm for the wind was strong enough to sway her on the top step and force her to snatch at her bonnet.

'Come along to the library. I believe Sir Clayton is to be found in there. I saw him enter the room not long ago.'

With her heart racing, Ruth followed the manservant. Darting glances roved the hallway, alighting on cool white marble and rich mahogany surfaces. Her fiancé's house was tastefully and expensively equipped, yet as Ruth walked amid Clayton's possessions she doubted she would ever be chatelaine of such splendour. She drew level with a magnificent gilt-framed mirror and, just before passing it, slipped a glance sideways. Her reflection startled and dismayed her—her huge dark eyes looked to be set in a complexion so pale as to be wraithlike. And then Hughes stopped and opened a door.

'Ah…he is not here,' the butler said with a frown, retreating from the room. Despite that setback, he ushered Ruth over the threshold of the library. 'If you would care to wait within, Mrs Hayden, I shall go and find Sir Clayton. I know he has not gone out.'

'Thank you,' Ruth murmured.

'Would you like some refreshment, ma'am?' Hughes remembered to ask before he fully closed the door.

Ruth shook her head and managed to murmur a polite declination.

Once alone, she loosened her bonnet and removed it, then took a few faltering steps over polished boards. She stepped on to a claret-coloured rug, then pivoted slowly about on the spot so she might fully see the grandeur of her surroundings. Her sepia eyes soared up and over the cased books. There were thousands, she guessed, ranging from tomes that looked to be over two feet tall and almost as wide, to tiny hide-bound booklets that refused to stand upright. Along the centre of the room were three sturdy library tables. Bulbous legs of turned oak supported leather tops of the same rich red hue as the rug she trod upon. Two of them bore a few scattered titles as though somebody had chosen them, finished with them, but not yet bothered to slide them home. Ruth's dark eyes flitted to the third table. There were no books, but it had on it an open wooden case…

Ruth felt her heart cease its erratic hammering and vault to her throat. She had seen such a box before. Her papa had owned a set of pistols.

Her clammy palms were dried on her skirts as swift steps took her closer to see if her fears were realised. She gazed down and, even to her inexperienced eye, guessed the guns were awesomely expensive duelling weapons. She extended a finger and touched the deadly cold metal, wonderfully chased in silver, before she slid her palm over polished wood and lifted one from where it innocently nestled.

'Are you going to use that?'

Ruth swished about with the weapon still gripped in her hand. Her denial was wordless and barely perceptible, yet set her dark tresses to trembling.

'Are you going to use it on Dr Bryant?' she returned in a whisper.

He didn't reply immediately; as he came towards her, she obliquely studied his appearance. She'd never seen him look so casually attired in buff breeches and a white linen shirt, agape at the throat, with the sleeves shoved back on solid muscle. When he reached her he removed the gun from her hand. His grey eyes roved her features with such solemn yet vivid desire that Ruth felt tempted to sway against him and let him erase all her anguish with draining kisses.

Ashamed that she could crave passion at such a time, she repeated breathily, 'Are you intending to use these tomorrow?'

'He's chosen swords,' Clayton said and replaced the pistol in the box.

Spontaneous heat scalded the backs of Ruth's eyes, making her blink rapidly. 'Close combat?' she croaked, almost to herself. 'Why?'

'I'm not sure,' Clayton answered with quiet truthfulness. 'But as a doctor he would know what damage a lodged bullet can do.'

'And a stab wound is harmless?' Ruth choked out in fierce frustration. 'This is madness.' Her tone was thick with despair. 'You knew I would come here and ask you not to fight. Your butler said you were expecting me.'

'Did he?' Clayton muttered. 'He's got too much to say for himself.'

'And what have you got to say?' Ruth begged to know in a husky choke. 'Please tell me you won't do this. I know it is a great deal to ask of you. I know honour and ego and all those things that gentlemen find so very difficult to deny are at stake…but surely you can see the disgrace in it, too?'

When he remained silent, she spontaneously grabbed at his jaw and jerked his face so he must look at her. As though startled by her audacity, and by the sensation of his angular abrasive flesh beneath her fingers, she just as quickly let him go. 'Can you bear to have on your conscience that tomorrow you might make a motherless little boy an orphan?' she demanded brokenly. 'I know I cannot. Joseph Bryant is only a year old…'

'I won't kill Bryant…I swear that to you.'

'But you are going to keep the appointment.'

'I must.'

'Why? Why must you? You have a choice,' she burst out in exasperation.

'Name it,' he said gently.

'Withdraw…please. Ian forced a kiss on me. I am the injured party and I ask you to forget what happened, as I have.'

'He insulted you. I heard him,' Clayton said.

'I have forgotten that too,' Ruth lied again.

'I haven't,' Clayton returned in the same placid tone. He stared down at the boxed weapons as he said softly, 'I've fought over a faithless wife and, had Pomfrey not seen sense, I would have fought over a scheming mistress. By God, I'll fight for you, Ruth, or know myself for the worst type of fool.'

'But I don't expect or want you to fight for me,' Ruth reasoned swiftly.

'I know, sweetheart…that's why I must.'

She could tell from his quiet steady tone that he wouldn't be swayed from what he'd decided. He might have issued the challenge to Ian on the spur of the moment, but it was obvious that, on reflection, his conscience was clear over it all.

'If you want to prove something to me, and please me…give me what I want,' she said huskily and came closer to him. 'I want the future you promised me.' Her slender hands rose to his shoulders, splayed over contoured muscle sheathed in cambric. Her head tilted to a perfect angle to tempt his mouth, her eyelids lowering in innate seductiveness. From beneath an inky web of lashes she could see the need start to smoulder at the backs of his eyes. 'I know you're an experienced duellist but…terrible accidents can happen. I might lose you.' Her warning was impressed on him as her straying fingers straddled his forearms. Abruptly she tossed her pride to the wind. 'How then will you give me that common ground we like to share, or a lengthy engagement?'

Clayton smiled slowly and with a hint of rueful humour. 'That's not what you want, Ruth. Nor should you,' he said gently, his grey gaze merging with her profoundly soulful eyes. He lowered his head and touched his mouth very lightly, very briefly to hers before moving away from the lure of her warm lush body. 'Go home, Ruth,' he said hoarsely. 'I swear to you Joseph will soon have his wretched papa back in one piece.'

Frost was glittering on the grass when the coach stopped and two men got out.

The vehicle scrunched away to halt beneath an arc of trees hemming a small clearing on Beech Common. Gavin immediately ran a booted foot back and forth, testing the white surface beneath it. 'Icy as hell,' he said and tossed Clayton a bleak look.

Clayton grimaced, then pivoted to look towards the sound of an approaching vehicle. The ghostly outline of a carriage emerged from the wispy mist. 'It's Francis Wells,' he told Gavin as his friend continued to walk back and forth over the treacherous turf, searching incessantly for a less perilous patch. But the yellow orb in the east had barely quit the horizon and was in no position to disperse the rime with its weak rays.

Gavin extended a hand as the surgeon marched over solid ground towards them. 'Gentlemen,' Francis intoned in solemn greeting, and shook hands with them both. 'Pistols or swords?' He looked at Clayton sharply for an answer.

'Swords,' Clayton informed him. 'But, unless Bryant's a master fencer, I wouldn't be surprised to hear him change his mind.'

'It's a foolish choice indeed,' Francis Wells said disapprovingly. 'Every morning this week has seen severe hoarfrost. It's not easy walking on such terrain. It would need to be a fool indeed who'd choose to fence on it.' He sent a grim gaze to rove over the crisp white environment.

Clayton smiled thinly. 'It obviously didn't occur to Bryant to take into account prevailing weather conditions. I think the doctor is probably inexperienced in these matters.'

'Whereas you are not.' Francis cast on him a jaundiced eye.

The sound of hooves and a creaking axle precluded any further debate. Another carriage loomed into view from beyond the screening trees.

It came to a stop on the opposite side of the clearing. Ian Bryant got out and shot a long stare Clayton's way. A dandified-looking fellow jumped down after him and immediately blew in his cupped hands to warm them.

'I didn't know Ian Bryant was on friendly terms with Claude

Potts.' Gavin made that observation as he stuck his hands into his coat pockets to protect them from the sting in the air.

'I doubt he is,' Clayton returned. 'I'd heard Christine Beauvoir has recently become Claude's mistress. Perhaps she thought it her duty to persuade him to offer his services to the doctor as she's helped to embroil him in this mess.'

'There's no chance of the matter being kept quiet now,' Gavin grimly remarked. 'Potts is the worst sort of blabbermouth. I doubt Bryant knows that about him, or much else. I'll warrant he'll not be pleased to discover all and sundry might soon know his business.'

Clayton didn't respond. He was watching the two men as they talked earnestly in between casting glances at their surroundings. Clayton had already guessed the outcome to their debate. A moment later Claude Potts picked a path across the hazardous terrain towards them and promptly confirmed Clayton's suspicions.

'Gentlemen,' he said and flourished a deep bow. 'My principal has asked that, if Sir Clayton is agreeable, weapons should be changed to pistols. The ground appears treacherous for fencing…' He slid an indicative look sideways.

'I make no objection to that,' Clayton agreed. 'Have you brought pistols?'

Already aglow from the cold, Potts's cheeks became brighter. He'd recognised immediately the light irony in Clayton's tone. 'I believe Dr Bryant was wondering…that is…have you brought a pair with you? We did not anticipate…'

'Clever fellows,' Clayton commented caustically.

'We'll settle for swords, if you have not,' Potts snapped. He knew, as the doctor's second, he should have thought to cover all eventualities. He knew too that, if something untoward were to occur, he could be called on to fight in the doctor's stead. The idea of combat of any sort with Clayton

Powell as his adversary was enough to make beads of cold sweat decorate Claude's bony forehead.

'I've a pair of pistols in the coach.' Clayton took pity on his blushing confusion.

Potts swallowed squeakily in relief. Having executed a less flamboyant bow, he started off treading daintily back across the frost.

Before Claude had reached the doctor's side, the assembled company were distracted by the noise of another coach. In seconds it was thundering into view through the mist. The horses were snorting from exertion and the vehicle shuddered to a halt in the middle of the clearing. Several gentlemen tumbled out, looking rather the worse for a night's roistering. The coachman then got off his perch and it was as he shoved his hat back on his head that Clayton recognised him.

'What in damnation…!' he expostulated in sheer exasperation.

'I said Potts has got a big mouth…' Gavin ejected through his teeth.

Ralph Pomfrey was already striding across the grass towards Clayton. He grabbed at his hand and pumped it up and down. 'Rum do, this, Powell. Any support needed…glad to give it, you know…'

Clayton snatched back his fingers and looked past Ralph to his spectator chums. He knew that they were simply rounding off a night's entertainment by coming here to watch the spectacle. 'If you want to be of use,' he enunciated curtly, 'keep them quiet and out of the way.' He turned to Gavin and they started to walk back towards their coach. 'Let's get this under way before the authorities turn up.'

'This is turning in to a farce,' Gavin muttered.

'Indeed…but make no mistake about it. Bryant is deadly serious and out for my blood.'

'And you?' Gavin asked shrewdly.

'Fetch the pistols,' Clayton said.

Chapter Nineteen

'Have you been sitting there all night?' Sarah asked softly on seeing Ruth's still figure perched fully clothed on the edge of a chair.

Ruth stirred her numb mind enough to give Sarah an answer. 'I woke about an hour ago.'

'You managed to get some sleep?' Sarah asked gently. She came further into Ruth's bedchamber.

Ruth nodded. 'A little.' She'd surprised herself by falling in to a deep dreamless sleep for a few hours before waking with a start and blinking at the darkness. Then the ghastly memories had crowded in on her and no further rest had been possible. She'd washed and dressed, with nausea rolling in the pit of her stomach, then sat down to wait for the dawn and news of the duel. But sunrise had come many hours ago and still there was no word of what had happened. Again her eyes were drawn to the small mantel clock. It was after eight o'clock.

'Is Gavin back yet?'

Sarah shook her head. 'I doubt he'll be long now… unless…' She hesitated to say any more.

'Unless something terrible has occurred.' Ruth sprang to her feet and paced to and fro. Her dread that a disaster had caused

Gavin's tardiness prompted angry futile words to explode from her lips. 'Men are such arrogant, egotistical brutes!'

'Indeed,' Sarah wryly agreed. 'Yet still we love them…'

Ruth's silence was answer enough, but Sarah probed gently, 'You do love him, don't you?'

'I hate him, too, for doing this.'

'The feeling won't last,' Sarah advised gently. 'There were things that occurred between Gavin and me that I thought too serious to be forgiven or put right.'

'But…if he is dead…or badly hurt…how can that be put right?' Ruth asked with a sob in her voice.

Sarah was about to attempt an answer when the noise of a vehicle in the street sent her rushing to the window instead.

'It's Gavin!'

Ruth collapsed back in to the chair, her face ashen. 'Is he alone?' she whispered.

After a moment Sarah answered, 'Yes…he is…' Sarah let the curtain drop and turned to Ruth. 'Will you come downstairs and hear the news or would you rather I—?'

'I'll come with you now,' Ruth interrupted in little above a whisper.

As they entered the parlour they came upon Gavin agitatedly prowling the room. His grim features made Ruth's heart thump with such force that she felt momentarily suffocated and unable to speak. 'Is he dead?' she finally gasped out.

'No,' Gavin answered quickly. 'But he is wounded… though not fatally,' he added immediately on seeing Ruth clutch a chair for support and turn so pale that he feared she might swoon. 'We've taken him back to the surgeon's house. Francis has stopped the bleeding and luckily the bullet did not lodge. The wound is clean.' His features tautened in ferocious anger. 'Bryant shot before the signal, then ran with his tail between his legs. He didn't even have the decency to offer to assist the surgeon in attending to Clayton's wound. He'd no idea what damage he'd caused and made no move to find out.'

'Was Clayton not able to get his shot in before the coward fled?' Sarah demanded, sounding as incensed as her husband.

'Oh…Clayton got a shot in. He put a bullet in the tree behind Bryant. It must have passed the caitiff's head with an inch to spare.'

'Thank God he missed him,' Ruth muttered so faintly the comment was almost inaudible.

'Clayton doesn't miss,' Gavin told her with bleak humour. 'He deloped. And why I'll never know. The fellow deserved some damage for what he'd done. At least he was frightened witless on knowing what he might get next time.' It was scant consolation and Gavin knew it. 'I have just come to put your minds at ease. I knew you would be desperately worried.' He passed a hand over his stubbly jaw. 'I must go back. Pomfrey is with Francis Wells and eager to assist. As soon as Clayton is fit to make the journey, we'll get him home and straight to bed.'

Ruth opened her mouth to speak, moistened her lips, desperately trying to think of some heartfelt message to send with Gavin. In the end all she could manage to croak out was, 'Please tell him I wish him well.'

'The gentleman's here, ma'am.'

Ruth turned from where she'd been sorting and labelling tubs and bottles in her larder. She gave Cissie a puzzled look while wiping flour from her hands on to her pinafore.

'The gentleman…you know…the one from London you said as might come back,' Cissie whispered, her eyes round as saucers.

Ruth froze in to immobility for a moment. She'd not

expected him to come so soon. She'd thought that perhaps in a month, when he was well enough, he might visit her. But it was not yet a week since she'd left Mayfair on the afternoon of the day of the duel. The Tremaynes had not tried to persuade her to stay, but had put every comfort at her disposal for the return trip to Willowdene. The parting from Sarah had been quiet, but intensely tactile and emotional.

Quickly Ruth started from her daze. She snatched off her pinafore and dropped it on to the table. 'Where is he?' she gulped.

'In the front sitting room, ma'am. I didn't know where you'd want him took...'

Ruth forced a smile. Her panic had transferred to Cissie and the poor girl looked quite scared. 'Thank you, Cissie, you may go home.'

Cissie nodded, but made no move to leave. Suddenly she darted to a row of hooks, grabbed her cloak and slipped out of the kitchen door.

It was too late to wish she'd chosen another afternoon to spring clean her kitchen cupboards. Ruth looked down ruefully at her dowdy attire. Since she'd returned home she'd plunged into energetic occupation, in and out of doors, simply to keep her troubles from tormenting her mind. And now the cause of her frantic daily activity was here...too soon. In no way was she prepared to see him yet. But desire to see him she most certainly did. With an inspiriting deep breath, and a nervous hand fiddling with wisps of glossy dark hair, she quit the kitchen.

He looked the same; the fine cloth of his charcoal-grey jacket fitted snugly to a back as wonderfully broad as she remembered it to be. His long athletic legs looked to be as sturdy following his ordeal. As he turned towards her she searched his dear profile for signs of any lingering pain but found nothing to concern her. He was facing her now and her eyes slipped shyly over him. Had she no knowledge of his recent threat to carry her struggling out of the Storeys' drawing room or to fight a duel over her, such assertions about his behaviour would have seemed preposterous. He looked cool civility incarnate and the picture of health and vitality.

'You look well,' she remarked and forced her hungry gaze away from him.

'So do you,' Clayton returned softly and brought an immediate blush to her cheeks. He watched as she self-consciously brushed a slender hand over the work dress she wore.

'You must excuse my appearance,' Ruth said on a little laugh. 'I didn't expect you to come so soon.'

'But you were expecting me, your maid told me so.'

Ruth's colour increased. 'She's got too much to say for herself,' she said lightly.

Clayton smiled; he knew she was echoing his words about his servant, spoken on the last occasion they'd met.

The expectant quiet lengthened, so she told him what she was sure he was politely waiting to hear. 'I knew you'd come as there is important unfinished business between us.' She frowned slightly. 'The matter of the engagement is still unresolved.'

Again her eyes darted to his body, seeking clues as to his injury. 'Has your wound healed so soon?'

Clayton pressed a few fingers to his right side and winced very slightly. 'It's well enough…'

'Well enough?' Ruth echoed, aghast. 'You have travelled so far with a bullet wound that still pains you?'

His eyes merged with hers. 'I wanted to see you,' he said gruffly. 'I couldn't wait any longer.'

'You want to know if I meant what I said, about…a lengthy engagement.' Ruth raised limpid dark eyes to his face. 'I did…and, if it's still what you want, I'm willing—'

'It isn't what I want,' Clayton interrupted in a voice that sounded harsher than he'd intended.

Ruth's eyes slanted immediately to his, her heart squeezing in anguish. He was rejecting her. He had come to end things between them and do it as quickly and courteously as he could. 'I see,' she finally choked out.

'I don't think you do, Ruth.' Clayton came a little closer to her. He made to reach for her then dropped tightly furled fists to his sides. 'If a man may be known by the company he keeps…what do you know about me? Tell me what you think of a man who has kept in style Loretta Vane, then considered you suitable as her replacement.'

Ruth felt a flush stealing under her skin. Within a moment of studying him she realised he wasn't waiting to hear that she could equal any service Loretta had provided. His expression and stance were bashful, boyishly endearing. He still wanted her good opinion and he thought his association with Loretta had ruined the chance of having it.

'Do you want my forgiveness?' she asked quietly.

'Yes, and more besides.'

'Is she in your past now?'

'She's been in my past since the day I travelled through snow to Willowdene Manor with Gavin. I swear it to you,' he added gruffly on seeing scepticism cloud Ruth's eyes.

'Then I think your past is your affair,' she said simply. 'I also think you astonishingly honourable and brave. You allowed Dr Bryant to go home, unharmed, to his son despite his despicable cheating. Once I considered that cheat a worthy man, and a friend. I considered accepting his proposal to improve my lot in life. What do you think of a woman so easily duped, so easily bought?'

'Do you want my forgiveness?'

'Yes…and more besides,' Ruth echoed his words wistfully.

'Name it. It's yours.'

Ruth allowed her lids to fall and felt the words teeter on her tongue tip. But pride kept them there for the moment. She wouldn't beg him to say he loved her any more than she'd demand he give her that lengthy engagement he'd offered. 'I'm so sorry,' she blurted. 'I haven't offered you refreshment and you've travelled far.' Her lack of manners made her feel worryingly inhospitable. Immediately she went to the decanter of port and, whether or not he wanted it, poured him a glass of rich ruby wine.

'I thought you were to use swords. Yet you have a bullet wound,' she said as she placed the glass on a table close to him.

'The ground was hard and slippery. Bryant changed his mind.'

'And you let him?' she said in wonder.

'It made no difference to me.'

'Because you knew you would not fight back whatever weapon he chose,' Ruth said with strengthening perspicacity.

'Something like that,' Clayton said diffidently. He picked up the glass of port and took a sip.

'The coward shot you, yet you deloped and allowed Joseph to have his papa back in one piece. You did it for me, because you'd promised me you would.'

There was no need for him to give a reply. The solemn intensity in his eyes, the stillness in him, told her the truth. He'd been intolerably lenient for her rather than for Joseph.

'Did you name your daughter?' Clayton asked huskily as though his mind tracked hers and he knew she thought of infants.

For a moment silence throbbed between them. Since that worrying evening at the Manor when little James had been poorly and Ruth had told him about her daughter, the matter had never again been mentioned between them. Her soulful dark eyes flicked up to him. 'Yes,' she eventually murmured. 'I named her Elizabeth.'

'Did your husband know her name before he died?'

Ruth swallowed, but the blockage remained in her throat so she nodded a reply. That was another matter that had remained unspoken between them. Yet instinctively she'd known he'd spoken to Keith Storey about the manner of Paul's death. 'Paul held Elizabeth before she was buried. He went back to his regiment of his own volition,' Ruth quietly volunteered. 'I didn't want him to leave. I feared what they might do to him. And so did he. But honour was everything to him, too. It was nothing to me but another body to bury. He was only twenty-two.'

'A man might live for his three score years and ten and never be as fortunate,' Clayton said softly. 'He had you. And you loved him.'

Ruth felt tears welling in her eyes at his quiet comfort. 'Did you want children?' she asked huskily.

'No,' Clayton said immediately. 'A child should have a good mother. A good father, too.'

'You would be a good father!' she cried spontaneously, then pressed together her lips. 'I'm sorry, I didn't mean to pry.'

'I want you to,' Clayton said with a coarse laugh. 'I want you to demand that I tell you why I've so long been wallowing in bitterness and unwilling to escape the shadow of a doomed marriage.'

'You don't need to tell me,' Ruth replied. 'I know it must have been a miserable time for you...' Suddenly the hurt she'd dammed behind pride and politeness exploded in harsh words. 'I don't want to know about her! I hate her! You're mine now! Why don't you want me now?' she keened in frustration. 'Is it because I tried to trap you to marry me?'

'Did you?' Clayton asked, but the wonderment in his face was put there by hope, not censure.

Already Ruth regretted what she'd done. She'd crumbled her own defences and the last bastions of her pride. Slowly she nodded and a watery little laugh bubbled in her throat. 'I didn't realise it at first. I thought I'd done it nobly for Sarah's sake. And of course I wanted to wipe the smirk from the face of that awful mistress of yours. But mainly I did it for me. I said we were to be married because I wanted it to be true.' She began to raise her head, feeling shy and apologetic. But by the time their eyes merged hers were vivid with challenge. She knew she had no bridges left to burn.

'So...you really don't mind that your affianced husband was once a maudlin idiot with very poor taste in women?' Clayton said gently. 'You don't mind that he was so sunk in self-pity he thought never in his miserable life would he have a chance with a woman as fine and beautiful as you?'

She shook her head, unable to speak for the wedge of emotion blocking her throat.

'Come here...' he ordered huskily and held out his arms.

Ruth stood rooted to the spot as tears spilled on to her lashes.

'I love you, Ruth. Please come here...' he begged huskily.

She flew across the room to him to hug him about the waist, then sprang back as she felt him wince. Immediately he drew her back against him and buried his lips in the scented mass of her hair.

'I'll take that pain and more just to have you in the same room as me,' he said hoarsely. 'God, I love you, Ruth. I love you so much.'

She lifted her watery countenance to his and touched a hand to his face. 'And I love you, Clayton.'

As though it was what he'd been waiting to hear his mouth plunged to hers with urgent need, sliding silkily back and forth. Ruth responded immediately, parting her soft lips beneath his sweet savagery. As his hands moved on her body she touched him back. Her fingers slid inside his coat, gently investigating. She felt the padding covering the wound and with infinite tenderness cupped her hand over it as though to protect him from any further hurt. Burying her face in the cosy nook beneath his shoulder, she asked with a throb of uncertainty, 'Do you want me as wife or mistress?'

'Both. I want only you. Will you marry me, Ruth?' he asked huskily.

'Are you sure it's what you want…?'

'Yes…and here's the proof.' He'd gently curtailed her anxieties while reaching in to a pocket and withdrawing a small box. With his arms about her, he opened it and turned the small casket to show her his gift. 'I came here, to beg on my knees if necessary, and make you have me and this ring. It belonged to my mother and now it's yours.'

Ruth gazed in awe at the fabulous round diamond. The shoulders of the shank were also encrusted with brilliant rectangular stones. 'Did Priscilla give it back?' she asked in amazement. It was the sort of gem any woman would be reluctant to part with.

'Priscilla?' He gave a bark of grim laughter. 'She didn't have it. My mother was still alive then and would never have allowed her to have it. She never liked Priscilla. I should have listened to her from the start.' His mouth touched her crown of silken dark hair. 'My mother would have adored you. She would be overjoyed to know she has at last a daughter-in-law to be proud of.'

'I'm most happy to accept it, and you,' Ruth said in a voice husky with tears. She took the ring then and slipped it on her finger, moving her hand to let the fading light in the room catch the stone and fire it to life. 'It's so very beautiful…I wish I had something equally precious to give you…'

As her thanks faded, her cheeks blossomed beneath the sultry heat blazing in his eyes.

'I think there's something…' he suggested wryly and dipped his mouth to seduce at the corner of hers.

She could sense the sweet wine on his breath, feel the heat of his desire warming her cheek.

'What about your injury?' she said softly, but turned her lips so they were ready to quickly couple with his.

'I trust you to be gentle with me,' he said and, with his mouth pressed to hers, took her towards the sofa.

Chapter Twenty

'There's somebody knocking on your door.'

Ruth stirred. She felt cosy and comfortable nestling against Clayton. His seduction had been wonderfully long and luxuriant and had culminated in a fiery ecstasy that had left her blissfully languid. Now she reluctantly lifted her head fractionally away from his warm chest and listened. There was an unmistakable sound of her knocker again being used. She squirmed against him to look into his eyes.

A groan escaped Clayton as she innocently tormented his hard sensitive body. Gathering back from her rosy face a fistful of tumbled chocolate-brown hair, he gently drew her face close and touched his mouth to the bruised bow of her lips.

'Did anybody see you arrive earlier?' Ruth whispered against his skin.

'Two women were in the street. They were stationed there last time I called on you,' he whispered back in amusement. 'Does this mean I must make good on my promise to marry you…or ruin your reputation?'

Ruth nodded. 'It does, I'm afraid.' She started slightly as the knocking became more insistent. In a flurry of petticoats, and tapping away Clayton's restraining hands, she scrambled to her feet. In a moment she'd smoothed down her crumpled skirts and arrived at the door to open it a fraction.

'Mrs Brewer…Mrs Stern,' she greeted breathily, thankfully unaware of the ravishing sight she made. Her bodice buttons were undone and displaying a creamy uncorseted cleavage. Her cheeks were flushed, her mouth plump and purple from Clayton's kisses and her rich dark hair waved about her face in artless disarray.

The two women goggled at her, then slid a speaking look at each other. Mrs Hayden might be unaware of how she appeared, but it was nevertheless quite obvious to them what she'd been about.

'We…we wondered…that is, we saw your gentleman visitor arrive some while ago and were concerned…' Mrs Brewer spluttered.

'Did you hear something?' Ruth asked, cringing from the possibility that her sighs and moans had been loud enough to travel through the wall.

'Why…no, Mrs Hayden. We could hear nothing at all,' Mrs Stern said disappointedly. 'So we decided to knock and make sure you were not in need of anything.'

'I have everything I need,' Ruth said with a simple serenity. Aware of the direction of Mrs Stern's gaze, she began to fasten her bodice.

The diamond flashed blindingly at the women, making their jaws simultaneously drop.

If Ruth had not known from a subtle caress on her hip that Clayton now stood behind her, the gawping ladies would have given the game away.

'You have not met my fiancé,' Ruth said with quiet pride. 'Sir Clayton Powell.' She turned against Clayton's body unable even now, under observation, to resist bodily contact with him.

'Sir Clayton…these ladies are two of my neighbours… Mrs Brewer and Mrs Stern.'

Clayton politely inclined his blond head and murmured an impeccably polite greeting, coupled with a farewell as he quietly closed the door. Just behind it he trapped Ruth against the wall and, placing a finger over her laughing mouth, trailed kisses on her joyous face from brow to jaw.

'Thank you for rescuing me,' she bubbled.

'Do you like me now?' he asked with a hint of gravity belying the wryness in his tone.

Ruth went on to tiptoe and brushed her mouth on his. 'I love you now. I also like you very much. In fact you have qualities I find irresistible, but you've always known that, haven't you?' she added softly.

'I'm equally captivated, sweetheart,' Clayton returned before transforming her gentle teasing of his lips into a deeply passionate kiss.

'Are you hungry? I can cook, you know,' Ruth finally said when their mouths parted. She cradled his hard handsome face between her soft palms. 'Would you like some dinner?'

'I'm hungry and tired. What shall we do first? Sleep or eat?' he asked hoarsely.

Ruth's eyes coupled with his. Gently, sweetly he had courted her on the sofa with kisses and caresses and tormented himself in the doing of it. Selflessly he had bestowed on her unbelievable pleasure while his own need went unrelieved. Wordlessly she gave her answer by slipping her arms about his neck and laying her head on his shoulder. She gasped as he swung her up into his arms as though she were featherlight.

'Have you truly carried a woman out of a drawing room over your shoulder?'

'She was more a girl than a woman,' he answered as he took the first stair.

'Who was she?' Ruth asked, steeling to keep jealousy from her voice.

'My sister, Rosemary. She was sixteen and professed to be desperately in love with a young poet. He'd written some ditties for her and she insisted on sharing them with the assembled company despite requests not to.'

'Did she marry him?' Ruth asked as she slipped sinuously sideways to scoop up the sconce from its holder and light their way.

'No…she married a Devon farmer without a romantic bone in his body.'

'Poor Rosemary.' Ruth sighed. 'Every woman needs a little romance in her life.'

'The poet's her lover,' Clayton said drily.

Ruth clasped his shady chin so he must look at her. 'Truly?'

'Truly.'

'Can you write poetry?' Ruth asked impishly.

'If I need to,' Clayton growled. 'But first let me show you an irresistible way I know of being romantic…'

'Did you see that diamond?'

'Did you see that gentleman?'

Mrs Stern and Mrs Brewer exchanged a look as they hesitated by the gate of Ruth's cottage.

'*Now* I understand those rumours I've heard about Dr Bryant going away.' Mrs Brewer crossed her arms over her chest.

'I said from the start he was going off to sunnier climes for his own good, not the boy's,' Mrs Stern added. 'Joseph looks to be a bonny little lad to me.'

'The doctor must be feeling most put out at being turned down by Mrs Hayden to go to such extremes!'

'It's a queer do, right enough.' Mrs Brewer huffed. 'She waits ten years for a decent man to happen by and two turn up at once.'

'Sons are the same,' Mrs Stern said darkly. 'I saw six daughters arrive before Stanley was born. Then Benjamin after him in less than eleven months.

'Look at that.' Mrs Stern nodded her head at the outline of the racing curricle gleaming in the dusk.

'Mayfair and devilish rich, I'd say,' Mrs Brewer whispered in awe.

'Devilish in every way, I'd say.' Mrs Stern dug her companion in the ribs and gave a scandalised gasp. 'It's as well Mrs Hayden will be moving away. She'd set tongues wagging doing *that* when it's not yet properly dark!'

The women watched as a wavering candle flame disappeared from the hall, only to reappear on the landing. As they waited with bated breath, it flared in the front bedchamber before being extinguished.

'You can't deny he is devilish handsome, too,' Mrs Brewer said charitably and cackled a laugh.

'I suppose she'd need to be a nun not to…' Mrs Stern generously agreed and, linking arms, they walked on home.

* * * * *

The Major And The Country Miss

DOROTHY ELBURY

Dorothy Elbury lives in a quiet Lincolnshire village—an ideal atmosphere for writing her historical novels. She has been married to her husband for fifty years (it was love at first sight, of course!), and they have three children and four grandchildren. Her hobbies include visiting museums and historic houses, and handicrafts of various kinds.

Chapter One

'The vultures are gathered, I perceive!' wheezed Roger Billingham, momentarily raising his consumptive body from his pillows, only to fall back in weary resignation as he gave way to another helpless fit of coughing.

'Try not to distress yourself, Roger,' his sister Eleanor beseeched him, motioning to the elderly manservant to mop the beads of perspiration from his master's brow. 'I have merely followed Hornsey's instructions—only those he named have been summoned—my son Jeremy, Jane's sister Marion and her son…'

She stopped as the old man struggled once more to rise.

'Young Maitland's here?' His bleared eyes eagerly raked the group at the foot of his bed.

'I'm here, Uncle.'

Will Maitland stepped forwards, his tanned and pleasant face full of concern as he bent over Billingham's bed.

'Got back without a scratch then, I see?' croaked his uncle, with a twisted grin, putting out his hand and gripping the younger man's. 'Ye'll do something for me, lad?'

'Of course, sir, if I can,' replied Maitland instantly and, without removing his hand, he lowered himself into a bedside chair. 'What is it that you require of me?'

Billingham flicked a glance at the listening group before carefully studying his nephew's open countenance.

'I have to put right a terrible wrong I've committed,' he cried, gasping for every breath. 'Otherwise there will be no peace for me beyond the grave! But answer me this, lad—are you prepared to forfeit your inheritance?'

Will Maitland frowned. 'I'm not after your money, Uncle Roger,' he said stiffly, his colour rising. 'Aunt Jane would have wished us to come—and you did have Hornsey send for us,' he gently reminded the old man. 'Now, what is it that you would have me do?'

As Billingham struggled to speak, he broke into another paroxysm of coughing. Just then another figure stepped forwards from the group.

'You may be assured that I, too, would be most happy to be of service to you, Uncle Roger.'

The Honourable Jeremy Fenton approached Billingham's bed, his handsome features carefully concealing the fastidious distaste he was feeling as he contemplated his uncle's death throes. He remained standing, his tall, rather too-slim figure meticulously attired in the current fashion, albeit that the calves within his buff-coloured pantaloons had been assisted with a little padding, as had the shoulders of his exquisitely cut, blue kerseymere jacket. Nervously fingering his intricately arranged neckcloth, he feigned a sympathetic smile at his dying relative.

Billingham took a sip from the glass that Maitland was holding to his lips and eyed his eldest nephew with undisguised contempt.

'Needn't tell me why you're here,' he snorted. 'In Queer Street again, shouldn't wonder—well, you're not getting at it without a bit of effort…'

'I'm sorry you feel that way, Uncle,' said Fenton, with a

pained expression on his face. 'Mother considered it my duty to attend—as your eldest heir…'

'Idle wastrel!' The old man struggled to rise, brushing away Maitland's attempts to pacify him. 'Already planning how to fritter away my hard-earned cash, are you? Well, let me tell you, you're in for a shock—all of you!'

He glared at the assembled company, then, twisting himself to face Maitland, he entreated him in urgent tones.

'Find the boy—please, Will—find Melandra's brat—if he lived! Help me make proper restitution for my sin—do this for me, lad—I know I can rely on you!'

At his nephew's puzzled but quite distinct nod, the old man's face contorted as he gave a little whimper and, breathing his last, he slumped back heavily on to his pillows.

Maitland laid his fingers over his uncle's face, gently closing the eyelids over the now sightless eyes before bowing his head in silent prayer. He then rose swiftly to his feet as Marion Maitland approached her brother-in-law's bedside. She stroked back the white, unkempt hair before bending to press her lips upon his brow.

'Poor Roger,' she said sadly. 'At peace, finally.'

'I'm somewhat confused, Mother,' frowned Maitland, standing back as one by one the rest of the little group came to pay their last respects to their dead relative. 'What is it Uncle Roger wants me to do? He mentioned Cousin Melandra—but she died over twenty years ago, surely? I can barely remember her.'

'Mr Hornsey will doubtless explain,' said Mrs Maitland. 'We are to attend him in the drawing-room—Eleanor tells me that Roger had instructed him to provide us with whatever information is available.'

They watched in silence as Ralph Sadler, the attendant physician, finally drew the sheet over Billingham's face and, at Lady Fenton's nod, Maitland turned to escort his mother from the room, followed by the small retinue of assorted cousins and elderly retainers who had also been present.

Jeremy Fenton caught up with them as they reached the door to the drawing-room and, grabbing his cousin by the arm, he said urgently, 'Got some bee in his bonnet, hadn't he—brain probably gave up at the end, shouldn't wonder. Think he's really changed his will, coz?'

Maitland shrugged. 'It's of very little interest to me what he's chosen to do with his money, Jerry—but no doubt you'll hear soon enough if you care to curb your impatience.'

'Yes, you can mock,' Fenton exclaimed hotly. 'Always the blue-eyed boy! Sucking up to him all these years…!'

'Allow me to remind you that I've been out of the country for the past five years,' returned Maitland drily, handing his mother into a seat. 'I haven't laid eyes on Uncle Roger since Aunt Jane died—so I'd say you've had a pretty clear field, if you'd a mind to curry favour. And, in case you had not noticed, I hasten to draw your attention to the fact that, unlike your own azure orbs, dear coz, my eyes are merely a nondescript shade of grey.'

'But I'm the eldest, by God!' Fenton scowled. 'My mother is the last of the Billinghams—this lot—' he gestured to the rest of the group behind them '—they're only distantly related through marriage.'

'As I, myself, am,' Maitland pointed out, with a grin. 'Aunt Jane having been my mother's sister.'

'Precisely!' returned Fenton triumphantly. 'Nary a blood relative present, apart from Mama and me—surely the old skinflint won't have left it out of the family?'

'Let's hear what Hornsey has to say, shall we? He seems very eager to begin.'

Fenton swivelled round to fix his eyes on the elderly man

of law, who was purposefully shuffling a sheaf of papers in his hands, apparently waiting for the subdued hum of conversation to cease.

'Well, get on with it, man!' he snapped, flinging himself into a chair. 'Are you going to sit there all day?'

Mr Hornsey eyed the heir-presumptive sourly, experiencing at the same time a feeling of unholy joy at the prospect of bringing the arrogant young dandy to his knees.

'Thank you, sir,' he said primly, adjusting his half-spectacles. 'I shall endeavour not to detain you any longer than necessary.'

Then, having declaimed that the document he held was, indeed, the last and completely valid testament of one Roger Billingham, Esquire, he proceeded to disburse generous annuities to Billingham's long-time servants and assorted bequests to the parcel of distantly related cousins who were also in attendance.

'—to my sister Baroness Eleanor Fenton, I leave our family home, Fetterfield, to dispose of as she sees fit, and to my sister-in-law Mrs Marion Maitland I pass on all of her sister Jane's jewellery, in grateful thanks for the loving care she devoted to my dear wife during her final illness.'

Here the lawyer paused and, after clearing his throat, he laid the set of papers down on the desk and looked over the top of his spectacles at the still expectant faces in front of him.

'At this point I am required to clear the room of all persons present, apart from the following…'

Then, in clear and precise tones, he proceeded to name Lady Fenton and her son Jeremy, followed by Marion and William Maitland. Then, having waited patiently until the last member of the departing group had vacated the room, he once again picked up his papers.

No one had spoken during this interval, Maitland merely

raising his eyebrows questioningly at his mother, only to receive a puzzled shake of her head in return. Fenton, rapt in his own deep study, stared moodily about the room, impervious to the concerned expression on Lady Fenton's face as she attempted to catch her son's eye.

'This part of the proceedings becomes somewhat unusual,' Hornsey then continued. 'Mr Billingham has put me in possession of certain facts, which he wishes to be kept within this small family circle. It concerns the rather delicate matter of his niece and ward, Melandra Billingham, now deceased, and the possible survival of the young lady's child.'

'Dear God!'

Lady Fenton let out a gasp and Hornsey's professionally impassive face suddenly became the focus of attention of four pairs of astonished eyes.

'Mr Billingham has required me to set in motion a thorough search to establish this child's existence. He apparently felt himself responsible for having abandoned it at birth and has left instructions that the bulk of his wealth shall be passed to this child should it prove to have survived...'

'No! No! I will not permit it!'

Fenton had risen to his feet, his face ashen.

'I shall contest it! The old man must have been insane!' Thrusting off his mother's attempts to restrain him, he strode forwards and tried to wrench the paper from Hornsey's hands.

'It is quite legal, I assure you, sir,' said Hornsey, savouring the moment. 'My client was perfectly sane—his own physician has borne witness. Do you wish me to continue?'

Fenton threw himself down on to his chair and glared at the lawyer.

'What does it matter—if we're not to inherit!'

'There are certain conditions, which may well affect you,' Hornsey was quick to point out. 'If the child is not discovered within a twelvemonth of today's date, the money is to be divided equally between yourself and Mr William Maitland.'

'And otherwise the damned brat gets the lot!'

'Not at all. He will receive, as I said, the bulk of the fortune—which I believe now stands in the region of some £500,000, not including the revenues from the plantations—but if you are prepared to make yourself instrumental in the search for the child's recovery you are to be awarded a one fourth share, as will your cousin Major Maitland, who, I understand, has already given his promise to assist in the search.'

He bowed his head towards Maitland, who smilingly nodded his acquiescence.

Fenton's eyes narrowed as he considered the lawyer's words.

'What you are saying, then,' he finally managed, 'is that I stand to get a quarter if this bastard is found now and a half if he isn't—but for that I will have to wait a whole year—is that it?'

'That is more or less correct, sir,' Hornsey said, enjoying this fleeting sensation of power. 'I believe Mr Billingham was anxious to atone for his having abandoned his young ward in her—how shall I put it—hour of need.'

'Never mind about that!' interrupted Fenton. 'Where is this child now? Good God—hardly a child—it's over twenty years since Melly ran off with that French tutor chap! D'you mean to tell us that he'd put her in the family way?'

'Since we're discussing the possible existence of a son, that would seem to be a fairly obvious conclusion,' his cousin pointed out, good-humouredly. 'However, I, for one, would be most interested to hear something of the story—if you could just forbear from interrupting at every turn, Jerry!'

He motioned Hornsey to continue, but the lawyer shook his head dolefully and indicated the single sheet of paper in front of him.

'Sadly, there is very little known of Miss Billingham's movements after she absconded with her tutor—Mr Billingham apparently received a plea for assistance some months later. I understand he would have ignored this had it not been for his late wife's insistence…?'

Seeing both Lady Fenton and Marion Maitland nodding at one another at this point, he invited her ladyship to elucidate.

'Both Roger and Jane adored Melly,' she said, 'not having children of their own. They had brought the girl up since Henry—our older brother—and his wife Patricia were killed in that dreadful carriage accident, along with their two little boys.'

'They spoilt her dreadfully,' put in Maitland's mother, 'but Jane would have it that the child had, after all, lost her whole family and they were only trying to make up for that—but she became very headstrong, I remember.'

'She was rather lovely, though,' recalled Maitland, leaning back in his chair and closing his eyes in reminiscence. 'I can remember when she was about to make her come-out—her first drawing-room appearance, I believe, and Uncle Roger had invited us all to see her in her finery before they left. She looked like a princess in a fairytale—with her beautifully powdered hair, that white-and-silver crinoline and all those diamonds—I swear I fell in love with her on the spot!'

'You *were* only six years old,' his mother laughingly reminded him, 'but it's true, she was an exceedingly lovely girl. Unfortunately, she knew it and was terribly flirtatious, too. It's always been my belief that Étienne never really stood a chance after he set eyes on her, poor man. I am convinced that their elopement must have been Melly's idea—he wasn't at all the sort of young man to suggest such a thing.'

'He was only a miserable tutor,' said Fenton scornfully.

'Hardly top-drawer and not a penny to his name—his cuffs were always frayed, as I recall.'

He viewed his own pristine cuffs with pride and flicked a non-existent fleck from his coat sleeve.

'No, Jeremy, you're quite wrong there,' said Mrs Maitland, shaking her head. 'He came from a most aristocratic family. They had fled the Terrors, of course, and he was forced to make his own way in the world. I always found him to be a perfect gentleman and I was very surprised to learn that he had abandoned Melly.'

Jeremy Fenton leaned forwards impatiently.

'Let's get back to that,' he said. 'Uncle Roger presumably answered her cry for help?'

His mother nodded. 'He went off into the wilds of Warwickshire somewhere,' she explained. 'Jane had persuaded him to fetch Melandra home—whatever situation he found her to be in—but he returned two days later and told us all that she was dead.'

She paused momentarily, her brow wrinkling in pensive remembrance of the stark, angry expression on her brother's face as he had curtly informed his shocked family of their niece's death. 'He made no mention of a child, however, nor do I recall the whereabouts of his destination. He always refused to speak of it.'

'His own recollection was merely that the building itself was reached by a long driveway with lime trees on either side,' offered Hornsey, once more perusing his papers. 'And, also he believed that the hotel he stayed in was a coaching inn in the market town of Dunchurch—I understand that this town is situated on the London Road, somewhere in the vicinity of Coventry.'

Maitland digested this information.

'She must have been buried, you know,' he observed. 'There

will be parish registers. It should not be too difficult to discover her last resting place—she had a most unusual name, remember. There can't be many Melandra Billinghams recorded as having died in—when was it—1795, I suppose?'

'You really intend to seek out this bastard, then?' Fenton, rising, eyed Maitland curiously. 'Said you weren't interested in Billingham's fortune—changed your tune now you know how much there is to gain, eh?'

Maitland also rose to his feet, facing his cousin squarely. The two were of equal height, but Maitland had the weight, his shoulders and limbs needing no tailor's assistance to fill out his coats and trousers and his clear grey eyes were unspoiled by the reckless dissipation that marred the older man's.

'I shall do you the service of ignoring that remark, Jerry,' he said carefully. 'I gave Uncle Roger my promise and I intend to do my best to find out what became of Melandra's child. If you wish to join me you will, of course, be welcome—but I advise you to keep such opinions to yourself, otherwise I may well forget that you are my kinsman!'

Jeremy Fenton's handsome face flushed slightly as, with a self-conscious laugh, he lowered his eyes.

'No offence, Will,' he stammered. 'Of course I shall accompany you—I bow to your military efficiency—I should hardly know where to begin! When are we to set off on this quest, may I ask? I shall require several days to settle certain—matters—and my man Pringle will need time to see to my wardrobe…'

Maitland burst out laughing and gave his cousin a friendly clap on the shoulder.

'I don't intend to drag about the countryside with carriageloads of your finery, Jerry!' he chuckled. 'We can't leave until after the funeral, of course, but then I mean to take off first thing and ride for Dunchurch—it can't be more than sixty miles away. If you want to accompany me, you'll need to keep your baggage to a minimum!'

'You surely don't expect me to travel all that way on horseback!'

The Honourable Jeremy was visibly horrified at the idea. Out of necessity he had learned to be a fairly competent rider, in as much as the daily canter in Hyde Park was concerned—for one had to be *seen*, of course—but the prospect of being in the saddle for several hours at a time appealed to him not in the slightest degree. His expensive riding coats and breeches were cut more for display than practicality and he shuddered to imagine what damage would be done to his new top-boots if he were to subject them to the rigours of country-lane mudbaths. Also, he had to have his man to help him into his jackets and see to his linen! He was no fool, however, and quickly realised that if there were to be any hope at all of maintaining his chosen way of life, he was going to have to make some sort of push to get hold of his share of old Billingham's money as soon as possible. Recurring visions of the likely alternative helped him to make up his mind.

'I'm not the cavalryman you are, coz,' he said, in explanation for his outburst. 'I'll have to follow you up in my chaise—I'll get Pringle to scrabble a few things together and we shan't be much behind you, you'll see. Will you order the rooms?'

'Good man!' Maitland gladly gave his hand to this arrangement then, turning to the man of law who had been sitting silently listening to this interchange, he asked, 'Is there nothing else which might be of use to us, Mr Hornsey? There must be hundreds of villages in that area—each with its own church and graveyard, I shouldn't wonder. No clues to that, I suppose?'

'You are welcome to copies of the papers,' Hornsey offered. 'I was most careful to take down everything in Mr Billingham's exact words but, of course, the event occurred a great many years ago and his memory was failing. I believe I have furnished you with all the relevant information…' His eyes scanned the sheets in front of him. 'He *did* leave a considerable sum of money for the young lady's funeral but he said that when the nun questioned him—'

'Nun! Are you sure?'

Maitland pulled the paper towards him and ran his eyes quickly down the close, spidery handwriting, finally giving an exclamation of triumph when he found the information for which he was seeking.

'Yes! Uncle Roger quite definitely said "nun"!' He spun round eagerly to face his puzzled family. 'Do you see what this means? It must have been a convent, or a priory—Roman, in any event—that will surely be easier to trace!'

'The young man Étienne,' said his mother, in growing realisation, 'he would have been a Roman Catholic.' She turned to Lady Fenton. 'What *was* his name, Eleanor? I've been racking my brains trying to recall it.'

The older woman's brow furrowed in concentration. "Dela"—no—"du" something—or "Des" something…..?'

'Doubly!' cried Fenton, in sudden excitement. 'His name was "Doubly". You remember, Will—we used to call him "Bubbly Doubly"—after we saw him sobbing away behind the church, that time?'

'*You* may have called him that,' said Maitland shortly, still intent upon scrutinising the lawyer's scribbled testimony. 'I remember him only as *monsieur*. Doubly doesn't sound very French to me—more likely to have been "D'Arblay" or "de Blaise".

'Yes, I remember now!' cried Mrs Maitland, clapping her hands. 'D'Arblay! Étienne D'Arblay—I'm sure that was it! Oh, Eleanor! Do you think he could have been there, too—with Melandra?'

There was a heavy silence for a few moments as the two ladies stared at one another, each of them considering the implications of this possibility.

'Doesn't look like it.' Maitland shook his head and indicated some more information he had managed to decipher. 'Apparently, the nun told Uncle Roger that Melandra had extracted a promise from them that her child would be given its dead father's name, but when they asked him—Uncle Roger, that is—what *he* wanted them to do, he informed them that he had no further interest in the matter and that they must place the child in a foundling home—he gave them money with which to give Melandra a decent burial, then he left.'

'And he never breathed a word to any one of us—not even Jane,' said Marion Maitland, in wonder. 'He must have known she would have wanted to keep Melandra's child!'

'No wonder he was so distressed at the end! To have carried this burden all these years!' Billingham's sister turned her eyes, now wet with tears, towards her son. 'You must find the boy, Jeremy—Roger was right—a dreadful wrong has been committed! The money is no longer important!'

Fenton raised his eyebrows. 'I regret to say that the money is very important, Mama,' he said witheringly. 'Most of my creditors have held out for so long only because they have been under the assumption that Maitland and I would soon be sharing Uncle Roger's estate between us—and I'm afraid that I have done little to discourage their belief. This recent development has dropped me right in the suds. I don't have a year to wait for my full share—I shall likely be in Marshalsea by the end of the month if I can't lay my hands on some serious blunt so, quite frankly, the sooner we can find this boy—or prove him dead— the quicker I shall be able to climb out of the basket!'

Maitland looked sharply at his cousin, his well-formed features full of concern.

'Perhaps you would allow me to help you out, Jerry,' he offered almost diffidently. 'I dare say I could manage to cover some of your most pressing debts—you can't owe so much, surely?'

'Enough to make a very large hole in any fourth part I might receive, old man,' said Fenton, smiling faintly as Maitland issued a soundless whistle. 'With the best will in the world, I doubt you could even buy up my vowels—but I'm obliged for the offer. I shall just have to put my faith in your ability to hunt down our quarry—to which end you seem to be progressing pretty well!'

'Good of you to say so, coz,' laughed Maitland, clapping him affectionately on the back. 'Although I don't care much for your terminology—the lad we're seeking is our young cousin, remember, not a wily old fox!'

'Well, let's hope he'll appreciate the sacrifices we're making for him,' returned Fenton drily and, turning to Hornsey, he asked, 'No chance of an advance, I suppose?'

The lawyer pursed his lips. 'I can probably arrange something of that nature by next week, sir,' he said. 'Your expenses will be met, of course, but I would first like to be assured that some progress has been made.'

'Perfectly in order.' Maitland smiled in agreement, then he frowned as he caught the muted oath that escaped Fenton's lips. 'Come now, Jerry—Uncle Roger told you that you'd have to earn your share. That's only fair, surely? Certainly, the fresh air won't do you any harm and a few days in the country will keep you out of those gaming hells you seem to spend your life in. I would have said that a repairing lease might be just what you need at the moment!'

Jeremy Fenton eyed the younger man truculently for a moment or two then, with a slight lift of his shoulders, he reached out to grasp his cousin's outstretched hand and shook it firmly. 'I'd almost forgotten what a good-natured fellow you are, Will,' he said, with an awkward grin. 'I swear I'm looking forward to spending some time with you again, after all these years!'

Chapter Two

Four days later, having agreed that he would meet up with his cousin at the Dun Cow at Dunchurch, Will Maitland headed north from his home in Buckinghamshire and made for Dunstable, from where the newly metalled Watling Street would take him into Northamptonshire and eventually on to join up with the Coventry turnpike. He had sent his bags on ahead of him and had every intention of making quite a leisurely journey of it, since he reckoned that it would take him something in the region of six hours to accomplish the distance, including a couple of halts for refreshment and to water Pegasus, his chestnut stallion.

The summer day was fine and fair, with sufficient breeze to make a steady canter enjoyable and, to begin with, having set out at such an early hour, he had the road much to himself, skirting past the occasional rosy-cheeked milkmaid as she dreamily followed her charges from their field to the milking-shed, and exchanging smiling greetings with the farmers' wives he encountered driving their laden gigs to the local marketplaces.

The morning wore on and the volume of oncoming traffic increased and, having more than once been forced to hug the hedge as a lumbering stagecoach bore down upon him, he judged the moment suitable to make his first stop, choosing a pretty little wayside inn just outside the village of Stony Stratford. After instructing an ostler to rub down and water his horse, he chose to partake of his own refreshment seated on the wooden bench that the landlord had thoughtfully provided beneath the shade of a nearby leafy chestnut tree.

His hunger satisfied, he leaned back in comfortable tranquillity against the tree's great trunk and closed his eyes and, whether it was the lulling sound of the insects droning above his head or the effect of 'mine host's' strong home-brewed, coupled with his early rising, he would never know, but in just a few moments his head nodded on to his chest and he was sound asleep.

A tentative tap on his shoulder startled him out of his pleasant doze.

'Begging your pardon, sir,'

The sound of the landlord's voice dragged Maitland from his slumbers and it did not take him long to realise that the sun was no longer directly overhead, which irritating circumstance meant that he would have to press on very quickly if he wanted to make up the time he had lost. Cursing under his breath, he called for Pegasus to be saddled, hurriedly paid his shot and, mounting in one swift movement, he wheeled the horse out of the yard and urged him into a fast gallop towards Towcester.

Two hours later, by mid-afternoon, he had reached the Daventry turnpike where he ascertained from the toll-keeper that a further eight miles would see him at the Dunchurch pike.

'An' ye'd do well to stop the night there, sir,' warned the keeper, pocketing Maitland's two pence and handing him his ticket. ''Taint wise to be crossing Dunsmoor Heath at sundown—been a fair few travellers robbed there lately.'

Maitland thanked the man for his solicitude, assuring him that Dunchurch would, in fact, be the end of his journey and, with a cheery goodbye, set off once more at a spanking pace.

Hardly a mile or so up the road, however, Pegasus suddenly faltered in his stride and, gradually slowing down, he began to limp on his left foreleg. Maitland, after five years in a cavalry regiment, had no trouble recognising the ominous signs and he immediately reined in, dismounted and led his horse on to the grass verge where he carefully examined the hoof and found, as he had expected, a small sharp flintstone lodged under his shoe. Since he always carried with him the necessary implements for dealing with such an emergency, it did not take him long to extract the offending object, but, knowing that the horse would still be in considerable discomfort for some little while, he looked about him for inspiration and, spotting a small stream not far off, he led the still limping animal over to the bank and into its soothing shallows. He patted his neck with sympathetic encouragement as the thirsty animal eagerly gulped the refreshing water, then, taking out his pocket-handkerchief, he soaked it in the fast-flowing stream and wiped his own perspiring face before lowering himself to sit on the grass verge while his mount gratefully cooled his sore foot.

There was still a considerable amount of traffic making its way in both directions along the road. Several carters went by, touching the brims of their felt hats in greeting as they passed, and a pedlar's wagon, hung all about with pots and pans, brushes and broom-handles and the like, brought a instant smile to Maitland's face as it rattled and clanked its way onwards. This was followed, shortly afterwards, by a well-sprung, open-topped landaulet, drawn by a pair of beautifully matched greys.

Having seen that the owner of the carriage was frantically

signalling to his coachman to check his horses, Maitland leapt to his feet. Almost before the vehicle came to a stand-still, its owner was out of his seat and hurrying back down the road, a slight limp impairing his otherwise swift progress.

'Will Maitland!' he cried, in obvious astonishment. 'By all that's holy! What in the name of goodness are you doing here?'

Grinning widely, Maitland strode quickly to meet him, both hands outstretched to grasp the other man's.

'Eddie Catford!' he said. 'My dear fellow! I had quite for-gotten that your place is hereabouts. How are you, old chum? How's the leg?'

The Honourable Viscount Edwin Catford beamed back at his ex-army comrade.

'Not worth a mention, dear friend,' he replied, with studied nonchalance. 'But why are you lolling about at the side of the road? Lost your way, old chap?'

'Very amusing,' chuckled Maitland, giving the viscount a light-hearted punch in the arm. 'Actually, I'm heading for Dunchurch, but poor old Pegs picked up a flint a while back, obliging us to rein in for a few minutes.'

'Oh, bad luck!' Catford was instant sympathy. 'Can we take you up?'

He gestured towards his carriage and Maitland, turning, saw that the vehicle held other occupants.

'That would be useful,' he confessed, 'but I see that you have ladies with you—I must not detain you.'

'Nonsense! They'll be delighted to meet you,' avowed Catford, steering his friend to the side of the landau. 'Ladies, this roadside vagrant is none other than an old comrade from my regiment—one William Maitland, Esquire. Will, allow me to present my cousin, Miss Georgianne Venables, and our neighbour's granddaughter, Miss Stephanie Highsmith.'

His two young passengers had been consumed with curiosity as to the identity of the stranger but, upon hearing Maitland's name, the viscount's cousin's face lit up with a welcoming smile.

'Major William Maitland!' she exclaimed. 'But surely you are the hero himself?'

'The very same,' replied Catford, grinning hugely at his friend's discomposure. 'Dragged me from the Jaws of Death without a thought for his own safety…'

'Cut line, Eddie,' begged Maitland, laughing. 'That's old history now—your servant, ladies.'

Turning, he made his bow to the occupants of the carriage, both of whom regarded him with unconcealed interest, for the tales of Earl Gresham's son's exploits in the Peninsula had long held the locals spellbound, and there would have been few who would not have heard of Will Maitland's daring intervention in what might well have been their young hero's final action.

Having had his horse shot from under him on the field at Waterloo, the viscount had found himself pinned beneath the dying animal, unable to extricate his shattered leg. Notwithstanding the fact that their company had, by this time, been in hasty retreat, Maitland had wheeled back and leapt from his mount to heave his comrade out of the mud and up on to his own horse's back. Miraculously avoiding both shot and cannon, he had managed to re-mount and head the animal in a frantic gallop back to their lines, for which courageous action he had been promoted and mentioned in dispatches.

'Aunt Letty will be overjoyed to finally meet you face to face,' said Georgianne. 'She was so full of your bravery when she brought Edwin back from the military hospital at Chatham.'

Maitland smiled. 'Her ladyship has been kind enough to write to me on several occasions during the past year,' he replied. 'I look forward to calling on her.'

'Which I hope you will do, as soon as may be,' interrupted Catford. 'But, for the moment, where are you bound? Tie Pegasus to the rear of the carriage and we will take you up as far as we can—give him a much-needed rest from your tiresome weight, at any rate,' he added, with a grin.

Maitland, returning the grin, acquainted Catford with his destination. On learning that the viscount was travelling to within two miles of Dunchurch, he gratefully availed himself of his offer and, having secured his mount's halter to the rear of the landau, climbed into the vacant seat beside his friend.

'You are bound for Gresham Hall, ladies?' he enquired with interest, as soon as the coachman had whipped up the horses. 'May I ask if you live hereabouts?'

Although he had addressed his questions to both of Catford's female passengers, it was the young lady seated directly opposite him who had captured the better part of his attention.

Whilst Maitland was willing to concede that the viscount's cousin, with her light brown hair drawn neatly back under a simple chip-straw and her placid grey eyes set in pleasant features, was far from unattractive, her looks paled almost into insignificance when compared with the breathtaking loveliness of Miss Highsmith.

A tumble of golden curls, half-hidden beneath the frivolous confection of a wide-brimmed, beribboned bonnet, framed Stephanie's utterly bewitching features. As he gazed, wholly entranced, at the girl's adorable face, complete with cornflower-blue eyes, a pert little nose and the most kissable lips he had ever come across, Maitland found himself instantly captivated.

'Since Georgianne is also my mother's ward, Gresham Hall has always been her home,' replied Catford, on the girls' behalf. 'And Lady Highsmith has done us the honour of allowing her granddaughter to stay with us whilst she herself takes the waters at Harrogate.' He turned to the still slightly bemused Maitland, explaining, 'My parents are about to celebrate their fortieth wedding anniversary and we are quite a houseful at the moment. You, of course, will be more than welcome to a bed. Had I known that you intended to be in Warwickshire at this time, I would have invited you earlier. Why *are* you here, may I ask?'

Hurriedly redirecting his mind to the viscount's question, Maitland replied, 'Thanks for the offer, Cat, but I'm racking up in Dunchurch—with my own cousin, as it happens, if he arrives as planned. We're set on the trail of a long-lost relative of ours who was, apparently, born in these parts—fulfilling a sort of a deathbed promise, you might say.'

'How intriguing!' Georgianne leaned forwards, her eyes alight with interest. 'May we be privy to this search? Or, is it a deep secret?'

'Well, there are family secrets involved, I must confess, but it is highly probable that in the end I shall be thankful for whatever assistance I can get, Miss Venables,' replied Maitland with a laugh. 'The mystery goes back before you were born, I hazard, and I suspect that it will be more of a chore than I had realised. I fear that I shall be poring over old parish records for some weeks to come.'

Stephanie's pert little nose wrinkled in distaste. 'Oh, that does, indeed, sound boring in the extreme, Mr Maitland—I do hope that you will be able to set aside a little time to come and visit us all at the Hall, as Lord Catford has suggested?'

Although Maitland merely promised that he would do his best, he was inwardly determined that wild horses would not prevent him from furthering his acquaintance with the lovely Miss Highsmith. Now twenty-eight years old, he had, of course, indulged in many light-hearted adventures of the romantic kind but, having spent the previous five years of his life in a somewhat ramshackle military life on the Continent, he had always been careful never to allow himself to become too emotionally involved. For, truth to tell, he thoroughly enjoyed his bachelor existence.

A man of independent means, with a solid family background to his name, he was almost totally lacking in personal conceit, although he could hardly have been unaware that the eyes of many a hopeful mother lit up when he chose to single out their daughters, for he was what was known as a 'good catch'. In point of fact, though, he had no idea of marrying for some time to come, being perfectly content to spend his days assisting his father in the management of the Maitland family's large estate in Buckinghamshire and involving himself in the many sporting activities available to gentlemen of his wealth and status. His previous amatory excursions had left his heart more or less unscathed, with the possible exception of that which had involved a certain somewhat exotic *demoiselle*, to whom he had been obliged to bid a rather reluctant farewell upon his unit's embarkation from Belgium. A few weeks back in the swing of the victory celebrations in London had soon cured him of that particular malady, however, and, although he had subsequently danced and dined with many a fair damsel, he had not, until this moment, discovered any good reason for altering his single state.

Sitting back, he allowed his eyes to play over the creamy perfection of Stephanie's complexion and, as he marvelled again at the curling length of the sooty black lashes that framed the deep azure blue of her eyes, the neat little nose and the sweet rosebud lips, a deep sigh seemed to tug at his heart. But then, suddenly conscious that he had, perhaps, been staring at the lady rather longer than was circumspect, he forced himself to drag his gaze away from Stephanie's all-encompassing loveliness and allowed it to drift across to her companion, only to discover that, if the curve of her lips was anything to go by, Catford's cousin appeared to be regarding him with a certain amount of amusement.

Feeling somewhat like a naughty schoolboy who had been caught with his hand in the biscuit jar, a slight flush appeared on his face and he hurriedly dropped his gaze and endeavoured to concentrate his attention on the ongoing conversation.

'His lordship is being most kind,' Stephanie was enthusing, as she cast a warm smile at the viscount. 'He has chosen to accompany us on our afternoon excursions almost every day since my arrival—he insists that it is good exercise for him—although I am sure he would rather be off shooting with the other gentlemen.'

'Not at all, my dear,' demurred Catford graciously. 'I'm not yet up to tramping the heath—more than happy to be of service, I assure you.'

'Cat keeps us entertained with his endless fund of droll anecdotes about his travels,' said Georgianne, shooting her cousin a fond glance. She had been somewhat taken aback at Maitland's response to her smile, which had been merely been offered as a gesture of friendliness on her part. His reaction to Stephanie's loveliness had come as no surprise to her, since it was very little different from that of the majority of others of his sex when they first set eyes upon her friend. Having known Stephanie all her life, Georgianne had learned to regard such behaviour with patient equanimity, experience having shown her that this sort of awestruck admiration was inclined, for the most part, to be fairly short-lived. She was well aware that her friend took such adulation as her due, deriving much enjoyment from playing off one hopeful contender against another. It was not that Georgianne particularly approved of Stephanie's somewhat cavalier attitude towards

her fluctuating band of admirers, but rather that she felt that
any man who allowed himself to be treated in such a way was
no man at all and must, therefore, deserve all he got. Furthermore, although she had no personal interest in him, she did
feel a slight sense of disappointment that the man who had
risked his own life to go to her cousin's aid should turn out to
be as shallow as the majority of Stephanie's previous devotees.

'You must know the area pretty well, Eddie,' ventured
Maitland, reluctantly hauling his thoughts back to the real
reason he had set out on this journey. 'Do you have you any
idea where might I procure a list of the local churchyards? I
suppose that ought to be my first objective.'

Catford pursed his lips in thought, then, 'Reginald Barkworth is your man,' he nodded. 'Used to be the curate at the
parish church in Dunchurch. Veritable encyclopaedia when
it comes to local history—oh, botheration! Here we are at the
Willowby turn, old man. Time to bid you farewell, I fear!'

Not at all sorry to extract himself from Georgianne
Venables's somewhat pointed scrutiny, Maitland opened the
door, leapt nimbly from the landaulet and untied Pegasus
from his tether. Catford leaning out, waited for his friend to
mount before adjuring him not to fail to present himself at
the Hall with all speed as soon as he was settled in.

'Reginald Barkworth,' he called, in reminder, as Maitland
turned his horse's head towards his destination. 'Tell him I
sent you and be sure to let us know how you get on with your
quest, dear fellow.'

Maitland had no difficulty in giving his promise, since he
had every intention of finding his way to Gresham Hall and
the fair Miss Highsmith at the earliest opportunity but then,
as he suddenly remembered that he had prevailed upon
Chadwick, his man, not to bother to pack his decent dress-
clothes, he cursed himself for a fool. Determined to reach the

inn in time to send off for reinforcements to his meagre wardrobe, he reluctantly waved farewell to his travelling companions and set off up the turnpike.

Chapter Three

Georgianne viewed Maitland's departing figure with an odd mixture of curiosity and disappointment.

'It will be very pleasant for you to have Mr Maitland's company again after so many months, Eddie,' she then observed.

'Capital fellow,' replied the viscount enthusiastically. 'Served with him for almost five years. A superb horseman and very handy in a bare-knuckle spar, he can shoot out a pip at twenty-five feet and hold his liquor with the best of them!'

Georgianne's lips twitched. 'High recommendations, to be sure!'

Catford laughed. 'Perhaps not to the ladies, dear coz—but I, for one, will never forget that I owe Will Maitland my life.'

His eyes grew bleak momentarily and there was a heavy silence. Stephanie sighed and a small frown creased her brow as Georgianne leant once more towards the viscount.

'You never speak about those times, Eddie,' she said in a tentative voice. 'I know that they must have been very bad, for Uncle Charles allowed me to read some of the dispatches.'

Stephanie shot a fulminating glance towards her friend.

'I'm sure Edwin would rather not be reminded of his

dreadful experiences, Georgianne,' she said pointedly. 'I have never understood why he felt it necessary to join the military in the first place—but, now that he is home again, it is surely finished with and best forgotten, I believe.'

'It certainly doesn't do to dwell on the matter,' agreed Catford, quickly recovering his composure and smiling across at his young companions. 'As to forgetting, of course, I shall be hard pressed to do that while I still have this gammy leg—but Stephanie is quite right, Georgie. War is not a suitable topic for social discourse and, most certainly, never for young ladies' ears.'

Ignoring Georgianne's affronted expression at this last remark, he turned the conversation to the coming celebrations and listened with cheerful interest as Stephanie, her face glowing with delight, described in detail the utter perfection of her newest gown.

'And you, Georgie?' he enquired, in a teasing voice. 'What stunning creation has Madame produced for you?'

Georgianne laughed, her good humour immediately restored. 'You know perfectly well that I do not have Steffi's enthusiasm for such matters, Eddie. Madame Henri and I have reached an understanding and I am usually very happy with her work.'

'I find it quite extraordinary that Georgianne never takes even the tiniest bit of interest in the latest fashions,' said Stephanie, complacently smoothing the pleats of her smart blue velvet carriage-dress. 'I swear that she'd wear the same outfit on every occasion if someone did not take her in hand!'

But her eyes twinkled at her friend as she spoke and Georgianne smilingly nodded in agreement.

'Very probably,' she said, looking down at her own well-worn, but still perfectly serviceable russet-coloured pelisse. 'I like to be comfortable; provided that I don't look an absolute fright, then I'm perfectly happy!'

Catford grinned. 'I'd like to be at that unlikely event, dear cousin, but I cannot see it ever happening. Both of you always look quite delightful and you will no doubt be surrounded by the usual bevy of admirers fighting to be included on your cards. I dare say I might be amongst them if my leg holds out—I could probably manage the odd stately minuet.'

Stephanie giggled deliciously. 'I doubt if anyone can remember the steps,' she said. 'The waltz is all the rage nowadays. How odd to think that only two years ago it was considered shocking and young ladies were forbidden to dance it in public!'

'You will allow, then, that the war was of some benefit to society?' said Catford, his lips twitching in amusement. 'At least our success in importing the German dance seems to have won your approval. Sadly, I fear that it will be too strenuous for me at present, but I look forward in great anticipation to seeing the pair of you twirling about the room.'

'A full-dress ball, at long last!' breathed Stephanie rapturously. 'I had almost given up hope of ever attending a real one! I am so grateful that you managed to persuade Grandmama to allow me to stay at the Hall for the month, Georgie—the thought of yet another season in Harrogate was beginning to drive me quite insane!'

'It is Aunt Letty who really deserves your thanks,' demurred Georgianne. 'She was the one who eventually convinced Lady Highsmith that she would benefit much more from her visit to her sister in Yorkshire if she did not have to concern herself with having to see that you were sufficiently entertained.'

'I have been forced to endure Harrogate's so-called "entertainments" ever since I was sixteen years of age,' grimaced Stephanie. 'They consist of morning promenades to the pump-room, afternoon visits to Grandmama's dreary old acquaintances and long, tedious evenings at the card tables.'

'But you did get to attend the assemblies last year,' her friend reminded her, with a smile. 'I seem to recall you mentioning that a rather dashing young lieutenant paid you a great deal of attention!'

'Richard Loxley,' Stephanie nodded glumly, 'He was quite sweet but, as usual, Grandmama did her utmost to discourage him—it sometimes seems as if she cannot bear to see me enjoying myself!'

'Oh, come now, Stephanie!' protested Catford, who had been following the girl's conversation with polite interest. 'You are being a little hard on Lady Highsmith, surely! Whilst it is certainly true that your grandmother takes her role as your guardian rather more seriously than would some, you cannot fault her for her generosity. Only five minutes ago you were describing to me the "simply gorgeous" ballgown that Madame Henri—whose creations, I might add, are hardly cheap—has produced for you. If her ladyship discouraged one of your suitors, you may be sure that she had very good reason for doing so.'

'Yes, but she *always* discourages all of them,' pouted Stephanie. 'That is why I was so astonished when she actually agreed to let me stay with you this year. She normally never lets me out of her sight for more than five minutes at a time!'

'Her ladyship is merely concerned for your welfare,' put in Catford gently, as he reached across to press her hand. 'Having devoted the best part of her life to caring for young ladies whose lives have been less fortunate that your own, she is probably more aware than most of the dangers that might easily befall one who is as lovely as you are, my dear.'

Although she was not remiss in offering the viscount a tremulous smile in recognition of his compliment, Stephanie could not forbear from thinking that it was all very well for those whose lives were as free as a bird's to chastise her for grumbling about her own rather more restricted one. After all, she reasoned to herself, none of the viscount's family had been obliged to suffer her grandmother's long-term dedication to her Refuge for Genteel Ladies in Distress—or Home for Unmarried Mothers, as some of the less enlightened members of the local populace tended to refer to Highsmith House. Highly commendable though Lady Highsmith's commitment to her project might be, it did seem to carry with it the unfortunate side effect of causing the home's founder to be uncommonly strict as regarded her granddaughter's upbringing. And, even though she had taken extreme measures to ensure that the girl was shielded from the more unsavoury aspects involved in overseeing the welfare of the continual stream of those young ladies who were housed in the west wing of the building—referring to them only as "our guests"—it would have been difficult, if not downright impossible, for an inquisitive child, such as Stephanie had always been, not to have learned the real truth of the situation.

Owing to the fact that Georgianne's aunt, Lady Letitia Gresham, served on Lady Highsmith's board of trustees, the two girls had been acquainted since early childhood. Having both been orphaned at birth, it was hardly surprising that they should have forged the bonds of friendship, even though their temperaments could hardly have been more different.

Not long after the two girls were out of leading-strings, it had been arranged between their guardians that Stephanie would take her lessons with Georgianne, in the schoolroom at Gresham Hall, and this she had done until both girls had turned eighteen. Georgianne's subsequent departure to London to make her formal début into the high society to which her family belonged, had filled her lifelong friend with both envy and rage, since Lady Highsmith had flatly refused to countenance the countess's very generous offer to bring the two girls out together.

Her grandmother's inexplicable refusal to allow her to accompany the Greshams to London had come as a bitter blow to Stephanie for, as with a certain amount of resentment, she had quickly pointed out to her friend, it was not as though the old lady was short of funds. 'It is all part and parcel of her refusal to admit that I have a good deal more common sense than any of those pathetic creatures to whom she devotes so much of her time!' she had complained at the time.

'I hardly think that sense has had a lot to do with any of your grandmama's ladies' falls from grace,' Georgianne had mused. 'I am rather inclined to the belief that they simply allowed their hearts to overrule their heads.'

'Allowed themselves to be totally taken in by some mendacious philanderer, you mean!' Stephanie had retorted scornfully, ignoring her friend's pained expression. 'Well, I for one, find it extremely galling to discover that my own grandmother appears to labour under the misconception that I am going to throw myself into the arms of the first man who crosses my path!'

'Stranger things have happened,' Georgianne had pointed out, with a smile and a shake of the head. 'Especially if you were to fall in love.'

'*Fall in love!*' her friend had scoffed. 'You do talk such nonsense at times, Georgianne! I have no intention of ever indulging in such a feeble-minded activity! Why limit one's favours to just the one gentleman when there is so much more satisfaction to be gained from having several of them at a time vying for one's attention?'

'Well, if the various routs and assemblies we have attended this past year have been anything to go by,' the laughing

Georgianne had then replied, 'there have certainly been more than enough of them queuing up to vie for yours!'

'Local squires' sons and impoverished preachers!' Stephanie had sniffed disparagingly. 'Just think how many earls and viscounts I might have added to the list had not Grandmama been so adamant in her refusal.' Then, having extracted herself from her friend's sudden but heartfelt hug of sympathy, she had added, somewhat despondently, 'By the time this Season is over, Georgianne, I predict that you will have netted a peer of your own and will be all set for your big society wedding, while it seems more than likely that I shall be stuck in this boring backwater for the rest of my days. Life is so unfair!'

Three years had passed since she had made that prediction, however, and, as the Gresham carriage rolled up the winding drive towards the Hall's front door, Stephanie found herself recalling how very astonished she had been when Georgianne had, in fact, returned from her sojourn in town not only quite unattached but, as it happened, several weeks earlier than had been anticipated. Short of a rather brief and terse account of her presentation at Clarence House, and, despite Stephanie's eager questioning, Georgianne had proved strangely unwilling to satisfy her friend's curiosity as to the success or otherwise of her London début. In addition to which, there had been no further talk of any future Seasons for Lady Letitia's niece.

Stephanie had been forced to deduce that some distressing event must have occurred to change the formerly positive and fully self-confident Georgianne from the girl that she had once been to the much quieter and far more reserved female that she was today. Whilst it was true that rare glimpses of her friend's once quite infectious sense of humour might still be occasionally observed, it saddened Stephanie to think that the girl whom she had always regarded as her soulmate no longer chose to confide in her.

Later that same evening, as she sat on Georgianne's bed, watching her friend brushing back her soft brown waves into the rather severe chignon that she favoured nowadays, a small frown marred Stephanie's smooth brow, as she pondered over the fact that Georgianne had surely had more than enough time to get over the unexplained mystery surrounding her London début.

'How is it that you never let your maid see to your hair, Georgianne?' she asked, fingering her own bright locks. 'Emily always thinks up such clever arrangements.'

'Too true,' nodded Georgianne, as she jabbed another hairpin into place. 'The trouble is that she chooses to ignore my specific requests and will insist upon arguing for "just the odd little tendril here" or for "softening the line just there"—to use her expressions—while I myself prefer this much less troublesome and, to my mind, far neater style.'

'I recall a time when your ringlets were even longer than my own,' Stephanie reminded her. 'We used to measure each other's every month, to see whose had grown the most, do you remember?'

'Yours always seemed to grow far more quickly during the summer months, as I recall,' said Georgianne, a little smile playing about her lips. 'My own hair, for some obscure reason, appears to favour the springtime.'

'Am I right in thinking that it was after you came back from London that you decided upon this particular style?' asked Stephanie, adopting a deliberately casual tone whilst, at the same time, appearing to give her full attention to a minor adjustment to the low-cut bodice of her dinner gown.

A slight frown flitted across Georgianne's brow and a wary

expression crept into her eyes. 'You probably are,' she murmured, as she reached for her gloves and rose from her seat. 'I really cannot recall the exact occasion.'

'Well, I can, Georgianne!' retorted Stephanie crossly, as she leapt to her feet and planted herself squarely in front of her friend. 'It's been over three years now—surely we have been friends long enough for you to trust me with whatever happened then to change you so!'

Georgianne let out a deep sigh. 'Honestly, Steffi,' she protested, 'I swear you are like a dog with a bone over this matter. No sooner do I think that I have cast it all out of my mind than you insist upon bringing up the whole beastly affair once again.' Then, after a moment's hesitation, she gave a resigned shrug, lowered herself down on to her bed and motioned to her friend to join her. 'What happened was really nothing so very dreadful,' she began tentatively. 'I fancied myself in love and so was over the moon when he—the gentleman concerned—petitioned my uncle for my hand in marriage. But then, on the very day that our engagement was due to be announced in the *Post*, my suitor begged to be excused!'

'Oh, how truly ghastly for you!' cried Stephanie, instantly reaching out to clasp her friend's hand in sympathy. 'But, did the dastardly creature give you no reason for his craven withdrawal?'

'He wasn't such a dastardly creature really,' said Georgianne, with a wan smile. 'In fact, I would have been prepared to swear that his intentions were totally sincere. Sadly, however, it transpired that my—er, lineage—was not up to the standard that the gentleman required in a wife and he therefore felt himself obliged to withdraw his suit.'

'But, that is ridiculous!' exclaimed her friend, her eyebrows raised in astonishment. 'Your lineage, as you call it, must be second to none! The Venables family history goes back hundreds of years—even the royals themselves could not claim a more distinguished pedigree!' She paused, frowning in contemplation, then, drawing in a deep breath, she asked excitedly, 'Was that it, Georgianne? Was your reluctant suitor a member of the royal family?'

'Absolutely not,' Georgianne hastened to assure her. Then, rising to her feet once more, she added, 'It really would be better if you forgot everything that I have told you this evening, Steffi. Since the gentleman in question swore never to disparage my name, I feel that he too is entitled to assume that his identity will remain my secret.'

'Hardly a gentleman, in my opinion!' sniffed Stephanie. 'Especially since you seem to have been carrying a torch for him all this time—'

'Oh, no, Steffi!' Georgianne interrupted hurriedly. 'You may relieve yourself upon that score, at least! I ceased to think of his—*him*—in that particular way some time ago. Further to which, I understand that the gentleman has since found himself a wife who would appear to have all the necessary qualifications.'

But then, as she fixed a stern eye upon her friend, she added quietly, 'Now that I have done my best to satisfy your curiosity, you must give me your promise that you will never refer the matter again.'

'But, of course you have my promise,' returned Stephanie, somewhat affronted that her friend should even consider otherwise. 'Although, I must confess that I still find it hard to understand why the matter should have wrought such a change in you.'

'I am bound to admit that the whole unfortunate business did have rather a sobering effect on me,' returned Georgianne, with a shrug, as the two friends made their way down the magnificent oak staircase to join the rest of the countess's guests. 'Which was due, most probably, to my self-esteem having suffered rather a setback!' At the foot of the staircase, she paused momentarily then, with a slightly rueful smile, added, 'It certainly taught me that it does not do to take anything for granted.'

Just as I had always done until that time, she recollected, with an inward shudder, as they walked across the marble-tiled floor towards the drawing-room.

Whilst it was true that Lord Tatler's retraction of his offer of marriage had affected her greatly, her initial distress had been as nothing compared to the painful humiliation that she had felt on being made aware of the real reason that lay behind her suitor's reluctant withdrawal. Her uncle's somewhat embarrassed explanation that she had, in fact, been born before her parents had exchanged any marriage vows had delivered a devastating blow to her self-confidence, and was certainly not something that she would ever be prepared to share with Stephanie, no matter how much her friend might tease and cajole her!

As a result of her uncle's disclosures and despite her aunt's protests to the contrary, Georgianne had, forthwith, resigned herself to a life of spinsterhood. Having already known the pain of rejection, she had done her best to protect her heart from any further such damage. While she had always been perfectly charming and agreeably polite to every one of the several prospective suitors who had attempted to win her hand during the past three years, she had been equally dogged in her determination that the unfortunate facts of her birth should not become common currency and had, thus far, refused to allow her heart to be swayed by any of those young men's eager blandishments.

Nevertheless, as she found herself wistfully recalling, for perhaps the third or fourth time that evening, the rapt look that had appeared on Will Maitland's countenance, as he had sat drinking in Stephanie's loveliness, it was with considerable difficulty that she managed to control the sudden longing that welled up inside her, its very presence threatening to destroy her hard-won equanimity.

Chapter Four

Leaping from his mount, Maitland passed the reins to a waiting ostler and was just about to make his way into the Dun Cow when he heard a voice from the far side of the stableyard calling out his name. Turning swiftly, he beheld a very familiar face from his not-so-distant past.

'Sergeant Andrews!' he grinned, reaching forwards to grasp the other man's outstretched hand. 'What in the name of fortune are you doing here? I was under the impression that you hailed from Essex!'

Pete Andrews, an ex-sergeant from Maitland's own Light Cavalry regiment, was a tall, lanky individual whose once-handsome features had been severely marred by the vicious sabre slash that he had received while on the field at Waterloo.

'Didn't fancy goin' back home with this 'ere, guv,' he grunted, ruefully fingering the puckered scar that ran diagonally across his face. 'Frighten my poor Rosie to death, so it would!'

'You would rather that your wife believed you dead?' exclaimed the astonished Maitland. 'But what about your children—you have two young sons, I believe?'

'Aye, that I have.' Andrews nodded, his bright blue eyes clouding over. 'Tommy and Billy—ain't set eyes on the pair of 'em for nigh on four years now—but I do my best to send 'em all bits of cash whenever I gets the chance, guv!'

'Very commendable, Andrews,' returned his former major, raising an eyebrow. 'However, I would be prepared to gamble that your good lady would as lief have your presence, rather than your pennies!'

'Not possible at the moment, guv,' shrugged Andrews. 'Us old soldiers 'ave got to go where we can find the work— two of my old muckers are up 'ere, too, as it 'appens. I dare say you'll, no doubt, recall Privates Skinner and Todd?'

'Only too well, Andrews!' replied Maitland, with a reminiscent grin, as he brought to mind the pair of rather shady individuals to whom his ex-sergeant had referred. Although they had always been up to some devilry or other, their ingenuity at ferreting out provisions for the communal pot had been second to none. Had it not been for the pair's amazing scavenging abilities, there had been more than a few occasions when he and his men might well have been forced to face the enemy with empty stomachs.

'So, what brought you to this part of the country?' he enquired.

'Matty Skinner used to work 'ere when 'e were a lad,' explained Andrews. 'Put in a word for us, so 'e did—seems coachin' inns can always find work for them as knows their way round 'orses.'

'Well, your employers will surely not be able to fault you on that score, Sergeant,' nodded Maitland, as he turned to go. 'I just wish you would give some more thought to returning to your family.' Then, after a thoughtful pause, he added, 'I dare say I could find you a place in my own stables—probably run to a cottage, too, if needed. What do you say?'

At first, the man's eyes appeared to light up in eager

interest but then, after a brief hesitation, he gave a careless shrug, saying, 'Thanks for the offer, Guv; I'll certainly bear it in mind!'

Later that same evening, Maitland, comfortably en-sconced in the small parlour that had been set aside for his private use, swirled the remnants of the brandy in his glass and, gazing down into the amber liquid, spent some little while ruminating over the day's happenings. That his ex-sergeant had not immediately jumped at his offer of employ-ment had surprised him somewhat, since it would seem that the man, if his almost skeletal frame and shabby appearance were anything to go by, could hardly be earning enough to support himself, let alone contribute to his deserted family's welfare. Sipping thoughtfully at his drink, Maitland could only suppose that, in order to send them any meaningful amount, Andrews must be reduced to sleeping above the stables and taking what he could get, in the way of suste-nance, from the inn's kitchens. Shaking his head at the man's baffling obstinacy, Maitland then turned his mind to the far more pleasurable subject of the deliciously lovely Miss Highsmith and wondered whether the following afternoon would be considered too early to pay the promised visit to Gresham Hall.

As luck would have it, however, shortly before noon on the following day, the Honourable Jeremy, complete with valet, arrived, along with one very large trunk and several bulging valises strapped to the rear of his smart chaise. This quickly put an end to Maitland's plans to ride over to Gresham Hall and so, leaving Pringle to organise his master's belongings, Maitland invited his cousin to accom-pany him down to the parlour, called for two bumpers of ale and proceeded to share with him the meagre bits of information that he had already manage to obtain from his previous day's enquiries.

'Sounds as if this Barkworth fellow could be worth a visit.' mused Fenton, as soon as Maitland had concluded his short report. 'Sure to be able to tell us where we might find nuns, at any rate.' And, tossing back the remains of his drink, he got to his feet, saying, 'Let's get on with it, then—nothing like striking while the iron's hot, as the saying goes!'

Accordingly, the cousins presented themselves at Reginald Barkworth's little cottage, which was situated close to the parish church at which he had once been incumbent, and were ushered into the cramped and dusty room that the elderly cleric had designated as his office. Hurriedly removing the untidy piles of papers and books from the decidedly rickety-looking chairs upon which they had been perched, he invited the two men to make themselves comfortable.

'Sit down, sit down, please, gentlemen,' he exhorted them, taking his own seat behind a desk that was covered in such an assortment of miscellaneous clutter that Maitland, who was a great believer in orderly arrangement, began to doubt whether this shaggy-haired venerable could possibly have anything to impart to them that might help them in their quest.

Half an hour later, however, he realised that his doubts were unfounded for Barkworth proved to be, as Catford had informed him, an inexhaustible fount of local history and folklore. However, since the elderly curate was only too eager to impart to his listeners far more on the subject than they might have wished to learn and was, clearly, not to be hurried, Maitland resigned himself to listening patiently to his host's apparently inexhaustible supply of local anecdotes.

The Honourable Jeremy, however, was in no mood to

prolong what seemed to him to be an extremely dull and tedious waste of time. 'Yes, yes, most interesting,' he muttered, fastidiously brushing away the particles of dust that settled upon his new yellow pantaloons every time Barkworth moved a book or lifted a map to point out yet another fascinating detail in relation to one of his stories. 'But it's churchyards we came to see you about—grave-stones and suchlike—it's nuns we're looking for, ain't it, Maitland?'

As Maitland shot his cousin a disapproving glance, the old curate pursed his lips and regarded Fenton with a frown.

'If it's nuns you're after, my boy,' he said scathingly, 'I doubt that you'll find any hereabouts. All the local priories and convents were disbanded a good many years ago, even though several of the villages, such as Priors Kirkby and Monkswell, still carry their original names. Even the old Mercy Houses, which the Poor Clares ran, gradually fell out of use well before the turn of this century.'

'Poor Clares?' Maitland asked with interest, while Fenton heaved another sigh and gazed dispiritedly out of the begrimed window beside which he was seated.

The cleric nodded and a wide smile lit up his cragged face.

'Aye, that's what they called them,' he said reminiscently. 'The Ladies of St Clare, to give them their proper title— part of what was left of the Franciscan order, I understand. Lived in small groups, helping the needy and tending the sick—usual kind of thing, but they wouldn't accept payment, hence the name.'

'And were there any such Mercy Houses in the vicinity of Dunchurch?' asked Maitland eagerly, convinced that he had, at last, hit upon something that might prove useful.

'More than likely,' nodded Barkworth. 'Couldn't advertise themselves, of course, being of the Roman faith—which, in those days, was like waving a red rag to a bull in certain sections of the community.'

After studying his visitors thoughtfully for some minutes, he dipped his quill into the inkwell and began to scratch out some names on a piece of paper.

'Try these, he said. 'Most of these village churches do have their own curates but, as to whether they will be able to lay their hands on such records, is hard to say. Nice little church-yards some of them have, too—worth a look, at any event.'

Having succeeded in scattering sand over paper, desk and floor before eventually passing the list to Maitland, he then rose stiffly to escort the two men to the street door, dismissing Maitland's grateful thanks with a careless wave of his hand.

'Happy to be of service, my dear boy,' he smiled. 'Don't hesitate to come and see me again if there is anything further you require.'

'Doubt if the old fool has had such a captive audience for years,' muttered Fenton, as the cousins made their way back cross the street to their hostelry. 'Shouldn't think that room's seen so much as a duster since the blessed Gun-powder Plot itself!'

Maitland laughed. 'You could be right there,' he nodded, in cheerful acquiescence. 'Nevertheless, it is just faintly possible that our loquacious friend might well have provided us with some rather useful information.' And, indicating the list in his hand, he then enthused, 'These villages, for instance—I see that Willowby is amongst them—an ex-military friend of mine lives in that vicinity—promised I'd look him up, if I got the chance. Fancy a trip over there tomorrow morning, Jerry?'

'Consider me at your service, dear boy,' returned his cousin, carefully picking his way across the straw-strewn forecourt of the Dun Cow. 'Only too happy to let you organise this campaign in whatever way you see fit—wouldn't have the vaguest idea where to start, meself!'

And so it was that, shortly after eleven o'clock the following morning, the Honourable Jeremy's well-sprung chaise, along with both of the cousins, found its way to Gresham Hall, which turned out to be an imposing early Georgian residence situated on a small rise on the far side of Greenborough village.

'Fancy-looking pile,' remarked Fenton enviously, as he brought the carriage to a halt at the foot of the Hall's front steps. 'Worth a pretty penny, I'll be bound.'

Having been alerted by the sounds of their approaching vehicle, a stable lad appeared from the rear of the property to take hold of the horses' heads, while the two men jumped to the ground and ascended the steps up to the wide front door, which was quickly opened by a tall, stately-looking individual, dressed in plum-coloured livery.

Upon learning the identity of the visitors, the manservant's haughty demeanour vanished immediately, to be replaced by an expression of deep respect.

'Mr William Maitland!' he exclaimed, in an almost reverent tone of voice, as he ushered the pair into the large black-and-white tiled hallway. 'May I say what a great privilege it is to come face to face with you at last, sir!'

'Good of you to say so,' murmured Maitland, not a little embarrassed at the serving man's effusive attitude, which must stem, as he now realised, from his having learnt about the part he himself had played in his young master's rescue and recovery.

To his further consternation, the elderly butler then thrust out his hand, saying, 'Allow me to shake you by the hand, sir! Oswald Moffat, at your service, sir!'

Reaching out to take hold of the other man's hand in a firm and friendly grip, Maitland could only pray that he was not about to be subjected to this sort of unwanted adulation from very many more of Earl Gresham's staff.

Inclining his head, he said graciously, 'I'm very pleased to make your acquaintance, Moffat. Perhaps you would see if her ladyship is receiving visitors this morning?'

Hurriedly remembering his place, the manservant gave a courteous bow and, after showing the two men into an anteroom, bade them to take a seat. Then, after bowing to Maitland once again, he exited, his eyes alight with pleasure, as he hurried to impart the good news of the hero's arrival, not only to his mistress, but also to his colleagues below stairs.

'What the devil was that all about?' demanded Fenton, in astonishment, as soon as the door had closed behind the departing butler. 'Damned funny way for a servant to go on, if you ask me!'

''Fraid it looks as though we might have to put up with quite a bit of that sort of thing,' said Maitland, with a rueful grin. 'Cat seems to have put it about that I had a hand in saving his life.'

'Seems there's no end to your blessed talents, Will!' exclaimed Fenton, eyeing his cousin sourly.

'Stow that, Jerry!' returned Maitland, reddening slightly. 'I only did what any fellow would have done in the circumstances, which hardly warrants remarks of that sort, surely?'

Fenton gave a careless shrug. 'If that butler chap's performance is anything to go by,' he observed, 'it strikes me that the odd sarcastic remark from yours truly might well serve to help keep your feet on the ground!'

Before Maitland could reply, a soft tap on the door heralded Moffat's return and the two men were escorted up the stairs to the morning room, where a smiling Countess Gresham, her son at her side, was eagerly awaiting their arrival.

'My dear Mr Maitland!' she exclaimed, rising from her seat and hurrying forwards to greet him. 'I have so wanted to meet you face to face! How can I ever thank you for saving my son's life?'

Doing his best to ignore his cousin's disdainful sniff, Maitland reached forwards and took Lady Letitia's out-stretched hands into his own. 'Eddie is my friend,' he said gently. Then, looking up and catching sight of the viscount's sober expression, he added, 'Had the roles been reversed, I know that he would have done nothing less!'

Tears glistened in her eyes as, releasing her hands from his clasp, the countess threw her arms around him and hugged him tightly. 'You dear, dear boy!' she cried. 'I beg that you will always consider Gresham Hall as a second home!' And, raising herself on tiptoe, she reached up and kissed him on his cheek.

Maitland returned her hug in much the same way as he was often wont to embrace his own mother and, after allowing her a few moments to regain control of herself, led the countess back to her seat. Then, having complied with her request that both he and his cousin should sit themselves down, he enquired as to the whereabouts of her ladyship's other guests.

'My father took several of the gentlemen out on a drag-hunt early this morning,' answered Catford, on his mother's behalf. 'The rest of our party are sunning themselves in the garden.'

'We were out there ourselves until Moffat brought news of your arrival,' added the countess, with a warm smile. 'But I did so want to speak with you alone before you were besieged by the others.'

'I trust that you are making a jest, your ladyship!' exclaimed Maitland, in horror, doing his best to ignore the nearby viscount's smothered laugh. 'I must assure you that I have no desire to be besieged by anyone!'

'Then I fear that I shall have to apologise in advance, my dear boy,' returned Lady Letitia, leaning forwards to pat his hand. 'Your exploits have become somewhat legendary within the family. It would be well nigh impossible for me to try to prevent any of them from wanting to shake you by the hand and offer you their thanks. If you could just grin and bear it for a few minutes, I promise you that it will soon be over and done with!'

Assuring the countess that he would do his best, Maitland rose and, offering her his arm, led her out of the room and down the stairs. Fenton, whose earlier fit of pettishness had not been improved by her ladyship having, apart from her initial greeting, virtually ignored his presence, followed the pair, unaware that his revulsion at the thought of having to stand by and witness Maitland basking in hero-worship was not entirely dissimilar to his cousin's own feelings at being obliged to submit to it.

Chapter Five

Some little while later, having endured all the effusive praise
and hearty backslapping with as much good nature as it was
possible for him to bring to bear in such trying circumstances, Maitland was at last released from his ordeal and
allowed to catch his breath. Stepping down from the terrace,
he swept his eyes across the manicured lawns in search of
Stephanie who, along with Georgianne, had desisted from
joining in the general mêlée that had greeted the cousins'
arrival. Eventually, having spotted her sitting in the shade of
a large chestnut tree on the far side of the garden, he was just
about to make his way over to her, his heart thumping in
joyful anticipation when, with a start of annoyance, he perceived that the Honourable Jeremy had already forestalled
him. Miss Highsmith, if her mischievous glances and ripples
of laughter were anything to go by, appeared to be very much
impressed by Fenton's blond good looks and well-practised
charm. And, as he watched Stephanie picking up her sketchbook and executing a few swift strokes with her pencil,
Maitland could not help but notice that three or four of the
other young men of the company had also started to drift over
in her direction.

Since he could not bring himself to be merely one amongst the many of those who had congregated about the clearly popular Miss Highsmith, he sauntered across to another part of the gardens to join Catford, who was engaged in a spirited conversation with his cousin Georgianne.

'Ah, there you are, Will!' cried the viscount, with a huge grin. 'Finally managed to stave off your devoted admirers, I see!'

'No thanks to you, dear friend!' grunted Maitland, as he threw himself down on the grass next to his ex-comrade. 'Next time you've a mind to fall off your horse, kindly call on someone else to drag you out of trouble!'

'Wouldn't dream of it, old chap!' chuckled the viscount, with a sly wink at Georgianne.

Although her lips curved in amusement as she listened to the two comrades' teasing repartee, Georgianne, who was well aware that her cousin's affable friend would far rather be sitting next to Stephanie than where he was at present, was unable to hold back the slight pang of longing that had suddenly invaded her heart. Bending her head, she tried to concentrate her mind on the piece of sewing that, for some time now, had lain idle in her lap but, even as she proceeded to execute the small neat stitches, she found her attention wandering across to where Maitland lay sprawled elegantly on the grass beside the viscount.

What a very fine physique the fellow has, she thought admiringly, as her eyes swept over him. *How broad his shoulders are!* But then, as she found herself dwelling rather too long upon how well his breeches clung to his muscular thighs, her face grew quite hot and she rummaged hurriedly in the basket beside her in search of the small fan that she always carried.

Noticing her sudden discomfort but, unaware of the true reason behind it, Catford scrambled to his feet, saying, 'This sun getting a bit too much for you, Georgie? Let me fetch you a cooling glass of Mrs Barnet's lemonade.' And, looking down at his friend, he added, 'What about you, Will? Fancy a drop of ale?'

After intimating that a glass of ale would, indeed, be most welcome, Maitland raised himself from his prone position and, casually draping his arms over his drawn-up knees, focussed his attention upon the opposite side of the lawn, where Stephanie was still holding court to her rapt audience.

Georgianne, having observed his melancholy demeanour, could not help but feel a flash of compassion for him. 'Poor Mr Maitland,' she said gently. 'Stephanie has so many admirers—you will need to arrive at a much earlier hour if you wish to be first in line!'

At her words, Maitland gave a sudden start and an embarrassed flush began to cover his cheeks, but then, having realised that there was little point in denying the obvious, he gave a dismissive shrug, saying 'So it appears! I did hope to get the chance to ask her if she would care to join me in an early morning ride tomorrow morning—but it looks as though I shall have to settle for writing her a note, instead.' Then, getting to his feet, he turned to go, saying, 'If you will excuse me, Miss Venables, I believe I shall go in search of Catford, in order to ascertain where I might lay my hands on some writing materials.'

Georgianne's smile did not waver, nor did her expression betray her inner disappointment. 'You will find paper and ink a-plenty in the library,' she said brightly, indicating one of the sets of doors leading out on to the terrace above them. 'Pens, too, I should think, for I mended several myself only yesterday. Do, please, go and write your note and, if you care to trust me with its delivery, I shall see that Stephanie receives it at the first possible opportunity.' Then, pausing, as a slight frown puckered her brow, she added hesitantly, 'However, I do feel that it is only fair to warn you in advance that Miss Highsmith does not, in fact, ride!'

Maitland's steps faltered and he turned back to face her. 'I beg your pardon?' he said, staring down at her in astonishment, for this was a possibility that had certainly never crossed his mind. 'Did I really hear you say that Miss Highsmith does not ride?'

Georgianne nodded. 'I'm afraid not,' she replied, with a sympathetic smile. 'She took a tumble when she was just a child and has refused to mount ever since—she actually has a great fear of horses, although she does enjoy being driven about the countryside. Perhaps you could invite her to take a ride in your carriage, instead?'

Maitland's heart sank. 'Unfortunately, as you are no doubt aware, I travelled up to Warwickshire on horseback. And the carriage in which we drove here this morning belongs to my cousin.' He nodded towards Fenton, who was still in the thick of those enjoying the exquisite Stephanie's favours. 'It should be possible to hire one, I suppose,' he went on, more to himself than to his companion. 'It's getting one's hands on a half-way decent one that might pose the biggest problem, though.'

Weighing up the various pros and cons of the unexpected dilemma, he stared moodily across the lawn, a hot spurt of jealousy running through him every time Stephanie bestowed her vivacious smile upon one of her admirers. But then, suddenly conscious of Georgianne's eyes on him, he remembered his manners and, hurriedly collecting himself, lowered himself to the ground at her side.

'And how about yourself, Miss Venables?' he asked, more out of politeness than from any real interest. 'May I take it that you do not share your friend's aversion?'

'Oh, absolutely not!' replied Georgianne, her eyes immediately lighting up and, to Maitland's surprise, completely transforming her face. 'It is quite my most favourite pastime and one that I indulge in at every possible opportunity. Uncle Charles—Lord Gresham, I should say—has only just recently purchased the most delightful new mare for me—I had quite outgrown my dear old Meg. Fortunately, we have no need to put her out to pasture quite just yet, since she is so gentle that Cat's two sisters are perfectly happy to trust her with their youngsters.'

A smile crept across Maitland's face. 'I have been fortunate enough to hang on to my own Pegasus for more than six years now,' he said, in reply. 'I have other mounts, of course, but none so dear to me. One grows so attached.'

Georgianne gave an enthusiastic nod. 'Oh, I do so agree,' she said fervently. 'I have to confess that I already find myself sharing many a secret with Puss!'

His smile deepened. 'Puss? An unusual name for a mare, surely?'

Catching his twinkle, she returned the smile. 'Her name is Olympus really, but it became too much of a mouthful when I was urging her over a seven-footer, so she became Puss, which does seem to suit her temperament rather well, I feel.'

'I'm sure that it does,' he returned, somewhat absentmindedly, for his eyes had strayed once more to the group on the far side of the lawn.

Swallowing her regret at his sudden change of manner, Georgianne refused to allow her disappointment to show. 'Steffi enjoys many other pastimes,' she said stoutly. 'She sketches and paints quite beautifully and plays the pianoforte far better than anyone I know. And, look—'

Reaching over into the basket by her side, she drew out a

carefully folded piece of material and held it out for his inspection. 'Her embroidery is perfectly exquisite.'

Somewhat taken aback, Maitland eyed the small flannel garment that she was holding up to him. 'What is it?' he asked curiously. 'It looks not unlike a doll's petticoat!'

'It's to be a nightdress, silly!' She laughed and, seeing his lack of comprehension, pointed to the pile of garments in her sewing basket. 'A newborn babe's nightdress—we sew them for Lady Highsmith's charity home, only…' as, with a self-conscious smile, she hurriedly folded the small garment and returned it to her basket '…I fear that I am no embroiderer—a simple seamstress, that's me!'

'Your work is very fine,' he replied. 'And of far more practical use than the usual traycloths and tea serviettes, I should imagine.' Then, reaching out, he ran his fingers through the finished garments. 'Why is it that not all of the garments have this small rosebud embellishment? Does it have to do with the status of the recipient?'

Georgianne looked shocked. 'Good heavens, no!' she disclaimed hotly. 'When they are finished, they will be identical! It is simply that I have been at liberty to forge ahead with my part of the task, while Steffi has had rather more calls upon her time, so she has a little catching up to do. You gentlemen must take the blame for that,' she added, eyeing him mischievously. 'Not you personally, I grant, but, I dare say as soon as you are given the opportunity…?'

'As a matter of fact,' he countered, somewhat impulsively. 'I was rather wondering whether you yourself would consider allowing me to join you on one of your morning rides?'

For the briefest of moments, she stared at him, her face quite impassive, then, giving a swift nod, she smiled, saying, 'Yes, of course, although Cat and I go out very early—you will have to be here by seven, if you mean to join us! Oh, look! Uncle Charles and the others have returned; I must go and see if Moffat has everything ready—it seems that we are to lunch "al fresco" today, which, while it is intended to provide a great deal of enjoyment for Aunt Letty's guests, does, of course, rather involve the staff in a great deal of extra work. If you will excuse me?'

As he scrambled to his feet, Maitland's eyes followed Georgianne's graceful figure as she crossed the grass, mounted the steps leading on to the terrace and disappeared around the corner of the building. Then, wondering where the devil Catford had got to with the promised drinks, he lowered himself down on to the grass once more and stared thoughtfully at the abandoned sewing basket. Why Georgianne's apparent lack of enthusiasm to include him in her morning ride should have come as such a disappointment to him, he could not imagine, since, as far as he had been concerned, his impromptu gesture had come about more out of good manners than for any real desire for her company. Not that the young lady had not proved herself to be excellent company, he hastened to remind himself, a swift grin creasing his face as he recalled Georgianne's impassioned listing of her friend's numerous accomplishments. Added to which, he thought good-humouredly, it had been a good many years since anyone had had the temerity to label him 'silly'!

His contemplative reverie was soon interrupted by the belated arrival of the highly apologetic viscount, bearing a pair of foaming tankards. 'Dreadfully sorry, old chap,' he puffed, as he joined Maitland on the grass. 'Bit of a domestic crisis, I'm afraid—one of the kitchen maids tripped over the blessed cat and suffered a broken ankle—had to call the doctor out!'

'Ooh, nasty!' returned his friend, with a sympathetic grimace. 'Nevertheless, if my impression of Lady Letitia is anything to go by, the poor lass is sure to have the benefit of the best of treatments.'

The viscount gave an emphatic nod. 'Quite right, too!' he exclaimed. 'The welfare of our employees has always been high on the list of Mater's priorities. Although, to be fair, Georgie's pretty amazing too, as a matter of fact. She'd grabbed a hold of a teacloth and a tub of ice and had a cold compress on the girl's foot before any of us could say "Jack Robinson"!'

Maitland sipped thoughtfully at his ale. 'Seems a very pleasant girl, your cousin,' he ventured, almost carelessly. 'Would have thought she'd have been snapped up by now!'

The viscount was silent for a moment. 'Mmm, well, you might think so,' he said, eventually. 'She's an absolute gem, is our little Georgie. Don't care to talk about the lady behind her back, but the fact is that she suffered a severe disappointment some years back and now does her damnedest to keep all the fellows at bay—still carrying the proverbial torch, if you want my opinion—not that any of us ever mention the subject, of course,' he added hastily.

'Nuff said,' acknowledged his friend while, at the same time, finding himself thinking that it was clear that the un-accommodating suitor, whoever he was, must have been in dire need of having his head examined.

While the two men were conversing, the servants had been setting up trestle tables and laying out a selection of cold meats, raised pies, platters of fruit and other mouth-watering delicacies. Chairs were brought out for the older members of the party, whilst rugs and cushions were thrown on the grass for those youngsters who might wish to avail them-selves of them. Shortly afterwards, a footman appeared on the terrace striking a gong, signalling to those guests still in the furthest reaches of the grounds that luncheon was about to be served. In answer to the summons, the ongoing games of cricket, tennis and croquet were brought to a swift close, couples ceased their aimless wanderings about the gardens, and everyone began to make their way back towards the terrace area.

Triumphantly waving the piece of paper that he held in his hand, the Honourable Jeremy sauntered over to join his cousin. 'What a creature!' he breathed. 'So talented and such rare insight!'

Catching hold of the paper, which he quickly recognised as a page torn from a sketchbook, Maitland found himself staring at a remarkably well-executed likeness of Fenton.

'One of Miss Highsmith's, I collect?' he said, feeling not a little put out that his rather dandified cousin had apparently captured Stephanie's undivided attention with such apparent ease.

'You should consider yourself highly honoured,' grinned Catford, as he leaned across and studied the sketch. 'Steffi usually only bestows those on her favourites.'

'Do you say so!' Fenton beamed, carefully rolling up the paper and tucking it into the inside pocket of his jacket, an action that caused Maitland considerable astonishment, knowing, as he did, his cousin's normally fastidious attention to the smooth, uncluttered line of his dress. 'I shall treasure it always! And, now, gentlemen, if you will excuse me, I am commissioned to select a few tasty morsels for the lady's enjoyment!'

'Well, he certainly seems to have found favour with our little beauty,' remarked Catford, as the Honourable Jeremy drifted off towards the refreshment tables. 'Wonder how long that little caper will last?'

Maitland frowned. It was not like his friend to cast disparaging remarks about a member of the opposite sex. 'Steady on, Cat!' he protested. 'That's a touch near the knuckle, surely!'

'If you had been acquainted with the delectable Miss Highsmith for as many years as I have, Will,' observed the viscount, with a wry smile, 'you, too, might have learnt to be a little sceptical—I do hope that you were not thinking of casting out a lure in that particular direction!'

'Well, you have to admit that she *is* rather dazzling,' returned his friend, giving a slightly self-conscious shrug.

The viscount stared across at him, his forehead puckered in dismay. 'Keep away, old chap, if you value your sanity!' he cautioned. 'There's not a fellow in the vicinity who hasn't fallen under her spell—have to admit that I went down the same road myself, a few years back. Luckily, I soon found out that the adorable Miss Highsmith enjoys nothing better than playing off her admirers one against the other—take a look, if you're disinclined to believe me!'

Not entirely convinced by Catford's friendly words of caution, Maitland allowed his eyes to travel across to where the object of their discussion sat, still surrounded by half-dozen or so eager gallants. But then, as he registered the mischievous way in which she smilingly reached out a finger to chuck one man under his chin whilst, at the same time, fluttering her long, curling lashes over his shoulder at another, it became horribly clear to him that the viscount's ruthless shredding of Stephanie's character had been entirely justified.

Stifling a pang of regret for all those earlier hopes and dreams that had, all too quickly, crumbled into dust, Maitland silently cursed himself for allowing his usual good sense to be swayed by the sight of a pretty face. Offering up a prayer of thanks to his lucky stars for his friend's most timely warning, he resolved to put aside all thoughts of romance and apply himself to the job in hand—namely, the search for young Étienne Billingham, always supposing that the unfortunate lad had survived his birth.

However, since it was clear that any attempt to hurry Fenton away from Stephanie's side at this juncture was likely to meet with fierce resistance and, uncomfortably aware that he was obliged to rely upon the clearly besotted Jeremy for his own transport back to the inn, Maitland realised that he had no choice but to wait until his cousin decided the moment of their departure. And, since the unexpected set-back to his own romantic hopes had somewhat diminished his appetite, he declined Catford's invitation to join the family for luncheon and, somewhat disconsolately, wandered off into the lower reaches of the gardens, towards the lake.

As the noisy hubbub of conversation and laughter began to fade into the distance, to be replaced by the rather more agreeable sounds of rippling water and birdsong, his inner turmoil gradually lessened and he could feel his mind growing calmer with every step. Pausing only to smile at the antics of the disorderly line of mallard duck chicks, each of them noisily jostling for position in their mother's wake, he made his way along the path towards the hexagonally shaped summerhouse that he had spotted on the bank a little distance ahead.

He had barely set his foot onto the bottom step of the building, however, before he became conscious of the fact that he was, clearly, not the only one who had chosen to leave the clamour of the garden party behind them, in search of a moment's solitude.

'Miss Venables!' he exclaimed, standing stock-still in the doorway. 'I beg your pardon! I had no idea that there was anyone here!'

Georgianne, who had, in fact, been observing Maitland's leisurely stroll along the lakeside path with a peculiar mixture of panic and excitement, carefully laid down her plate of, as yet, untouched food on to the bench at her side. 'I fear that you have found me out, Mr Maitland,' she said, with a rueful smile. 'I had a sudden urge to get away from all the hullaba-loo for a few moments' peace and quiet on my own.'

'And here I am, depriving you of your well-earned rest!' grimaced Maitland, stepping back hurriedly and turning to go. 'Please accept my apologies for having intruded upon your privacy.'

'No, please don't go, sir!' begged Georgianne, leaping to her feet. 'There is more than enough room for the two of us here and, as you can see…' she indicated with a sweep of her hand '…the view from this spot is simply marvellous.'

Maitland entered the summerhouse and sat down on the bench opposite. 'It's hardly surprising that you felt the need to catch a few minutes' respite from your labours, Miss Venables,' he ventured, with a gentle smile. 'Cat has told me all about your sterling efforts with the unfortunate kitchen maid.'

She flushed. 'I had heard that it is preferable to limit the swelling in such cases,' she replied diffidently. 'It apparently makes it easier for the physician to reset the bone.'

'Far less painful for the patient too, I believe. How is the poor lass?'

'Fast asleep by now, hopefully—Dr Travers had to admin-ister quite a hefty dose of laudanum to calm her. I shall look in on her later this afternoon to see how she does.'

Maitland's eyes travelled to the heaped plate at her side. 'I appear to have interrupted your luncheon,' he observed, suddenly feeling quite peckish himself. 'Please do not allow my being here to prevent you enjoying your meal.'

'Perhaps you would care to join me?' invited Georgianne, lifting up the plate and holding it out to him. 'Cook piled on far more than I can possibly manage.'

Quickly transferring his position to her side of the sum-merhouse, Maitland thanked her and helped himself to a slice of game pie. 'I have to admit that I was somewhat disinclined to join in the general scrimmage around the refreshment tables, but that little walk along the lake path seems to have done wonders for my appetite!'

'I have often thought that picnics are not nearly as much fun as we keep telling ourselves!' she said, with a dimpling smile.

'Oh, I cannot agree there, Miss Venables,' he protested, a wide grin on his face. 'I have to say that I am finding this particular alfresco meal rather pleasant!'

At his words, Georgianne felt her cheeks grow quite warm and, in an attempt to hide her growing confusion, she turned her head away, appearing to busy herself with choosing a titbit from the plate. Maitland, studying her profile, suddenly found himself wondering how it was that he had ever considered her to be merely 'nice-looking'. With her clear grey eyes and softly flushed cheeks, not to mention the several gently waving tendrils of warm brown hair that had escaped their rigid confinement from their pins to fall, in graceful confusion, over her brow and down the nape of her neck, he could see that it was well past time to revise his former opinion of his friend's young cousin.

'Your hair appears to have come somewhat adrift, Miss Venables,' he pointed out softly, lifting up his hand in an attempt to tuck one of the curling wisps back behind her ear.

Almost as if she had been stung, Georgianne started back in alarm. 'Yes, I know,' she acknowledged breathlessly. 'I had intended to deal with it before going back to the house.'

'Pity,' he drawled, her sudden reticence not having escaped his attention. 'It suits you much better that way.'

Then, getting to his feet, he strolled across to the doorway, endeavouring to give her the impression that he was admiring the view. *Great heavens above!* he was thinking. *You have surely not been extricated from one bumblebath only to fall straight into another!* Then, shaking his head, he came to the conclusion that it must have something to do with the much talked-about rebound effect, a circumstance with which he was unfamiliar. Or, could it be that, having registered Cat's remark about his cousin 'keeping the fellows at bay', he had regarded Georgianne as something of a challenge to his masculinity?

'I really need to get started on this blessed search,' he murmured aloud. But, on turning to face the silent Georgianne, to enquire as to the whereabouts of Willowby's church, his breath caught in his throat and he found himself quite lost for words.

Still seated on the bench, Georgianne had taken advantage of his protracted meditation to unpin her hair and was, at this very moment, hurriedly combing her fingers through the flowing waves, prior to coaxing them back into their usual neat chignon and quite determined to have the job done before Maitland should turn around.

Alerted by the sounds of his booted feet on the stone floor of the summerhouse, she swept back the curtain of hair from her face and, to her consternation, looked up to find him standing directly in front of her. Biting her lip in annoyance at having been caught out, she quickly attempted to bundle up her locks into some semblance of tidiness, only to find Maitland's hand on her own, preventing her from continuing.

'Please don't,' he said softly, running his own fingers through the silken strands. 'Your hair is so very lovely—must you drag it back into such an unbecoming style?'

Finding herself, momentarily, transfixed by both the sensation of his fingers on her head and his unconcealed expression of admiration, Georgianne could neither move nor think but then, as Maitland, having relinquished his hold, lowered himself on to the bench at her side, she drew in her breath and said, somewhat shakily, 'It is not, usually, quite as troublesome as it has been today—I must crave your indulgence while I attend to it.'

And, much to Maitland's regret, she proceeded to coil her hair into a tight loop and, with the help of the few remaining pins at her disposal, set about attaching the heavy chignon to the top of her head. Then, picking up the chipstraw bonnet that she had lain aside on the bench, she settled it carefully over her newly arranged hairstyle and quickly tied the ribbons under her chin.

'There, now,' she said, with a smile of satisfaction. 'That should hold it in place—I dare say all that rushing up and down stairs caused it to come adrift—I must make a point of securing it more firmly in future.'

Although he was obliged to shelve his disappointment that Georgianne had chosen to ignore his plea that she might adopt a less severe style, Maitland could not help but be impressed at the calm, matter-of-fact way that she had attended to her somewhat embarrassing predicament. He was well aware that a good many of the young women of his acquaintance, by exhibiting a more-than-usual quota of fluttering eyelashes, simpering blushes and highly irritating giggles, not to mention a pretended mortification, would have used such an opportunity to turn what had been merely an unfortunate mishap into a full theatrical performance. Having observed Stephanie Highsmith's earlier display of dramatic ability, it was not difficult for him to visualise how she would have reacted, given a similar circumstance.

Unfortunately, Maitland's failure to reply to her light-hearted comment only gave Georgianne the impression that her somewhat nonchalant behaviour had caused him to think badly of her. As an unexpected sense of despondency swept over her, she rose hurriedly to her feet, fighting back the impulse to offer her apologies for having acted in so unladylike a manner in front of a gentleman, who was, after all, still little more than a stranger.

But Maitland, finding himself suddenly loath to part with her company, at once leapt up to join her, saying, 'Please do not rush away, Miss Venables. I was hoping that you might point me in the direction of your local church—this would seem to be an excellent opportunity for me to have a few words with the incumbent there.'

'Oh, that would be our curate, Mr Childs,' the much-relieved Georgianne was delighted to be able to inform him. 'And you are in luck, for there is a shortcut to the church through that spinney just ahead of us—the family often make use of it. If you will permit me, I would be happy to take you there myself.'

'The pleasure will be mine, I assure you.'

And, so saying, Maitland leapt nimbly down from the summerhouse and held out his hand. After a scarcely discernible hesitation, Georgianne placed her hand in his and allowed him to help her descend the three shallow steps on to the pathway. Why this simple action should have had the effect of setting up such a trembling inside her, she could not imagine but, when Maitland then chose to tuck her hand firmly into the crook of his arm, she was powerless to prevent the rosy blush that formed instantly upon her cheeks.

Fortunately for Georgianne's peace of mind, her escort seemed not to have noticed her brief moment of confusion. Indeed, as far as she could tell, he appeared to be heavily engrossed in studying the courtly behaviour of the pair of swans who were sailing majestically across the lake.

'Such beautiful creatures,' he observed chattily, as they turned off the path and strolled through the sunlit spinney, at the far end of which the church's squat tower could be seen. 'I'm told that they mate for life.'

'A particular habit amongst a good many members of the bird family, I believe,' replied Georgianne, with a sudden smile. 'Strange, really, when one considers that their brains are said to be not nearly as well formed as our own.'

He shot her a quick glance and was relieved to see that she seemed to have overcome her momentary attack of agitation, which, contrary to his companion's firm belief, had not, in fact, escaped his attention. 'I believe their choices are made more by instinct than by the decidedly unreliable methods we humans tend to employ,' he said, a rueful grin forming on his lips as the unwelcome memory of his own recent and rather foolish lapse over Stephanie sprang into his mind. 'It is possible that we might be far better off endeavouring to emulate their ways, rather than allowing our hearts to rule our minds, as we are frequently inclined to do.'

Georgianne gave a thoughtful nod. 'A fair point, Mr Maitland,' she conceded. 'Although the swans' lifetime devotion to their partners does seem to suggest that something more than mere instinct must be involved. For instance, I have heard it said that a bereaved swan simply pines away after having lost a mate, which rather begs the question insofar as the basic instincts for survival and self-preservation are concerned.'

'Both of which we humans, too, are all too often apt to thrust to one side when it comes to matters of the heart,' he pointed out. 'So, perhaps, when all is said and done, the various species are not really so different, after all!'

'That may well be so,' replied Georgianne, with a little laugh. But then, after a slight pause, she frowned and added, 'Although, to my mind, the greatest difference between us and the rest of the animal kingdom lies in the fact that they appear to be allowed the luxury of selecting their own mates without outside interference.'

'Well, the male of the species, quite possibly,' acknowledged Maitland, with a broad grin. 'But even they are often obliged to do battle to gain that privilege!'

Georgianne came to a sudden standstill, exclaiming, 'Good grief, so they are! I had quite forgotten that particular aspect. And, while they are locking horns—or what you will—' she then riposted pithily, 'the female of the species is obliged to wait patiently on the sidelines in order to learn her fate!'

'True, but then she always gets the champion and never has to settle for second best,' he argued, taking her by the elbow and gently urging her forwards. '"Faint heart never won fair lady", as the saying goes, or, if you prefer it, "To the victor the spoils!"'

Biting back the smile that threatened, Georgianne gave a little sigh. 'Still,' she said, 'I find it hard to believe that male swans would allow other swans to influence their choice of mate.' She hesitated for a moment, as though gathering courage, then, taking a deep breath, she blurted out, almost defiantly, 'Nor indeed are they likely to call their partner's ancestry into question!'

At her words, and just for a second or two, it was Maitland's turn to be thrown into confusion, but then, after storing that particular phrase into his memory for deeper consideration at some future point, he felt constrained to point out that, since neither he nor she were ever likely to find themselves in a position to discover the truth of the matter, there was little point in continuing that particular line of discussion. 'For all we know, animals may well have their own systems of justice,' he reasoned, before adding, with a quick grin, 'Think of parliaments of owls and—er—kangaroo courts!'

When Georgianne did not reply, he cast a quick sideways

glance at her and, although her face was turned away from him, he was perturbed to see that her shoulders were shaking. *Good God!* he thought. *Has my insensitive raillery reduced the poor girl to tears?* Lifting his free hand, he reached across and swung her round to face him. Her wide grey eyes were, indeed, brimful of tears but, as he very quickly realised from the expression on her face, they were not tears of sadness, but of laughter!

'What an odd sense of humour you do have, Mr Maitland,' she gasped, her eyes still alight with laughter as she delved into her skirt pocket in search of a handkerchief. 'Kangaroo courts, indeed! You know perfectly well that that expression has nothing whatsoever to do with what we were discussing!'

'Possibly not,' he said, with an unrepentant grin and, pulling out his own, much larger and far more suitable, linen handkerchief, he drew her gently towards him and, taking her chin in his hand, proceeded to dab all vestige of the tears from her cheeks. 'But it did cause you a certain amount of amusement, so I consider myself well served!'

'There now,' he said jokingly, as he stood back and surveyed her. 'I pronounce you as good as new. It would hardly do to give your Mr Childs the impression that I am in the habit of reducing young ladies to tears!'

'Oh, you have no need to concern yourself,' replied Georgianne, making every effort to keep her tone nonchalant, for Maitland's gentle touch seemed to have had the effect of turning her insides to a mass of quivering jelly. 'Mr Childs has a fine sense of humour—we have had many a laugh together.'

At these words, a slight frown creased Maitland's forehead, and as he held open the gate that led into the rear of the churchyard, he was somewhat perturbed to discover that, for some reason, and even before he had met him, he had already developed a marked dislike for the unsuspecting clergyman.

Chapter Six

After a somewhat confusing conversation with the cleric's rather elderly and slightly deaf housekeeper, Georgianne and Maitland found themselves directed across to the village green where, minus his neckerchief and with his sleeves rolled up, they eventually discovered the Reverend Philip Childs, surrounded by a rowdy group of squabbling urchins.

''Taint fair, sir!' one small lad was declaiming. 'Freddy Pritchard's side allus gets ter go in first!'

'S'my gear, innit?' retorted the tallest of the group, smugly tossing the badly scuffed ball into the air. 'Wouldn't 'ave a game at all iffen my pa's boss 'adn't give the stuff to 'im. Stands ter reason that my side should be first in!'

'If not precisely in the spirit of the game!' murmured Maitland under his breath.

Clapping his hands, the young reverend attempted to bring the group to order. 'Come along now, boys,' he cajoled them. 'We are wasting precious time. Do sort yourselves out and let us get on.'

'Perhaps I might be of assistance here, sir,' said Maitland, stepping forwards and shrugging out of his jacket, which he handed to the astonished Georgianne.

'Right, now stand still, all of you!' he commanded, in a tone that immediately brought about a hushed and respectful silence. Having got their attention, the ex-major then had little difficulty in dividing the pack into two reasonably equal teams, based mostly upon a combination of height and weight. Ignoring the barely suppressed mutterings of the one or two dissatisfied youths who found themselves on their opposing team of choice, he then gave the players a short, but succinct reminder that the game of cricket was a sport and, as such, should be played in a sporting manner. He then went on to point out that, notwithstanding the fact that some of their friends might be on the opposing team, every man's allegiance and loyalty must be reserved for his own side. The biggest challenge, he told his, by now, eager listeners, was not simply to beat their opponents, but to beat them fairly and squarely. Then, casting a fulminating glance at the self-proclaimed owner of the bulk of the equipment, he asked him if he had any objection to the other boys making free with his property for the duration of the game. After a wide-eyed and rather nervous shake of the head supplied him with the expected result, he leaned forwards and, gripping the lad's shoulder, said, 'Good man! For that, I shall appoint you captain of team "A", and you, my lad…' here, he beckoned to another likely looking youth '…as captain of the opposing team, may stand ready to call the toss!'

'I cannot imagine who the man may be,' the Reverend Childs whispered to the now dumbstruck Georgianne, as they watched Maitland withdraw a coin from his pocket and toss it into the air, 'but I am certainly grateful for his assistance!'

'His name is William Maitland and he is a good friend of Catford's,' Georgianne whispered back to him, her admiration for the ex-major increasing by the minute.

'Not *the* William Maitland?'

Georgianne gave a brief nod. 'The very same,' she replied, in a somewhat abstracted manner, for her eyes were glued to the subject of their conversation, now heavily involved in directing operations on the green in front of them.

Having taken a lead from the curate's example, Maitland had divested himself of both waistcoat and cravat, unbuttoned his shirt and rolled up his sleeves, displaying his well-proportioned physique to the utmost effect, the unexpected spectacle of which was causing Georgianne's heart to behave in the most unruly manner. And, whereas she had viewed the—albeit far less well-endowed—Reverend Childs's similar state of undress with total equanimity, the startling vision of the super-fit ex-military man striding up and down the green in front of her, the ripple of his muscles barely concealed beneath his closely fitting garments, had the effect of rendering her quite breathless.

Fortunately for its two equally spellbound spectators, a certain lack of skill in the finer techniques of the game on the part of its young players, very quickly brought the impromptu match to a close but, even though the final score was an abysmal 17 runs to 14 in the 'B' team's favour, Maitland's insistence that each team should give the other three rousing cheers for effort soon had every one of the lads clapping each other on the back and commenting on what a jolly good game it had been!

'I doubt that you'll have any further trouble with them, sir,' remarked the grinning Maitland, as he joined the waiting pair and retrieved his discarded clothing. 'They are good-hearted lads and, now that they have learned to play by the rules, all they need is a little dedicated coaching.'

'Dare I presume to suggest that I might press you into volunteering your services in that direction, Mr Maitland?' enquired Childs hopefully.

'I dare say I might be able to fit in a few sessions,' replied Maitland, after giving the curate's request due consideration. 'Certainly, while I am staying in the vicinity. However, I do have to point out that it is possible my visit will not be of a very long duration. In which respect I was rather hoping that *you* might be in a position to assist *me*!'

After assuring Maitland that he would be more than pleased to help him in whatever way he could, the curate waved away the still excited youths and led his visitors back to the vicarage where, in the relative comfort of his small sitting room, the elderly housekeeper served them tea, during which procedure Maitland outlined the task that his uncle had set him.

'Billingham?' The reverend shook his head. 'I'm afraid that it's not a name that I am familiar with and, to my certain knowledge, there is no young man of that name in the immediate vicinity. However, the best place to begin such a search would surely be in the Parish Registers for the year in question—ours are kept locked in a cupboard in the vestry—if you would care to accompany me?'

Seeing that the curate had risen to his feet, Georgianne set down her teacup and followed suit, saying, 'If you will excuse me, gentlemen, I fear that I must leave you to your endeavours. My aunt's picnic lunch must be long since over and she will be wondering what has become of me.'

With a sharp sense of disappointment, Maitland, too, leapt to his feet. 'Oh, must you go?' he beseeched her. 'I was hoping that you might care to assist us in our search.'

'In the normal way, there is nothing that I would enjoy more,' she hastened to assure him. 'But, I fear I have been absent from my other duties overlong. Another time, perhaps?'

'No, wait!' interrupted Maitland hastily. 'You must, at least, allow me to escort you back to the house.'

'Thank you, but that really is not necessary,' replied Georgianne, smiling up at him. 'Once through the wicker gate, I am on Gresham land—it is a journey I am well accustomed to making on my own.'

'Yes, indeed!' Reverend Childs nodded his affirmation. 'I am happy to say that Miss Venables is a frequent visitor—I assure you that she will come to no harm on the bridle path.'

Although it did not sit well with him to think of his young companion returning to her home unescorted, Maitland, re-alising that it would hardly do to make an issue of the matter, was obliged to stand back and watch Georgianne disappear into the spinney.

'Miss Venables visits you often, you say?' he asked, turning back to the waiting curate.

'Almost every day,' beamed Childs, as he led Maitland across the churchyard and through a side door into the vestry of the church. 'She teaches the little ones in the village school and, in addition, since I am not, as yet, blessed with a helpmeet of my own, she has been good enough to offer to accompany me on my visits to the sick.'

As he followed the curate into the vestry, a little frown creased Maitland's brow. It would have come as no surprise to him to learn that the Reverend Childs had already picked out his so-called 'helpmeet' in the shape of the rather comely Miss Georgianne Venables. Though what the devil her family were about to allow their young relative to visit the man so freely, he could not begin to understand. Just because she had suffered one disappointment all those years ago was hardly any reason to allow the girl to throw herself away on a mere parson, he found himself thinking, as he watched the unsus-pecting curate cross the room and unlock a large oak cupboard in the far corner.

'I'm told these records go back over forty-five years,' said Childs, as he rummaged through the dusty tomes. '1795, I believe you said? Yes, here it is—slightly battered, I fear, and it looks as though it might have been stored in a somewhat damp environment at some point in its history. Still, we can but hope!'

Dragging out the mildew-speckled leather-bound volume, he laid it on a nearby table and, pulling up a chair, indicated that Maitland should follow suit. 'The records include not only all the births in the parishes of both Willowby and Greenborough, but the marriages and deaths also. However, to be on the safe side, we might just as well cover the lot,' he suggested, with what might well have been termed a con-spiratorial grin and, for a few fleeting moments, as he returned the benevolent gesture, Maitland found himself ex-periencing a slight pang of regret in regard to his earlier somewhat uncharitable assessment of the young man.

Well over an hour later, after running his finger down the names on the final page, Reverend Childs closed the book with a disconsolate sigh. 'Not a Melandra nor a Billingham nor an Étienne to be seen in any situation, I'm sorry to say! Clearly, neither of our two parishes can have been your uncle's port of call on that sorry night all those years ago. I'm afraid it would appear that your search looks likely to prove a good deal more wearisome than you might otherwise have imagined.'

'You may well be right, sir,' nodded Maitland, easing back his shoulders in an attempt to relieve the unaccustomed stiff-ness that poring over the records had brought about. 'It was too much to hope that I would light upon a result at my very first attempt and I am much obliged to you for sparing me so much of your time.'

'Why, good heavens, man!' declared the curate. 'After your sterling efforts earlier, I could hardly do less. And, when the identity of the man who took charge of their match reaches the lads' ears, I swear that there will be no holding them back! We will find ourselves inundated with volunteers, I have no doubt!'

'I'll have you know that I don't altogether approve of all this misplaced adulation,' groaned Maitland, as he stood up to stretch his cramped limbs. 'Especially since the whole event seems to have been exaggerated out of all proportion!'

'I'm afraid that you will just have to grin and bear it,' returned the other, with a sympathetic grin. 'Folks love a hero and it might just as well be you as the next chap—although it does mean that you are for ever obliged to make sure that you are not found to have feet of clay!'

'Well, I can't promise you that,' laughed Maitland. 'But I shall certainly make every effort to join you again next Saturday. And now, I suppose, I had better get back and see what my cousin has been up to in my absence—the last I saw of him, he was languishing at the feet of the local beauty!'

At his words, a dark flush stained the young curate's cheeks and he turned hurriedly away. 'That would be Miss Highsmith, I imagine,' he said, in a low voice.

'That's right,' nodded Maitland, somewhat surprised at the other man's sudden change of manner. 'I dare say you are acquainted with the young lady?'

'Whilst it is true that I number Lady Highsmith and her granddaughter among my parishioners,' returned Childs flatly, as he bent to return the heavy volume to its former place in the pile, 'I fear I cannot claim to be actually acquainted with them.'

So the poor devil's affections lie in that quarter! thought Maitland, experiencing a curious sense of relief at this discovery, not to mention a considerable warming towards the unfortunate curate.

'I take it that Miss Highsmith does not share her friend's

dedication to charitable works, then?' he found himself asking, not that he was in any doubt as to the answer.

Getting to his feet, the reverend swivelled round and stared at him, a pained expression on his face. 'I would have you know, sir,' he replied stiffly, 'that Miss Highsmith spends a good deal of her time assisting her grandmother in that good lady's most admirable endeavours up at Highsmith House. And, since I am fortunate enough to have my own little team of willing helpers, I do not feel the need to impose upon her generosity.'

'No, indeed!' returned Maitland hurriedly, it not having been his intention to cross swords with the young curate who had devoted the greater part of the afternoon to his own quandary. 'And, I must thank you again for your own sterling efforts—at the very least, it means that I can now cross two parishes off my list.'

With a promise to do his best to return on the following Saturday, he then bade farewell to the reverend and retraced his steps back through the spinney to Gresham Hall.

Although Maitland's somewhat prolonged absence from the gathering had been starting to cause him a certain amount of anxiety, Viscount Catford could not prevent himself from bursting out laughing when Georgianne, upon her own return, acquainted him with the reason for his comrade's non-attendance.

'No change there, then,' he grinned, shaking his head. 'He was just the same in Portugal—for ever organising the local youngsters into some activity or other!'

'Well, Mr Childs was certainly impressed with his capabilities,' she assured her cousin, as they took a stroll through one of the Hall's many flower gardens. 'Both of them were up to their eyes in dusty parish registers when

I left. I doubt you will see your Mr Maitland much before dinnertime.'

'That's quite a task he seems to have taken on,' remarked Catford thoughtfully. 'I just wish we could be of more help to him—that Fenton chap he brought with him looks to be about as much use as a parasol in a cloudburst!'

'There does seem to be something of the dandy about the man,' agreed Georgianne, with a soft chuckle. 'Although, oddly enough, Steffi looks to be rather taken with him.'

'Merely the novelty of a new face, I'll be bound,' returned the viscount sagely. 'Having the same old admirers falling at her feet day after day must get pretty wearisome after a time, I would imagine. What surprises me, though, is that she didn't instantly make a dead set for Will—him being the conquering hero and all!'

'Don't be so beastly, Eddie!' she admonished him. 'These visits to Gresham Hall are practically the only opportunities that Steffi ever gets to exercise a little freedom—so it's hardly surprising that her behaviour is sometimes a little—er—*extravagant*, shall we say? As you well know, Lady Highsmith keeps her on such a tight leash in the normal way that the poor girl is more or less bound to want to kick over the traces when she gets the chance.'

Catford glanced down at her fondly. 'Whatever the young lady's faults, dearest Georgie,' he smiled, 'it is clear that she has a good friend in you. I just hope that she knows what she is doing.'

'Oh, you may be sure that, no matter how flirtatious she appears to be to the average onlooker, our Miss Highsmith has her head screwed on most securely,' stated Georgianne with conviction. 'Having had to endure her grandmother's constant homilies regarding the devious mentality of the predatory male, as well as having been obliged to have the sad effects of dozens of other girls' misfortunes thrust under her nose day after day for most of her life, it is hard to imagine how she could not!'

'One would have thought that getting the poor girl married off would have been in Lady Highsmith's best interests,' mused the viscount. 'Yet, if what Steffi says is true, it seems that her grandmother goes out of her way to positively discourage all such relationships.'

'From the little that I have been able to gather,' replied Georgianne, shaking her head, 'it would appear that Lord Highsmith was not the most pleasant of husbands, which would, perhaps, go a long way towards explaining her ladyship's attitude to marriage. And, since Steffi never talks about her parents, it has been impossible for me to reach any conclusion about them.'

She paused, as her cousin squeezed her hand encouragingly. 'Not that I am in the habit of discussing my own forebears, of course,' she went on hurriedly. 'But, since it has often occurred to me that Steffi's parents' circumstances might well have been similar to those of my own, I can well understand her reluctance to enter into any discussion about them.'

Catford gave a thoughtful nod. 'If your assumption is correct,' he said, 'it would certainly explain Lady Highsmith's rather obvious antipathy towards the opposite sex—once bitten, twice shy, as the saying goes.'

'Precisely!' returned Georgianne, in a somewhat abrasive tone.

He pulled up short and swung her round to face him, his expression full of concern. 'Good God, Georgie!' he exclaimed. 'You must not suppose that that foolish remark was directed at you! Your case is entirely different and, if I could just lay my hands on that blackguard who so insulted you, I swear that he would be lucky to escape with his life—regardless of how much you still care for him!'

The wry smile that had been forming on her lips was replaced with a look of startled bewilderment. 'Care for him?' she repeated, in astonishment. 'My dearest Cat! It is years since I gave him a second thought! And, in view of your somewhat belligerent attitude towards the poor fellow—whilst I have to admit that your championing of my cause is greatly appreciated—it is, perhaps, just as well that my uncle refused to divulge the gentleman's name to you!'

At these words, the viscount blinked several times and took a deep breath. 'But, if you are not still carrying a torch for the man, why have you gone to so much trouble to keep all the other fellows at bay since he cried craven?'

Georgianne was silent for a moment or two. Then, with a brief shrug of her shoulders, she said diffidently, 'Because I am not prepared to face the prospect of further mortification, I suppose. Apart from which, how can I be sure that any other prospective suitor would prove to be as accommodating as the first, as regards the keeping of secrets? Being part of such a close-knit neighbourhood as we are, surely the fewer people who are privy to such knowledge, the better?'

Catford frowned and shook his head. 'You appear to have taken it for granted that every fellow is bound to pull out as soon as my father acquainted him with your history!' he protested.

'I am simply not prepared to take the chance that he might not,' replied Georgianne, casting him a rueful smile, before adding hastily, 'Not that I have been sufficiently enamoured of any one of them to put the matter to the test.'

'I refuse to believe that any man who truly loved you would concern himself with such a piddling topic as your ancestry—I know that I, for one, would not give a fig about such a thing!'

Smiling, she stretched up on tiptoe and kissed his cheek. 'For which I thank you, dearest Eddie,' she said gently. 'But, since we have always been as brother and sister, I fear that you have a somewhat blinkered attitude towards me. Sadly, not all men are as open-minded as you are.'

At that moment, for some unknown reason, a sudden vision of Will Maitland's laughing visage presented itself to her, causing her to catch her breath in confusion. All the way back from the vicarage, she had done her best to put her cousin's friend out of her mind, by trying to concentrate on such matters as the best disposition of the guests at tonight's dinner table—arranging for the ongoing care of the injured kitchen-maid—the acquisition of fresh flowers for the drawing-room—anything, in fact, to stop herself dwelling on the highly disconcerting feelings that had swept through her in that one brief moment in the spinney.

From the first moment that Maitland had stepped up into Catford's landaulet, Georgianne had felt herself curiously drawn to him but, having witnessed his immediate capitulation to her friend's loveliness, she had done her best to quash her own interest—a practice with which she was now well nigh perfect, having had more than three years in which to refine the procedure.

Unfortunately, despite her best endeavours, she had been unable to prevent the sudden jolt that had hit her when he had unexpectedly appeared on the terrace that morning. Nor had she seemed to have a great deal of control over the breathless tingles of excitement that had coursed through her body when he had stepped up to join her in the summerhouse. Biting her lip in mortification, as she recalled what had followed, she mentally chastised herself for having allowed her carefully constructed guard to slip. But, even as she pledged to redouble her efforts, she could not help feeling that it was going to take a good deal more than mere dogged determination to banish all thoughts of the highly personable Will Maitland from her daydreams!

As a soft sigh escaped his cousin's lips, Catford looked down at her in concern. 'Overdoing things as usual, Georgie?' he asked, as they climbed the terrace steps. 'Mother tells me that you never seem to stop.'

'I like to keep busy,' she murmured. 'It helps to pass the time.'

'But, are you happy, Georgie?'

She stared up at him in surprise. 'Happy? Well, yes. Of course I am happy. What an odd question, Cat!'

Pursing his lips, he shook his head and ushered her into the drawing-room.

Chapter Seven

Having spent the whole of Sunday and Monday engaged in a fruitless search for some proof of his cousin Melandra's death all those years ago, it was not until shortly before seven o'clock on the Tuesday morning that Maitland was eventually able to carry out his intention to join Georgianne and Catford on their morning ride. He found himself tingling with anticipation, as he cantered into the stableyard at Gresham Hall, in full expectation of finding the pair still in the process of collecting their gear. To his surprise, the groom who ran out to take his horse's head informed him that his lordship and Miss Venables had left some ten minutes earlier.

Hurriedly ascertaining the riders' direction and urging Pegasus into a swift gallop, the somewhat put-out Maitland set off in pursuit of the couple. Doing his best to dismiss the uncomfortable thought that one or other of the pair might not want his company, he could only surmise that his suggestion that he might be allowed to join them on their morning ride must have slipped Georgianne's mind.

Upon his return from the vicarage on the previous afternoon, he had been immediately commandeered by his lordship, the earl, who had, very naturally, desired to make the acquaintance of the young officer who had saved his son's life. Following this somewhat embarrassing interlude, it had then taken Maitland quite some time to track down and persuade Fenton to extract himself from the charms of the fair Miss Highsmith, on the grounds that neither he nor his cousin were suitably dressed for the dinner invitation that had been pressed upon them. All of which had left him very little time to speak with either Georgianne or Catford again, other than to offer his friend sincere thanks for their kind hospitality, along with a promise that he would see them again soon.

This last Maitland could remember quite clearly. 'See you soon!' he had called over his shoulder, as Fenton had driven his carriage away from the front steps where Stephanie and the viscount, along with several of the other guests, had chosen to congregate to wave the two of them farewell. Georgianne, as he had been chagrined to observe, had not been amongst their number.

Having then been obliged to spend the remainder of the evening listening to his cousin's over-fulsome praise of Stephanie Highsmith's now rather obvious attributes, it had been with a certain amount of relief that Maitland had, eventually, managed to excuse himself and retire to his bed. Unfortunately, his plans for a relatively early night, in order to meet this morning's early appointment, were destined to come to naught as, toss and turn though he might, sleep persisted in eluding him, his mind being fully engaged in trying to disentangle the perplexities of the day's events.

His lips curved in appreciation as he recalled the spirited conversation between Georgianne and himself and it was not long before it came to him that his inability to get to sleep was due, in part, to a rather curious desire to renew his acquaintance with his friend's somewhat enigmatic young cousin.

Thus, to learn that Georgianne had paid scant attention to

his request to ride with her was somewhat belittling and, when he did, at last, managed to catch up with the errant pair, Maitland was not in the best of tempers.

'What the devil do you mean by going off without me?' he panted, as he reined in alongside the startled viscount.

'I beg your pardon, old boy!' returned his friend, with a puzzled frown. 'I was not aware that you intended to join us.'

'Then it is clear that Miss Venables must have omitted to inform you of our arrangement!' said Maitland, casting a darkling look towards Georgianne, whose sudden high colour, he was gratified to note, was a reasonable indication that she did, at least, acknowledge her culpability.

'Oh, I would hardly call it an arrangement, Mr Maitland,' she flashed back at him. 'As I recall, you merely expressed a desire to join us—"one morning", if my memory serves me right. I could hardly be expected to know to which morning you were referring!'

'No matter,' interposed Catford in haste, for he had spotted the instantly recognisable gleam of fury that had appeared in his friend's eyes. 'You are here now and that's all that counts. Let us not spoil such a lovely morning by arguing the toss—speaking of which,' he then added, with an adept change of subject, 'I hear that you have taken over the running of Mr Childs's fledgling cricket team!'

Since the bridle path was rather narrow at that point, barely sufficient for even two to ride abreast, Georgianne gladly opted to ride ahead, urging her mount past the two men, in order to allow them to indulge in what appeared to be their favourite occupation of casting increasingly damning aspersions on each other's capabilities. This manoeuvre, as she very quickly discovered, was not without its problems, for she then had the most disconcerting feeling that Maitland's eyes were boring into her back, which had the effect of making her feel extremely uncomfortable. She was well aware that it had been very remiss of her not to have told Catford that his friend might be joining them and it had required a good deal of persuasive grumbling on her part to get her yawning cousin out of the stable yard on two successive mornings well before the clock struck seven.

Nevertheless, having suffered the torments of a night spent alternating between, on the one hand, a total inability to sleep, due to uninvited images of Will Maitland invading her thoughts and, on the other, several rather vivid and highly disconcerting dreams about him, she had awoken quite unrefreshed and, worse, with her self-composure now seriously undermined.

Thus, as soon as the path widened out into an open meadow, she determined to make use of the opportunity to leave the two men behind and, spurring her little bay mare into a faster gait, she moved off at speed, calling over her shoulder, 'I need to shake off the cobwebs—I'll catch up with you slugabeds at the other side of Toler's Wood!'

'Dammit!' cursed Catford, as he watched horse and rider take the far hedge with ease. 'You'd better go after her, this damned leg of mine is not up to those sort of tricks yet—I'll have to stick to the bridle paths—see you on the other side!'

With a quick nod, Maitland dug in his heels and charged after Georgianne, who had now disappeared from his view. Two fields later, however, he was obliged to bring his horse to a halt, since he had no idea in what direction she might have chosen to go. And, where the devil *were* Toler's Woods? he wondered, as he stood up in his stirrups in an attempt to better his view of the surrounding countryside. As he craned his neck, a slight movement on the side of a wooded hill some distance ahead caught his attention. Yes, there was no doubt about it! That flash of dark red was definitely Georgianne's riding habit! With a satisfied grin, he urged Pegasus forwards, crossed the three intervening fields, along with their accompanying hedges, and, in fewer than five minutes, found himself at the foot of the hill, on the crest of which grew a great stand of young oak trees—the aforementioned Toler's Woods, he presumed.

Georgianne, as he could see, having reached the brow of the hill, had dismounted and was sitting on a tree stump, her mare cropping peacefully nearby. He hesitated, unable to decide whether a surreptitious flanking manoeuvre would have a better chance of success than an all-out frontal attack. From her earlier demeanour, he had little doubt that Georgianne would try to make a break for it the moment she spotted him. He, however, was just as determined that she would not escape him, for there were, in his opinion at least, one or two small matters that the pair of them needed to address.

At last, having managed to skirt the base of the hill unseen, Maitland had little difficulty making his way up to the rear of the summit and into the woods. Once he was within sight of the clearing, he quietly dismounted and, after tethering Pegasus to an overhanging branch of a nearby tree, he crept silently towards the spot where, he hoped, Georgianne would still be sitting.

Unfortunately, his lack of local knowledge brought him out of the woods at a point well to the left of his objective where, to his exasperation, Georgianne was able to spot him the moment he left the cover of the trees. Before he managed to gather his wits together, she had leapt to her feet with a cry of vexation, mounted the tree stump and thrown herself up on to her saddle, feverishly applying her crop to the mare's rump, as she urged Olympus back down the steep slope.

Rearing in protest at the uncustomary harsh treatment, the startled mare took off like a bullet, her hooves slipping and sliding on the dew-wet grass. Within seconds, her right fore hoof met with a concealed rabbit hole and the terrified animal collapsed, instantly catapulting its rider on to the ground.

His heart in his mouth, Maitland sped across the grass and threw himself down on his knees beside Georgianne's recumbent form where, by sliding his arms under her unresisting body, he painstakingly succeeded in easing her away from the animal's violently threshing hooves.

'Oh, God!' he panted, as he cradled her against his chest. 'Open your eyes, Georgianne! Say something, please, for pity's sake!'

Somewhere in the darkest depths of her consciousness, Georgianne could hear a voice calling her name but, for several moments, although she tried her hardest, she was unable to persuade her eyelids to carry out her requirements. Eventually, by giving the matter her utmost concentration, she managed to achieve a slight flutter, the accomplishment of which brought about a heaving groan of relief from whoever was clutching her in so intimate a fashion. No sooner had her mind taken note of this extraordinary phenomenon than her eyes at once flew open and, with an exclamation of dismay, she thrust herself away from the sanctuary of Maitland's arms and staggered to her feet, whereupon she immediately swayed forwards and would have fallen to the ground again had he not been standing at the ready.

'You really need to sit down and take it easy for a moment or two,' he advised her. 'You may well have a concussion— perhaps you would allow me to examine your head?'

Without waiting for her reply, he placed his hands under her armpits and, before she knew what he was about, she found herself sitting on the grass once more, with his hands running across her scalp, her hat, it seemed, having dislodged itself during her fall.

Although the feel of his fingers on her head was oddly pleasant and comforting, Georgianne knew that there was something she should be doing—something important—and she could not, for the life of her, bring to mind what it could be.

Suddenly, it all came back to her and, as she forced herself to turn her head, her eyes lit upon the ghastly spectacle of her beloved Olympus, lying on her side, snorting and writhing in apparent agony. She closed her eyes and a low moan left her lips. 'Oh, Puss,' she whimpered. 'What have I done to you?'

Maitland stood up and held out his hand to help her to her feet, doing his best to ensure that his bulk obscured her view of the distressing scene. 'Nothing broken, as far as I can tell,' he said, striving to sound light-hearted, in a vain attempt to draw her attention away from the injured animal. 'But we need to get you to a doctor, just to be sure.' Jerking his thumb over his shoulder, he added, 'Do you think you could manage to make it back up to the tree stump, if I give you my arm?'

Numb with misery at what she had done, Georgianne made no attempt to deter him as he put his arm around her waist and guided her the few steps up the hill, in order to lower her on to the stump, with the tree behind providing a convenient back rest.

'Now, don't you move,' he commanded, stepping away from her as soon as he had satisfied himself that she was safely ensconced. 'It will take but a minute for me to fetch Pegs—then I can get you home.'

'Never mind about that!' she gasped in protest, as she reached forwards to clutch at his sleeve. 'Go and see to Olympus! She needs your help far more than I do!'

Undecided for a moment, Maitland stared down at her anguished expression then, gently extracting himself from her grip, he turned towards the injured animal, which had, by this time, managed to scramble upright, but was clearly unwilling or unable to place any weight on its right foreleg. A brief inspection of the leg was enough to convince Maitland that nothing was broken and that the main damage appeared to be restricted to the fetlock joint.

'Looks to me like a bad sprain,' he reassured the anxiously waiting Georgianne, on returning to her side. 'They'll soon sort her out, I'm sure, although I would guess that she's likely to be out of action for several weeks.'

Although her mind was still somewhat befuddled, it did not take long for Georgianne to register the fact that her beloved mare's injury had come about as a result of her own foolishly impetuous behaviour. Staring up at Maitland in mute appeal, she stumbled to her feet. 'It's all my fault,' she whimpered brokenly.

Maitland shook his head in protest. 'The blame is entirely mine!' he returned vehemently. 'Had I not pursued you and crept up on you as I did, it would never have happened!'

At his words, Georgianne's eyes filled with tears and her entire body began to convulse with huge shuddering sobs. Reaching out, she collapsed into his hurriedly outstretched arms.

In the face of such overwhelming anguish, Maitland was almost unmanned but, steeling himself, he wrapped his arms about her and held her tightly against him, murmuring nonsensical disjointed phrases of comfort into her ear, in an effort to still the heaving spasms that racked her body. Slowly and very gradually, the heartrending sobs at last subsided into little more than a breathless whimper.

As relief flooded through his body, Maitland raised a hand and gently stroked her head, pressing his lips against her brow, in the way one might comfort a small child. But then, when Georgianne raised her tear-drenched eyes and gazed into his, an unexpected *frisson* of desire shot through him and he became only too aware that this was no child he was holding in his arms, but a fully grown and decidedly well-formed young woman!

Hurriedly loosening his hold, he moved slightly away from her, but kept his hands on her elbows, conscious that she might still fall. Deprived of the warm comfort of his arms, Georgianne began to shiver. With a muttered oath, Maitland pulled her towards him once more, desperately striving to control his wayward body and dismiss the prurient thoughts that insisted upon crowding into his brain. He tried to concentrate his mind on how he might best tackle the problem of the injured filly, prior to getting the traumatised girl back to Gresham Hall but, with Georgianne in her present state of confusion, it was difficult to see how he was going to accomplish either of these tasks. Added to which, he could not help but feel that, if he was obliged to stand here for much longer with the soft curvaceousness of her trembling body pressed so tantalisingly against his own, he was not entirely sure that he could be answerable for the outcome!

Luckily for both his willpower and his stamina, help was soon at hand in the form of Viscount Catford who, having arrived at the previously arranged meeting place some fifteen minutes earlier had, with scant regard for the well-being of his injured leg, ultimately elected to ride up the steep slope to ascertain the pair's whereabouts. The discovery of Maitland's tethered horse had merely served to intensify his growing anxiety and, flinging caution to the wind, he had completed the final few yards through the woods in a frantic dash, only to bring his mount to a skidding halt when he broke through the trees.

'Good God!' he called out in horror and, hurriedly dismounting, he limped awkwardly across the grass, rapidly taking in his cousin's dishevelled appearance and the mare's still obvious distress. 'What the devil happened?'

'Caught her foot in a rabbithole and came a cropper,' returned Maitland tersely as, with an inward sigh of relief, he uncoupled himself from Georgianne and stepped to the side, keeping one arm around her waist to hold her steady. 'Cursed bad luck, really.'

Georgianne's eyes widened and she took in a sharp breath, clearly ready to refute the veracity of this assertion. Digging his fingers into her back in a patent warning, he gave her a barely perceptible shake of the head and went on, 'Nothing we could do, I'm afraid.'

'And you, Georgie?' queried her anxious cousin, coming to her side and gathering her into his arms. 'Are you hurt?'

'Just a little bruised, that's all, Cat,' she replied. 'And, hopefully, Olympus seems to have suffered no more than a bad sprain.'

Looking down at her still-white face, Catford frowned and drew Maitland to one side. 'I'd appreciate it if you'd take Georgie back to the house, if you wouldn't mind,' he murmured into his friend's ear. 'Seems to me that she ain't looking at all the thing! If you could get Everton to send up some of the lads—he'll know what's needed. I'll just hang on here until they arrive.'

After a hurried consultation between the two men, it was decided that, since it was, of course, quite out of the question to ask Georgianne to travel astride, she would have to sit up in front of Maitland. Within minutes, she found herself balanced precariously on a folded blanket, which had been placed across the saddle's pommel, in an attempt to make her ride a little less uncomfortable. No amount of padding, however, would have been enough to alleviate the discomfort she suffered when, after Maitland had climbed on to the horse, she realised that she was virtually sitting in his lap! Not only that, but in order to keep her balance, she was obliged to put one arm around his waist, whilst clutching at his jacket lapel with her free hand! Her feelings of embarrassment were not aided by the discovery that Maitland's waistcoat and shirtfront were both considerably damp, thanks to her earlier torrent of tears!

Needless to say, this somewhat awkward state of affairs was enough to curb any conversation and, other than occasionally enquiring as to his passenger's welfare, while endeavouring to ignore the fact that her lower half was draped across his left leg, it was as much as Maitland could do to concentrate his attention on guiding his horse.

After they had travelled some distance in this rather disconcerting manner, Georgianne, in an almost feverish attempt to distance her thoughts from their constant awareness of Maitland's warm muscles rippling beneath her, had taken to replaying the morning's horrendous events. It was still difficult for her to comprehend how she, who had never struck an animal in her life, could have acted in such a way.

And then, as a sudden thought occurred to her, she jerked up her head, saying, 'Why did you let Cat believe that it was an accident, when you know perfectly well that it was not?'

He shrugged. 'I had no desire to see you suffer further,' he replied. 'Besides which, there was nothing to be gained by going into details.'

When she did not reply, he added, 'In any event, I still maintain that the real blame is mine for having sparked off your irritation—for which I can only apologise, most humbly.'

'Please don't,' she returned, the words barely distinguishable, as she leaned her cheek upon his chest in an attempt to stem the fresh bout of tears that threatened. 'My foolhardiness was beyond understanding—I cannot begin to imagine what led me to do such a thing. Cat would never forgive me if he knew the truth!'

For some minutes, as they continued to ride on in silence, Maitland was given ample opportunity to contemplate the nature of this outburst and it was not long before he reached the conclusion that Georgianne's out-of-character ill temper had been brought about by his having turned up so unexpectedly to interrupt her customary ride with her cousin. That the two were very close was plain to see—they had grown up together, after all. Could it be possible that she was carrying a torch for him? Catford had told him that she had spent the past three years 'keeping all the fellows at bay', as he had termed it. What if the viscount had been mistaken in his supposition that Georgianne was still fretting for her lost love? As Maitland considered this possibility, another thought occurred to him, one that caused him to clench the reins tightly in his fists, an action that had the effect of discomposing the already unsettled Pegasus who, in skittering sideways, almost unseated Georgianne from her none-too-secure perch.

'Why—wh-what's wrong?' she cried in alarm, as she tightened her grip around his waist and clutched at his jacket.

'Nothing—sorry—lost concentration for a moment. Didn't mean to alarm you!'

Mentally kicking himself for having allowed his mind to wander, Maitland steadied the horse and swiftly brought him back in line.

'Won't happen again, I promise you,' he assured his passenger. 'Not far to go now. I can see the drive gates from here—barely a couple of hundred yards ahead of us—dare say you won't be sorry to get your feet on terra firma again!'

Five minutes later, he wheeled his horse into the stable-yard where several stable hands hurried over to help Geor-

gianne down, firing anxious questions at him as to the whereabouts of their young master. After directing a curious
dairymaid to fetch the housekeeper to attend to Miss
Venables without delay, he sought out Everton, Gresham
Hall's head groom, and explained the situation as briefly
and as calmly as he could.

No sooner had the groom gone into action, issuing orders
left, right and center than Maitland took the opportunity to
rearrange his blanket-roll back into its accustomed position,
behind his saddle. He was trying to make up his mind whether
it would be more circumspect for him to go into the house,
in order to clarify Georgianne's explanations, which he suspected might be somewhat muddled, or to return to Toler's
Wood, along with the rest of Everton's minions, to assist in
bringing the unfortunate Olympus down from the hill.

In the end, he did neither, having persuaded himself that
now that she was in Lady Letitia's competent hands there
was no further need for him to concern himself about Georgianne's welfare, particularly since he had the distinct feeling
that she would be unlikely to welcome any further interference on his part. As for the injured mare, he concluded that,
since the groom seemed to have matters well in hand, any
additional assistance from himself would be entirely superfluous. And so, after leaving an explanatory message with
one of the remaining stable hands, he remounted and made
his way back to the Dun Cow.

Chapter Eight

No sooner had the highly shocked housekeeper, Mrs Barnet, delivered her into her aunt's care than the still somewhat dazed Georgianne was stunned to learn that, despite all that had happened since she and Catford had ridden out of the stable-yard, only little over an hour had elapsed since that time. Lady Letitia, she discovered, was still dressed in her peignoir, sitting at her dressing-table, partaking of her usual morning cup of hot chocolate. Most of the other guests, it appeared, were only just beginning to make their way down to the breakfast room.

Even as she related the distressing events that had brought her to her aunt's boudoir at such an early hour, she could not help feeling that it was strange that something that had had such an impact on her own life seemed not to impinge upon the lives of those around her. Aunt Letty was as solicitous as it was possible for anyone to be, of course, but her concern was all for Georgianne's comfort and the fact that Olympus had been injured seemed not to bother her ladyship in the slightest—in fact, she advised her deeply subdued niece to put the matter out of her mind, hastening to assure her that her Uncle Charles would be sure to provide her with a new mount as soon as she was pronounced fit to ride again.

Much too dispirited to take her aunt to task for exhibiting such a matter-of-fact attitude to what she herself considered to be a good deal more serious, Georgianne meekly submitted herself to her ladyship's sympathetic ministrations. In next to no time, she found herself bathed, annointed all over with a soothing emollient and tucked up in her bed, with a flannel-wrapped, stone hot-water bottle at her feet, despite the warmth of the day. Ignoring her protests, her aunt had summoned Dr Travers, having informed her that, since the physician was due to attend the injured kitchen-maid that afternoon, it would do no harm to have him give Georgianne a quick examination, just to satisfy them all that she had suffered no lasting damage.

'In the meantime,' she added, with a gentle smile, as she turned to leave the room, 'it would be as well for you to try to forget all about it and just snuggle down and enjoy a little cosseting, for a change!'

Although she did her best to comply with her aunt's bidding, Georgianne found it impossible to shut out the troublesome and often incomplete images that would persist in crowding her brain and, before long, the tears she had succeeded in keeping at bay since her return home began to flow in earnest. Alone in her room, she pressed her face into her pillow, in an attempt to silence her racking sobs. The hands of her bedside clock moved steadfastly onwards but still she wept, until finally, a state of sheer exhaustion, along with the sodden wreck of her pillow, brought her anguish to a shuddering close.

Tossing the offending article to one side, she heaved a long quivering sigh and, closing her eyes, now red-rimmed and badly swollen, she eventually drifted off into a restless, dream-filled sleep.

Shortly after noon, she was awakened by her maid, Emily, bearing messages of sympathy from various members of the house party and informing her that Dr Travers was on his way up to see her.

'Would you like to sit up to receive him, Miss Georgianne?' she asked, as she fussed around her mistress, straightening the bedcovers and plumping up the pillows, only to utter a startled, 'Good grief, miss! Did you upset your water carafe—this here pillow is saturated—I'd best change it for a fresh one!'

Struggling up into a sitting position, Georgianne was dismayed to find that, despite the earlier application of bruise-reducing ointments, every single part of her body ached. Clearly, she had landed more heavily than she had supposed, although it was gratifying to note that her head now seemed to be free of the confusing fog that had previously invaded her thoughts.

'Now, then, my girl!' came the doctor's booming tones, as he strode into her room. 'What's this I hear? Falling off a horse, at your age, my dear! I'm surprised at you!'

Although she had known Dr Travers since her early childhood, Georgianne found it difficult to conjure up the expected smile at his heartening sallies, which were intended, as she had learned long ago, to raise his patients' spirits. Not that this attempt at bonhomie always had the desired effect, of course, and she was not entirely sure that her present situation called for such joviality. Nevertheless, it was beyond her to snub the elderly physician, for she knew that his intentions were thoroughly well meaning.

'Yes, it was very silly of me, Doctor,' she acquiesced. 'But you really had no need to trouble yourself—I ache a bit, it's true, but I dare say a day or so in bed will soon put an end to that.'

'Allow me to be the judge of that, young lady!' returned the doctor, drawing up a chair at her bedside. 'Any sickness? Visual disturbances?'

Having ascertained that she had suffered none of the usual signs of concussion, Dr Travers then set about examining the rest of Georgianne's body for sprains and fractures and so on until, with a satisfied nod, he sat back in his chair and pronounced that, apart from a good shaking up—which was no more than one might expect, if one went about falling off horses—she appeared to be as fit as the proverbial fiddle.

'You may get up as soon as you feel up to it,' he declaimed, as he tossed his instruments back into his valise. 'Just take it easy for a couple of days and have your maid keep applying the hamamelis lotion.'

With that, he departed, but no sooner had he quit the room than the door was flung open again and in bounced Stephanie, her cornflower-blue eyes wide with curiosity.

'Oh, Georgie!' she exclaimed. 'We have all been so worried! Catford has told us what happened! It must have been dreadful for you! Thank goodness you weren't badly hurt!'

'Just a few bumps and bruises, which will soon mend, I'm sure,' Georgianne assured her friend, with a brave attempt at a smile. 'Doctor Travers says that I am to be allowed up whenever I choose.'

'Oh, thank goodness! How dreadful it would have been if you had been obliged to miss the ball!'

'No fear of that, I promise!' replied Georgianne, keeping her tone light although, at this moment, there was nothing that she felt less like doing than assisting her aunt with the hundred and one things that were going to have to be attended to, if the success of the forthcoming grand event was to be guaranteed. 'Aunt Letty is depending upon me to help her organise the decorations.'

Stephanie frowned. 'I can't think why Lady Letitia doesn't leave all that sort of thing to the servants,' she said, lowering herself on to the bed next to Georgianne. 'If ever I marry and have a house of my own, I shouldn't wish to be involved in such maudlin domestic affairs—that's why one employs a housekeeper and a retinue of other employees, surely?'

'These things do not arrange themselves,' countered Georgianne, with a light laugh. 'They require a highly proficient hostess, such as my aunt, to bring together all the infinitesimal details that are involved in orchestrating what is—even given the most dedicated staff—a most frightfully complicated business. If you do not intend to involve yourself in the running of your own residence, we must just hope that the man that you marry—whoever he may be—will prove wealthy enough to provide you with a skilled staff who have no difficulty in interpreting their mistress's requirements, without her prior instruction!'

'I suppose you're right,' sighed Stephanie, jumping to her feet and pacing restlessly about the room. 'I shall never be as practical as you are, no matter how hard I try and, as for being wealthy—I just wish there were a way I could find out how rich he is without actually asking him point blank!'

'Who—w-what?' faltered Georgianne, staring across at her friend with a puzzled frown. 'Who are on earth are you talking about?'

'Jeremy Fenton, of course!' returned Stephanie, with a defiant toss of her blonde ringlets. 'He has been describing his life in London to me and I do so envy him. Trips to the theatre and the opera house, visits to pleasure gardens and parties almost every night! And, you can tell by the cut of his jacket that his tailor cannot be cheap.'

'But you can't possibly contemplate marrying a man based purely on the cut of his jacket!' exclaimed the startled Georgianne, whose own impression of Maitland's dandified cousin had left her with the distinct feeling that he was something of a mountebank and, more than likely, given to indulg-

ing in wild flights of fancy. 'Besides which, I thought you
had your heart set on capturing a duke or an earl!'

'Fat chance I have of coming across either one of those
stuck in this awful backwater,' shrugged the disaffected
Stephanie. 'An heir to a baronetcy looks to be about the best
I can do—for the moment, at any rate.' Pausing, she pondered
her reflection in the looking-glass, absent-mindedly rearranging a stray curl, before adding, 'I sometimes wonder if
I didn't make the most dreadful mistake in not snapping up
Catford when I had the chance! In fact, if it weren't for that
horrid gammy leg of his...'

'Steffi!' gasped her dismayed friend. 'I won't have you
saying such beastly things about poor Cat!'

'Well, you can't argue with the fact that he's not nearly so
attractive as he was three years ago,' returned the unrepentant Stephanie. 'Whereas, Mr Fenton, as well as being remarkably handsome, has a decidedly dashing air about him.
I just wish I could find out if he has enough money to make
him worth my while!'

'Oh, honestly, Steffi!' chortled Georgianne, as she collapsed back on her pillows in a fit of giggles. 'You are quite
incorrigible! What Lady Highsmith would say, if she were
to hear you making that sort of remark, I cannot imagine!'

'If you really must know,' retorted Stephanie abruptly,
turning around to confront her friend, 'my dearest grandmama has given me every reason to suppose that she will
never countenance my marrying anyone, regardless of his
rank or station. Some few weeks ago, I took the opportunity
to snatch a quick look at her will, while she was out of her
office.' Ignoring Georgianne's shocked face, she went on, 'It
appears that she has left her entire estate to me—but only on
the proviso that I continue running Highsmith House as
always and that I never marry—otherwise the estate goes

straight into a trust fund and I get a paltry five hundred pounds a year annuity!'

For several minutes, Georgianne stared at her friend in silence, unable to think of anything to say. She was finding it difficult to believe that Lady Highsmith would be so cruel as to treat her granddaughter, her only living relative and one whom everyone could see she petted and spoiled most dreadfully, in such a callous and heartless way.

'But, why?' she eventually managed. 'Why would she do such a thing?'

'Oh, she's always had this weird belief that all men are inherently evil.' Stephanie shrugged. 'My grandfather was a bit of a beast, by all accounts, and involving herself with all these fallen women must have given her a rather distorted view of the opposite sex, I suppose. In any event, I mean to do something about it all before she gets back from Harrogate—it's merely a question of considering where my best options lie!'

Shaking her head in disbelief, Georgianne was just about to remonstrate with her friend, when the door opened and Lady Letitia entered, bearing a tray. Upon seeing that her niece already had a visitor, she gave a little frown.

'Now, off you go, Stephanie,' she directed, as she laid down the tray on Georgianne's nightstand. 'I believe I told everyone that Georgianne was not to be disturbed for the rest of the day—I find it rather surprising that you chose to disregard my instructions.'

'I only just popped in for a minute to see how she was faring, ma'am,' came Stephanie's swift rejoinder, as she hurriedly made for the door. 'I won't bother her again, I promise you.'

'Ridiculous child!' tutted Lady Letitia, as she straightened her niece's coverlet. 'I swear that she sometimes tries my patience to the limit! How are you feeling, my dear?'

'Much better, Aunt Letty,' Georgianne was happy to assure her.

Her aunt gave a satisfied nod. 'I am very glad to hear it, dear girl,' she said. 'And, if it will ease your mind, Eddie has instructed me to tell you that Olympus is now safely ensconced in her stall and her injuries have been attended to.'

Nodding smilingly at the expression of relief on her niece's face, she then added, 'And now, my love, Cook has sent up some tit-bits to tempt your appetite—a bowl of her delicious chicken broth and a tiny piece of grilled salmon. Do try to eat a little of it, dearest—she will be so upset if you don't. Emily will be along shortly with the lotion and a fresh hot-water bottle and then you can settle down for the night, without fear of anyone disturbing you again.'

To her surprise, Georgianne discovered that she was, in fact, quite hungry and soon managed to polish off Cook's offerings, along with the glass of wine that her aunt had so thoughtfully provided. Following which, her maid's gentle massaging with the soothing lotion gradually had the effect of making her feel quite drowsy again and, snuggling down once more into the lavender-scented softness of the newly replaced pillows, she readied herself for sleep.

As she slowly drifted off, she was unable to prevent her thoughts from wandering over the day's events. Although she had been shocked by Stephanie's unexpected confidences, she could not help wondering whether it might not be preferable to be in her friend's shoes rather than in her own at this point in her life. At the very least, she reasoned sleepily, Stephanie did have the option of marrying or not, as she chose, whereas she herself would never be given that luxury. Due to some foolish indiscretion on the part of parents whom she had never even known, their daughter appeared to be condemned to lifelong spinsterhood. And, even though Cousin

Eddie had insisted that there were a good many men around who would dismiss the murky details surrounding her birth as being of little consequence, how was she to recognise such a man? Would he be tall or short, fat or thin, or would he have broad shoulders, a fine physique and clear grey, laughing eyes like…?

With a hint of a smile upon her face, she fell into a deep sleep.

Chapter Nine

Upon his return to Dunchurch, Maitland was greeted by his excited cousin, who was all agog with the news that yet another hold-up had taken place on the heath during his absence.

'Would you credit it—in broad daylight, too!' Fenton declared as, wilfully ignoring the other man's muttered expletives, he strutted backwards and forwards, preening himself in front of the pier glass in Maitland's room, while his cousin struggled to arrange his neckerchief. 'Made off with every penny they had, so the landlord tells me!'

'Do get out of my way, Jerry!' exclaimed the now highly infuriated Maitland. 'Has it escaped your attention that I'm trying to tie this blessed cravat? Why can't you go and study your reflection in your own damned mirror?'

'Just thought you ought to know, old man,' replied Fenton, continuing with his aimless perambulations, quite undaunted by his cousin's ire. 'Personally, I don't much care for the idea that we're going to be dashing back and forth across the pesky place, in search of Mel's elusive brat! Practically asking for it, if you want my opinion! P'raps we should confine our investigations to the villages on this side of the heath, until these beggars are apprehended—I'm told that the local constable is drafting in a troop of dragoons from the military barracks in Coventry.'

'Well, they'll soon see the blighters off!' laughed Maitland, as he stood back from the looking-glass with a satisfied nod. 'Although, from what I've heard, the chaps who are doing this are not exactly in the style of your average highwaymen.'

'How do you mean?'

'Well, for a start, they seem to steer clear of the more obvious targets—fancy crested carriages, with bags of luggage and so on—and choose to hit on fairly ordinary folk instead. I understand that this morning's attack was on that inoffensive-looking pair who sat near us at dinner last evening. Shouldn't have thought that any highwayman worth his salt would have given them a second glance, let alone gone to the trouble of holding them up—do you happen to know what they made off with, by the way?'

'Sizeable amount of coin, I believe—or so the chap told the landlord,' supplied Fenton, as the pair made their way down to the inn's breakfast parlour. 'Oh, and a couple of rings his wife was wearing—hardly worth a fortune, if my memory serves me correctly.'

Settling themselves at a table near the window, the two men tucked in to the hearty meal with which they were soon provided. Any further attempts at conversation were kept to a minimum as the pair of them made short work of several slices of glazed gammon and a couple of succulent pork chops apiece, followed by a dish of devilled kidneys topped with poached eggs.

'I shall have to have all my jackets let out, if I keep this up!' gasped Fenton, finally pushing his plate aside and reaching for one of the foaming tankards of ale that the serving-maid had just brought to their table.

'You could do with a bit more flesh on your bones,' grinned

Maitland, surveying his cousin genially. 'Added to which, I'm glad to observe that your complexion is already beginning to lose its usual pasty look—this country air appears to be having a most beneficial effect upon your constitution!'

'Well, I have to admit that it ain't been as bad as I feared it might be,' returned Fenton, leaning back in his chair, with a contented smile on his handsome face. 'Where are we headed today, old chap? Bit too soon to pay another visit to your chums at Gresham Hall, I suppose?'

'Out of the question!' retorted Maitland, somewhat sharply. After his rather disconcerting experiences earlier that morning, he felt that he needed a little time to himself to marshal his incoherent thoughts. The unfamiliar and rather disturbing emotions that he had found himself experiencing in regard to Georgianne Venables had perturbed him greatly and he had every intention of quashing them in the bud without delay. For, having replayed Saturday's conversation with the viscount over and over in his mind, he had eventually come to the conclusion that Catford appeared to be just as enamoured of Georgianne as she was of him and, that being so, there was absolutely no way on earth that he would allow himself to do anything that might queer his friend's pitch.

Hoisting himself out of his chair, he tossed a coin on the table for the serving wench and, followed by the now yawning Fenton, strode towards the door.

'Better get on with it, I suppose,' he said. 'Tell them to have your carriage ready in ten minutes and we'll tackle some of the villages to the south of the town.'

Having collected their hats and gloves, the two men made their way round to the back of the inn into the stableyard, where they found Maitland's ex-sergeant, Pete Andrews, standing ready at the horses' heads.

'Picked a fine morning for your little jaunt, sir,' he grinned, steadying the sprightly pair of greys as the men leapt up on to the driving seat. 'Going somewhere nice?'

'Just round and about, to take in a little of the magnificent scenery,' returned Maitland, smiling down at the man. 'Thought any more about my offer, Sergeant?'

'Still considering it, sir, if you don't mind!'

'Well, let me know when you've reached a decision—I think you'd be a fool not to accept it.'

With a brisk nod, Andrews executed a smart salute, his bright blue eyes following the smart chaise as it bowled out of the yard. Then, turning, he made his way back to the tack room, where he had been cleaning saddles.

What a miserable coil he had got himself into, he thought, as he settled himself back down on his stool and reached for the saddle-soap. Discharged from the army hospital without a penny to his name and scarcely a rag to his back, he had been obliged to make his own way home, along with the many hundreds of other unfortunates whose military services were no longer required by their units, the war between England and France having reached its bloody climax on the field at Waterloo less than a year ago.

Had it not been for running into Matty and Josh, God only knew what might have become of him. Deeply self-conscious of the ragged scar that marred his once-handsome face, he had been unable to bring himself to return to his wife and children in Essex, initially having decided that it would be far better for them to believe that he had perished in the final battle.

However, after having spent the past few months cloistered with Josh Todd up in the tiny garret that the pair of them shared in Matty Skinner's uncle's cottage, which was situated just around the corner from the inn, he had been given ample opportunity to reconsider the wisdom of his former decision.

The trouble was, as he had very soon realised, that any attempt to extract himself from the web into which Skinner's harebrained chicanery had entangled him was bound to prove difficult, if not well nigh impossible.

Already there was talk of bringing in the militia and, being an ex-soldier himself, Andrews had no delusions as to what methods would be employed, once a troop of trained dragoons laid hands on their quarry. Furthermore, it wasn't even as if any of them had profited greatly from Matty's ill-conceived scheme. Whilst it was true that, in shunning the flashier coaches and carriages, they had avoided the likelihood of having their heads blown off by an armed guard's blunderbuss, his own share of the miserable pickings that they had achieved, by directing their activities at a more lowly set of travellers, had so far provided him with less than half the cash needed to buy his ticket home—which was now his constant dream.

To begin with, he had regarded the escapade as little more than a bit of harmless fun, since he had been adamant that there should be no violence involved, having seen more than enough of that during the past five years. The plan had been, to begin with, fairly simple. Every so often, when a suitable target had been agreed upon, one of the three would help himself to a mount from the inn's commodious stables, where there were never fewer than a couple of dozen horses available at any one time. Then, whilst the remaining two of the trio set about employing a series of delaying tactics upon the unsuspecting travellers, their elected member would make off for the disused charcoal-burner's hut, where the tools of their nefarious trade—cloak, hat and mask—were kept secreted. Having disguised himself in this time-honoured fashion, the intending highwayman would then make for a suitably secluded spot on the heath, well in advance of the approaching carriage. By using different mounts on each occasion and continually switching places in this way, any descriptions that the beleaguered travellers had been able to supply to the authorities had been, thus far, highly confusing and somewhat contradictory.

Unfortunately, any enjoyment that Andrews might have derived from the activity at the start had long since evaporated. On top of which, the ringleader Skinner, whom the ex-sergeant suspected of helping himself to a greater share of the meagre pickings than was dealt out to Todd and himself, had grown overly confident and was now insisting that the time had come to step up the operation and try for bigger game. The mere thought of the inherent dangers involved in so doing was enough to send cold shudders down Andrews's back, with the result that he now lived every day in the very real fear of finding himself at the end of the hangman's noose, should the trio's activities be discovered, a circumstance that seemed to him only too likely to occur rather sooner than later!

From Andrews's point of view, his ex-major's offer was an absolute godsend and could not have come at a more auspicious moment. If he could just find a way of leaving the area without either of his two accomplices being made aware of his ultimate destination, he could put all this jiggery-pokery behind him, collect his wife and boys and set about making a fresh start.

With a bitter sigh, he reapplied himself to his task, reasoning that, whatever decision he came to, none of his plans could be put into action until Maitland showed signs of quitting the area.

The number of villages to the immediate south of Dunchurch proved to be singularly few, obliging Maitland to direct his attention to those situated on the western fringes of the heath, much to his cousin's apprehension.

'Ain't sure that it's wise for us to be travelling in this vicinity,' he muttered, glancing fearfully into the bushes that lined the narrow lane upon which they were travelling. Having elected to hand over the reins to Maitland some time ago, he was now wondering whether he would not have done better to keep them in his own hands, since it went without saying that, should the two of them be called upon to defend themselves, his cousin was by far the better shot.

Maitland laughed. 'I doubt whether any self-respecting highwayman would care to chance his arm twice in one day,' he said reassuringly. 'Mark my words, the fellow will lie low for at least a couple of days before he strikes again— probably tucked up in the arms of his doxy, even as we speak. Try not to trouble yourself about such things.'

Then, in an effort to direct his cousin's thoughts in a more cheerful direction, he asked him what he had done with the sketch with which Stephanie had presented him.

'Thinking of getting it framed, as a matter of fact,' proclaimed the Honourable Jeremy, with a self-satisfied nod. ''Taint every day a fellow gets his likeness done by a lass who is not only an out-and-out beauty, but turns out to be rolling in lard, to boot!'

A disapproving frown appeared on his cousin's face. 'Where did you get that idea from?' he asked. 'I was given to understand that Miss Highsmith was under the guardianship of her grandmother, who ploughs all her funds into her charitable institution.'

'Not quite *all*, if I'm any judge,' replied Fenton, with a sideways grin. 'That gown her granddaughter was wearing must have cost a pretty penny, not to mention that string of pearls!'

'Clearly, then, your interest in the lady is not exactly what one might call altruistic,' retorted Maitland grimly. 'May I enquire whether you are thinking of setting your cap at her?'

'What a sweet old-fashioned expression!' replied Fenton, wrinkling his nose. 'Unlike yourself, dear coz, I am obliged to keep my options open. Who knows how long it may take to ferret out this blessed brat of Melandra's—given that he still exists, of course? Every day brings the threat of prison closer—not to mention the fact that no less than three of my creditors have threatened me with violence for having failed to meet their deadlines. I'm only too glad that none of them have managed to track me down thus far!'

'Good God, man!' exclaimed Maitland, quite taken aback. 'Why on earth did you not tell me that things had got to this point? My offer of help still stands—surely your creditors would be prepared to take something on account?'

Fenton gave a wry smile. 'I do appreciate your offer, Will, but I fear that, from what I have gathered on the grapevine, it would seem that several of them have lost all patience with me and intend to exact satisfaction one way or another if I don't pay them off in full.'

'But surely your father must be aware of your situation?' asked Maitland, as he turned the chaise back into the Dun Cow's stable yard.

'He is,' sighed his cousin. 'But he sent me to the devil some time ago. It was old Billingham's legacy I was depending upon to get me out of this scrape.' He paused, shaking his head. 'But since that is no longer in the immediate offing, it is just faintly possible that getting myself shackled to an heiress might bring about a temporary cessation in hostilities!'

Having recalled Catford's remarks in regard to Stephanie Highsmith's somewhat capricious nature, Maitland found himself hard pressed to believe that his rather pretentious cousin was likely to find favour with her for very much longer, let alone join herself to him in marriage! Since the little baggage had already turned down a viscount, it seemed clear to him that she was after a much bigger fish than a mere baronet's son. Nevertheless, imparting information of this sort to Fenton was a task that Maitland was not entirely sure that he was willing to undertake, not just at this precise moment, at any rate. Comforting himself with the thought that the matter would, more than likely, resolve itself in the not-too-distant future, he tossed the reins to the waiting stable-hand and jumped down from the chaise's perch and, together with his cousin, made his way towards the inn's rear entrance.

Upon reaching the taproom, he was accosted by the landlord, who handed him a missive from Gresham Hall. This proved to be an apology from the countess for having failed to speak with him this morning, coupled with her effusive thanks for bringing her niece safely home, along with an invitation for both Fenton and himself to join the family at dinner the following evening.

Chapter Ten

No sooner had the two cousins set foot inside the Hall's drawing-room than Maitland found himself obliged, once again, to suffer the embarrassment of being hailed as a hero. This time, however, the fêting turned out to be for his precipitate action in coming to Georgianne's rescue. Unfortunately, since he knew himself to be almost entirely responsible for the distressing events of the previous morning, he felt deeply uncomfortable at being the object of so much unwarranted praise and backslapping and it was as much as he could do to stop himself blurting out the truth of the matter. Added to which, the problem of not knowing exactly what details Georgianne had chosen to impart to her relatives made it increasingly difficult for him to conjure up satisfactory answers to the awkward questions that were being fired at him in regard to the accident. Doing his utmost to make light of his part in the affair—having decided that discretion was definitely the better part of valour—he endeavoured to concentrate his remarks on how fortunate it was that Miss Venables's injuries had not been more severe and how happy he was to have been of service to her.

Of Georgianne herself there was no sign and when he did,

at last, get a few moments to himself, he made a point of seeking out Catford to enquire as to her progress.

'Oh, she's doing pretty well, all things considered,' the viscount was happy to assure him. 'Thank heavens you were so near at hand—it hardly bears thinking about what could have happened had the blessed creature rolled on top of her!'

Maitland's face was expressive. 'You're pretty fond of her, I imagine,' he then ventured, in as non-committal a tone as he could drum up.

'Fond!' expostulated the viscount, staring at his friend in astonishment. 'Why, I'll have you know that I love Georgie most dearly—I could not bear that anything bad should happen to her...' The sudden cessation of conversation in the room caused him to turn his head towards the room's entrance and his eyes lit up. 'Well, I'll be damned. It would appear that the lady has decided to join us after all! What a trooper!'

Maitland's eyes flew to the doorway where, surrounded by a bevy of welcoming admirers, each vying for the privilege of escorting her into dinner, stood Georgianne. Wearing a gown of eau-de-nil crepe, the deceptively simple lines of which merely served to emphasise the soft womanly curves of her figure, she looked more heartrendingly lovely than he could possibly ever have imagined. Her cheeks were pale, it was true, and he was certain that he could detect just the faintest of shadows beneath her eyes. And her hair! He drew in a sharp breath. Gone was the former tightly controlled chignon and in its stead, held in place by a delicate circlet of pearls, was a glorious cascade of waves and curls!

His heart pounding, he watched in silence as Catford limped hurriedly across the room, forced his way through the crowd and, throwing his arm possessively across Georgianne's shoulders, claimed for himself the honour of escorting her and earning, for his efforts, the sweetest of smiles from his much-relieved cousin.

With a wry twist of his lips, the scene at the doorway merely having reinforced his belief that Catford's love for his cousin was rather more than platonic, Maitland turned away, thereby missing the look of eager delight that had appeared on Georgianne's face the moment she spotted his presence.

'I am so glad that Mr Maitland agreed to join us for dinner,' she said, as she tucked her hand into the crook of her cousin's elbow. 'I was afraid that I wouldn't get the chance to thank him properly for all his efforts yesterday.'

'Shouldn't worry about it,' averred Catford stoutly. 'Will has always been the sort of fellow you can count on in an emergency and, if I know him, he'll have been more than happy to oblige.'

Having had more than enough time to play and replay the embarrassing events of the previous morning and despite Maitland's protestations to the contrary, Georgianne had been unable to dismiss the belief that her beloved mare's unfortunate accident had been brought about by her own headstrong conduct. Despite the fact that her breathless reaction to Maitland's innocent attentions had caused her not a little confusion, she was painfully aware that to harbour feelings of that sort towards her cousin's friend was quite out of the question. In fact, no sooner had she realised the effect that Maitland seemed to be having on her normally tightly controlled demeanour, that she had determined to steer well clear of him. It had been for this reason that she had urged the viscount to make haste out of the stableyard, her intuition telling her that, since Maitland had failed to show up on the previous day, it was increasingly likely that he might well choose that morning to carry out his promise to join them in their early morning ride. An intuition that had soon proved to be quite correct.

Nevertheless, she could not escape the fact that, had she not reacted so childishly to his accusation, it was unlikely that he would have felt the need to chase after her to demand some sort of explanation. Unfortunately, the real truth of the matter was not something she cared to share with anyone, least of all Maitland himself!

Her niece's unexpected arrival having thrown the countess's carefully balanced seating plans into slight disarray, some little time elapsed before Moffat's stately tones announced that dinner was now served. Hence, it was with a confused mixture of anticipation and uneasiness that Maitland discovered that Lady Lavinia, having elected to place him, as guest of honour, at the top of the table to her left, had seated Georgianne on his other side. Catford, of course, having escorted his cousin to her place, took up his usual place at his mother's right hand, with Stephanie and Fenton seated next to him.

Having only just undergone a considerable cross-examination in regard to the disturbing events of the previous morning, Maitland, only too relieved to learn that her ladyship's attention had now switched to the subject of his missing relative, was more than happy to supply her with the rather paltry summary of his lack of success thus far. The details of which, as he was soon to realise, were quickly picked up by several of the other guests within earshot of his remarks, resulting in a barrage of, generally speaking, not very helpful suggestions as to what his next move might be. Consequentially, it was some little time before he found himself in a position to turn his attention to Georgianne.

'I trust that you are quite recovered from your ordeal, Miss Venables,' was the best he could manage, however, when a suitable opportunity eventually did arise.

'Oh, yes, indeed, Mr Maitland,' replied Georgianne, in as

cheery a tone as she could muster. Although the ongoing discussions regarding his abortive attempts to discover any information about his missing cousin had not failed to capture her interest, she had, at the same time, been racking her brains as to how the subject of her appalling behaviour of the previous morning might best be broached without arousing any undue interest from their near neighbours. 'Apart from a few bruises here and there, I swear that I am almost as good as new, all thanks to your kind offices!'

Maitland flinched. 'No thanks, please, I beg of you,' he protested, in an anguished undertone. 'I hold myself totally responsible for the entire business. It was wrong of me to impose myself on your ride with Catford and, as for pursuing you in the way that I did…' He shook his head and his voice trailed off.

Georgianne took a deep breath. 'That is utter nonsense and you know it, Mr Maitland,' she answered quietly. 'Now, however, is not the time to cross swords about the matter—perhaps another topic would be more suitable at this moment?'

Hesitating only momentarily, it being something of a relief to him to find that Georgianne had not offered him the cold shoulder which, in the circumstances, he could not help thinking, was no more than he deserved, his lips curved and his eyes brightened. 'Would a mention of your rather becoming new hairstyle be considered a suitable topic for the dinner table, may I ask?' he whispered, in a conspiratorial tone.

Although a slight flush stained her cheeks, Georgianne could not prevent a smile from forming. 'As a matter of fact, the bruises on my head must take some credit for that. I found that pulling my hair back into my usual style caused me a certain amount of discomfort.' This was not, of course, the entire truth, since she had practically driven her maid Emily into a frenzy over the number of times she had changed her mind prior to settling on this new style before finally venturing downstairs. But at least he *had* noticed and that, for the moment at any rate, made the effort well worthwhile. 'I am happy that it meets with your approval.'

'Oh, it does indeed,' Maitland hastened to assure her. 'Although I am very sorry about the bruises, of course, I cannot help but feel that we have all gained from their presence!'

Almost without being aware of his action, he lifted his hand and was just on the point of reaching out to finger one of the soft curls that caressed the back of her neck when he was suddenly conscious of Catford's eyes upon him. The viscount was smiling, it was true, but his left eyebrow was raised in that self-same quizzical fashion that the ex-major knew of old. Cursing inwardly, Maitland's hand fell to his lap and he made a great play of rearranging his table-napkin before turning to the countess to compliment her on the floral arrangements around the room.

Having been unaware of this brief moment of interplay between the two men, Georgianne was puzzled as to Maitland's abrupt change of direction. She could only assume that, since the topic of her new hairstyle had clearly run its course, added to the fact that she had made absolutely no effort to further the conversation, he must have reached the conclusion that she was boring in the extreme! Her other neighbour, cousin Elizabeth's husband Daniel was, as usual, more concerned with what was on his plate than with troubling himself to engage in polite chit-chat with her. She was at a loss to understand why it had become so important to her but, all at once, she felt a wild compulsion to divert Maitland's attention back to herself once more. She cleared her throat, straight away causing him to turn his head in her direction, his eyes full of concern.

'Miss Venables?'

Rather gratified, albeit slightly ashamed, that her little

charade had effected such an immediate reaction, she shot him a quick smile before lifting her glass to her lips. 'Merely a crumb, Mr Maitland—I am not about to swoon at your feet again, I promise you!'

'Rest assured that it would be my pleasure to catch you should you do so,' he said, a mischievous grin lighting up his face. 'Although I rather get the feeling that I should have to take my place in the queue if that crowd of admirers who rushed to escort you earlier is anything to go by!'

'It is true that I do have a good many cousins who express a certain fondness for me,' she admitted, casting him another heart-stopping smile. 'But, since most of them are somewhat younger than myself and rather fancy themselves as veritable Corinthians in the making, I would hazard a guess that such fondness might well vanish utterly should one of them find himself in the embarrassing position of being required to scoop me up off the floor!'

He let out a deep chuckle, the sound of which caused Georgianne to experience the oddest sensation in her mid-region.

'I refuse to believe that all of your admirers come into that category, Miss Venables. I know that Catford, for one, would dash to your aid if you needed assistance of that sort.' He was aware that he was putting out feelers, but he could not help himself. He was merely looking for more substantial confirmation of that which he felt he already had good reason to suppose.

Georgianne's eyes softened as she looked across the table and returned her cousin's smile.

'Dearest Cat!' she said. 'I love him dearly. He was always there for me when I was younger—getting me out of scrapes and patching me up when I'd hurt myself. You are perfectly correct in your assumption there, of course, although I wouldn't be prepared to swear on the poor darling's ability to "dash" exactly!'

Twin dimples formed on her cheeks as she turned back to face the, by now, totally confused but wholly captivated Maitland. 'And so, my friend, should I choose to slide gracefully out of my chair, I fear that there is nothing for it but to place my trust in your strong hands!'

'My dear Miss Venables!' he expostulated, as a look of horror gradually dawned. 'Allow me to beg that you do no such thing!'

'Put my trust in you or slide out of my chair, do you mean?' she enquired, her face the picture of innocence, although she was well aware that she was behaving in a highly outrageous manner.

The moment her words sank in, a wry grin began to form on Maitland's lips. 'Fell straight into that one, hook, line and sinker, didn't I? Clearly, my wits have gone begging!'

She beamed at him. 'That is always a possibility, I suppose, but I'm glad to see that your sense of humour is still intact!'

As he looked into her eyes, now sparkling with mischievous laughter, he felt his throat tighten. It was no wonder that Catford was so enamoured of his delightful cousin, he reflected despondently. How could anyone not be? The creature was entrancing! None the less, if what he believed proved to be the case—as was looking more and more likely—the occasional friendly interchange with Georgianne Venables would be as much as he could hope for in the circumstances, since trespassing on another fellow's preserve had always been wholly foreign to his nature. Still, he reasoned, surely the odd ride about the countryside would not be considered out of order—if Georgianne could be persuaded, perhaps?

'I trust that you don't intend to allow what happened yesterday to put you off riding for good,' he said.

A slight shadow crossed Georgianne's face and she gave a vehement shake of the head, although there was a small pause before she eventually replied, 'I do hope not. Riding is such a huge part of my life and I would hate to think that I might never again experience that unbelievably exhilarating sense of freedom that one gets on a wild gallop across the fields. The trouble is that I'm finding the idea of going off on another mount quite difficult while my poor darling Puss is confined to her stall—I still feel so terribly guilty, you see. But I know that I must make the effort soon, before I completely lose my nerve.'

She looked across at her cousin who, with his usual good humour, was giving every appearance of being completely engrossed in Stephanie's animated retelling of Fenton's vastly exaggerated social life in London. Frowning slightly, she went on. 'I shall have to ask Cat to pick out a suitable mare for me— I dare say that I will have no trouble persuading him to accompany me, although…' pausing, she bit back the smile that was forming '…for the time being, at any rate, all thoughts of a gallop are quite out of the question for the poor lamb.'

Quickly seizing the opportunity, Maitland assured her that he would be more than happy to volunteer his own services in that respect should she so wish it, adding, 'The sooner you get back in the saddle, you know, the quicker your confidence will return—it's a well-known fact.'

Georgianne gave a decisive nod. 'You are quite right, Mr Maitland and, as to your generous offer, I swear that I would be hard put to turn down such a tempting inducement.'

Offering him another of her dimpling smiles, she found herself thinking that the 'tempting inducement' was rather less the idea of the 'wild gallop' than the thought of spending some time alone with this fascinating man! Although she had, long ago, resigned herself to the fact that it was her lot to remain an old maid all her life, Maitland's unexpected appearance on the scene had jolted her out of her usual equanimity. His very presence caused an inner turmoil such as she had never before experienced and, while she was very well aware that nothing could come of such a limited friendship with him, she could see no reason to deprive herself of the pleasure of his company for the short time that he would be around. In a week or so—possibly even less!—his search for his young relative would be complete and, no matter whether his endeavours brought about success or failure, he would have no further need to remain in the district. Surely, no one could begrudge her this one brief interlude in her, otherwise, rather regimented existence? After all, she persuaded herself, it was not as though she could be accused of throwing herself at him, since it had been he who had suggested that they might ride out together.

'If you are quite sure that you are up to it,' replied Maitland, his heart leaping with anticipation as he returned her smile, 'shall we say tomorrow morning, then? I shall look forward to it.'

Shooting a quick glance across the table, he was not surprised to find Catford's intent gaze upon him. Then, all of a sudden, his friend's face broke into a wide grin and, to Maitland's utter bewilderment, the viscount raised his glass in a salute to him!

He had little time to ponder over this rather puzzling turn of events, however, in view of the fact that a little flurry of movement to his right indicated that Lady Lavinia was about to rise from her seat, giving the cue for the rest of the ladies in the party to depart to the drawing-room, so as to leave the gentlemen to their port and cigars. Fortunately, despite his thoughts being otherwise occupied, he still retained sufficient presence of mind to scramble to his feet in time to hand Georgianne out of her chair and offer her a bow of respect as she made to follow her aunt out of the room.

Chapter Eleven

'I really can't see why we ladies have to sit in here sewing and drinking tea night after night while the men carry on having high jinks elsewhere,' complained Stephanie, as the sound of hearty laughter filtered through the drawing-room doors from across the hallway. 'I'm sure they would much prefer that we remained with them.'

'I take leave to doubt that,' murmured Georgianne, putting aside her own needlework and fixing her friend with a sympathetic smile. 'Like us, they need a little private time to— er, *refresh* themselves, as it were. It's just one of those things that you will have to get used to, if you mean to be the mistress of a big house.'

Stephanie made a discontented moue. 'But even when they have finished with their drinking and merriment, half of them disappear into the billiard room, or sit around playing their silly card games!'

'We can play some hands of *vingt-et-un*, if you like,' suggested Catford's sister, Lady Elizabeth, having overheard the girl's petulant remark. 'There are more than enough of us and it would help to pass the time until the gentlemen join us.'

'But that's precisely my point,' glowered Stephanie. 'We

are just obliged to *pass the time* until they deign to stop what they are doing to join us! When I run my own house I shall order things quite differently. I shall make sure that whatever is going on where *I* am is a more attractive prospect than mere cards or billiards!'

'Such as what?' laughed Georgianne, as several of the other ladies in the group leaned forwards, interested to hear how Stephanie intended to entice the prospective men in her life from their preferred pursuits.

Stephanie shrugged. 'Well, for one thing, we could have dancing!'

'In the drawing-room, my dear!' put in the countess's elder daughter Lady Charlotte, a shocked expression on her face. 'I hardly think so! Besides which, if you really suppose that the thought of dancing would draw our spouses from their chosen amusements, you clearly have a great deal to learn about the opposite sex!'

As a laughing murmur of agreement rippled around the room, Georgianne hoped that she was the only one who heard Stephanie's muttered observation that it would, surely, depend upon with whom the gentlemen hoped to dance!

'Perhaps we might take a turn out on the terrace?' she suggested, in an endeavour to rally her restless friend who, as she was gradually beginning to discover—to her abounding sorrow—seemed never to be truly happy unless she was basking in the admiration of one or another group of males. 'The evening is still quite warm—we could walk down to the lakeside, if you would like?'

'Better than staying in here listening to that awful female's attempts to murder yet another Beethoven sonata!' returned the other girl disconsolately, as she carelessly tossed aside the tiny bodice with which she had been fidgeting and reached for her Paisley silk shawl. Having had the best and most expensive music tutor that her grandmother could find, her own expertise at the instrument was somewhat more exemplary than the performer who was presently fumbling at the keyboard. Miss Highsmith, however, always made a point of never being pressed into displaying her not inconsiderable talent unless there was a suitable number of members of the opposite sex around to admire her performance.

Outside on the terrace, the air was, as Georgianne had predicted, still pleasantly warm and, since an almost full moon shone high in the sky, the two girls had little difficulty making their way across the lawn down to the lakeside.

'It isn't at all as I had expected, you know,' observed Stephanie, as she stood staring gloomily at the moon's rippling reflection in the dark waters.

Georgianne was puzzled. 'What isn't as you had expected?' she asked.

Stephanie gave a disaffected shrug. 'Oh, my visit—the house party—the guests—I don't know! When Grandmama agreed that I should be allowed to attend, I could hardly wait to get here, but it has all been rather disappointing. I am just as tied down to a lot of ridiculous rules and regulations as I was back at Highsmith House. Even Saturday's ball doesn't stir up as much excitement as it did when I first heard about it, especially now that I know that it will be made up of the same prosy collection of tedious old bores and tiresome juveniles.'

'I presume that you are referring to the dearth of suitable males,' retorted Georgianne, somewhat stung by her friend's disparaging remarks. 'Well, I'll have you know that I don't consider Cat, for one, to be in the least bit tedious or tiresome! Why, he has kept his carriage at your disposal since the very first day you arrived here! And, to my certain knowledge, every one of my male cousins has been at your complete beck and call daily! Honestly, Steff, you really are the limit, sometimes! I simply cannot imagine what more you could expect of us!'

'Oh, don't get into a huff, Georgianne,' returned Stephanie, in a placatory tone. 'I wasn't including Cat—he has been a real sweetie, I know, but I can't count *him*. I just mean that I was expecting to meet a whole host of other available viscounts and earls, but all of those who *are* here have turned out to be either married to one or other of your cousins or still in the schoolroom. And while I grant you that Mr Maitland is quite presentable, I doubt that he is sufficiently wealthy to be recognised by those in the upper set. All of which leaves me with Jeremy Fenton—an heir to a mere baronetcy—with a perfectly healthy father to boot, by all accounts!' she concluded, with a petulant sniff.

Georgianne was not sure whether to laugh or cry at her friend's disconcerting outburst. 'Well, I wouldn't have said that you were at your last prayers, exactly,' she said. 'You are young and beautiful and—who knows—your Mr Right could suddenly turn up out of the blue and sweep you off your feet.' *A fantasy not nearly as impossible as one might have imagined less than a week ago*, she could not help thinking.

Stephanie stared at her in disgust. 'A *Mister* Right would be no earthly good to me!' she riposted crossly. 'And, I've already explained to you why I need to find someone very soon. I've already wasted two whole weeks of Grandmama's proposed month in Harrogate and, knowing her fractious nature, I wouldn't be at all surprised if she suddenly changed her mind and turned up tomorrow!' She shook her head. 'No,' she declared. 'There's nothing for it but to settle for the Honourable Jeremy, at the moment!'

'But, surely Mr Fenton hasn't yet asked you to marry him?' returned Georgianne, now reeling in shock at her friend's quite outrageous suggestion.

'Oh, pooh to that!' said Stephanie dismissively. 'The poor man is totally besotted with me. I have only to suggest that we might run away together and he would have his carriage at the door before I could turn round!'

'Steffi!' cried Georgianne in horror. 'Surely you can't possibly mean to elope! That would put you both well beyond the pale, as far as society is concerned—and what about your grandmama—have you thought how she will feel?'

Stephanie gave an indifferent shrug. 'It will teach her a lesson,' she said coldly. 'Besides, I don't need her permission. I am gone twenty-one and can marry whomsoever I choose. I just have to get Fenton alone for a few moments and the deed will be done!'

For several moments, Georgianne could only stare at her friend in disbelief but then, on hearing the sound of male voices in the distance, she turned and, to her dismay, observed Maitland and his cousin coming across the lawn towards them. A sudden feeling of panic threatened to overcome her. Reaching out, she clasped Stephanie's hands in her own. 'Please tell me that you're joking, Steffi!' she said urgently. 'You can't possibly mean to ask him to do such a thing!'

'Well, the matter probably does need a little more thought,' returned Stephanie warily. Having taken note of Georgianne's clear distress, she had quickly arrived at the conclusion that sharing her plans with her friend might, possibly, not turn out to be the wisest course of action. 'I dare say it would be wise to shelve it for the moment.'

Having drunk more than his fill of port, it not being a particular favourite of his, Maitland could scarcely wait for the other men at the table to decide they had had enough and make a move to join the ladies. But, as tradition had it, it was necessary to sit through the usual round of coarse jokes and ribald humour before a general consensus could be expected. Hence, a good half-hour elapsed before the earl rose to his feet and declared that, tedious though it may seem, the time had come to present themselves to their womenfolk.

Catching up with Catford as the group of men strolled across the hallway, Maitland sought the viscount's opinion as to the advisability of carrying out his offer to ride with Georgianne on the following morning.

'She seems pretty keen to get back into the saddle,' he ventured, trying, at the same time, to gauge his friend's reaction to the idea of his intended going off alone with another man. But, to his surprise, Catford gave a huge grin and nodded in agreement.

'Great idea, man!' he replied, clapping his friend on the back. 'Best thing for her, after that dismal business yesterday. She needs to put it right out of her mind and a good gallop should see to that! Would do it myself, as you know, but I'm not quite up to it yet. Just you leave it to me, Will, old boy. I'll have Everton sort out a suitable mount for her.'

Not quite sure what to make of his friend's somewhat cavalier attitude, Maitland followed the viscount into the drawing-room where, on sweeping his eyes around the collection of ladies seated there, he realised that Georgianne was nowhere to be seen. Disconsolately throwing himself down on a vacant sofa near the window, he allowed his eyes to wander over the moonlit lawns outside. Then, in one swift movement, he was back on his feet.

'Fancy a stroll outside, Cat?' he asked nonchalantly. 'Need a bit of fresh air after all that smoke.'

'Not me, old chap,' replied the viscount, who had plonked himself down next to one of his many female cousins and was admiring her tapestry. 'Had enough exercise for one day. You go, though. I believe Georgie's out there somewhere, along with Miss Highsmith.'

On hearing Stephanie's name mentioned, Fenton, who had been mooching about the room half-heartedly examining the various pictures on the walls, came at once to his cousin's side. 'I'll come with you,' he offered with what was, for him, decidedly uncharacteristic enthusiasm.

The truth was that the Honourable Jeremy was finding himself quite smitten with the lovely Miss Highsmith and, since he had generally been in the habit of taking his pleasures from the lowly type of female that he came across in London's many gambling dens, he had not had a vast amount of experience when it came to dealing with the more gentle members of the opposite sex. Consequently, having been rather bowled over by Stephanie's onslaught upon his senses, he found that he could not stop thinking about her. Not only had she been blessed with more than her fair share of nature's bountiful assets, but it also appeared that she was sole heir to a wealthy grandparent. Could any fellow ask for more? he reasoned. If she could just be persuaded to throw in her lot with his, not only would all his immediate financial problems be resolved but, with her on his arm, he would also be the envy of every red-blooded male in the capital!

'A beautiful evening for a stroll, gentlemen,' observed Georgianne, as soon as the two cousins eventually reached the lakeside. 'I take it that you were unable to persuade Catford to join you in your perambulations?'

'Too busy admiring Lady Alice's handiwork,' replied Maitland, conjuring up a cheerful smile, although his pulse seemed to be racing nineteen to the dozen. *How is it possible*, he was marvelling to himself, *for a woman to look even more desirable in the moonlight than she had done in a room lit by a hundred candles?* He was finding it impossible to take his eyes off her. Her hair was a halo of burnished bronze; her skin had taken on an almost translucent sheen and stray moonbeams appeared to have taken up residence in her eyes, transforming their normally placid grey into a myriad of silvery sparkles.

Thrusting his hands deep into his pockets, for it was all he could do to keep them to himself, he walked down to the water's edge and stared, somewhat disconsolately, into the unfathomable depths below.

Georgianne, not a little confused at his action, stepped forwards to stand at his side and placed her hand on his arm. 'Would you care to wander round to the boathouse?' she asked hopefully, indicating a wooden structure further along the bank to their right. Stephanie, she knew, had virtually dragged Fenton off in the opposite direction towards the pavilion and, fearful as to her friend's intentions, Georgianne had no desire to come upon the pair of them in any sort of compromising situation.

At her touch, Maitland started back as though he had been stung. *For God's sake get a hold of yourself, man!* he commanded himself angrily, as he tugged his hand out of his pocket to offer her his arm. 'Not thinking of taking a boat out, I trust?'

She laughed. 'Hardly! It can get quite chilly out there in the middle! I once fell overboard when I was a child and dearest Cat was obliged to jump in to fish me out. He was absolutely furious with me, for he ruined his brand new boots in the process!'

Maitland could not prevent a smile from forming at the image that presented itself. 'I take it that you had never learned to swim?'

'Not then, but I can now,' she assured him. 'After his

ducking, Cat made jolly sure that I would be able to save myself should I ever have the misfortune to fall in again.' Head on one side, she smiled reminiscently. 'An hour every day for six entire weeks,' she confided. 'Almost the whole of his school holidays and he refused to give up on me until I could swim unaided right across the lake and back!'

'Stout fellow!' returned Maitland, with a grin, having done much the same for his two younger sisters. 'I had a word with him about that gallop we agreed on, by the way, and he seems quite happy for me to accompany you. Everton will have a mount ready for you at seven—if you are still of a mind, that is?'

'Yes, of course I am,' Georgianne replied almost absently, for she was wondering why Maitland had found it necessary to seek her cousin's blessing in the matter. 'I am looking forward to it.'

By now, they had reached the boathouse, where Maitland was swift to take cognizance of the fact that there was a varied selection of small craft available.

'Perhaps we could take a boat out on another occasion,' he suggested. 'Now that I am fully confident of your swimming ability, I dare say I might even wear my best boots!'

'Oh, how churlish of you to remind me, sir!' retorted Georgianne, her eyes sparkling with suppressed laughter. 'After such a remark, you may find that your boots failed to survive the wetting, should you find yourself tipped over the side!'

Grinning widely, Maitland held up both hands in surrender. 'Pax! Pax!' he cried. 'I apologise, most humbly, and promise never again to mention your fall from grace!'

'My fall from a boat, you mean,' returned Georgianne, smiling up at him, causing his heart to turn several somersaults. 'Very well, you may consider yourself forgiven. However,' she added, pointing across the lake to where

Fenton and Stephanie were presently making their way—arms closely intertwined, as she observed with some misgivings—back towards the house. 'It is getting late and you will, no doubt, be wanting to get back to your hotel.'

Since getting back to his hotel was, at this moment, the very last thing in the world that Maitland either wanted or needed, he could do little more than answer with a laconic, 'As you say.'

'And, thank you for being such pleasant company, Mr Maitland,' she hastened to add. 'I know that having your friendship has always meant a great deal to Cat and I would like to feel that we, too, can be good friends.'

Maitland briefly closed his eyes and gritted his teeth before once again offering her his arm. 'I can't think of anything I would like better,' he lied, as he led the blissfully unsuspecting Georgianne back along the path.

Chapter Twelve

When he rode into Gresham Hall's stableyard the following morning, however, Maitland was not exactly overjoyed to discover Catford mounted and ready to join Georgianne and himself in their ride.

'I'll come with you as far as Brinkley's cottage,' said the viscount, gesturing to some vague point in the far distance, as the three riders exited the yard. 'Father has asked me to have a word with one of the cottagers.'

Swallowing his disappointment, Maitland held back his mount, in order to allow Georgianne to move in front, next to her cousin. Having received a number of highly confusing and conflicting messages during his recent conversations with each of them, he had hoped that this morning's excursion would provide him with the opportunity to discover, for once and for all, how things really stood between Georgianne and his friend.

For several minutes, the trio rode in a companionable silence, then, to Maitland's surprise, Catford dropped back to join him.

'I just wanted to ask you to keep an eye on Georgie,' the viscount advised him, in an undertone, although the sound of the horses' hooves on the gravelled roadway was more than enough to prevent any third party from making out his words. 'She seems to be doing all right, at the moment, but I'd like you to be sure that she has the measure of her mount, before you let her take to the gallop, if you would?'

'I think that you can rely on me to make sure that she comes to no harm, old chap,' replied Maitland, rather taken aback that his friend had found it necessary to caution him on such an obvious point. 'Your cousin will be perfectly safe in my hands, I assure you!'

'Good God, Will!' exclaimed Catford, a horrified expression appearing on his face. 'Don't you think that I know that? There's not a safer pair of hands in the whole world to whom I would rather trust her than your own! It's just that, well, um…' he glanced up ahead to make sure that Georgianne could not hear his words '…knowing her as well as I do, I know how headstrong she can be on occasions and I just felt that I needed to warn you to keep your wits about you. After that business on Tuesday, she is quite liable to push herself too far, just to prove some stupid point or other and—as I've mentioned before…' here he paused and a wistful look crossed his face '…she *is* rather precious to us all!'

Reaching across, Maitland squeezed his friend's arm. 'Please don't concern yourself, Cat. I shall watch her like a hawk—she won't get away from me this time, I promise you!'

'A thousand thanks, Will.' With a satisfied nod, the viscount turned his horse's head to the left, where a narrow lane led down to a row of estate cottages, one of which was his intended destination. 'I'm off now, Georgie,' he called to his cousin. 'Enjoy your ride!'

'See you later, Cat!' she called back to him, as she slowed her pace to allow Maitland to come alongside. 'I'd lay a pound to a penny that I can guess what all that havey-cavey chat was about,' she said, with a sideways peep at his rather sober expression.

Raising an eyebrow, he stared at her in astonishment. 'Havey-cavey? I can't think what you mean!'

She laughed. 'Liar!' she challenged him. 'I know perfectly well that Cat has been telling you to make sure that I don't kick over the traces! He still thinks that I'm the same uncontrollable scamp that I was when I was in pigtails, bless him!'

'Well, he *was* keen to make sure that I didn't allow you to push yourself too far on this occasion,' admitted Maitland, with a guilty grin.

'I doubt if anyone could push themselves too far on this little slugabed,' she grimaced, flicking her reins in an effort to urge the docile chestnut mare into a trot. 'Everton must have been ordered to pick out the most passive mount in the entire stables!'

'It's just until you get your confidence back,' he assured her sympathetically. 'Perhaps, if we cut though this copse just here, we could take a quick canter across those couple of fields over yonder?'

'What, not even a little gallop?' she said, pouting her lips in mock dismay.

'Well, possibly,' he chuckled. 'If you give me your word that you will not make off without me!'

'On this pesky creature?' she returned, her eyes twinkling with laughter. 'Very unlikely!'

Turning into the little copse, they were obliged to walk in single file along the narrow bridle path, giving Maitland ample opportunity to admire Georgianne's trim waist and shapely rear end, a spectacle that caused him to experience a certain stirring somewhere in the region of his lower abdomen. Mindful of Catford's exhortations, however, he gritted his teeth and endeavoured to concentrate on the task in hand.

Several minutes later, the two riders reached the first of the aforementioned fields, whereupon Georgianne was quick to point out that, to cross into its neighbour, would involve them stopping to unlatch and then refasten the five-bar gate that separated the pair.

'Unless you can trust me to take a four-foot jump without falling off and breaking my neck, that is!' she said, confounding him with another of her provocatively dimpling smiles.

'It's actually your mare that I wouldn't trust, on this occasion,' he grunted, at the same time wondering what the devil had possessed him to suggest this damnfool idea in the first place! She was driving him slowly mad and, if she didn't cease from tormenting him with her eyes and her lips, he would be unable to prevent himself from dragging her out of her saddle and kissing her and kissing her until...

'So, have you reached a verdict, Mr Maitland?'

As Georgianne's laughing voice cut across his lustful fantasy like an icy blast, he was obliged to take several deep breaths to bring himself back to earth. Hurriedly turning his attention back to the current problem, he cast an eye across the field to the gateway and estimated the distance to be about two hundred yards or so. Then, having hazarded a guess that the width of its neighbour would be something in the same region, he figured that the total distance across both fields would be roughly a quarter of a mile.

'Tell you what we'll do,' he suggested. 'If the gate were open and you carried on through, that would give you a good four hundred yards to work up steam. Would that suffice for this morning, do you suppose?'

Her eyes sparkling with excitement, Georgianne raised one finger and tipped her hat to salute him. 'What a very clever man you are, Mr Maitland,' she beamed. 'I would never have thought of such a thing!'

He gave a diffident shrug, at the same time feeling rather smugly satisfied that his suggestion had met with such a delighted reaction. 'If you'll just wait there while I go over and sort out the gate,' he called, as he took off across the field. 'Then you'll be able to breeze on through without a hitch.'

Watching him go, Georgianne could not help thinking that life, at times, could be decidedly unfair. There was Steffi, cold-heartedly scheming and plotting to entice the poor unsuspecting Fenton into running away with her and here she was, alone with the most desirable man she had ever met in her life and, despite all the provocative signals she had attempted to throw him, he had not attempted any sort of response. It was true that she had, more than once, caught him staring at her with a rather disturbing expression in his eyes—an expression that had the effect of causing her mind to go completely blank whilst, at the same time, turning her insides into a quivering mess—but he had remained, at all times, the perfect gentleman. Clearly, despite his cheerful willingness to escort his friend's spinster cousin around the countryside, he was not in the least bit interested in her as a woman which, to Georgianne, was a somewhat dispiriting thought. But, then, with a defiant toss of her head, she decided that she could not allow such an insignificant consideration to mar the few precious hours that she did get to have him all to herself. It was not as though there was any harm in what she was doing and, when the time came for him to leave, as it surely would, she would simply creep back into her shell and nurse her battered heart without anyone being any the wiser!

Maitland's distant shout, from the far side of the field, interrupted her pensive reverie and, with a guilty start, she realised that he had probably been standing by the gate for some time, for he was madly gesticulating to her to get a move on! Digging her left heel into Brandy's side, she flicked the reins and, after a moment's hesitation—heavily mindful of what had happened on the previous occasion—tentatively brought her crop down on the mare's rump. Instantly obeying her rider's command, the animal set off across the field.

At this point, the somewhat concerned Maitland had just been on the verge of swinging the gate back into position and returning to Georgianne, fearful that she had lost her nerve but, no sooner had he registered the expression of pure joy on her face as she swooped past him, than he knew that all was well. He breathed a sigh of relief as she reached the far side of the second field without mishap and wheeled back towards him with the utmost competence.

'Well done!' he cried, reaching out to grab hold of the bridle as, laughing breathlessly, she reined in at his side.

'Oh, that was absolutely marvellous, Will!' she panted, her face aglow with happiness. 'It would seem that I did the poor creature a disservice! Can I go again?'

'As many times as you care to,' returned Maitland with a self-satisfied smile, Georgianne's inadvertent use of his given name not having escaped him.

For some five minutes he stood by his own mount, poised to leap into the saddle to rush to her aid, should she have the misfortune to come a cropper. Eventually, however, having reached the conclusion that Georgianne was more than capable of carrying out the exercise without any interference from him, he swung himself up on to the top bar of the gate and simply allowed himself the sheer pleasure of just watching her. She was like no other woman he had ever come across: vibrant, quick-witted and so full of life yet, at the same time, it was clear that she was possessed of a quiet but steely determination. He let out a deep sigh of longing. If only she had not belonged to another man!

Having replayed the activity several times more, until both

she and her mare were thoroughly spent, the highly exhilarated Georgianne finally allowed Maitland to leap down from his perch and refasten the gate.

'I really can't thank you enough, Mr Maitland,' she exclaimed, as they retraced their way back across the field towards the copse. 'It must have been incredibly boring for you to sit there all that time and watch me making a fool of myself.'

'Hardly,' retorted her escort. 'You were magnificent! I promise you that it was a pleasure to witness such fine horsemanship!'

Then, after pausing for a moment, he added, 'However, I'm not altogether sure that I approve of the return to "Mr Maitland". I believe you called me "Will", not so many minutes ago.'

Georgianne's cheeks flamed. 'D-did I, really?' she stammered. 'I do beg your pardon! I tend to think of you—that is, I have become so used to hearing Cat refer to you by your given name that I...' Her voice trailed off in embarrassment.

'Oh, please don't think that I'm complaining!' he hastened to assure her. 'If we are to be friends, I should have thought that it was the obvious thing to do. I was rather hoping that you would allow me to call you Georgianne—or, perhaps, Georgie...?'

'Oh, no! Not Georgie, please!' was her hurried reply. 'That has always been Cat's pet name for me!' As a matter of fact, she had always disliked the diminutive, although she had no intention of admitting this to her beloved cousin's friend.

Despite the considerable sinking of his heart at these words, which merely served to confirm his suppositions, Maitland was determined not to allow such a trifling drawback to spoil the moment. *After all*, he reasoned, as he held back his mount to allow her to precede him into the copse, *it's not as though I have any intention of turning the situation to my advantage!*

'Then Georgianne it shall be,' he said, with a wide smile, as she made to overtake him.

'But only when we are by ourselves, if you please,' she returned hastily. 'My aunt would not think it at all seemly for us to be on first-name terms after so short an acquaintance.'

Before he could think to retort that, in his opinion, it was well past time that such archaic conventions were done away with, Georgianne was already out of earshot.

On reaching the lane that led back to Gresham Hall, where they were, once again, able to ride abreast, Georgianne turned towards him and asked if he would be free to ride with her again the following morning.

'I realise that I am taking up an awful lot of your time, Mr—er—Will,' she said. 'But it is so long since I had so much fun as I've had today!'

'My mornings are entirely at your disposal, I assure you,' replied Maitland who, having spent the past few minutes pondering on the various ways that he might introduce the topic, was more than delighted that it was she who had suggested it. 'My dear cousin Fenton rarely surfaces before half-past ten.'

'It would seem that you are not having a great deal of success in your search for the missing Miranda,' she then remarked.

'Melandra,' he corrected her absently, as they trotted in a leisurely fashion up the quiet country lane. 'We have pretty well scoured the whole of the immediate vicinity—I had never realised how many churches there were in this part of Warwickshire. If I have to read through many more parish registers, I swear I shall go cross-eyed!'

Her lips curved and she let out a rippling laugh, the very sound of which sent a *frisson* of desire shooting right through him. 'Now, that *would* be unfortunate, for then you would be obliged to stare at twice as many names!' Pausing, she then added, 'Melandra? It is a very unusual name, isn't it?'

'It translates as "Little Honey", I believe,' he replied, with a wide grin. 'Her father—my Uncle Henry—was something of a scholar, I'm told.'

She returned his smile. 'And to think that all this time I had been under the impression that you were saying "Miranda".'

Raising his eyebrow, he gave a short laugh. 'Doesn't say much for my powers of articulation then,' he observed drily.

'Well, it's not as though I have ever had a face-to-face conversation with you about your missing relative,' retorted Georgianne. 'Most of what I have accumulated has been hearsay—would it bore you to tell me the whole story?'

'Not at all,' said Maitland. 'Although it will probably bore you to hear it!'

Notwithstanding, he then gave her a brief outline of the events that had led to his recent arrival in the area, followed by his singular lack of success in laying his hands upon any trace of the unfortunate Étienne.

'Twenty-one years ago,' she repeated, almost to herself. 'That would make him roughly the same age as I am.'

'*If* the child survived,' Maitland could not forbear from pointing out. 'Although, having explored more or less every possible avenue in this neck of the woods, I am fast coming to the conclusion that my late uncle's memory of the whole business must have been decidedly awry, in which case, the lad could be anywhere!'

'But you won't give up just yet, will you?' she asked, holding her breath. Having felt herself totally at one with him, she did not think that she would be able to bear it if he left so soon. *Just a few more days*, she pleaded, sending up a prayer to whichever invisible deity might be smiling down on her at that moment, *and then I swear that I will put him out of my mind for ever!*

Not while I have the opportunity to spend a few more hours alone with you, was Maitland's immediate thought, as they rode into the stableyard.

'No, I shan't give up until every vestige of hope is gone!' he replied, his lips twisting in a brief smile as he handed her down from her horse.

Chapter Thirteen

As soon as luncheon had been cleared away, Georgianne sought out her friend and suggested that she might like to take a walk down to the lakeside.

'Then you can tell me what happened between yourself and Mr Fenton,' she declared, as she selected one of a collection of straw hats from the row of hooks in the back lobby and tossed another to Stephanie. 'I trust that he managed to persuade you to forget your ridiculous proposal?'

'As a matter of fact,' replied Stephanie complacently, as she tied the ribbons under her chin, 'he didn't think that it was in the least bit ridiculous, but he did say that it would require quite a bit of organisation and—as he so charmingly put it—a fair bit of blunt!'

'Perhaps Mr Fenton is not quite as well heeled as you supposed him to be?' observed Georgianne quietly.

'Oh, he clearly has plenty of money,' returned Stephanie, with a careless shrug. 'It's just that—not expecting to be in need of it on this trip—he didn't bring a great deal with him. So, it would appear that our plans will have to be put on hold until he can have some funds transferred up to the Town & County in Dunchurch. Plus, it seems that he will need to apply to some bishop or other for a special licence.'

Georgianne, who had, long since, reached the conclusion that she would not care to trust the sickeningly over-confident Mr Fenton any further than she was able to throw one of the marble busts that stood on the hall plinths, took hold of her friend's hand and regarded her searchingly. 'Are you certain that this is what you want, Steffi?' she asked.

'Of course it's not what I *want*!' exclaimed Stephanie, angrily tugging her fingers away from Georgianne's clasp and turning her head away. 'I *want* to marry a duke or an earl and have a huge society wedding in Hanover Square! I *want* to host huge balls in my own grand mansion and be the envy of every female in the *ton*, but—for the moment, at any rate—I shall have to make do with a clandestine affair in some shabby back-street registry office!' Her eyes glistened with unshed tears. 'It's so unfair!'

'But if you are so unhappy about the whole thing, why are you so determined to carry on with it?' queried her bewildered friend.

'Oh, Georgie, you will never understand,' said Stephanie, with a weary shake of her head. 'I just can't put up with this same boring humdrum existence for another minute. I simply have to get away—if I stay here any longer, I shall run quite mad!'

Privately, Georgianne was on the verge of thinking that her friend had already run mad but then, as she contemplated the succession of long dreary days ahead of her once Maitland had departed, she began to feel a good deal more sympathetic towards her friend. Whilst it was true that Stephanie was simply in love with the idea of life in high society—which could in no way compare with her own feelings for Will—she had no difficulty in relating to her friend's utter despair.

'Perhaps Aunt Letty's ball will help to cheer you up a little,' she said, trying to coax a smile from Stephanie's gloomy face. 'I am sure that your lovely gown will far outshine any of the others on display and—who knows—it's just vaguely possible that your elusive earl might turn up, after all. One should never give up hope, you know!'

'You really are the best of creatures, Georgie,' replied the slightly mollified Stephanie, immediately struck with the idea that, in her magnificent ballgown, she would undoubtedly be the Belle of the Ball—not that she had ever supposed otherwise, of course, but still…! 'How you can carry on day after day, sticking to the same boring old routine, I will never understand.'

'I don't actually find it all that boring,' returned Georgianne, somewhat defensively. 'I have my riding and I usually manage to fill my days quite productively. Added to which, it isn't every day that one gets to help organise such a big affair as Saturday's promises to be!'

'Well, if you want my opinion,' said her friend in reply, turning back towards the house, 'you would do far better taking more of an interest in sorting out your own outfit than concerning yourself with such mundane matters as floral arrangements and candle quantities!' she then added, as she followed her friend through the side door.

Once inside the house, however, it appeared that something of a heated argument was going on between some of the younger guests and their elders and no sooner had Georgianne put her nose round the drawing-room door than she was immediately dragged into the room by her cousin Delphine, a plump and pretty seventeen-year-old.

'Georgianne and her friend Miss Highsmith are sure to want to go!' declared the girl, with all the confidence of youth.

'Go where?' asked her cousin, mystified. But then, finding herself surrounded by a bevy of excited youngsters, each of whom was intent upon having his or her say, she placed both hands over her ears, crying, 'Do stop, please! One at a time, I beg of you!'

'They are trying to rake up your support to attend tonight's assembly at the Dun Cow in Dunchurch,' volunteered Catford, in the ensuing silence. 'Ma did wonder whether it might not be a bit too close to Saturday's proceedings, but some of the youngsters are quite determined. What do you think, Georgie?'

'The Dun Cow?' repeated Georgianne, a sudden spurt of excitement coursing through her body. But then, as common sense prevailed, she shook her head doubtfully. 'An assembly? I shouldn't have thought—'

'Oh, yes!' cried Stephanie, clapping her hands. 'The very thing! Do let us go, Georgianne!'

Georgianne looked across to her aunt, a question in her eyes. In reply, the countess simply smiled and gave a slight shrug. 'How many of you would like to attend?' she then enquired.

Seven or eight hands were immediately raised, which, as Georgianne quickly realised, comprised almost the entire group of youngsters present—those of an eligible age that was, since anyone under the age of sixteen would not be permitted entry to a public gathering.

'Fairly unanimous, I'd say!' chortled the young Lord Berkeley, a cousin from her uncle's side of the family.

'But you will need chaperons and carriages,' complained his mother, the Countess Darrowby. 'And I, for one, am not of a mind to spend the evening sitting in some stuffy assembly room, listening to a motley assortment of village fiddlers scraping away!'

As several of the other mothers leaned forwards to declare their support for the countess's declaration, Georgianne turned towards Catford, hoping for some guidance in the matter.

'Well, the carriages certainly ain't a problem,' he observed.

'And, I dare say I could drag myself there, if I had to. Ought to have at least one of you ladies in attendance, though,' he added pointedly, casting a frowning glance around the room.

An embarrassed silence followed until his grandmother, a very elderly dowager, let out an exasperated 'tsk!' and grunted, 'It looks as though it had better be me then, I suppose!'

'Bless you, Grandmama!' twinkled Catford, while three of the girls rushed to the old lady's side, threw their arms around her neck and showered her with kisses.

'Away with you all,' she chuckled, flapping her hands at them. 'And, you need not think that just because I am getting on in years, I am likely to turn a blind eye to any shenanigans, for my eyesight is as good now as it has ever been, so you had all better be on your best behaviour!'

'Oh, we will, we will!' came the effusive chorus from her youthful descendants.

'Well, if I am to stay up half the night,' remarked the dowager, rising to her feet with surprising alacrity for one of her advanced years, 'I had better get my head down for a couple of hours.' Then, making her way towards the door, she flung over her shoulder, 'I dare say this change of events will herald an early dinner, Letty?'

'I shall attend to it directly, *Belle-mère*,' replied the countess, in reply to her mother-in-law's query. 'Five o'clock would suit, I should imagine.'

Riding into the coaching yard at the end of another unsatisfactory day spent searching for the elusive Étienne Billingham, Maitland was surprised to find the place thronged with an unusually high number of assorted vehicles. Upon enquiring of Pete Andrews the reason for all this activity, he learned that it was all to do with the assembly that the Dun Cow held on the last Thursday of every month.

'A lot of the guests drive in from the outlying villages and prefer to stay overnight,' volunteered the ostler, as he took hold of Pegasus's halter while Maitland swung himself down from the horse's back.

Local assemblies being of very little interest to Maitland, he gave an indifferent shrug and asked, 'I suppose you don't happen to know if Mr Fenton has returned?'

It having been his normal practice to rap heavily on his cousin's door in order to drag him from his slumbers, he had been rather taken aback to discover that the Honourable Jeremy appeared to have forestalled him. Hurrying down to the dining room, in anticipation of finding his cousin tucking into what, by this time, had become his customary hearty breakfast, Maitland had been met by one of the waiters, who had handed him a note from the mysteriously absent Fenton. In it, his cousin, apologising for leaving Maitland to carry on with the search without him, had explained that he had a rather pressing matter to attend to and would, no doubt, catch up with him again at dinnertime!

'Drove in some time ago,' said Andrews, in response to Maitland's question. 'Got quite annoyed with me when I told him that I'd have to put his carriage on one of the back lots—need to keep the front clear for these overnighters, y'see.'

Naturally, the ex-sergeant was not about to divulge the fact that this particular arrangement had been at Matty Skinner's behest, in order that the crafty devil might be in the best position to select his next potential victim. Instead, since he was growing more and more anxious about the possibility of discovery, he enquired as to how much longer Maitland expected to remain in the area.

Given that, following today's fruitless journeying, he had picked just about every churchman's brain and thoroughly exhausted every possible venue for miles around, Maitland, as reluctant as he was to admit it, was beginning to find himself very close to giving up the quest altogether. He was fast coming to the conclusion that either Mr Hornsey had misheard his client's mumbled instructions or that Uncle Roger's memory had, rather unsurprisingly, after all these years, failed him.

He pursed his lips, considering the stableman's question. Then, 'Probably some time early next week,' he responded, with a decisive nod, having realised that it would be quite out of the question for him to leave before the Greshams' ball— not forgetting the following morning's ride he had promised himself! 'Have you finally made up your mind to accompany me, then? A very wise decision, in my opinion.'

'I doubt if I'll get a better offer, Major!' responded Andrews, with a quick look over his shoulder in order to ascertain that this rather unusual conversation between himself and one of the hotel guests had not been overheard. Then, eyes alight with gratitude, he added, 'Very much obliged to you, sir!'

Lifting his hand in dismissal of the man's thanks, Maitland gave a quick nod and turned to follow the highly excited group of newcomers that was presently making its way into the hotel's rear entrance. *Clearly*, he thought to himself, with a wry grimace, *it looks set to be a pretty noisy evening!*

Fenton, who had been sitting in the taproom, nervously contemplating his next move, leapt up eagerly as soon as Maitland stepped through the doorway.

'Extremely sorry to leave you in the lurch today, Will,' he said, as he signalled to a passing waiter and pulled out a chair for his cousin to join him. 'Had a rather pressing matter to attend to.'

'More money problems, Jerry?' returned Maitland, offering his cousin a sympathetic smile. 'Haven't I told you to come to me, if you find yourself in difficulty?'

'That's very true,' acknowledged Fenton. 'Dashed handsome of you, too, in the circumstances. As a matter of fact,' he then went on, his cheeks reddening slightly, 'I could do with a small loan—a couple of hundred—if you could manage to lay your hands on that amount?' *It was all very well for Stephanie to come up with this mad idea about elopements and such*, he thought morosely, *but these things didn't come cheap!*

'Consider it done, old man,' said Maitland, with a careless grin. 'I'll write you out a banker's draft and you can take it across to the Town & County first thing in the morning.'

'I swear I'll return it as soon as I'm in funds again, dear chap,' Fenton assured him fervently.

'Don't fret yourself, Jerry,' replied his cousin, turning his attention to the foaming tankard of ale that the waiter had placed in front of him. 'It's of no consequence.'

There followed a few minutes silence as the two men sipped at their drinks then, 'I forgot to ask you how you got on today, Will,' said Fenton. 'Drew the usual blank, I imagine?'

Maitland nodded. 'It's beginning to look as if the old fellow must have made a mistake in the location of this blessed convent or nunnery, or whatever. No one around here has ever heard of such a place. There seems to be nothing for it but to go back to Hornsey and admit defeat.' He looked across at his cousin, his eyes full of concern. ''Fraid that does mean that you're going to have to wait a full year before you can get your hands on any of Uncle Roger's blunt, old man. Is that going to pose a problem for you?'

Fenton gave a non-committal shrug. 'Dare say I might be able to weather the storm,' he replied. *As soon as Stephanie's old lady comes up with the dibs, that is!* he told himself reassuringly.

'Think I'll go on up,' said Maitland, quaffing back the last of his drink and rising to his feet. 'This place is getting a bit too crowded for my liking. I see that they're serving dinner in a smaller side room, so I don't think I'll bother—maybe just have a tray of bread and meat sent up and then try to get an early night. It's been a tiring day and I'm pretty well done in.'

'Doubt if you'll get much sleep when all the racket from the assembly room gets going,' replied his cousin, getting up to join him. But then, as a sudden thought struck him, he asked eagerly, 'You don't suppose any of the crowd up at Gresham Hall is likely to attend a function like this, do you?'

Maitland shook his head. 'Shouldn't think so for one minute,' he returned.

Chapter Fourteen

In the event, the landlady's plentiful selection of meats and cheeses remained scarcely touched as Maitland, reaching out for the bottle of brandy he had ordered along with his meal, refilled his glass for the third time and moodily lounged back in his armchair.

He wished to God that he had never allowed himself to be dragooned into volunteering his services for what had turned out to be, in all respects, a complete wild-goose chase. And, if that were not sufficiently demoralising, he thought, savagely, as he tossed back yet another mouthful of the fiery spirit, there was the added ignominy of having fallen head-over-heels in love with a girl who was, without doubt, the future intended of one of his dearest friends!

Having spent much of the day puzzling over why the pair seemed so set on preserving what was, to him, a rather unnatural silence about their attachment, he could only suppose that they were acting in accordance with some ancient family ritual or other that obliged them to wait for an official announcement. And, having followed this line of reasoning to what seemed to him to be the most logical end—given that the matrimonial intentions of the heir to the title were likely to be of considerable interest to a good many of the landed gentry in the area—he had arrived at the conclusion that the coming Saturday's ball would make an ideal occasion for such an announcement. All the more reason for him to cry off, he chastised himself, although he knew that he could no more do that than fly to the moon. As he had told Georgianne, it was not in him to admit defeat until every vestige of hope was gone—a quality that had always served him well enough in his days with the military, but one which, in the present circumstances, looked set to be of no use whatsoever!

The clatter of carriages pulling up to the hotel's front entrance brought him to his feet in an instant. Muttering imprecations under his breath, he strode over to the open window, intending to latch it shut against the worst of the noise. But then, as he focussed his somewhat bleary eyes on the two vehicles just below, he immediately snapped to attention. Gresham carriages, by Jove! And who should be stepping down from the first of them than the very subject of his melancholic reverie!

Carefully placing his still half-full glass back on the table, he walked across the room to the marble washstand, poured the entire contents of the jug into the washbowl and thrust his head into it, gritting his teeth as the chill of the water crept up over his ears.

The cold ducking having left him a good deal more alert than he had been five minutes previously, he towelled himself off briskly and, flinging open the wardrobe door, dragged out his dress-clothes. Ten minutes later, he was standing in front of his mirror, wrestling with a third attempt to arrange his necktie to his satisfaction and thanking a divine providence for the hotel's excellent laundry service!

His hair still slightly damp, he flew down the stairs to join the bustling crowd of noisy revellers that was presently making its way into the assembly room, the larger of the hotel's two dining rooms wherein, as he was soon able to see, the tables and chairs had been arranged around the walls in order to leave the centre of the floor clear for dancing.

Since there was still a good deal of movement going on around him, it was some little time before he managed to spot the Gresham party and he was somewhat taken aback to see that his cousin, Fenton, was already engaged in a deep conversation with Stephanie Highsmith. Doing his best to appear totally nonchalant, Maitland strolled across to the group and, with a courteous bow, paid his respects to the dowager countess.

'I must confess that I hardly expected to find you frequenting such a mediocre gathering, ma'am,' he said, endeavouring to keep his eyes off Georgianne, who looked quite entrancing in a simple chiffon gown of the palest green and her hair, as he was delighted to note, still dressed in the new softer style.

'I hardly expected to be here myself until a couple of hours ago,' replied the old lady, giving him what he could only describe as a rather searching look. 'But, the young folk would have it and, since it would seem that every one of my cow-hearted relations considered themselves far too high in the instep to put in an appearance, here, as you see, I am, young man!'

'For which I am quite certain that your young ladies are most grateful,' he said gallantly. 'Do I have your permission to solicit a dance with one or other of them?'

'Help yourself, Mr Maitland,' she chuckled, waving him away with her fan. 'Although, I dare say you might find that one or two of them are a little on the young side for you!'

'Not too young to dance with, I assure you, ma'am,' he grinned, as he turned to greet Catford who, having selected a nearby seat, was presently doing his best to assure two of his pretty young cousins that he was perfectly content to sit and watch, while they took to the floor.

'But couldn't you just try a line dance, Eddie?' cajoled Lady Alice, the more buxom of the pair. 'It's mostly only walking and I really shan't mind if you don't feel up to doing the twirling around!'

'Maybe later, Alice,' he replied, giving her a gentle smile. 'But, since the reason I agreed to bring you all here was so that you could all let off a little steam, I would feel happier to see you tripping the light fantastic with someone who is a little more sprightly than I am at present.' Cocking his head at Maitland, he raised a questioning eyebrow, to which signal his friend gave an immediate nod. 'I'm sure that Will here would be more than happy to twirl you around the floor.'

'Nothing would give me greater pleasure, Lady Alice,' lied Maitland, as he offered the girl his hand and led her across the floor to join the line of waiting couples. 'Although, I have to admit that it is some time since I indulged in one of these.' Groaning inwardly, he wondered why it had never occurred to him that country assemblies meant country dances.

'I hear that it was all cotillions and waltzes when you and Cousin Eddie were in Belgium,' said his young partner, as the fiddlers started up and the dance began. Looking across the room to find her cousin regarding her with a slightly wistful smile on his face, she added, 'The poor lamb was always such a good dancer!'

'And he will be again, I promise you,' replied Maitland reassuringly, as he stepped forwards to twirl the lady opposite around before returning her to her partner, then collecting his own partner again and moving on to change places with the pair on their left, in accordance with the movements of the dance. Out of the corner of his eye, he had caught a glimpse of Georgianne, some four or five couples further down the line and, mentally crossing his fingers in the fervent hope that the music would continue long enough for him to reach her, he tried to convince himself that a couple of twirls with her was better than nothing!

Sadly, when that moment did at last arrive, there was barely enough time for the two of them to exchange more than the briefest of greetings before the music compelled them to move on again.

To his great relief, the dance reached its conclusion on the next change and he was able to return his flushed and laughing partner to her grandmother's side.

'Thank you so much, Mr Maitland,' said Lady Alice, dipping her knee to him in a dainty curtsy. But then, as she turned to see her cousin rising stiffly to his feet, she cried, 'Oh, Eddie! You really must try to stop getting up every time one of us comes anywhere near you. At this rate, you will be up and down like a Jack-in-the-box all evening!'

'Can't be helped, my dear,' returned Catford, with a wry grin. 'I'm afraid I'm far too long in the tooth to change my ways now.'

'Then I shall stay here beside you and make sure that you do sit still,' she averred, as she plonked herself down at his side.

'I'm not a cripple, Alice,' the viscount reminded her gently. 'I wouldn't have brought you if I had known that you intended to waste the whole evening sitting next to me. Apart from which, I need to have a word with Will. Look, I see young Berkeley signalling you. So, do run along and enjoy yourself, there's a good girl.'

'You wanted to speak to me, Cat?' asked Maitland, unable to prevent a slight feeling of unease, as he lowered himself down on to the seat that Lady Alice had recently vacated. He could not help wondering whether Catford had taken offence at some aspect of the friendship that was developing between himself and Georgianne, but he need not have concerned himself, for the viscount merely wanted to thank him for all the time and effort he had put in that morning on his cousin's behalf.

'She was quite her old self again, when she got back,' he declared gleefully. 'I swear that it's been some time since I've seen her looking so happy. Whatever you are doing to bring her out of her shell, old chap, I beg you to keep up the good work!'

Maitland's eyes travelled sideways to where Georgianne was sitting, several places away, cheerfully chatting to her grandmother. Making up his mind, he rose quickly to his feet. 'Then, if you're sure you have no objection, Cat, I believe I might ask Miss Venables if she cares to take to the floor?'

'Why on earth do you think I would have any objections,' asked Catford, a puzzled frown on his face. But Maitland, his mind keenly focussed on the matter in hand, was already out of earshot.

'I trust that you will give me the pleasure, Miss Venables?' he said, holding out his hand and willing her to accept.

'Off you go, Georgianne,' ordered the dowager, pointedly digging her granddaughter in the ribs. 'You didn't come here to sit nattering to me all night!'

'Don't talk nonsense, Grandmama!' laughed Georgianne, as she rose to her feet and placed her hand into Maitland's. 'You know perfectly well that I hang on your every word!'

'Humph!' retorted the old lady, making skilful use of her fan to hide her smile. 'Take her away, young man!'

With a contented grin on his face, Maitland was only too happy to oblige her ladyship. It was, however, somewhat disheartening to discover, as he was shortly about to do, that the dance into which he was leading Georgianne was nothing more than an eightsome reel, a fairly boisterous dance that rendered conversation impossible. Nevertheless, it was better than nothing, he told himself.

Georgianne, for her part, had been delighted to find

Maitland in attendance at the assembly for, as she had frequently heard her older cousins remark, 'Most gentlemen are hardly likely to opt for dancing if they are faced with a selection of other manly pursuits!' Therefore, she was more than gratified to be dancing with him, eightsome reel or no.

After her visit to the stables that morning, when Everton had assured her that Olympus was responding very nicely to her treatment, followed by the highly exhilarating gallop that had quickly restored any possible loss of self-confidence that she might have suffered, she had made up her mind to make the most of every one of the precious minutes in which she found herself alone with her cousin's friend. For, if she were any judge, there were bound not to be that many left. Along with the rest of her family, she was well aware that he and his cousin had scoured the whole area and beyond for some clue as to his missing relative and, whilst she could not help but be sorry that all of Maitland's hard effort had come to nought, her most pressing regret was that this failure to turn up any useful information would mean only one thing. His imminent departure!

With that rather depressing prospect now uppermost in her mind, she then proceeded to fling herself wholeheartedly into the dance, bestowing upon him the widest of smiles at every turn and retaining hold of his hand for the merest fraction of a second longer than was, perhaps, altogether necessary. All of which rather unexpected behaviour on her part being more than enough to render her already highly vulnerable partner into a state of utter confusion.

In truth, Maitland was finding that he could scarcely take his eyes off her, so completely mesmerised was he by her curving lips, her dimpling cheeks—not to mention the highly provocative swaying movements of her body as she chasséed gracefully across the circle! And what in God's name was that challenging expression in her eyes all about? he asked himself in bewilderment. Had he not known better, he would have been prepared to swear that his good friend Catford's future bride was actually flirting with him!

It was with a certain amount of relief that he heard the fiddlers executing their final tuneful flourish, signalling not only the end of that particular set of dances, but also the call to the supper room.

Unfurling her fan, Georgianne wafted it to and fro in an effort to cool her heated cheeks. 'That was almost as invigorating as this morning's gallop, Mr Maitland,' she proclaimed breathlessly, as she tucked her hand into the crook of his arm and gave him another of her captivating smiles. 'I can hardly wait for tomorrow's run!'

'You are still intent upon repeating this morning's exercise, then?' ventured Maitland, in a vain attempt to divert his mind from the prurient fantasies that were presently taking shape therein.

'Goodness me, no!' she replied, with a gurgling laugh that did nothing to help Maitland's struggle to maintain his composure. 'I was rather hoping that we might take a run across the heath—Brandy proved not to be too bad, as it happens, but we can really put her through her paces out on the heath.'

'You aren't nervous about meeting up with this dreaded highwayman, then?' he asked curiously. Every other female he had come across had blanched with fear at the very mention of the subject.

'Well, I might be, if it were later in the day and if I were travelling in one of Gresham's carriages, with a few hundred pounds' worth of jewellery slung round my neck.' She twinkled up at him. 'But, in my opinion, no highwayman worth his salt is going to drag himself out of bed at sunrise to accost a couple of mere riders when some of this potential booty—' she waved her hand around the room, indicating the large number of females present who were quite happily displaying their largesse upon their necks and fingers '—could well be his for the taking a couple of hours later.'

'That's quite true,' he acquiesced, as he shepherded her into the crowded supper room where, upon looking around, he perceived that Catford had already commandeered a table for his party. 'But the man would be a fool if he chose to strike tomorrow. I believe that the local watch committee has already drafted in the militia. As a matter of fact, I have it on good authority that there is a troop of dragoons quartered around the town.'

'Well, that's settled it, then,' replied Georgianne, taking her seat, with a satisfied nod. 'And, since it is highly unlikely that any of this present company will rouse themselves from their slumbers much before ten o'clock, we will have the heath to ourselves and be back home long before the rest of the world is even stirring!'

'I look forward to it,' returned Maitland, with a slightly forced smile, not entirely sure whether, in fact, he did or not. However, he was more than certain that the feeling of utter helplessness that had threatened to engulf him not five minutes earlier was not an experience that he cared to repeat. And if, on the morrow's outing, Georgianne chose to continue her pitiless bombardment on his fragile emotions, he might well find himself to obliged to disregard the fact that he was a gentleman and teach her a lesson that she would not easily forget!

Chapter Fifteen

❦

Despite the thoroughly depressing pall that hung over the sky, doubtless heralding a bout of heavy rain at some point in the not too distant future, it was a determinedly cheerful Maitland who rode into Gresham Hall's stableyard at precisely five minutes to seven on the following morning. Having spent a decidedly restless night pondering over Georgianne's far from usual behaviour during the assembly, he had reached the conclusion that, in all probability, his earlier over-indulgence with the brandy bottle might well have caused his imagination to run wild. He hadn't *felt* tipsy, it was true—not until she had flashed him one of her bewitching smiles, that was—but, nevertheless, the whole extraordinary experience had been, in many ways, not a great deal different from partaking of one too many shots of strong spirit!

Upon his arrival, an equally cheery Georgianne greeted him with a welcoming smile. 'Everton reckons we might be due for a shower or two,' she called, as the groom hoisted her up on to her saddle.

'Would you rather not go?' asked Maitland, a sudden disappointment washing over him.

'Good heavens, no!' Georgianne laughed. 'Do you take me

for some sort of milksop? I won't melt, I promise you—a little spot of rain never hurt anyone!'

'So be it.' He grinned. 'But don't blame me if that perky feather of yours gets ruined!'

'Well, I dare say a feather can easily be replaced,' she said, complacently fingering the flaming red cockade that decorated the front of her jaunty shako and thanking Providence that she had allowed her aunt to talk her into having Madame Henri design her this dashing new habit which, to her immense satisfaction, had been delivered late yesterday afternoon. Quite severely cut and based upon the prevailing fashion for all things military, the midnight blue jacket clung to her curves like a second skin and she was sure that she had not imagined the flash of admiration in Maitland's eyes when he had first caught sight of her. On the previous morning, she had been obliged to wear the shabby old habit that she had worn on the day of the accident, but the unpleasant memories it had conjured up had left her feeling quite uneasy and she had been only too glad to instruct her maid, Emily, to finally dispose of it. After all, she reasoned, if one does intend to indulge in a little harmless flirtation, one might as well look one's best whilst one is at it!

'Off to the heath, then?' she called back to him, as she headed out of the gate in front of him. 'We can cut across the fields and skirt around Dunchurch.'

They rode off in a companionable silence, Maitland holding back slightly, to allow her mare to keep pace with his own mount. By the time they had reached the fringes of the heath, however, the ominous rumble of thunder could already be heard in the distance.

'Looks to be moving in this direction, I'm afraid,' declared Maitland, pointing over to the heavy bank of clouds on the low horizon just ahead of them. 'Are you sure that you want to carry on? We could be in for a jolly good soaking, you know!'

For the briefest of moments, Georgianne hesitated, torn between the prospect of getting her smart new outfit wet and losing out on this precious hour or so alone with Maitland. Then, reminding herself that new riding habits were far easier to come by than once-in-a-lifetime opportunities like this one, she gave a decisive nod.

'There's an old shepherd's bothy by the quarry over there,' she said, indicating the direction with her crop. 'If we set off now, we would be sure to reach it well before the storm hits— I dare say that we could shelter there until it blows over.'

'How far?' he asked, still eyeing the ever-darkening clouds and trying to gauge the speed at which they were moving.

'Oh, about three to four miles or so, I should think— are you game?'

Poised to spring her mare, she tilted her chin at him, a challenging gleam in her eyes and her lips curved in a beatific smile and, even though Maitland was vaguely aware of the sound of alarm bells echoing through his brain, signalling to him that what he was about to do was not at all wise, he chose to ignore the warning.

'I'm game,' he answered, with a grin, as he gathered up his reins. 'Off we go, then!'

Heads bent and bodies crouched well down in their saddles, the pair set off at a gallop. Pointing their horses' noses in the direction that Georgianne had indicated, meeting up only with the occasional group of sheep, they sped across the heath, with the occasional shallow stream they encountered posing no difficulty and the frequent clumps of gorse that grew in random confusion about the place merely providing them with an added challenge to their horsemanship.

Unfortunately, Georgianne's rather casual estimation of the distance to the shelter turned out to be somewhat on the optimistic side. Added to which, the band of murky weather appeared to be moving towards the two riders at a much greater rate than Maitland had originally anticipated. The disused shelter was still several hundred yards ahead of them when a blinding flash of lightning, followed almost instantly by a tremendous thunderclap, announced that the impending storm was now almost directly overhead.

'Can you make it, do you think?' Maitland yelled at Georgianne, as the pair raced towards the bothy. Having already been obliged to cut back his speed, in order to allow the little mare to keep up with Pegasus—who was well used to headlong charges of this sort—he was afraid that the wetting he had predicted was about to become an uncomfortable reality.

Since the first spatterings of the promised deluge were already lashing against her face and running down the back of her neck, Georgianne did not bother to reply. Instead, she determinedly applied her crop to Brandy's rump, urging her, 'Come on, girl—you can do it!'

Less than five minutes later, both horses skidded to a halt outside the windowless bothy, the walls of which were constructed of stone that had been roughly hewn from the nearby quarry a good many years earlier. Having long outlived its original purpose of providing shelter for sheepherders, it was now used only by the odd passing vagrant—apart from its recent use as a bolthole for occasional highwaymen!

Leaping from his own mount, Maitland bounded to Georgianne's side where, without further ceremony, he proceeded to haul her out of her saddle in a far from gentle manner and, thrusting open the cabin's still solid oaken door, he hustled her inside.

'Get your jacket off!' he ordered her, hurriedly stripping off his riding gloves and easing his shoulders out of his own. 'No point in letting the damp seep through to our shirts! We can hang them over there,' he then added, having spotted a series of nails sticking out of the wall on the far side of the cabin. 'Luckily for us, much of the gorse thatching seems to have survived intact.'

He had been so occupied with investigating their surroundings that, apart from his instruction that she remove her jacket, he had not paid Georgianne a great deal of attention but now, turning to face her, with the intention of relieving her of her damp garment, he stood momentarily transfixed at the scene in front of him.

Having removed both her jacket and her hat, Georgianne had unfastened several of the buttons on her blouse and was now in the process of unwinding her neckcloth, intending to use the article to towel off her face and hair.

'I found a nail of my own,' she said complacently, nodding to where her own jacket now hung on the wall beside her. 'You were right about the feather, though—I fear that it is sadly ruined!'

Maitland took a step towards her, then stopped. 'I dare say that it can be replaced,' he said, his tone deliberately flat. *Of all the places to find myself holed up with her*, he was thinking, as he stared grimly out of the open doorway at the rain-swept landscape beyond. *And, by the look of things, we could be here for hours!*

'Oh, no, I shouldn't think so,' came Georgianne's reply as, with a sudden start, he realised that he had spoken his last thought out loud. 'These summer storms seldom last more than a quarter of an hour or so—we have them regularly. It helps to clear the air, so I'm told.'

She was trying her utmost to appear cheerful which, in the circumstances of feeling decidedly damp and dishevelled, was not easily achieved. But, since she was well aware that the pair's enforced wetting had been brought about by her own stubborn refusal to either postpone or turn back from the ride across the heath, her conscience was beginning to trouble her. Added to which, it was becoming increasingly apparent that Maitland was not best pleased to have found himself in this situation—a situation which, as she was well aware, could easily be construed by those of a salacious turn of mind as being somewhat compromising! As the disquieting thought that her actions might have found disfavour with him filtered itself into her brain, a feeling of complete desolation came over, causing a sudden tremor to run through her body.

'I'm really very sorry,' she began, looking across at him, the beginnings of tears already glistening in her eyes but, before she could finish her sentence, a muttered expletive had slipped from his lips and, in two short strides, he was at her side where, enveloping her in his arms, he hugged her closely to his chest.

'Good God, you're shivering, you poor darling!' he murmured, doing his utmost to ignore the tantalising scent of jasmine that nearly threatened to destroy his self-control. With their bodies separated by only a few thin layers of fabric, it was impossible to discern whether it was his own or Georgianne's heart that was pounding so violently. Unable to prevent himself, he tightened his hold and buried his face into her perfumed tresses, his lips pressed against her brow.

Georgianne who, until that moment, had been in something of a seventh heaven to find herself nestled so tenderly within the circle of Maitland's arms, gradually became aware of the gentle movement of his lips against her skin, at which totally unanticipated turn of events, her eyes flew open in astonishment. Was it possible that he was actually going to kiss her? she wondered, in disbelieving awe. At which incredible notion her heart gave a wild jolt of combined joy and anticipation. Even Cedric Tatler, her erstwhile suitor, despite having declared his undying love for her, had never actually gone so far as to offer her more than a surreptitious peck on the cheek. Although she scarcely dared to take a breath, lest she ruined the spell, she tilted her head slightly, powerless to prevent either the expectant gleam that lit up her eyes or the hint of the smile that threatened to form.

As he raised his head, Maitland's questioning eyes sought hers and, even though he found it impossible to comprehend what he believed he saw in their depths, a shudder of longing ran through him. He let out a little groan and, without a second thought, he lowered his mouth to meet hers. Almost tentative, his kiss was sweetly gentle to begin with, for he was still sufficiently in command of his senses not to wish to alarm her. But then as, with a sudden leap of excitement, he became aware of Georgianne's hands slowly creeping up around his neck, his desire mounted and the kiss deepened. His arms tightened compulsively as, pulling the provocative softness of her yielding curves to fit more snugly against his own taut masculinity, he lost himself completely in the magic of her eager response.

Equally spellbound, Georgianne could hardly believe what was happening. Whilst it was true that she had hoped for another day or two of Maitland's free-and-easy companion-ship, any real romantic involvement between the two of them had not entered the picture—it being totally out of the question, in any event. That she had fallen hopelessly in love with the man was beside the point, since he had given her no reason to suppose that he regarded her as anything more than his friend's rather tiresome young relative. Putting aside the disquieting likelihood that it might well have been her own rather outrageous behaviour that had encouraged him into this precipitous course of action, she surrendered herself to the moment and returned his kiss with vigour.

Very gradually, the full enormity of what was happening

began to seep into Maitland's brain until suddenly, as though a bucket of ice-cold water had been flung over him, he snapped to attention. With an odd guttural sound that was halfway between a sob and a groan, he uncoupled Georgianne's hands from his neck and thrust himself away from her.

'Oh, God, I'm so sorry!' he panted, staring down at her, his expression an odd mixture of self-revulsion and utter chagrin. 'Catford will never forgive me!'

Still reeling from the shock of the unexpected abandonment, it took Georgianne some little while to register his words. *Catford?* she thought, her brow furrowing in a puzzled frown.

Taking a deep breath, having just experienced the most heady and fulfilling moments of her life, she was not yet entirely in control of her senses. Fumbling hopelessly with her top buttons in an effort to focus her mind, she blurted out, somewhat irritably, 'I doubt that he is likely to find out, unless one or other of us feels obliged to inform him!'

He spun round to face her, a questioning look in his eyes. 'And you don't intend to?' he asked, rather too eagerly for Georgianne's liking.

Her heart plummeted and she was filled with a deep sense of humiliation. Whilst she was well aware of the close camaraderie that existed between Maitland and her cousin, she found it hard to believe that the two men confided every single one of their innermost secrets to each other and, as for what had actually happened—*well, dammit*, she thought, with an angry shrug, *it was only a kiss!* And, whilst it was true that, to her, it had been a truly heart-stopping experience, she was reasonably sure that it could not have affected Maitland to any similar degree. He was, after all, a man of the world and although it had not escaped her that he had, for a short while at least, shown rather a partiality for her friend, Stephanie—for whom that state of affairs was an almost everyday occurrence— Georgianne still could not find it in her heart to think him a philanderer.

'It was only a kiss!' she retorted, reaching for her still-damp stock and, with a slight grimace, winding it quickly around her neck. 'Hardly a hanging matter, in my opinion. Why you would think that I should wish to mention the matter to anyone else, I simply cannot imagine!'

Somewhat stunned to hear that Georgianne appeared to be perfectly content to dismiss what had just happened between them as having been of little account, Maitland, unable to conjure up a suitable reply, thought it best to remain silent. In point of fact, for one fleeting moment, he began to wonder whether it was possible that she actually made a habit of flirting with the friends of her prospective groom—a thought that he quickly dismissed as soon as it entered his head! Probably just a last grasp at freedom before she ties the knot, he persuaded himself, for he could not bear to think of her as perfidious. Nevertheless, if she had no intention of broadcasting the event about the place, then he would do as well to put it right out of his mind—if he could, that was! The recollection of her deliciously yielding lips pressed against his own was a memory that he would find nigh on impossible to forget!

In an effort to distract his mind from the impious thoughts that persisted, he strode to the doorway to determine the state of the weather.

'It seems that you were right,' he said, turning back to Georgianne. 'There's a distinct lightening in the sky and the rain has eased off considerably. Another five minutes or so should do it.'

'That's good,' she replied, in a purposefully non-committal tone, as she continued to do up her jacket buttons. 'Our poor horses will be glad to get back in the dry. They won't have enjoyed being out there in all that rain.'

'I dare say they will have managed to find themselves a bit of shelter somewhere or other,' he said, in an effort to reassure her. 'Horses are usually pretty good at making the best of things, whatever the weather—a-hah! The rain has finally stopped, I see! I'll just go and give your saddle a quick wipe and then we can be on our way.'

Grabbing his jacket from its improvised hook, he shrugged himself into it and made his way round to the corner of the building where, as he had supposed, the two horses had managed to huddle together under the overhanging eaves of the thatch and were now quite contentedly cropping the wet grass at their feet.

'Good lad!' he said, giving Pegasus's nose a swift pat then, pulling out his handkerchief, he proceeded to apply it vigorously to Brandy's saddle. By which time, Georgianne had reached his side.

'All ready to go?' he asked, in as cheery a tone as he could muster.

At her brief nod, he put his hands around her waist and, willing his mind to blank out everything but the job in hand, he tossed her up on to her saddle, steadying the mare's head while her rider rearranged her skirt and settled herself into her seat.

Then, without further ado, he leapt up on to his own mount, gathered up the reins and, with Georgianne at his heels, started to head back in the direction they had come.

The ride back to the stableyard was completed in total silence. And, not in a breathless gallop as their outward journey had been, but in an unsatisfactory jog-trot, with each of them choosing to make his or her own way through the multitude of deep puddles that had collected in the hollows of the scrubland as a result of the storm.

* * *

When, at last, they reached the Hall, an anxious-faced groom ran out to take Brandy's head, while Georgianne let herself down on to the mounting-block.

'We was all gettin' a bit worried about you, miss,' he confided, his young voice filled with concern. 'His lordship has been talking about sending out a search party!'

'Thank you, Dick,' she replied, and although she was feeling singularly tired and depressed, she managed to give the lad what was intended to be a smile of reassurance. 'Mr Maitland and I did manage to find shelter for the worst of it. I suppose I had better go and inform Lord Catford of our safe return.' Then, turning to face Maitland, who had remained in his saddle, she asked, somewhat hesitantly, 'Will you be free to ride again tomorrow morning, Mr Maitland?'

For several moments he made no response, fighting with his conscience while every nerve in his body willed him to answer in the affirmative then, very reluctantly, he shook his head. 'I think not, Miss Venables, if you will forgive me. I believe I shall be leaving in the next day or so and there are one or two matters that need my attention before I go.'

She stepped closer, the distress in her eyes plain to see. 'But you will still be attending my aunt's ball tomorrow night, I trust?'

It was only with considerable strength of will that Maitland managed to restrain himself from reaching out his hand to caress her cheek.

'I shall certainly endeavour to put in an appearance,' he replied. 'If only to bid you all *adieu*!'

As her eyes followed his progress out of the yard, Georgianne's heart made a rapid descent into her boots. *Gone, and without even a backward glance*, she thought glumly, as she trudged towards the back porch, trying to console herself with the fact that, no matter how much she wished it to the contrary, it would all have come to nought in the end. Fighting back the tears that threatened, she reminded herself of the vow she had taken—to simply enjoy every moment of Will Maitland's company while she could and then return to her normal way of life, hugging her precious secret to her heart. Now, due to a foolish indiscretion on her part, the whole affair had gone badly wrong! Even the still vivid memory of his kiss failed to jolt her out of her fit of the dismals, since Maitland had given her every reason to suppose that he deeply regretted the incident, even seeming to be more concerned with what his friend might think of his behaviour than of any feelings *she* might have on the matter!

But then, with a determined toss of her head, she pulled off her boots, straightened her shoulders and padded across to the library where, according to his usual custom, Cat was sure to be ensconced with the morning papers. And, whilst her normal good sense was telling her that she would simply have to put the whole miserable business out of her mind and chalk it down to experience, her innermost self was pointing out that this course of action, in fact, looked likely to prove a great deal more heart-wrenching than she had originally supposed.

Chapter Sixteen

Unable to face the prospect of returning to the Dun Cow where, after the previous evening's social gathering, he knew that he was only too likely to find himself surrounded by hordes of noisy, rumbustious strangers, Maitland sought out a small inn some distance away from the little market town and ordered up a hefty breakfast.

After just a few mouthfuls, however, he was obliged to push the plate away, the continual recoiling of his stomach, as the morning's disastrous happenings played and replayed themselves in his mind, preventing him from doing justice to the landlady's tasty offerings.

If only he could get away right now, he thought to himself, he could no doubt find plenty to occupy his mind when he got back to Ravenhill, the family estate in Buckinghamshire. Or, perhaps, he could collect a few of his friends and spend a couple of weeks up at his hunting lodge in the Lake District, or maybe even pay a visit to London—it had been some months since he had spent any time in the capital.

But then, as he well knew, none of these diversions would serve to cure him of this painful ache deep within his heart. Not only had he committed the cardinal sin of falling in love with a one-time comrade-in-arms's betrothed, he had actually had the temerity to try to make love to her! And, despite Georgianne's casual reference to it having been 'only a kiss', he knew better. For him, at least, it had been an earth-shattering, never-to-be-forgotten moment of unalloyed enchantment! Nevertheless, whilst he realised that putting in an appearance at Lady Letitia's ball on the following evening was not something that he could, in all conscience, avoid, he could not, for the life of him, see how he was ever going to look Catford in the eye again!

Sunk in the pit of his own sense of hopelessness, he failed to notice the passage of time until, jerked back to dismal reality by the noisy arrival of a group of excited and highly voluble individuals, he leaned back in his chair, stretched and got to his feet, anxious to leave as quickly as possible. His way, however, was blocked by one of the aforementioned individuals who, after raising his glass to him, exclaimed, 'Great news, eh? Now we can all sleep safely in our beds again!'

Maitland gave a puzzled frown. 'I beg your pardon?' he said, in the most courteous tone that he could muster, in his present frame of mind.

'Good God, man!' cried one of the man's companions, turning from the bar in surprise. 'You mean you haven't heard? They've finally caught the slippery little devil!'

'Slippery little devil?' repeated Maitland, still perplexed, but then, as the man's meaning suddenly dawned upon him, his face cleared and he gave an appreciative smile. 'I take it that you are referring to the notorious highwayman? Caught him at last, have they?'

The first man nodded. 'Better than that!' he crowed excitedly. 'Dead as the proverbial doornail, he is! Young Jack Stamford—Squire Stamford's lad, that is—whipped out his pistol and shot the beggar clean through the head!'

'Good for him!' said Maitland approvingly. 'Have they managed to identify him—the highwayman, that is? There was some talk of him being a local man.'

'Yes, indeed,' returned the man. 'Turns out he was one of the stable hands at the Dun Cow—ideal base from which to plan such capers, if you want my opinion. The devil was an ex-army chap too, by all accounts!'

He then went on at some length about what he had seen and what he had heard, but Maitland was no longer listening to him.

An ex-army chap! Surely to God he can't be talking about Pete Andrews, he thought in dismay and, turning swiftly on his heel, he made for the door, rudely cutting off his would-be raconteur in mid-sentence.

Having already paid his shot, he collected Pegasus and hurried back to the Dun Cow, where he found the stableyard, much as he had feared, swarming with a huge press of individuals, including a full troop of dragoons, complete with their mounts. Of Pete Andrews, there was no sign. Indeed, as Maitland very quickly realised, when he looked for someone to relieve him of his horse, there was not a single ostler or stable-hand to be found.

Hurriedly looping Pegasus's reins over a convenient hitching-post, he shouldered his way through the crowds of curious bystanders who had turned up—no doubt hoping to catch sight of the dead highwayman's grisly remains, he thought grimly—and headed for the equally crowded taproom.

Craning his head, he spotted his cousin Fenton, who was loudly giving forth to anyone who cared to listen that he was not at all sorry to hear of the fellow's demise, since he himself had always known him to be a villain! 'Why, only the other day,' he declared, his face full of indignation, 'the damned scoundrel knocked over a bucket of horse dung directly in my path and almost ruined a perfectly good pair of boots!'

'Did you get the man's name?' demanded Maitland who, having eventually succeeded in reaching him, clutched at his arm with some urgency.

Turning to see who was handling his best jacket with so little respect, his cousin exclaimed, 'Oh, there you are, Will!' Then, after drawing him to one side, he demanded, 'Where on earth have you been all this time? The most amazing thing has happened! You know that chap who used to—'

'Yes, I've heard all about it,' Maitland cut in curtly. 'Do you happen to know what the fellow's name is?'

Fenton looked affronted. ''Course I know what his name is! Should've thought the whole town knows what his name is! Haven't I just been telling you?'

Maitland closed his eyes, willing himself to keep his temper. 'Is it Pete Andrews?' he asked quietly.

'Pete Andrews?' Confused, Fenton stared at his cousin. 'No, of course it ain't Pete Andrews! The fellow's name is Skinner—Matthew Skinner—if I have it correctly.'

Relief swept through Maitland like a breath of fresh air. 'Thank God for that!' he murmured, almost to himself, then, 'What's happened to all the other stable hands?' he enquired.

'Been taken over to the magistrate's house for questioning,' answered his cousin, jerking his head in the direction of the church, next to which the house of the town's guardian of the law was situated. 'Dare say they figure that there might have been others involved!'

Head bent and hands clasped tightly between his knees, Pete Andrews stared down in moody silence at the black-and-white marble tiles beneath his feet. Along with the rest of the stable staff, some twelve men in all, he was waiting his turn for the expected grilling. Since those who had gone before had been taken out of the house by a different exit, it had been impossible for him to quiz any of them as to the exact nature of the questioning, which made it rather difficult to prepare acceptable answers in advance. Added to which, having been taken completely by surprise at the sudden turn of events following Matty's fateful decision to make Squire Stamford his next objective, Andrews had been unable to get hold of Josh Todd to make sure that their stories tallied. And Josh, as he well knew, had never been the sharpest knife in the box! God only knew what tale he might be spinning in there at this very moment!

He took his mind back through the course of events that had led up to the precarious situation in which he now found himself. Despite the fact that both he and Todd had voiced strenuous objections to the scheme, on the perfectly reasonable grounds that the whole area was now crawling with dragoons, Skinner, pointing out that they were never likely to get such a golden opportunity as this looked set to be, had dismissed their cautions with a contemptuous sneer. Swiftly pointing out the many advantages to be gained from such a choice, the gang's ringleader had then selected the mild-mannered Squire Stamford as his intended target, saddled up a horse and, after issuing the uneasy pair with the usual instructions, had ridden off several minutes before the squire's carriage was ready to leave the yard.

Having been regarded as something of a whip in his salad days, the easygoing squire still liked to take the reins himself, which meant that, in the event of being told to 'Stand and deliver!', there would be no time for him to prime his weapon, if indeed he carried one! In addition, the man's concern for the safety of his buxom young wife and two lovely daughters would surely preclude him from putting up any sort of a fight. As to the presence of Stamford's sixteen-year-old son, Jack, Skinner had already dismissed him as being of little consequence, having observed that the rather scrawny youth had spent the better part of the previous evening vainly trying to persuade one of the barmaids to give him a kiss.

What he had not realised, however, as he later found out to his cost, was that the squire, in an effort to instil a sense of heritage into his son and heir, had lately arranged for the boy to accompany his estate manager on his daily rounds. Since the estate manager was, by necessity, something of a crack marksman, it was hardly surprising that he should have elected to pass on some of his expertise to his highly enthusiastic pupil. In fact, after less than three weeks of this skilled tuition, Jack Stamford had developed into quite a fair shot and, although his father had instructed him to leave his newly acquired pistol at home, he had, nevertheless, tucked it into the side pocket of the family carriage. Unobserved by his mother and his two sisters, who had been deeply engrossed in their discussion of the various merits of the girls' partners at the previous evening's assembly, he had been covertly tinkering with his latest acquisition, loading and unloading it, in an effort to see just how quickly he could prime it up for action—a proficiency that his mentor had assured him might well save his life one day!

For Matty Skinner, unfortunately, that day turned out to be rather sooner than the youngster had expected. As a result of which, having previously been dismissed as a spotty, somewhat weedy individual of little account, Jack Stamford now found himself regarded as one of the greatest heroes in local history—with pretty barmaids a-plenty simply begging for his attention!

Insofar as the magistrate, Sir Joseph Kerridge, and his two colleagues were concerned, Squire Stamford's sworn statement was really all that they needed to declare the matter an open-and-shut-case—especially since a large cache of money and several previously purloined valuables had been found hidden away under a floorboard in Skinner's bed-chamber. Nevertheless, since the affair had attracted a great deal of attention in the town and neighbouring districts, these three worthies, ever conscious of their public image, were also inclined to the belief that it would do them no harm at all to puff up their consequence by appearing to deliberate more solemnly on an issue of such magnitude.

In the event, all they actually did was to ask each of the respondents whether they had ever seen Matty Skinner borrow a horse from the Dun Cow's stables or advertise an unusually plentiful amount of cash. Since the answer in every case was, as they had supposed from the start, always in the negative, by the time the tribunal got to Josh Todd and Pete Andrews, Sir Joseph and his fellow councillors were beginning to get rather bored with the whole proceedings. Added to which, since the hour was now approaching five o'clock, it was well past their dinner time.

As a result of this somewhat dilatory approach to what should have been a much more thorough investigation, when Pete Andrews finally stepped out of the front door of Sir Joseph's town house, it was with a far lighter step than he had entered it some hours earlier. On returning to the stable-yard, he was immediately accosted by the rest of the stable hands, demanding to know what questions he had been asked and whether he had given the same answers as they had. However, they were given no time to speculate upon the matter, due to the arrival of Cunliffe, the inn's somewhat harassed landlord who, along with several of his bar staff, had been obliged to deal with the comings and goings of four stagecoaches, in addition to their normal workload.

'Now, come along!' he chivvied them. 'We're all glad the

whole nasty business is over and done with, but your absence has put us well behind-hand! A good many of our customers have been waiting for their carriages for several hours—so step to it, lads!'

Maitland, too, had hurried out to enquire as to Andrews's welfare.

'Skinner getting shot like that must have come as a bit of a shock to you, old chap,' he said, fixing his ex-sergeant with a sympathetic smile. 'The sooner the two of us are out of here the better, as far as I can see. If you could make yourself available to travel on Monday morning, I'll see about organising you a horse from the livery stables.'

'Thank you, sir,' came Andrews's heartfelt reply. 'It'll take me no time at all to put my few bits and pieces together. I'll be ready to leave as soon as you are, I promise you!'

Could it be that Lady Luck was about to smile at him at long last? he then wondered, as Maitland, with a satisfied nod, left him and strode back into the hotel. It just remained to have a quiet word with Josh Todd and then he would be free to go and put all this foolhardiness behind him.

Unfortunately, it was not until the last of the delayed carriages had been sent on their way, the stables mucked out and all the horses fed and watered, that Andrews was finally able to confront his fellow partner-in-crime.

'You're certain that they didn't suspect you?' he asked, as the paired trudged back to their shared lodgings.

Todd shook his head. 'Shouldn't think so,' he replied. 'After all that 'anging about, I were only in there for about five minutes and then all I got to say was "No"! Just the same as the other fellows, it seems. They all think that Sir Joseph was just tryin' to make a meal of it.' Pausing, he shot a quick sideways look at his companion, before muttering, 'Rotten shame about poor old Matty, though!'

'Well, he wouldn't be warned,' replied Andrews quietly. 'And, don't you forget that it could well have been either one of *us* on the receiving end of that lad's pistol! I'm only too relieved that the whole business is over and done with at last—I was never that keen on it, in the first place!'

'You and me both!' exclaimed Todd. 'Didn't make much out of the caper, at any rate—although from what I've 'eard, Matt's pickin's seem to 'ave been a sight better than ours ever was!'

'So I heard.' The ex-sergeant nodded. 'I just hope that they found everything.'

'How d'yer mean?' demanded Todd as, standing stock-still in the lane, he turned and faced his companion. 'You think 'e might 'ave stashed some more somewhere?'

'Well, I wouldn't put it past the greedy beggar,' returned Andrews, with an indifferent shrug. 'But I was really wondering about the old bothy—I've a mind to go out there just to make sure that none of us left anything incriminating lying around.'

'Well, there'll be no more 'elpin' ourselves to 'orses from now on,' Todd was swift to point out. 'Old Cunliffe will be watchin' us all like an 'awk! So, it'll 'ave to be a five-mile 'ike each way. Don't fancy it meself!'

'Don't worry, I'll see to it,' averred Andrews, with a resigned sigh. 'We used to walk far greater distances than that when we were tramping over France and Spain. This should be a doddle, compared with that sort of terrain!' He paused, ruminating over the matter for a moment or two, before adding, 'Sunday morning will be the best time—most folks are at church then and, if you're prepared to cover for me, I should be able to slip away for a couple of hours without anyone noticing.'

'Sooner you than me,' retorted Todd, as the two men walked up the pathway to their lodging-house. 'Mind you, I'm not so sure that I wouldn't rather be doin' that than what we 'ave to do right now!'

Andrews frowned. 'How do you mean?' he asked, as he pushed open the door.

'Facin' up to Matty's old uncle, that's what,' muttered Todd. 'After you, mate!'

Chapter Seventeen

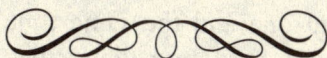

Georgianne was finding it increasingly difficult to concentrate her mind on the various tasks she had set herself. Contrary to her aunt's wishes, she had insisted upon seeing to the arrangement of the flowers in the ballroom herself, which was no minor undertaking.

'But I really would prefer it if you were to take yourself off and read a book or sit down and do your sewing, my dear,' Lady Letitia had protested. 'In my opinion, you are not looking at all the thing. I am quite sure that you have been overdoing things. First that nasty fall and then going off yesterday and getting yourself soaked—you really should be taking things easy! Mrs Barnet and I can manage perfectly well without you.'

'But I really do want to help, Aunt,' her niece had assured her. 'You have so many other things to attend to. And, when all's said and done, it's hardly a labour of Herculean proportions to stick a few flowers into a set of pots!'

'There is good deal more to it than that, Georgianne, and well you know it!' returned her aunt, with some asperity. 'However, if you really insist, it is true to say that I would appreciate your assistance. The flowers have all been deliv-

ered to the still-room—but be sure and get one of the
footmen to help you with the heavier arrangements.'

To which request Georgianne had been more than happy
to give her promise. Some two hours later, however,
having dismissed yet another arrangement as totally unsatisfactory, she had been obliged to pull out all of the
blooms and start anew. Why does everything always have
to go wrong at one and the same time? she wondered
dismally. It was hard to believe that only yesterday
morning she had felt as though she was walking on air.
Even the rain had failed to quench her exuberant spirits.
It had been enough just to be with him, to enjoy again the
friendly sparring and that inexplicable feeling of harmony
that seemed to exist between the two of them—culminating in that last frantic dash for shelter, and then the heady
rapture of that kiss! But then, as Maitland's hurtful words
had hit home, to have found herself, in the space of a few
short minutes, cast down from the highest of highs to the
lowest of lows!

And now, having spent the remainder of the previous day
as well as half the night going over and over what had
occurred in the old bothy, that feeling of gloom still persisted, even though she had finally formed the conclusion
that she had no one but herself to blame for Maitland's
unworthy conduct. Why, having flirted outrageously with
him for most of the past week, she had all but *begged* him
to kiss her, she chided herself, as she impatiently jabbed
another white lily into the burnished copper urn in front of
her, uttering a barely concealed oath when the fragile stem
snapped between her fingers.

Oh, this will never do! she told herself crossly. *Not content
with having allowed myself to become overly melodramatic*

about the whole affair, I am now beginning to behave like some star-crossed schoolgirl!

Taking a deep breath, she straightened her shoulders and set about trying to apply her mind to the task in hand. After all, she told herself, she had no reason to doubt her ability to put all those foolish thoughts of romance out of her mind—hadn't she had over three years to perfect that very technique? To that end, it was a blessed relief to know that Maitland would shortly be on his way and, she promised herself firmly—just as soon as she had had time to adjust to the idea that he was never coming back—she would be able to get back to the even tenor of her former existence. A little more withdrawn, perhaps, but far, far wiser!

Unfortunately, for her present peace of mind, there was still this evening's entertainment to get through. But then, giving a brisk shake of her head, she persuaded herself that, if she could just keep her mind focussed on fulfilling the many tasks she had set herself before that time, she need give no thought to what he might say to her when the hour arrived—if, indeed, he chose to speak to her at all!

As for the subject of Georgianne's earnest introspection, he too was feeling less than happy about the forthcoming festivities, although he knew that it would be downright churlish of him not to attend. But the thought of having to smile and make polite conversation—not to mention being obliged to dance with a whole collection of simpering, mock-modest females—was increasingly difficult for Maitland to contemplate. Especially since the only female that he really wanted to hold in his arms was Georgianne and that, as he knew, was out of the question.

Although the ex-major was not, in the normal way, a man who lacked spirit—indeed, he had proved himself on many occasions both on and off the field of conflict—summoning up the backbone to face Catford was proving to be a different matter entirely! It was not his friend's wrath towards himself that he feared but the thought that, should the tale of yesterday morning's clandestine embrace come to light, it might well damage Georgianne's future relationship with the viscount. As much as Maitland wanted her for himself, he had no desire to ruin his friend's happiness.

Whilst behaving in an underhand manner was totally foreign to his nature, he could not help but hope that Georgianne had meant what she had said about keeping the matter to herself. Whether or not she had done so was not something he was likely to discover until this evening!

Heaving himself up from the breakfast table, where he had been sitting ruminating over his misfortunes, he went upstairs in search of his cousin who, as he had expected, was still in the process of having his man dress him.

'Shan't be long, Will,' said Fenton, waving at Maitland to take a seat. 'Where are we off to today?'

'Nowhere,' returned his cousin shortly. 'At least, *I'm* off to play cricket—you may please yourself.'

'We're not dashing about the countryside on the track of this blessed Étienne fellow, then?' demanded Fenton, turning round in some surprise.

Maitland shook his head. 'Not a lot of point, now,' he replied. 'Pretty well scraped the barrel as far as all the parish registers go, which leaves us at point non-plus, as far as I can see!'

'Surely you don't mean to give up the search?' exclaimed his cousin in dismay. 'But you know how desperately I need to get my hands on that money!'

'Can't be helped, old man,' said Maitland, with another decisive shake of his head. 'I'm not giving up, exactly, but, since we're doing no real good here, I figured I might just as well go back to Fetterfield and see if I can't find some more useful clue amongst Uncle Roger's old papers.'

'How soon are you thinking of leaving?' Fenton asked guardedly.

'Monday morning,' returned Maitland, rising to his feet. 'You are welcome to stay on as long as you like, of course.' He shot his cousin a wry smile. 'How *is* the romance with the fair Miss Highsmith progressing, by the way?'

'Better than you might suppose!' retorted Fenton, a smug expression on his face. 'She seems to have taken quite a fancy to me, at any rate!'

'Well, you just watch yourself, my friend,' cautioned his cousin. 'Women can be capricious creatures at the best of times.' As he well knew to his cost! 'I shall be back around five in time to change for the Gresham ball—I take it that we'll be using your carriage?'

At Fenton's nod of confirmation, Maitland turned on his heel and exited the room, the stableyard his next objective. Having promised the young Reverend Childs that he would do his best to turn up and assist him in his efforts to organise the village boys into some more constructive pastime than that of throwing stones at passing carriages or tying tin cans to cats' tails—which were their normal pursuits when let off their usual labours for an hour or two on a Saturday afternoon—he now felt obliged to keep his word.

It was true that the church was perilously close to Gresham Hall, but Maitland was comforted by the fact that, since she was more than likely involved in helping her aunt with the arrangements for this evening's festivities, there was very little danger of Georgianne showing up on the village green. Nevertheless, despite the fact that his attention was almost fully occupied with keeping the lads in check, he found it impossible to stop his eyes from straying over to the little wicker gate that marked the entrance to the Gresham estate, in the forlorn hope of seeing her emerging through it.

Two hours later, exhausted but fairly well pleased with his afternoon's work, he eased himself down into one of the vicar's comfortable old armchairs.

'They're turning into quite a reasonable bunch of players,' he remarked, smiling his thanks up at the deaf housekeeper as she passed him a cup of tea. 'I shall be sorry not to see how they progress.'

'Off soon then, I take it?' asked Mr Childs, his chubby young face a picture of disappointment. 'No luck with your enquiries, then?'

'None at all, I'm afraid.'

The vicar gave a slightly distracted nod, then, leaning forwards, he said somewhat hesitantly, 'Don't know if it's of any consequence, old chap, but there was something that occurred to me the other day, after you left.'

Raising a questioning eyebrow, Maitland waited for the other man to continue.

'Well, the thing is,' went on the vicar, 'and, I'm not sure whether you are aware of this, but old Godfrey Freeman— my predecessor—was sometimes in the habit of taking the odd service at the chapel up at Highsmith House. Baptisms and burials and so on for those unfortunate little ones who didn't survive.'

His attention suddenly alerted, Maitland clapped his hand to his forehead 'The home for unwed mothers!' he exclaimed. 'Why the devil did that not occur to me before?' Then, leaning forwards, in great eagerness, he asked, 'Would this Reverend Freeman have kept any records of these births and deaths, do you suppose?'

'Oh, he would have been obliged to,' Mr Childs was swift

to assure him. 'Trouble is, there's no sign of them amongst any of the papers here, so that just leaves the chapel or High-smith House itself!' A slight flush crept over his cheeks. 'As you are no doubt aware, Lady Highsmith is away from home at present, but it did occur to me that, since you are in such close contact with everyone up at the Hall, it is possible that you may be able to elicit some further information from Miss Stephanie herself.'

'I shall have the pleasure of seeing Miss Highsmith this very evening!' Maitland replied, with a satisfied smile. 'And I can't thank you enough for bringing this piece of information to my attention. I was beginning to despair of ever finding anything of value.'

'Think nothing of it, my dear chap,' said the vicar, rising to his feet to see Maitland to the door. 'I trust that it will prove to be of some use to you. Indeed, it's the very least I could do after all your sterling efforts to knock my fledgling cricket team into shape!'

With a dismissive grin and a wave of his hand, Maitland mounted Pegasus and rode back through the village. Having previously paid scant attention to the Highsmith property, which was situated at the junction of the Willowby lane and the main pike road and some three miles or so distant from the church itself, he now realised, when viewing it at closer quarters, that the large house could well have been the one so vaguely described by his uncle. It even had a driveway bordered with lime trees. But a convent it was most definitely not!

Could it be possible that the house had changed its designation over the years? he wondered—maybe the fickle Miss Highsmith would be able to supply him with some answers on the subject? Suddenly the thought of spending the evening at Gresham Hall became a far more interesting prospect than it had been earlier in the day! Wheeling his mount around, he headed up the turnpike back towards the Dun Cow, barely able to conceal his eagerness to share this exciting information with his cousin.

Chapter Eighteen

The room was already becoming oppressively warm, even though the evening was barely yet into its stride. Standing at the top of the stairs, anxiously scanning the faces of the mass of individuals now milling around below him, Maitland was unable to locate either Georgianne or, more especially, for the moment at any rate, her friend Stephanie.

Catford, as he had just observed, was still in the receiving line, along with his parents and the rest of the Gresham family. Maitland had been surprised not to find Georgianne standing with them. Fortunately, for his own peace of mind, the press of people moving forwards to pay their respects had absolved him from giving his friend any more than the customary bow, for which the viscount had returned him a cheerful grin—this friendly salutation merely having had the effect of making Maitland feel a good deal more of a bounder than he had felt originally!

Standing at his side, his cousin Jeremy was also scouring the room for a sight of his proposed bride. However, Fenton's eagerness to find Stephanie was more to do with the fact that he wished to tell her that he had, after going to some considerable trouble and expense, finally managed to avail himself of the marriage licence that she had insisted he procure before she would commit herself to eloping with him.

Georgianne, having caught sight of the two men the moment they had appeared through the doorway at the top of the staircase, was doing her best to conceal herself behind one of the pillars that she had spent so much of the afternoon festooning with ribbons and posies. In the event, as even she was bound to admit, the final results of her labours had proved to be quite eyecatchingly dazzling. At least no one would be able to fault her in that respect, she thought, heaving a deep sigh of regret, as she allowed her eyes to linger upon Maitland's face.

In order to avoid a face-to-face confrontation with him in full public view, she had managed to persuade her reluctant aunt to excuse her from the family line-up. Although she knew that it would be impossible to avoid him entirely, she felt secure in the knowledge that, should he seek her out, the press of people around would serve to obviate all but the most cursory of conversations,

He looked so imposing and so full of self-assurance standing there, surveying the crowd. And, although he was not what one might describe as exactly handsome, his features were regular and well formed, his eyes clear and bright and his lips—but perhaps it would be as well not to dwell upon any thoughts about his lips at this particular moment, she thought hurriedly, doing her utmost to banish the memory of that breathtakingly heady embrace.

Like the vast majority of the other gentlemen in the room, Maitland was clad in a long-tailed evening suit, his crisp white shirt and neckcloth standing out in stark contrast to the coal-black superfine of his jacket. Unlike most of the others, however, his broad shoulders and upright stance were more than enough to make him stand out from the crowd. Small wonder that she had lost her heart to him, thought Georgianne sadly, as her eyes followed his progress down the stairs and, eventually, out of her line of vision. Stephanie, as she quickly observed, had wasted no time in making her way towards the Honourable Jeremy and the pair were, even now, heads together, involved in hatching some nefarious scheme or other. She hoped to goodness that Steffi was not about to ruin her aunt's big night by running off with the man in the middle of this evening's festivities!

'I trust that you are not hiding yourself away from me, Miss Venables!' came a soft voice from over her shoulder.

With an exclamation of dismay, she spun round, only to find herself face to face with the very person that she had been trying to avoid.

'N-not at all, Mr Maitland,' she stuttered, as the tell-tale colour rose in her cheeks. 'I was—er—merely adjusting one of the ribbons on the pillar—it seemed to have worked itself loose.'

He eyed the offending decoration with some scepticism. 'Looks pretty secure to me,' he pronounced. She was lying, of that he was quite certain, although why she should need to drum up such a paltry excuse to explain away her concealment was beyond him.

There followed a somewhat awkward pause as Georgianne desperately tried to think of something to say that did not sound as absurdly idiotic as her previous offering.

Fortunately, Maitland forestalled her. 'I was hoping that you would be able to tell me where I might find Miss Highsmith,' he said.

Georgianne's heart sank even lower. So, he was still intent upon pursuing Steffi, she thought glumly, not entirely sure whether she ought to be glad or sorry that, if the poor man truly had any designs in that quarter, he was about to have them cruelly shattered.

'She was over by the stairway, in conversation with your cousin, the last time I saw her,' she replied, pointing her fan in the direction she had indicated. 'In fact, I am almost sure that I saw them going towards one of the card rooms just behind the stairs.'

'Thank you.'

Bowing, he made as if to take his leave but then, gritting his teeth, he smothered the oath that had inadvertently slipped from his lips, stopped and spun round to face her again.

'It would pain me very greatly to lose your friendship, Georgianne,' he told her, his voice low, but full of urgency. 'I can't apologise enough for what happened yesterday morning but I swear that, if you would just consider return- ing our relationship to its previous happy footing, such a thing will never occur again!'

'Since you have given me to understand that you are about to leave the district,' she replied stiffly, 'I should think that any likelihood of it being repeated is somewhat remote!'

Momentarily stung by her frigid tone of voice, he was silent, then, 'True enough,' he felt bound to concede. 'But I should like to be assured that if I were to come to Gresham Hall again, at some time in the future, you would not find my presence unwelcome.'

She stiffened, the colour rising in her cheeks once more, but this time for a very different reason. 'I trust that I can always be relied upon to do my duty by my aunt's guests,' she retorted. 'And I have no doubt that Catford's friends will always be made welcome at the Hall.'

With that, she turned on her heel and, head high, she edged her way through the group of people who were conversing nearby and disappeared into the crowd.

His eyes grim, Maitland stared after her departing figure until it was no longer visible. Then, with a barely audible grunt of frustration, he started to make his way over to the anteroom of which she had spoken. *At least let me find some bright spot in this otherwise never-ending pit of gloom,* he prayed, closing his eyes briefly as he cast his mind back to the moment that he had spotted Georgianne lurking behind the pillar. Wearing a hip-skimming gown of cream-coloured satin, whose low-cut bodice revealed rather more of her luscious décolletage than was good for any man's pulse rate, and a simple pearl tiara fixed atop her glossy curls, she had looked so heart-stoppingly lovely that, despite his fervent promise to keep his distance, it had taken every ounce of his self-control to prevent himself reaching forwards and pulling her into his arms.

Gritting his teeth together, in an endeavour to cast that tantalising vision from his thoughts, he reached the stairway and, spotting the closed door of the aforementioned anteroom, he was just about to make his way towards it when he felt a tap on his shoulder. Turning, he was seized by a faint sense of alarm as he discovered Catford regarding him with a slight frown on his face.

'Let's get out of this crush for a minute, Will, old sport,' begged the viscount, as he edged himself sideways in an effort to preserve his injured leg from the swaying corpulence of a passing matron. 'There's a little matter I would like to have clarified, if you've no objection?'

Maitland's heart sank. *So, it's finally about to come out into the open,* he thought, as he hurriedly suppressed the groan of regret that threatened. *Still, perhaps it's time for 'cards on the table'—at least now I might find out, once and for all, exactly what the situation is between the enigmatic Miss Venables and her cousin!*

Directing his friend to follow him into the card room—which Maitland, to his surprise, discovered was empty of any other inhabitants—Catford bade him sit down and, perching himself on the arm of a nearby armchair, said bluntly, 'I dare say that you will tell me that it is none of my business, Will, but I have to ask you this. Have you and Georgie fallen out over something?'

Somewhat taken aback at this direct line of questioning, it took Maitland a moment or two to recover his composure. 'What's given you that idea?' he asked guardedly.

Catford pursed his lips. 'Well, she's been acting damned oddly this last couple of days,' he replied. 'Just when we were all beginning to think that she'd put all that sorry business behind her, she seems to have gone right back into her shell again.' He shook his head mournfully. 'I really don't care to see her like this, Will, and I couldn't help wondering whether you had had words—and just when I thought that the pair of you were getting along so famously, too!'

Maitland was now in something of a quandary. He could hardly tell his friend the real cause of the apparent dissension between Georgianne and himself but, since it was clear that the viscount had noticed something amiss, he felt obliged to conjure up an explanation of sorts.

'It may well be that Miss Venables was not best pleased with the wetting she took on our last ride out together,' he offered, affecting a shamefaced expression. 'My fault, entirely, I hasten to add! And then, when I was obliged to cancel our appointment this morning, I fear that I must have blotted my copy-book entirely!'

Catford shook his head. 'Georgie ain't the sort to get into a pet about that sort of thing—besides which, she's already told me that it was *she* who persuaded you to go out when that thunderstorm threatened—she's always been a bit of a daredevil in that respect!'

Both men were silent for a few moments then, 'Dare say she'll snap out of it, soon, old chap,' ventured Maitland, somewhat awkwardly. 'In any event, you should know by now that trying to fathom out what goes on in a woman's head is a waste of both time and energy—I gave up that course of action a good few years ago!'

'True enough, Will,' laughed Catford, as he rose to his feet. 'Still, I would hate you to part on such poor terms. Perhaps you wouldn't mind asking her to dance at some point? Pretty good way to mend broken fences, I've always found!'

'Certainly, I will,' Maitland assured his friend, although he could not help thinking that, after the earlier rebuff, it was doubtful whether Georgianne would be happy to countenance any such petition from him. But then, recalling his other problem, he added, 'I do have to seek out Miss Highsmith first, though—I have been told that it is possible that she may be able to shed some further light on what became of my missing relative.'

'Stephanie Highsmith?' exclaimed Catford, arching his eyebrow in scornful amusement. 'Doubt if you'll get much help from that fair damsel—head stuffed with fashion plates and cash accounts, if you ask me!'

'You may well be right,' returned Maitland, with a rueful grin. 'I mean to have a damned good try, nevertheless!'

Although finding Stephanie did not prove to be much of a problem, since she and her cohorts appeared to have set up their own court in one corner of the ballroom, getting near enough to hold a private conversation with her turned out to be a rather different matter altogether, as Maitland was soon to find out.

'Have you managed to have a word with Miss Highsmith about the chapel records yet?' he demanded of his cousin, whom he had discovered hovering, somewhat disconsolately, on the fringe of the circle of eager swains who were clamouring for Stephanie's attention.

'Er—no—'fraid not, old man,' replied the distracted Fenton, anxiously eying his intended bride's rather coquettish manner towards one of his rivals.

Following the agreement that he should 'spirit' her away during the Gresham family's ritual sojourn at the church service the following evening—she would invent a fictitious headache to prevent her from accompanying them—Stephanie had then insisted that, in order to avoid drawing undue attention to themselves, it would be best if she and Fenton were to stay apart for the remainder of this evening. At his protest, she had reached for his hand and, fluttering her eyelashes at him, had stroked his fingers, gently cajoling him with, 'Dearest Jeremy! Surely, you can't want the whole village hot on our trail before we even reach the turnpike?'

Since that was the last thing Fenton wanted, his main objective being to have Stephanie wedded and—if he had any say in the matter—bedded long before the sun went down, he had had to curb his objections. The result being that he now found himself obliged to stand by and watch while Stephanie danced and flirted with every Tom, Dick and Harry who happened to take her fancy. Having already received several pitying glances from one or two bystanders, who had, apparently, reached the conclusion that Fenton's term as current favourite appeared to have run its course, his growing resentment had wiped all thoughts of Maitland's earlier request right out of his mind.

'Well, what in blazes are you doing stuck at the back of this set of fribbles?' enquired his cousin, rather crossly. 'Only this morning you were giving me to understand that you and Miss Highsmith were as thick as two inkle weavers! Don't tell me that you've lost interest in claiming your share of Uncle Roger's fortune!'

Fenton looked affronted. 'You know damned well that I haven't, Will,' he retorted. 'But you said yourself that the whole thing was beginning to look like a lost cause. And, with the best part of a year still to go, I need to make the most of every opportunity that happens to come my way in the meantime!'

'You call this skulking about "making the most of your opportunities"?' snorted Maitland scathingly. 'Well, I'm afraid I've no time for such niceties!' And with that, he thrust himself forwards through the crowd of young hopefuls, blithely ignoring all the indignant protests with which he was being showered.

'Miss Highsmith,' he said, as soon as he reached her side. 'A word with you, if you please.'

Thoroughly startled by this sudden and rather forceful invasion, Stephanie's questioning eyes flicked towards Fenton. Surely, the fool had not been so naïve as to share their plans with his cousin, she thought in a panic, as every little cog in her brain spun wildly in a frantic endeavour to conjure up some sort of a solution that might rectify the potential damage. From what she had gathered about Viscount Catford's friend, she knew that it would require more than the usual amount of blandishment and cajolery on her part if she meant to save this perilous situation, since every one of her previous attempts to ensnare Maitland's interest had been met with complete indifference.

Rising from her chair, she plastered on her most winning smile and, holding out her hand, said, 'Perhaps we might take a little promenade about the room, Mr Maitland?'

Surprised, but none the less relieved that he was to be given the chance to question her without interruption, Maitland responded to her smile with a satisfied grin and, tucking her hand into the crook of his elbow, escorted her through her crowd of envious and gaping admirers.

'Maybe a little refreshment would be more in order, at this point,' he suggested, leading her over to one of the side salons where parts of the buffet were laid out. 'A cooling glass of champagne, perhaps?'

'Oh, how very clever of you!' she cooed, fluttering her eye-lashes up at him in feigned admiration, an action that had the effect of setting his teeth on edge and his toes curling up in revulsion. 'I absolutely adore champagne!'

He settled her into a seat and, after signalling to one of the footmen to fetch them some champagne, he took his place beside her.

'May I ask how long you have lived at Highsmith House, Miss Highsmith?' he then asked, quite bluntly.

Stephanie was clearly taken aback. 'H-Highsmith House?' she stammered. 'What is that to the purpose?'

Maitland smiled. 'I merely wondered if you had any knowledge of the building ever having been used as a convent—or religious seminary, even?'

It was beginning to dawn upon Stephanie that there seemed to be a distinct possibility that her concern for secrecy had, in this instance, led her to the wrong conclusion. Still, she thought, giving an inward shrug, it would certainly do no harm to keep her little band of love-struck devotees on tenterhooks for a few more minutes. In any event, she reminded herself, after tomorrow, who knew when her next chance to revel in such unconcealed adoration would present itself? Besides which, the champagne was very refreshing, after the heat of the ballroom! She would allow him five minutes of her precious time and not a second more. Taking a sip of her drink, she eyed him over the rim of the glass, and resigned herself to answering what seemed to her to be a per-fectly ludicrous question.

'As far as I am aware, Mr Maitland,' she replied, 'High-smith House has been in my family for several generations so why you should think that it might have once been a convent, I simply cannot imagine.'

He gave a quick nod. 'Never mind—it was just a thought. What I really wanted to ask you was whether you knew where the chapel records might be kept?'

A puzzled frown crept across her brow but then, after staring at him in some amazement for several seconds, her face cleared and she began to chuckle. 'Oh, I see now!' she said mockingly. 'This is all to do with that ludicrous search of yours, isn't it?'

Then, placing her unfinished glass of champagne back onto the table, she rose to her feet. 'Allow me to assure you, sir, that neither Highsmith House nor its chapel hold the answer to your mystery,' she said, with a petulant flounce. 'It has never been either an abbey or a monastery or a convent, nor have we ever harboured monks or nuns in any shape or form—'

Then, suddenly, she stopped, and a slightly disconcerted expression flitted across her face. As two scarlet spots of colour appeared on her cheeks, she bit her lip in embarrassment. 'Not unless one counts old Mother Mattie, that is,' she added lamely, her voice dropping to almost a whisper.

'*Mother* Mattie?' Maitland was all attention. 'A nun?'

'Well, some sort of novice, at any rate,' answered Steph-anie, as she subsided back into her seat, feeling somewhat foolish. 'Her real name is Marthe Matthilde, but the villag-ers couldn't get their tongues around the French pronuncia-tion, so she has been known as Mother Mattie for almost as long as I can remember.'

'And she still resides at Highsmith House?' asked Maitland eagerly.

Stephanie shook her head. 'Not any more,' she replied. 'She was with us for years but then, just a year or so back, it seems that she had a hankering for a place of her own, so Grandmama set her up in one of the estate cottages.'

Maitland could scarcely believe his luck. It hardly seemed possible that, after all those days of fruitless searching, the answer could well have lain right at his fingertips the whole time! He leaned forwards. 'I take it that this Marthe Matthilde worked in the—er—how shall I put it—?'

'Refuge for unmarried mothers!' she returned bluntly. 'There is no need to beat about the bush—everyone in the whole area is perfectly well aware of its function! And, yes, Mother M—I mean Marthe Matthilde, was actually Grandmama's right-hand man—well, woman, I should say!' she corrected herself, and let out a tinkling half-laugh. 'Still is, to a certain extent, I suppose.'

But then, having spotted the sullen-faced Fenton leaning against the room's doorpost watching them, she rose swiftly to her feet, saying, 'I'm afraid that's about all I can help you with, Mr Maitland. My grandmother has always made sure that I am kept well away from that part of her life and I promise you that I really do know nothing about chapel records and all that sort of thing!'

Seeing her get up, Fenton darted forwards, his face alight with eagerness. 'Allow me to take you back into the ballroom, Miss Highsmith,' he said, holding out his arm.

Stephanie heaved a sigh of annoyance. 'I believe I told you not to bother me this evening, Jer—Mr Fenton!' she returned impatiently. 'Mr Maitland is perfectly capable of seeing me back to my seat. Why don't you go and dance with one of those delightful young ladies who keep giving you the glad-eye?'

'You know perfectly well that I have no desire to dance with anyone but you,' mumbled Fenton, casting her a hurt look.

'Well, I can't help that!' Stephanie shrugged, giving the appearance of complete indifference although, in reality, she rather enjoyed the sense of power with which such admissions always filled her. Then, turning towards Maitland, she held out her hand, 'May we go now, sir?' she asked him prettily, totally ignoring Fenton's crushed expression.

Flashing his cousin a quick look of sympathy, Maitland stepped forwards and offered Stephanie his arm. But then, just as he was about to lead her out of the room, he turned his head towards Fenton and said, 'Stay here for a couple of minutes, if you would, old chap—Miss Highsmith has just provided me with some information that I feel might be of immense value to us.'

Some fifteen minutes later, having deposited Stephanie back amongst her faithful attendants, in addition to having acquainted Fenton with a quick resumé of what he had recently learned, Maitland went in search of Georgianne. From his seat in the anteroom, having caught several glimpses of her gliding past the open doorway on the arm of one or another of her dance partners, he was grimly determined to pursue Catford's suggestion that he should ask her to dance.

He approached her, just as her current partner was leading her off the floor.

'Ah, Miss Venables,' he said, sweeping her a courtly bow. 'I believe this next dance is mine?'

Momentarily confused, it took Georgianne several seconds to recover her composure but then, flicking open the dance-card that hung from a ribbon on her wrist, she was about to shake her head in denial at his claim when, upon observing that the next dance was, in fact, a waltz, a sudden mischievous whim leapt into her head. Why not? she thought, in stubborn defiance, thrusting every one of her previous good intentions resolutely to one side. This could be the very last chance she would ever get to feel his arms about her once more and, even though it was true that they would be on a dance floor, surrounded by dozens of others, it was a final indulgence that she simply refused to deny herself!

And so, to Maitland's joy and astonishment, she flashed him a smile and replied, 'I do believe you are right, Mr Maitland!'

Chapter Nineteen

~~~~~~~~~~~

Scarcely able to believe his good fortune, Maitland stepped forwards and, gathering her into his arms, swept her into the dance. For the first few minutes or so, it was enough for him to feel the soft warmth of her body so close to his own as, in perfect unison, they dipped and swayed together, their footwork echoing the compulsive rhythm of the music. But then, as he became more and more aware of the unmistakeable scent of jasmine rising from her hair, his pulse quickened and, almost unconsciously, his hand tightened its grip around her waist, pulling her even closer to him.

At the increased pressure, a startled gasp escaped Georgianne's lips and, conscious of the impropriety of his action, she was about to reprimand him for his flagrant disregard of the rules of the dance but, on raising her eyes to meet his, however, her heart almost stopped in its tracks. Maitland was gazing down at her with an expression of such—what was it?—wistfulness?—longing?—that her head was in such a whirl that she found it difficult to think clearly.

In her confusion, she missed the beat and stumbled, causing him to grasp her to him even more tightly before he swung her out of the path of another pair, gradually relaxing his hold as he did so. Not unlike Georgianne's own, his breathing was becoming more and more rapid with every movement.

'Sorry about that,' he muttered through gritted teeth. 'Wasn't concentrating.'

'That was all my fault and well you know it!' she pointed out softly, having finally regained her composure. 'Taking the blame for my constant *faux pas* seems to be growing into something of a habit with you, Mr Maitland!'

Registering the smile that accompanied her words, Maitland sent up a fervent message of thanks to whosoever might have been responsible for Georgianne's apparent change of heart and at once relaxed.

'As it happens, Miss Venables,' he said with a satisfied grin, as he skilfully guided her through a reverse turn, 'as far as I am concerned, you have no faults!'

'Oh, very smooth, sir!' she chuckled.

'Thank you, ma'am,' he replied, feigning a smug expression. 'I'm flattered that my dancing ability meets with your approval!'

She smiled up at him, her eyes sparkling with laughter. 'I was not referring to your dancing skill, sir, as you are perfectly well aware—although I do have to admit that you are a considerable improvement on my previous partner.'

As she whirled around the floor in the warm security of his arms, she could not help but feel both pleased and sad that—even after all that had happened to blight the tenor of their former friendship—they had both slipped back into the sort of teasing repartee that had formed so much a part of that earlier relationship. She felt so very much at ease with this man—so absolutely right!—and, if she could just persuade herself to put aside the bitter fact that there was no future in loving him, she could at least enjoy this uplifting camaraderie for the brief time that was left to her.

Maitland, for his part, was simply glad that Georgianne's earlier animosity towards him seemed to have evaporated. He was heavily conscious of the fact that she had had every right to take offence at his taking advantage of her the other morning. Nonetheless, since she appeared to have decided to forgive and forget his appalling lack of self-control, there was no real reason, as far as he could see, why he should deprive himself of these final few hours of her company. Now I understand how Cinderella must have felt, he thought, his lips curving in a wry smile as he shepherded Georgianne skilfully across the floor. At the stroke of twelve—or at whatever other hour the Greshams chose to end their ball—he would find himself saying his last goodbyes to them all and then have to do his utmost to put her out of his mind. This particular aspect of the situation would, as he well knew, be devilishly hard to accomplish. Nevertheless, he would just have to force himself to get on with his life and, if the heavens were just, tomorrow might well bring forth plenty to occupy him and then, before he knew it, it would be Monday morning and he could be on his way.

Skirting the edge of the floor, he tightened his grip once again and, as the musicians rendered their last pulsating chord, he swung Georgianne into a swirling flourish that left her at once breathless and laughing.

He was just about to lead her back to her seat when the resounding clang of the dinner gong rang out across the room. Looking over at the musicians' podium, from where the sound had erupted, he was intrigued to see Catford, along with his parents and two or three other members of his vastly extended family, standing on the podium.

'Dear friends!' cried the earl, holding up his hand for silence. 'If I might have your attention for one moment, please!'

At his words, the hub of conversation in the crowded

ballroom drew immediately to a close as all heads were turned in the direction of the stage.

'What can this be, I wonder?' he asked Georgianne, who seemed to be just as puzzled as he was.

Shaking her head, Georgianne made no reply. Instead, hoping against hope that what she had most feared had not come to pass, she tried craning her head, in a desperate attempt to see if she could spot Stephanie or, at the very least, the taller Fenton, anywhere near. Unfortunately, what with the press of people surging forwards to hear what Lord Gresham had to say, it would have been as much as she could do to keep her balance had not Maitland put a protective arm across her shoulders and pulled her towards him, which had the instant effect of making her forget everything but the feel of his warm, lean body so enticingly close to her own.

There was an expectant hush, as the earl, with a broad smile on his face, drew the blushing Lady Alice forwards and motioned to his son to join them.

'Ladies and gentleman,' he began, 'it is with the greatest of pleasure that my wife and I announce the engagement between Lady Alice Chetwynd and our dear son Edwin!'

After a moment's stunned silence, the room was filled with the deafening sound of applause, accompanied by jovial calls of 'bravo!' and 'well done!'

Maitland who, utterly bewildered, was finding it quite impossible to comprehend what the earl had just said, stared down at Georgianne in confusion, his heart flipping over with sorrow when he registered her anguished expression.

Every vestige of colour had gone from her face and she was biting at her lower lip, in a vain attempt to fight back the tears that were already glistening in her eyes.

'Pray excuse me!' she gasped, tearing herself from his grip

and, before he could stop her, she had thrust herself through the crowd and was gone from his view.

What in God's name is going on? he asked himself as, turning back to the musicians' dais, he was just in time to witness the extraordinary spectacle of his ex-army comrade placing a ring upon Lady Alice's finger. A simmering anger began to fill his chest, causing him to pay scant attention to the earl's smiling explanation that the two families had deemed it necessary to keep the betrothal secret until Alice had celebrated her eighteenth birthday which, 'as many of you will know, occurred only yesterday but, fortunately, well in time for our own little function!'

Fastening his eyes on the somewhat complacent expression on Catford's face, Maitland clenched his teeth and balled his fists in fury. It was beyond his understanding how any man with a shred of decency in him could stand there with such a self-satisfied smirk on his face, after serving such an unpardonable insult to the woman he had professed—in Maitland's own hearing—to love most dearly?

It had been plain to see that Georgianne had been even more shocked by the unexpected announcement than he himself had been. Her obvious distress had struck Maitland to the quick, but he was forced to face up to the fact that, however much he might wish to seek her out and offer her his support and commiseration, it was doubtful that she would welcome either his company or his interference in so personal a matter. His rage almost at boiling point by now, he determined to tackle Catford the moment he stepped off the podium.

Had he but known it, Georgianne's sudden uncharacteristic bout of self-pity had actually been brought about by the realisation that, not only was Stephanie—who, despite her capricious and often irritating ways, had always been a good friend to her—about to disappear out of her life for ever, but that Catford, too, the dearest and most beloved of her cousins, had also found himself a life partner, whereas she herself was condemned, through no fault of her own, to a future filled with nothing but loneliness.

Having fled to her room where, although a few moments spent in quiet contemplation soon restored her to her normal good sense, she still could not bring herself to return to the ball. After having behaved so abysmally, she cringed at the thought of being obliged to face Maitland again, for she could not begin to imagine what he had made of her vulgar and unseemly display of bad manners. He might well have gained the impression that she was suffering a fit of pique at having been kept out of the family secret or, even worse, jealous of Lady Alice's good fortune!

She paced backwards and forwards over the bedroom floor for a good half-hour, castigating herself for the unforgivable manner in which she had fled the party. Quite apart from the atrocious way she had treated Maitland, she was growing conscious of the fact that Catford must be wondering why she had not joined the rest of the guests to offer the newly be-trothed pair her congratulations.

Undecided, she stood, with her hand on the bedroom door, willing herself to make the effort to return to the ballroom. But then, having reached the conclusion that, with more than a hundred and fifty other people to contend with, her cousin would surely be far too occupied to remember whether or not she had formed part of that number, she made up her mind that she would wait until all the guests had departed before approaching the viscount and his fiancée. That decision taken, she wandered over to her window, which overlooked the back of the house, and gazed across at the myriad of lights flickering from the scores of Chinese lanterns that festooned the trees in the park.

The rear doors of the ballroom had been flung open and several groups of people were standing about on the terrace, taking advantage of the balmy evening air. Faint strains of music could be heard issuing forth from within the room and, at her sudden realisation that the musicians were playing a waltz, Georgianne's eyes moistened and a little lump lodged in her throat. Every fibre of her body cried out in protest at having to let Maitland go without even bidding him a final farewell. Dancing with him had filled her with the most in-credible feelings of delight, but then, as the sharp realisation that this enchanting memory would be all she had to sustain her in the long, dreary days ahead suddenly hit her, she let out a soft sigh of regret. Slumping wearily down into the window-seat, she pressed her brow against the windowpane and, closing her eyes, allowed her mind to drift back to that indescribable moment when she had found herself, once again, wrapped in Will Maitland's arms. *At least no one can take this away from me*, she thought, as the sound of the lilting music drew her once again into her own private world of make-believe.

Having been obliged to hang about cooling his heels on the fringes of the crowd pressing around the happy couple, Maitland's indignation at Catford's perfidy was increasing by the minute and, by the time that the viscount was finally free of well-wishers and able to be approached, his impa-tience had reached boiling point.

'What in God's name are you up to?' he demanded, his face like thunder as he confronted his ex-comrade.

Catford looked startled. 'Steady on, old chap!' he cried. 'No need to lose your rag! Would have liked to tell you but, as the dear old pater said, Alice's parents wanted to keep it all "hush-hush" until after her birthday!'

Maitland couldn't believe his ears. 'You're telling me that this was all arranged some time ago?' he demanded.

'Well, I suppose it's always been on the cards, really,' replied Catford, with a self-conscious grin. 'The parents got their heads together when she was little more than a babe-in-arms and, all things considered, I have to admit that she's turned into a pretty good sort of girl, really!'

'Pretty good sort of girl!' repeated Maitland, horrified. 'Do I take it that you're not in love with her, then?'

Catford stared at his friend in disbelief. 'You know damned well that fellows in my position seldom have the luxury of marrying for love,' he replied, somewhat stiffly. 'Our lives tend to be governed by rather more practical issues—such as increasing land and assets and maintaining bloodlines. Besides which, a good many of my peers are still of the opinion that what they like to think of as "the ruling class" would go to the dogs if people like me were allowed to let our hearts rule our heads!' He gave a little half-laugh, before adding, with a slight shrug, 'No doubt that's why so many of them have mistresses.'

Casting his eyes across to where his intended bride was standing, excitedly showing off her ring to a cluster of admiring female friends, his expression softened. 'Although, to tell the truth,' he added quietly, 'I've always been rather fond of Alice and I'm sure we will rub along famously.'

'Rub along!' Maitland was incensed. 'But what about Geor—Miss Venables?' he demanded.

'Georgie? Not sure I get your drift, Will!'

For a moment, Catford looked perplexed, but then, as it suddenly came to him that there had been no sign of Georgianne amongst the crowds of well-wishers, a worried look came over his face. 'Damnation!' he exclaimed. 'I'd almost forgotten about Georgie! After all she's been through, this won't have gone down very well!'

He scanned the room, searching for a sight of his cousin then, with a muttered oath, he turned back to Maitland. 'Did you happen to see where she went, old chap?' he enquired anxiously.

'Miss Venables left some time ago,' came Maitland's terse reply. 'And not looking at all the thing, if you want my opinion!'

Clapping his hand to his forehead, Catford let out a low moan. 'Oh, lor!' he said. 'The poor darling must be thinking that I'm about to desert her!'

Dumbfounded, Maitland stared at his friend in astonishment. 'You surely aren't intending to keep up your—liaison—with Miss Venables after you're married, do you?'

'Well, naturally I—' Catford's voice ground to a halt and his eyes widened in consternation. *'Liaison!'* he repeated. 'Dammit, man! You can't possibly mean what I think you mean!'

At the sight of the patently horrified expression on his friend's face, Maitland began to wonder if he might not have got hold of quite the wrong end of the stick, insofar as his supposition about some sort of clandestine relationship between Georgianne and her cousin was concerned.

'No such thing, old chap,' he put in hurriedly. 'I wasn't intending to accuse you of anything—I was simply concerned about how Miss Venables would go on without your support.'

His face clearing, Catford gave his friend a piercing stare. 'You really care about her, don't you?' he asked quietly.

At Maitland's reluctant nod, the viscount's lips twitched briefly and he went on, 'I was beginning to think so—hope so, as a matter of fact, and, unless I'm very much mistaken, I would say that Georgie feels pretty much the same way about you!'

Maitland's eyes widened and he could feel his heart setting

up a most irregular beat. 'What makes you think that?' he asked, in a studied monotone.

'Oh, only that she's been displaying much the same symptoms as you have yourself,' laughed Catford, clapping him on the back. 'Picking at her food and secret yearning glances and all that sort of thing! Thing is, old chap, what do you intend to do about it?'

'Well—if you really think I stand a chance—I'll declare myself straight away, of course!' returned Maitland, his expression brightening.

'Yes, well, there's the rub,' said the viscount, a deep frown furrowing his brow. 'Knowing Georgie as I do, I very much fear that she will feel obliged to turn you down.'

'Feel obliged?' Maitland stared at his friend in some confusion. 'Why should she feel—?' He stopped and a slight flush crept across his cheeks. 'Oh, I see! I'm not in the right league, is that it?'

'Rubbish, Will!' Catford retorted, with a swift shake of his head. 'That's far from the truth, as well you know. It's just that...' He hesitated, eyeing Maitland searchingly for several moments before going on, ''Taint really my place to tell you this, old man, but I can't see that anyone else is going to put you in the picture, so here goes! The thing is— that's to say, the *reason* Georgie goes out of her way to keep all the fellows at bay is because she's got it into her head, after that bounder in London backtracked on his offer, that no decent chap will want her!'

'Why on earth would she think that?' demanded Maitland hotly. 'She's quite the most adorable creature that *I've* ever met and I doubt that I'm the only man who finds her so!'

Distractedly chewing at his lower lip, Catford was silent for a moment or two. Then, seeming to have finally made up his mind, he took a deep breath and blurted out, 'The fact of the matter is that the fellow withdrew his offer because he discovered that Georgie's parents were never married and now she's of the opinion that every other chap she meets is bound to react exactly as he did!'

Although he could not help but be shaken at the viscount's somewhat startling revelation, Maitland was also somewhat curious. 'Am I to take it that she has never put that supposition to the test since this fellow reneged on his offer?' he asked quietly.

'Never!' returned Catford, with a hurried shake of his head. 'She's always made damned sure that she's never been in a position to do so!'

He eyed his friend keenly. 'Should I be regretting having shared this information with you, Will?'

Maitland gave him a pensive smile and shook his head. 'Hardly, Cat,' he answered firmly. 'Whilst I can't deny that it's come as something of a shock, I promise you that it doesn't have the slightest effect upon my feelings for your cousin. After all, the poor sweet can scarcely be held responsible for her parents' misdemeanours. In any event, surely no man worth his salt would give a tinker's cuss about that sort of thing—not if he really loved the girl. In my opinion, your cousin is well shot of the rotten coward who treated her in such an abominable fashion.' A sudden grin lit up his features. 'As to that, hopefully the miserable fellow's loss will prove to be my gain!'

'If I know Georgie, she won't give in without a fight, Will, old chap,' the viscount felt bound to warn his friend. 'Are you sure that you're up to the challenge?'

'Just give me the chance!' nodded Maitland, his eyes aglow with anticipation. 'You may expect me on your doorstep first thing—oh, devil take it!' Having just remembered the plans he had already made with Fenton, he screwed up his face in dismay. 'It will have to be a little later, I'm afraid. There's another rather pressing matter that I have to attend to first.'

Chapter Twenty

Shortly after ten the following morning, the two cousins made for the narrow lane behind Highsmith House where, they had been assured by Stephanie, they would find the woman for whom they had been searching. Having spent most of the night with his mind in a complete turmoil as to how he might best approach Georgianne, Maitland was only too keen to get the present interview over and done with as quickly as possible, in order that he might devote the whole of his attention to a subject that was a good deal closer to his heart than the mere discovery of Billingham's long-lost heir!

The men had no difficulty in locating the cottage, for its owner could plainly be seen in the tiny front garden, down on her knees painstakingly clearing the weeds from her flourishing herb garden. Small, plump and neatly dressed in a faded black garb, her head covered with a large black kerchief, the old woman did not look up at the carriage's approach. It was the lifting of the latch on the garden gate that caught her attention and, despite her age and obvious infirmity, she rose almost gracefully to her feet as the two men approached.

'Your pardon, ma'am,' said Maitland, removing his hat,

'We apologise for interrupting your work. You *are* Marthe Matthilde, I take it—or should I call you Mother Mattie?'

The old woman's face, deeply lined and weathered, creased into a smile as she carefully wiped her hands on her black apron.

'Marthe Matthilde, *messieurs*—one-time Sister of the Order of St Clare,' she replied. Although heavily accented, it was clear that her use of the English language was excellent. 'It is the children who 'ave named me Mother Mattie— it is simpler for them.'

'We are hoping that you may be able to help us, ma'am.' He spoke carefully, having noticed that she bent her head towards him, indicating that she was probably hard of hearing. 'We are anxious to trace the whereabouts of a young relative of ours and have been told that you may have information.'

'But *certainement*, *messieurs*, if I can assist.'

The old woman beckoned the two men to follow her into the cottage, which Fenton did with scarcely disguised reluctance, looking about him with distaste, although the little kitchen into which they were ushered was spick and span and the air was sweet with the aromas of mint and lavender, bunches of which were hanging in abundance from the rafters.

'Please to take a seat, *messieurs*.'

Indicating the cushioned settle that stood against the wall, she herself sat down on the rocking chair beside the glowing stove and moved the kettle further on to its hotplate. Then, turning her head towards her visitors, she enquired as to how she might be of assistance.

'I shall 'ave to ask you to speak up a little, *mes amis*,' she said cheerily, her face wrinkling into a smile. 'I fear my 'earing is not as it used to be.'

Having elected to sit himself at Marthe Matthilde's table, Maitland pulled out his chair and moved it forwards, in order that the old woman might hear him more clearly. Then, after having introduced his cousin and himself, he went on to elucidate, as quickly and as briefly as possible, the reason for their visit.

Leaning forwards and focussing her attention upon his lips, Marthe Matthilde followed his succinct explanation with a deep and concentrated interest, her only movement being, every so often, a slow and thoughtful nod.

When he had finished, she leaned back in her chair and studied him closely.

'You say that your uncle 'as charged you to find this lost relative?' she asked, her rheumy black eyes fixed on Maitland's face. ''Tis a pity that the man did not show such concern when *le pauvre enfant* came into this world!'

'My sentiments exactly, ma'am!' returned Maitland, with a smile. 'Nevertheless, I did make him a deathbed promise that I would do my utmost to find the youth and—if possible—restore him to the family.'

A little smile twitched at the corners of the old woman's lips then, swivelling her eyes across to where Fenton was distastefully inspecting his boots for any damage that the walk up the cinder path might have caused them. 'And you, Monsieur Fenton?' she enquired. 'You also 'ave made such a promise?'

Fenton shifted uncomfortably on his cushioned seat. 'Well, naturally, I'm just as keen to find the lad as Mr Maitland,' he said hurriedly. 'After all, there's a great deal at stake here—' He stopped, one look at his cousin's expression having told him that this was not, perhaps, the wisest remark to have made. 'I mean—er, that is to say—we're all keen to do the right thing by our young relative!'

But Marthe Matthilde was nodding. 'Ah, *oui*!' she said, pursing her lips. 'I begin to understand. There is, perhaps, a large sum of money involved in this undertaking of yours?'

'Oh, don't you fret!' exclaimed Fenton, leaning forwards eagerly. 'We're more than willing to pay you, if that's—'

'Oh, do hold your tongue, Jerry!' cut in Maitland, shooting his cousin a scathing glance. Then, turning once more to face the old woman, he said, 'Please excuse my relative's lack of manners, ma'am. But, as it happens and, as you have just remarked, there is a great deal of money involved—the bulk of which, let me hasten to assure you, is to go to our cousin Melandra's child.'

'Who is, *naturellement*,' Marthe Matthilde could not forbear from pointing out, 'no longer a child.'

She sat quietly for some minutes, digesting all that Maitland had told her but then, with a firm shake of the head, she prised herself up from her chair, saying, 'No, *messieurs*, I am truly sorry, but I cannot think that, after all these years, it would be at all wise for any of us to interfere in this—'ow you say—young person's life. Milady 'ighsmith 'as always gone to a great deal of trouble to protect the identities of her infant charges. I cannot think that she would be 'appy to see all her good work come to naught.'

'But, do you not perhaps think that this—young person, as you seem keen to refer to him,' put in Maitland gently, as he also got to his feet, 'is, at past twenty-one years of age, entitled to decide for himself whether or not to turn down the opportunity to win himself such a large fortune?'

The old woman frowned, her heart and her conscience clearly at loggerheads with one another. Then, 'Very well, *monsieur*,' she said, at last. 'It shall be as you desire but, I 'ave to warn you—on your own 'eads be it!'

Picking up her stick, she limped off towards the door, bidding them follow her but then, pausing on the threshold, she turned and faced them both. 'There is, however, one small matter on which I must put you right, *messieurs*,' she said, as the beginnings of an inscrutable smile started to form on her wrinkled cheeks. 'I fear you 'ave been badly mis-informed about the gender of the infant to whom your un-fortunate cousin gave birth—it was, in fact, a female child!'

'A girl!'

'Good Lord!'

Both Maitland and Fenton were stopped dead in their tracks, each of them staring at the other in dismayed confu-sion.

'And, to think that we've spent the last two weeks enquir-ing after a blasted "Étienne"!' exploded Fenton.

He scurried after Marthe Matthilde, who by this time had crossed the lane where, taking out a large key from the pocket of her apron, she proceeded to unlock the wrought-iron gate that led into the rear parkland of Highsmith House.

'So, are you going to tell us this female's name or not?' he demanded angrily.

'Patience, *monsieur*,' she urged him, with a little frown of admonishment. 'If you would care to follow me, I promise you that all will be revealed!'

She led them through a coppice into a small clearing where, surrounded by a number of headstones and other memorial tablets, stood a tiny chapel, not much bigger than the little kitchen they had just left. Then, picking her way through the proliferation of weeds and tall grasses that had been allowed to flourish among the gravestones, she lowered herself down to the ground at the foot of a small black marble tablet and, with a corner of her apron, proceeded to rub away the years of accumulated grime.

As soon as the carved out letters gradually began to reveal themselves, she sat back on her heels with a deep sigh. 'Now you shall see for yourselves, *messieurs*,' She nodded, pointing to the names on the headstone, which read:

Here lie the earthly remains of
Étienne-Georges St Cristophe
9th Conte D'Arblaise
aged 30 years
and his beloved wife
Melandra Patricia D'Arblaise
Aged 19 years
24.5.1795

'I myself was travelling in the carriage with them, when it overturned,' she went on, dabbing at her eyes with the corner of her apron. 'Both Milord *le conte* and the driver perished on the instant. *La pauvre madame* was also very badly injured. I myself was fortunate enough to escape with only a few cuts and bruises and so managed to make my way to Milady 'ighsmith's 'ouse to summon assistance. Sadly, for *la petite contesse*, giving birth to 'er child took every bit of the little strength she 'ad left and she died moments after the babe was born!'

With a sad shake of his head, Maitland stared down at the long-neglected headstone.

'Poor little Melly,' he said, reaching into his pocket for his handkerchief and hurriedly blowing his nose, in an attempt to prevent the sudden bout of tears that threatened. 'So beautiful and so very young.'

'Yes, quite! Dreadful tragedy, I'm sure!' interrupted Fenton, rudely pushing his cousin aside in order that he might get a closer look at the tablet's wording. 'So, the fellow's name was D'Arblaise, after all, and seems he was a count too, by jove!' He let out a low whistle. 'Well, who would have thought it!'

Determinedly ignoring his cousin's cross observations, Maitland was focussing his attention on the runaway tutor's given names. 'Étienne-Georges Cristophe,' he murmured, a puzzled frown on his forehead. 'But old Hornsey seemed pretty sure that the child was named for its—that is, her—father. Cristobel? Christine?' He shot an enquiring look at their guide who, having risen to her feet, was studying the two young men with an expectant gleam in her eye.

'No, by golly!' let out Fenton, his voice rising in sudden excitement. 'Don't you see? It's George! Georgianne! Georgianne Venables—or whatever she calls herself—it has to be!'

Georgianne? Maitland's heart thudded to a standstill and, as a rapidly descending spiral of hopelessness threatened to overcome him entirely, he struggled to gather his wits together. *Oh, God, no! Not Georgianne!* he pleaded silently. *Don't let it be Georgianne, I beg you!* Having done his utmost to hide his true feelings for her, how could he now approach her and beg her to be his wife? he asked himself, in weary resignation. Any declaration of love from him at this stage would, almost certainly, be construed as simply a wanton desire to get his hands on the considerable fortune of which she was shortly to find herself in possession! She was even more lost to him now than she had ever been!

Utterly crushed and unable to collect his thoughts, it was several minutes before he could do anything other than gaze at the indisputable inscription on the tablet in the grass below. But then, slowly as, one by one, his senses gradually began to recover from the mind-blowing shock they had just received, his eyes were drawn, once again, to his late cousin's name. He heaved a deep sigh, it having suddenly come to him that she too had paid a heavy price for falling in love. Suddenly, he stiffened. *Beloved wife*, he read. *Wife!* But hadn't Catford only just informed him that Georgianne had been born out of wedlock? He spun round to face Marthe Matthilde, renewed hope in his eyes.

'It isn't Miss Venables, is it?'

'*Mais non!* Of course not, *monsieur*,' she replied, in astonishment. 'I should 'ave thought the answer to your puzzle was plain to see. Just as Milady D'Arblaise requested, the infant was named for 'er father!' She paused momentarily and a slight frown sifted over her brow. 'Regrettably, since Étienne is not, of course, a name in common use in this country, we were obliged to settle for the English version which—as I should have thought you would have known—is Steven!'

'Steven?' repeated Maitland dully, his faculties still not entirely back on form. 'I'm afraid I don't follow.'

The old woman gave an impatient shrug. 'Steven—Stephen—why, Miss Stephanie, of course! Stephanie 'ighsmith! Milady took her for adoption soon after she was born and brought the child up as her own granddaughter!'

For a moment, totally dumfounded, Maitland could do nothing other than simply stare at her but then, as the implication of her words began to penetrate his brain, a slow smile spread over his face and, within minutes, he was laughing out loud!

'Stephanie Highsmith!' he chortled, shaking his head in wonder. 'By all that's holy! Did you hear that, Jerry?' And, spinning round to catch Fenton's reaction to this astonishing news, he was somewhat taken aback to discover that there was no sign of his cousin.

'Now, where the devil has he got to?' he muttered, half to himself.

'I fear the other gentleman left some little while ago,' Marthe Matthilde volunteered, pursing up her lips. ''e appeared to 'ave lost interest long before 'e found out the real truth of the matter and took 'imself off. I daresay you will find 'im waiting for you in 'is carriage.'

'No doubt.' Maitland smiled, offering her his arm to lean on, as they made their way back towards the park's entrance. Now completely at ease with himself, he added, 'It was very good of you to go to all this trouble to help us, ma'am—I really cannot thank you enough.'

She shook her head. 'I believe that it was only right that you should know the truth,' she replied. 'This uncle who 'as died—he was the gentleman who came 'ere, *non*?'

At Maitland's nod, she pursed her lips and went on, 'I could not like 'im. 'e became most violent when I was obliged to inform 'im that his niece 'ad perished. When I asked him what he intended to do about the *pauvre enfante* 'e merely slammed a bag of money on to the table and stated that, as far as 'e was concerned, we could all go to the devil! *Sacré bleu!* 'e refused even to look at the child—which is presumably why you were unaware that she was female!'

'But did you not tell him that Étienne and Melandra had married?' questioned Maitland. 'That surely would have made a difference to his attitude?'

'The man was not interested to 'ear anything that I 'ad to say,' replied Marthe Matthilde, with a typically Gallic shrug of her shoulders. 'We 'ad parcelled up milady's belongings and papers to give to 'im, but 'e simply tossed them aside and left!'

'It is possible that he was overcome with grief,' Maitland pointed out. 'We all have different ways of expressing our sorrow.'

'I am well aware of that, young man!' retorted the nun, with some asperity. ''ad your uncle shown even the slightest interest, I would have been glad to tell 'im that I myself was present at 'is niece's wedding and that *la mère superieure* of my Dublin convent 'ad bestowed upon me the 'onour of accompanying the young couple on their journey back to England!'

Maitland was curious. 'Have you never wanted to return to your previous calling?' he asked, in some surprise.

'Sadly, the opportunity 'as never arisen.' She sighed. 'But, as you know, there are many ways in which one may serve the Lord and I do not consider that I 'ave acquitted myself too badly during these past twenty years or so.'

'According to Miss Highsmith,' laughed Maitland, 'you have practically run the place single-handed!'

'Possiblement!' returned Marthe Matthilde, with a disaffected smile. 'Nevertheless, this discovery you 'ave just made may well 'ave—'ow you say?—put the cat among the pigeons. Miss 'ighsmith is not the sort of young lady to allow the grass to grow under 'er feet and I am very much afraid that once she gets 'er 'ands on this legacy that you speak of, there will be no 'olding her. She will be off before you can mention the proverbial Monsieur Robinson by name! I fear that it will break Milady's heart!'

'Perhaps we may be able to persuade Mr Hornsey, our solicitor, to find some way to restrict any tendency that Miss Highsmith may have to embark on a wild spending spree?' suggested Maitland, offering her a sympathetic smile, as he waited for her to lock the gate. 'My uncle may well have made certain—'

His words ended in an indignant intake of breath as, having glanced across the road to where his cousin's carriage had previously stood, he saw, to his growing consternation that, just as its owner, it was now nowhere to be seen! The confounded swine had taken off without him!

Couldn't wait to share the good news with his supposed lady love, thought Maitland sourly, as he pondered on what his next move might be. *Well, I wish the pair of them the joy of each other!*

But then, as the joyful prospect of finally being able to

declare his own feelings to Georgianne recaptured his attention, he resolved to put his cousin's self-centred conduct out of his mind. Instead, he thanked Marthe Matthilde once again, bade her farewell and, with shoulders back and arms swinging smartly to and fro, he set out to walk to towards Gresham Hall, whose drive gates were something in the region of two miles up the road.

It was only after he had travelled a distance of some half-mile or so, that the odd remark that Marthe Matthilde had made about Fenton's surprise departure suddenly came to him. The old woman had pointed out that his cousin had left the little graveyard *before* learning the real truth of the matter! As the reason for Fenton's furtive behaviour became hideously clear to him, Maitland rocked to a standstill, his fists clenched in a wild fury. The cunning bastard had taken off under the mistaken impression that it was *Georgianne* who had inherited the bulk of Roger Billingham's estate!

At this realisation, a fearful premonition leapt into Maitland's brain and he began to run as though his very life depended upon it—although it was, in fact, the impending threat to Georgianne's that added wings to his feet. He sped down the lane and hurled himself through the Hall's gateway, ignoring the shouts from the indignant gate-keeper. His heart almost bursting, he leapt up the front steps and hammered on the large oaken door.

The instant the door started to open, he thrust himself through the gap, pushed past the astonished Moffat and tore up the stairs into the morning room, where, as he had supposed, the entire family—with one ominously notable exception—was assembled.

Gasping for breath, he sought out his friend. 'Help me, Cat!' he croaked, as his hands reached out for the back of the nearest sofa, in an attempt to stop himself collapsing on to the floor. 'I think that Fenton may have abducted Georgianne!'

In an instant, the whole company was on its feet, a cacophony of voices raised in consternation, but it was Stephanie Highsmith's voice that finally penetrated the noise as, marching over to where the thoroughly shattered Maitland was still clutching at the sofa for support, she screamed at him, 'Nonsense! You are talking absolute drivel! Jeremy is eloping with *me* this very evening!'

At her words, a sudden hush fell over the room, but Stephanie, ignoring the raised eyebrows and pitying looks, gave a defiant sniff and exclaimed, 'Well, so what? You were all bound to find out sooner or later. It's obvious that Mr Maitland has just made a silly—'

'For God's sake shut her up, Mama!' pleaded Catford, as he limped over to his friend. 'And someone get the poor devil a drink!'

Putting his arm around Maitland's heaving shoulders, he drew him down on to the arm of the sofa. 'Now, Will,' he commanded softly, 'tell me what's happened.'

Shaking his head, Maitland heaved himself back on to his feet. 'We have to go after him, Cat,' he insisted. 'He believes that Georgianne is Billingham's heir! God knows what he intends to do with her!'

'But, what the devil has given him that idea?' asked the astonished Catford.

In short, clipped sentences, Maitland outlined the bones of his conversation with Marthe Matthilde, culminating in the discovery that Fenton had made off with the carriage. 'It's as clear as a pikestaff that he must have gone after her!'

'He could well have run into her when she was on her way back from the church!' put in Lord Gresham who, like the rest of the group—Stephanie, in particular—had been attending avidly to Maitland's hurried account. But then, as he looked at the clock, he shook his head, adding, 'Fairly unlikely, however, since Georgianne's little Sunday-School group never finishes until twelve-thirty, and it is now barely a quarter to one. I doubt if your cousin has even managed to accost the girl, let alone abduct her!'

'Georgianne is at the church?' demanded Maitland, a sudden gleam of hope springing into his eyes as he made for the door. 'Then she should be on her way back through the park by now. If you will all excuse me, I'll go and meet her myself!'

Taking the stairs two at a time, he made for the rear terrace and, after hurtling across the lawn and on to the path that ran alongside the lake, he cast his eyes anxiously over towards the bridleway that led to the church, desperately hoping to catch a glimpse of Georgianne's slender form as she emerged from the little copse.

Surely it was well past the time that she should be on her way home, he thought, his panic rising and although his lungs had, yet again, reached bursting point and the stitch in his side was already well nigh unbearable, he forced himself forwards at an even more punishing pace.

Arriving at the entrance to the church and unable to halt his rapid progress, he cannoned straight into Philip Childs, who was just on the point of departing.

'Why, Mr Maitland,' exclaimed the vicar, as he staggered back in surprise, grabbing at the door handle to prevent himself from falling. 'I had not expected to see you again so soon!'

'Miss Venables!' croaked Maitland, leaning over and clutching at his side in agony. 'Is she still inside?'

'Miss Venables?' repeated the Reverend Childs, in some confusion. 'Why, no! I'm afraid you have just missed her! A young man took her up in his carriage not ten minutes since!'

Clapping his hand to his head in despair, Maitland found himself obliged to think quickly. 'A horse!' he cried urgently. 'Do you have a horse I could borrow?'

'Well, yes, of course!' returned the vicar, with a puzzled frown. 'But, I don't understand—is something amiss?'

'I'm afraid there's no time for explanations at the moment!' gasped Maitland, reaching forwards to grab the other man by the arm. 'We have to hurry!' Then, dragging the highly indignant vicar towards the rear of his house, he demanded to know where he kept his horse.

Wordlessly, the goggle-eyed Childs pointed his finger in the direction of the small stable situated at the far end of the property.

Releasing his hold, Maitland made for the stall. 'I need you to get a message up to Lord Catford at the Hall right away,' he called over his shoulder, as he unlatched the stable door. 'Tell him that I was too late. Fenton has abducted Miss Venables and I've gone after them!'

'F-Fenton? Abducted?' stuttered the confused clergyman. 'Am I to understand that—?'

But, before he could finish his sentence, Maitland had ridden off in pursuit of his cousin's carriage.

Chapter Twenty-One

Having seen and heard more than enough to convince himself that Georgianne was indeed the principal heir to the bulk of Billingham's large fortune, Fenton had sneaked out of the Highsmith property and taken off with all the speed that he could muster. Intent upon reaching Georgianne before his cousin could be given the opportunity to acquaint her with this startling news, his sudden recollection of a remark that Stephanie had once made, regarding her friend's 'odd little pastime' of staying behind after the morning service to read Bible stories to the village children, had convinced him of the possibility of catching her before she left the church.

This latest development in the search for his uncle's heir had very quickly convinced him of the need to abandon his former plan to elope with Stephanie. Although the idea of being seen about town with such a tasty morsel on his arm had originally been more than enough to tempt him into relinquishing his previously cherished bachelorhood, it came as no hardship for him to cast the lovely Miss Highsmith out of his mind now that he had found a far bigger fish to fry. The only difficulty now, as far as he was concerned, was in conjuring up some plan that would persuade Georgianne to get into his carriage.

Whipping up his horses, he urged them down the winding lane that led to Willowby's little church where, to his great delight, he was just in time to witness Georgianne waving farewell to the last of her pupils. Pulling up sharply at the entrance to the church, he leaned out of his seat and gave her a frantic wave.

'Miss Venables! Thank God I have caught you!' he cried, as the now perplexed Georgianne came hurrying towards him.

'Is there something wrong, Mr Fenton?' she asked, having caught sight of his hurriedly adopted expression of deep consternation.

'My cousin has met with the most dreadful accident!' he informed her, in the gravest of tones. Then, having registered the look of horror on Georgianne's face, he began to warm to his theme. 'I fear that he has taken a bad tumble from his horse and is, even as I speak, lying close to death's door!'

Georgianne's hand flew to her mouth, her cheeks whitened and unchecked tears sprang into her eyes. 'I must go to him!' she whispered. 'Take me up with you, Mr Fenton, I beg of you!'

'That is why I am here, my dear,' replied Fenton, almost hugging himself with glee at how easily the foolish girl had been duped into accompanying him. Then, on another sudden stroke of genius, he added, 'He has been asking for you!'

And, without further ado, he reached out his hand, hoisted her up on to the seat beside him and applied his whip to his already heavily perspiring horses.

'But, how could such a thing happen?' she beseeched him, as the speeding carriage charged past the gates of Gresham Hall and on up the lane towards the turnpike. 'Your cousin is, far and away, the most accomplished horseman I have ever come across.'

Since keeping his horses at such a furious pace required most of his concentration, Fenton was forced to think quickly.

'Er—I believe a child ran out in front of him,' he improvised. 'Dare say he came a cropper while trying to avoid the nipper.' He was starting to feel somewhat ill at ease at having to weave such a tangled web of deceit and, as he felt himself getting deeper and deeper into the mire, slight pangs of conscience began to prick him. 'You know Will, he does not have it in him to harm a youngster,' he then added, trying to console himself with the thought that that much was true, at any rate.

At her vivid remembrance of Maitland's solicitous dealings with the recalcitrant lads in the Reverend Childs's fledgling cricket team, Georgianne's lips began to tremble and, closing her eyes, she sent up a fervent prayer that they would not be too late. It was bad enough that he was leaving the district but, if he—*died*—she could hardly bring herself even to think the word—what point would there be in her own survival? Without him, life would no longer have any real meaning. If she could see him just once more, just hold his hand, just let him know how desperately she needed him—wanted him—*loved* him!

As the rocking, swaying carriage approached the Dunchurch crossroads, her heart was in her mouth. Would they make it in time? Would he still be conscious? Would he be able to understand what—!

To her consternation and dismay, the carriage flashed passed the Dun Cow and carried on up the road towards the heath. Now totally confused, she swung round to face Fenton, causing the carriage to pitch dangerously. 'Why have we gone past the inn? Where are you taking me, Mr Fenton?'

'Do sit still, Miss Venables, please!' returned Fenton crossly. 'You will have us over, if you keep that up! Will isn't at the inn, he's—he's in a—er—woodman's cottage just along the road here.'

'Woodman's cottage!' Georgianne would have none of that.

The man was clearly lying! 'What woodman's cottage? I'll have you know that there are no woodmen's cottages anywhere in this vicinity!' As the sudden realisation hit her, her hand flew to her mouth and, staring at him in horror, she gasped, 'Just what are you up to, Mr Fenton? Will hasn't been injured at all, has he? I demand that you put me down this instant!'

Realising that he had been rumbled, Fenton chose to ignore her and simply applied his whip to his weary horses' rumps with even more determination than hitherto.

At his action, it became horribly clear to Georgianne that she was the victim of some sort of hoax—probably to do with Stephanie's ill-conceived scheme to run away with Fenton, she concluded heatedly. Although in what way her presence might be required in that venture, she could not even begin to imagine!

Clutching at the side rail, she tried to stand up, wondering if she dared to throw herself from the swiftly moving carriage.

'Now you're being silly!' exclaimed Fenton angrily, as he thrust out his hand to drag her back into her seat. 'You can't jump out and you know it! Just sit still and behave yourself!'

'I demand to know where you are taking me!' retorted Georgianne, as she reluctantly complied with his command. 'My aunt and uncle will be furious with you for dragging me off on such a false premise! If this was one of Stephanie's harebrained ideas, I promise you that she will live to regret it!'

'Oh, do be quiet, Miss Venables!' sighed Fenton, who was beginning to feel that kidnapping her might well turn out to be far more trouble than it was worth. He had the marriage licence, it was true, but was not at all sure whether it would be possible to substitute Georgianne's name for Stephanie's. But, if he could just keep her away from home for one night, he was confident that she would be only too glad to marry him, come the morning. Nevertheless, the thought of having to spend almost a full twenty-four hours in the company of this little hellcat appealed to him not in the slightest.

Georgianne, who had been sitting quietly at his side frantically trying to think up some way in which she could extricate herself from his clutches, suddenly detected the sound of horses' hooves approaching from the rear. Turning her head sideways, she took a quick peek over her shoulder, her eyes gleaming with hope at what she saw. Some half a mile or so behind the carriage were two fast-moving riders and it was becoming patently obvious, even to their infuriated owner that, despite all his efforts to press them into greater exertion, Fenton's exhausted horses were gradually beginning to lose pace.

She held her breath, hugging herself with anticipation and promising herself that, as soon as the two gentlemen were alongside, she would scream for help. It might well be that they would recognise her or turn out to be friends of Catford or his father, the earl. Whatever the case, they were surely bound to help a lady in distress?

The sudden sound of shots being fired brought her up short. 'It would seem that we are about to be waylaid, Mr Fenton!' she murmured, not entirely at ease with this latest development, although she could not help but wonder whether her failure to return home might already have set the wheels of a search in motion. Could it be that these riders were, in fact, racing to her rescue? 'I trust that you had the forethought to provide yourself with a suitable explanation before you set out on this wild scheme.'

Casting a nervous look over his shoulder at the rapidly approaching pair, Fenton found himself in a dilemma. With his whip in one hand and the reins in the other, there was no way he could reach for the pistol that was tucked away under a concealed flap in the driver's squab. Could these fellows be yet more highwaymen, out to terrorise the neighbourhood? he wondered fearfully, conscious that, after having cashed the draft that Maitland had so generously made out to him, he was carrying the greater part of that money in the inside pocket of his jacket!

When the two horsemen drew alongside, however, and commanded him to pull up, his heart sank to a new low. These were not highwaymen, as he very quickly realised, but two of Sir Maxwell Allardyce's henchmen! Mad Max, so called because of his predilection for exacting the most vicious of revenges from anyone who failed to honour his promissory notes, and the gentleman to whom Fenton owed the best part of thirty thousand pounds!

'I'm afraid that we are going to 'ave to ask you to come along with us, Mr Fenton,' said the first of the two men, a swarthy-looking individual whose squashed and broken nose gave a clear indication of his previous profession. 'Sir Maxwell is keen to 'ave a word with you, if you've no objection?'

'As a matter of fact, Biggins,' retorted Fenton, racking his brain for some way to forestall the inevitable, 'I object most strongly! Can't you see that I have a lady with me—at least let me escort her home, before you come the heavy on me!'

'Can't be done, sir,' put in the other man. 'And begging your pardon, Miss—' here he tipped his hat in Georgianne's direction '—Sir Max will have our hides if we let you slip out of our clutches a second time!'

'But I'm just on the verge of laying my hands on more than enough money to pay him what I owe!' protested Fenton. 'By this time next week, I swear that I'll be rolling in the stuff! Go back to your boss and tell him that he'll find me on his doorstep before the end of the month and that's a promise!'

'Seems your promises,' said Biggins, with a sorrowful

shake of his head, ''ave about as much value as the paper they're written on!'

'But if I come with you now,' cried Fenton, in desperation, 'I shan't be able to marry Billingham's heiress here and then Mad Max will never get his money!'

'Are you telling us that this young woman has inherited your uncle's fortune?' demanded the second of the two men, one Hopkirk, an ex-stockbroker by trade who, although he had served his time for fraudulent practices was, by far, the more intelligent of the pair.

'That's right!' nodded Fenton eagerly. 'And the minute we've tied the knot, every penny of hers will belong to me!'

Having been listening to this puzzling interchange with growing alarm, it did not require a great deal of ingenuity on Georgianne's part to arrive at the conclusion that Fenton owed someone—this Sir Maxwell character, presumably— a great deal of money. Clearly, he had thought up this ludicrous fabrication on the spur of the moment in the hopes that these men would let them go, which left her in something of a quandary. Although it was against her nature to tell deliberate falsehoods, she was quite sure that for her to deny Fenton's fantastic claims at this point in the proceedings would do little to help their present situation. Quickly making up her mind, she decided that it might prove rather more beneficial to go along with his story.

'What Mr Fenton has told you is perfectly true, gentlemen,' she said, offering the younger of the two men her most beguiling smile. 'And, whilst you may regard his word as being of little account, let me assure you that, as niece of his lordship, the Earl of Gresham, my word *is* my bond!'

Frowning, the two men eyed each other uncertainly. 'We wasn't told to put the squeeze on the nieces of earls,' muttered the ex-pugilist. 'Fellows 'ave been 'ung for less!'

'That's true,' returned his companion. 'Trouble is, Mad Max will play merry hell with us if we just let them go. There has to be a way we can hang on to them until we get word to him.'

'Stash 'em away somewhere, you mean?'

'Mmm,' Hopkirk nodded, then, pulling his accomplice to one side, he muttered into his ear, 'I believe that there's a shelter of sorts on the heath over to our right somewhere— place where that highwayman hung out, so I was told. Near a disused quarry, apparently so, if we keep our eyes peeled, it shouldn't be that difficult to make out signs of the old wagon track!'

Having thoroughly searched the bothy, both inside and in its immediate environs, and having found nothing that might incriminate either himself or Josh, Pete Andrews pulled the planked door shut behind him and set off to head back to Dunchurch. Barely fifty yards out of the little clearing, however, the sound of an approaching carriage halted him in his steps. His immediate thought was that it must be a group of law officers coming back to have another look at Matty's hiding place and thanked providence that he had had the foresight to check it out beforehand.

Nevertheless, knowing that it would hardly do for him to be discovered in the vicinity, he gazed hurriedly about him, in an effort to find somewhere to hide. To his consternation, he was very soon to realise that the scrubby heathland, with its proliferation of low-lying gorse bushes and occasional groups of rowan offered very little in the way of concealment. As the sounds of the horses' hooves grew louder, he grew more desperate and, finally, in a blind panic, he hunched himself up and backed into the narrow opening between a nearby pair of gorse bushes where, gritting his teeth in agony as the vicious thorns cut into his hands and face, he endeavoured to make himself as inconspicuous as possible.

Less than two minutes later, the carriage, accompanied by its two outriders, bounced awkwardly past his makeshift hiding spot. Screwing up his eyes, he could just make out the identities of its two occupants, the sight of whom was very nearly enough to cause the incredulous Andrews to exclaim out loud. What, in God's name, was the major's cousin doing here? he wondered, in astonishment—let alone his lordship's niece, Miss Venables! And, by the look of their two companions—a couple of none too savoury-looking characters, in his opinion—there appeared to be something decidedly fishy going on here!

He watched as the carriage trundled into the clearing where, pulling up in front of the old bothy, it ground to a halt. He saw Fenton leap to the ground, furiously gesticulating and, by straining his ears, Andrews managed to catch the better part of what was going on.

'…all but wrecked the damned springs!' Fenton was complaining. 'Think yourselves lucky the pole didn't fracture!' Then, looking about him in disgust, he added, 'What is this place, anyhow, and why have you brought us here?'

'Just a temporary stop-gap, until we're told what's to be done with you,' the taller of the two men grunted as, after leaning down to extract a coil of thick twine from one of his saddlebags, he slid down from his horse and walked across to Fenton.

'But you can't possibly mean to keep us here while you go off to London to confer with Allardyce,' protested Fenton, backing away nervously, as the man began to unravel the twine. 'You could be gone for days!'

'The guvnor ain't in London.' Biggins grinned as, at a signal from Hopkirk, he approached Fenton from the rear and, after grabbing at the horrified man's wrists, clasped them roughly together, ready for his partner to bind. 'As it 'appens, 'e's just down the road at 'is 'unting box in Little Stretton—which is 'ow he got wind of your presence—'im and the local vicar being such bosom bows and all!'

Fenton, by now thoroughly deflated and quaking with fear, allowed himself to be propelled into the little stone shelter where, after being pushed down to the floor in the far corner, he found his ankles being tethered together in a similar fashion to his wrists.

'Wha' we gonna do about the gentry mort, then?' asked Biggins, when he finally re-emerged from the bothy. 'Go' any more cord?'

'Just about enough to tie her hands, at any rate,' replied Hopkirk who, in his partner's absence, having ordered the greatly alarmed Georgianne out of the carriage, now held her firmly by the wrists. Relinquishing his hold, he pushed her towards the waiting Biggins and strode across the grass to where his horse stood quietly grazing and extracted a smaller coil of twine from his saddlebag. 'Take off her boots and stick her in the doorway, where you can keep an eye on her. She doesn't look the sort to give you any trouble.'

'I'm to stay 'ere, while you go off and report to Allardyce, then?' queried Biggins, as soon as they had completed that task.

Hopkirk gave a perfunctory nod. 'Might be a good idea to shift their carriage over to that stand of trees and uncouple the horses, as well—just in case one of them does happen to find some way to make a break for it.'

''ardly perishing likely!' scoffed the other man, as he watched his accomplice remount. 'No fear o' that while I'm on guard!'

Crouching well down until the obvious mastermind of this very sinister-looking operation had ridden out of his hearing, Andrews waited until his partner began to busy himself with the moving of Fenton's carriage. Then, as soon as the man's back was turned, the ex-sergeant wriggled painfully out of his hiding place and, using the occasional clump of gorse as his only means of cover, he crawled around to the rear of the shack. He was not entirely sure what it was he was going to do when he got there, but felt that it might be of some comfort to the two prisoners to know that their plight had been witnessed.

Despite her underlying anxiety, Georgianne, who had remained stoically silent throughout the whole of the extremely uncomfortable journey and subsequent ordeal, was gratified to learn that she appeared to have gained her objective in making the kidnappers believe that she was some timid miss of little account. Having been thrust down with her back against the rough stonework at the bothy's opening, in full view of their captor, she soon realised that any attempt on her part to try to extricate herself from her bindings was likely to prove a complete waste of effort. Fenton, as she could see, to her utter disgust, was still slumped on his side in the far corner of the bothy and, clearly, had no intention of trying to free himself.

'You might, at least, make some sort of effort to get us out of this!' she flung at him, in a scathing undertone.

'What's the point?' he replied wearily. 'There's no way that we'd be able to get away from that bully boy out there. In any event, Allardyce is sure to tell Hopkirk to release us. As soon as he gets wind of who you are, he'll be far too eager to get his hands on the money than in doing me—us, that is,' he corrected hastily 'any more harm!'

Furious at the man's cowardly acceptance of the situation, Georgianne was too dumbfounded to argue with him. Instead, she brought her wrists up to her mouth and, surreptitiously, tried to loosen the knots with her teeth. But then, as a sudden thought occurred to her, she swung round to face him again. 'And why on earth you had to come up with that ridiculous cock-and-bull tale about me being your uncle's heir is completely beyond me!'

Fenton stiffened. 'It's not ridiculous at all!' he retorted at once. 'Granted that you may not have been aware of the connection but, let me assure you that I saw the evidence with my own eyes—your father's name was Étienne-Georges D'Arblaise and Melandra Billingham, my late cousin, was your mother—it's all there on the tombstone outside the chapel up at Highsmith House!'

For several moments she was beyond speech but, then, 'Are you completely *mad*?' she exclaimed, staring at him in astonishment. 'I know for a fact that my father was the Viscount George Arthur Venables and my mother was a Miss Anne Yardley. Indeed, I have the birth certificate to prove it!'

'But you told Hopkirk that I was telling the truth!' cried the now thoroughly alarmed Fenton, finally straightening himself up into a sitting position and starting to wrestle violently with the twine that held his wrists together.

'Only because it seemed the most sensible thing to do at the time,' snapped back Georgianne, shooting him an indignant glare but then, having registered the look of total wretchedness that had appeared on Fenton's face, her eyes softened. 'Nevertheless,' she added, 'if it serves to get us out of this mess, I am prepared to keep up the pretence.'

Andrews, who by this time, had gingerly edged his way round to their side of the building, poked his head round the doorway with an urgent 'Psst!'

Georgianne's head jerked up and, by straining to her left, she was just able to catch sight of the tip of the speaker's nose. All at once, the faintest glimmerings of hope began to rise in her breast. 'Who's there?' she called softly.

After poking his head forwards briefly and instantly retracting it, Andrews dropped to his knees. 'Pete Andrews, miss,' he mouthed in a husky undertone. 'Ostler at the Dun Cow.'

'Have you brought help?' she asked eagerly as, impatiently motioning to Fenton, who, leaning forwards with excitement, was demanding to be told what was going on, to hold his tongue, she bent her head in the direction of the opening so as not to miss what their would-be rescuer was saying.

'Don't lean towards me, miss!' he begged her. 'Drop your head on to your knees so that, if yonder bruiser should happen to look in this direction, you won't give the game away.'

'How many of you are there?' she asked, hurriedly doing as he had bidden.

'Just me at the moment, miss, but I'm off to fetch help right away—I just wanted to tell you to sit tight and try not to worry.'

'Thank you, Pete,' came Georgianne's now somewhat tremulous reply. 'But, you will hurry, won't you?'

'Be as quick as I can, miss, I promise!'

And, with that, he was gone and all she could hear was the slight rustle of branches as their aspiring liberator slithered off into the undergrowth.

Barely half a minute later, Biggins's stocky form appeared in the doorway, pistol in hand. 'Tha's righ',' he nodded, surveying the two silent captives with a satisfied grin. 'You just si' there nice and tigh' and no 'arm'll come to yer. Time fer yours truly to 'ave a li'l blow, methinks!'

He then moved away again but, to Georgianne's intense disappointment, only to position himself against the wall of the bothy, scarcely three feet from the doorway, from which viewpoint, as she very quickly realised, it would be quite impossible for him to miss anyone who tried to approach the shelter. Added to which, she very soon realised, having heard the sounds of flint striking steel as the man lit up his pipe, his close presence now made it quite impossible for her to acquaint Fenton with the ostler's worthy intentions.

Unfortunately, the possibility of Hopkirk returning before Andrews managed to summon up assistance was growing more likely with every passing minute. Had the ostler been on horseback? she then wondered. If not, it could be well over an hour before they could even begin to expect any help! At this disheartening thought, unbidden tears sprang into her eyes. Angrily blinking them away, she tried to console herself with the notion that at least Maitland must now be wondering where his cousin had disappeared to, for it was unlikely that he would think of leaving the district without him. Not that this was of any great significance insofar as Fenton's and her own current situation was concerned, as she was only too well aware, but it was strangely comforting to think that Maitland was still somewhere close by and, with any luck, might even be at the inn when Andrews eventually showed up with his request for assistance! As the wildly imaginative vision of Maitland heading up a band of volunteers to rush to her rescue filtered its way into her brain, Georgianne could not help but raise a tiny smile. And, even though she was bound to admit that the whole idea was about as far-fetched as one could get from reality, it did, at least, give her something to concentrate her mind upon while she waited for the unknown destiny that Fate actually had in store for her.

Chapter Twenty-Two

No sooner had he satisfied himself that he was well out of Biggins's earshot, Andrews got to his feet and broke into a run and, by cutting across the heathland by the shortest route possible, he very quickly reached the turnpike.

Slowing down his pace to a brisk march, in order to conserve his breath, he set off down the road towards Dunchurch. Although he was determined to seek help for the two captives, he could not help being somewhat anxious about the uncommonly long time he had absented himself from his duties in the stableyard. Not that he actually gave a damn about the job itself, he reminded himself with a grin since, come the morning, he knew he would be quitting it anyway. His real concern at this moment was that Cunliffe might simply dismiss his tale of kidnappings and hostages as some sort of feeble explanation for having failed to show up at his workplace.

Breaking into a jog-trot, he pressed on determinedly, fully resolved that, no matter what it took, he would make someone hear him out. With less than a mile and a half to go, by his reckoning, he rounded a steep curve in the road only to find himself having to leap for the grass verge in order to avoid being mown down by an oncoming horseman, who was galloping towards him at full tilt. But, as the horse swept past him, he had no difficulty in making out its rider. Wonder of wonders! It was none other than the major himself! If he could just get him to stop! Frantically waving his arms, Andrews ran back up the road yelling out for Maitland to halt.

But Maitland, having recognised his ex-sergeant, had already pulled his horse up and drawn to a halt. Wheeling round, he was, even now, making his way back to Andrews but, before the groom could speak, he burst out with, 'Have you seen any sign of Mr Fenton's carriage on this stretch of road, Pete?'

'Thank God it's you, sir!' returned Andrews. 'I was on my way to find you—they've got your cousin and Miss Venables tied up in the old bothy!' He flung his arm in the direction from which he had just come. 'It's over by—'

'I know it!' interrupted Maitland tersely then, reaching into his pocket, he drew out a bag of sovereigns and tossed it down to the other man. 'Take this and hire yourself a horse— steal one if you have to—but get over to the Hall as fast as you can and pass this information on to their lordships!'

Then, almost before the stunned ostler had had time to digest his command, he had turned his mount and was off across the moor as though all the devils in hell were on his tail.

Having already sacrificed several precious minutes of his time to call in at the Dun Cow in order to enquire after his runaway cousin whilst, at the same time, exchanging the vicar's horse for his own, much more speedy Pegasus, it had been with a heavy heart that Maitland who, after emerging from the inn's stableyard, had then been faced with the prospect of choosing from three possible routes to pursue. Surely, somebody must have seen the damned carriage go through, he had thought, grinding his teeth in frustration and promising himself that, if his traitorous cousin had harmed so much as a single hair on Georgianne's precious head, the slimy toad would wish he had never been born.

Wearily casting these unproductive thoughts out of his mind, Maitland had then gazed about him for some sort of inspiration as to which road Fenton might have opted to take, since all three of them led to a major township. Unable to make up his mind, his eyes had fallen upon a noisy group of urchins who appeared to be squabbling over the rightful ownership of the heap of marbles that lay at their feet. Hardly daring to hope that one or other of these youngsters might have witnessed Fenton's carriage pass by, he had quickly dismounted and, leading Pegasus over to the grass verge where they were engaged in their tussle, he had enquired, without a great deal of hope, 'Any of you lads happen to notice a maroon carriage go by in the last fifteen minutes or so?'

'Pulled by a couple of showy-looking greys, was it?' one of the lads had returned, without looking up, his attention more fully engaged in the friendly pummelling of the young colleague upon whose back he had been straddled.

'That's right!' Maitland had exclaimed, stepping closer. 'Half a crown if you can tell me which way they went!'

Without hesitation, the boy's head had snapped back and he had jumped to his feet, his eyes wide. 'Shot straight over the crossroads without stopping, it did, and went up towards the heath!' he had answered without a pause, his grubby paw held out in readiness to receive the unexpected fortune.

After tossing the promised coin to the waiting youth, Maitland had lost no time in leaping back on to his horse, whereupon, having urged Pegasus to give him everything he had, he had set off up the turnpike towards Dunsmoor Heath.

* * *

Thanking God for having sent Andrews to point him in the direction and, spurred on by the very real fear that Georgianne might be hurt or in some sort of danger, Maitland headed for the little clearing that housed the bothy, trying not to let the highly poignant memory of his last visit to that spot cloud his ability to think straight. Casting his mind back to the type of terrain that surrounded the building, he soon realised that anyone on horseback would be spotted long before the rider could reach the spot so, reining in alongside a couple of stunted oak trees, he tethered Pegasus to an over-hanging branch and began to make his way on foot. In much the same way as his ex-sergeant had done earlier, he drew on the many surveillance tactics that had served him well during his years on the Continent and, making use of whatever cover the rolling moorland had to offer, he crept stealthily towards his objective.

Eventually, having reached the clearing, he managed to conceal himself behind the trunk of one of several beech trees that were dotted about the area and anxiously surveyed the scene in front of him. Insofar as he could make out, there appeared to be only one man guarding the shelter, but that did not mean that there might not be several more of them somewhere in the near vicinity. All at once, a flash of blue sprigged muslin suddenly claimed his attention and his eyes flew across to the bothy's threshold, from where a pair of shapely ankles, clad only in white stockings, revealed themselves! Realising that Georgianne's presence was now indisputable, his heart leapt into his throat but, as to how many others were also inside the windowless building, he did not care to hazard a guess.

Only too conscious of the fact that it would be impossible to alert her of his presence without drawing attention to himself, he inched his way round to the rear of the bothy and, after extracting his pistol from his pocket, quickly and silently primed and loaded it for action.

Dropping to all fours, he manoeuvred himself to the corner of the building where, after a quick look round to ensure that his presence had not been observed, he stood up and raised his weapon. He was just about to take a pot shot at the guard's shoulder blade when he heard Georgianne calling out.

'Do you think that you might loosen these ties just a little, Mr Biggins?' she was beseeching her captor. 'This thin cord is cutting into my flesh most dreadfully and I can scarcely feel my fingers!'

Biggins, who had been puffing away at his pipe, engrossed in his usual daydream of getting hold of enough money to leave this very unsatisfactory life behind him and set up his own boxing salon—just as Gentleman Jackson had done—tutted resignedly and dragged himself to his feet. Couldn't do any harm to slacken off the girl's bindings at this stage, he thought to himself. When all was said and done, she'd been as quiet as a mouse and, in any event, Hopkirk would be back at any minute. Apart from which, as he had realised some time ago, if—God forbid—they *should* happen to get caught, it wouldn't go well for either of them if the girl had been injured in any way—her being related to an earl and all!

Sauntering over, he bent down to inspect her wrists and could see that the twine was, indeed, just as she had complained, pressing cruelly into her tender flesh. Tucking his pistol into his belt, he began to fumble with the intricate knots, totally unaware of Maitland's presence directly behind him.

On the other hand, Georgianne, whose eyes had been focussed over Biggins's shoulder, as she had contemplated the pros and cons of trying to make a run for it, spotted him immediately. Her mouth dropped open and she let out a little squeak of surprise, only to have Maitland shake his head and press his finger to his lips. Hurriedly, she turned her excited squeak into a squeal of pain, causing Biggins to apply himself more diligently to his task. 'Beg pardon, miss,' he muttered. 'Can't seem ter ge'—OOF!'

He crumpled to the ground, the butt of Maitland's pistol having smashed into the back of his skull, rendering him immediately unconscious.

Doing her best to edge herself away from the unpleasant spectacle at her feet, Georgianne was almost too afraid to ask Maitland if the man was dead.

'Hardly,' replied her rescuer as, stepping unconcernedly over Biggins's prone form, he whipped out his penknife and began to saw at her bindings. 'But he'll have one hell of a headache when he comes to!' Then, drawing her to her feet, he asked anxiously, 'Are you all right? Did they hurt you?'

'Not really,' Georgianne hastened to reassure him. 'Slightly sore wrists, that's all.' Suddenly, her eyes lit up and her lips parted in a wide smile. 'I swear that I was never so glad to see anyone!' And, before Maitland had had time to register her intention, she had flung her arms around him and was clinging to him so tightly that he could scarcely take a breath. It took every ounce of his self-control to stop himself returning her embrace as, clenching his teeth, he was forced to keep reminding himself that, after having suffered such a dreadful experience, the poor girl was clearly overwrought. He could not help but feel that any attempt on his part to take advantage of the present situation, highly enticing though it was proving to be, would render him as bad, if not worse, than his scoundrel of a cousin—quite apart from the fact it was Georgianne's love that he wanted, not her gratitude.

Promising himself that he would wait for a more auspicious moment before declaring his true feelings, he gently disentangled Georgianne's arms and reluctantly eased himself away from her hold. Steeling himself to ignore the expression of hurt bewilderment that appeared on her face, he stepped hurriedly away from her and swung round to confront Fenton who, with increasing impatience, had been waiting to be released from his own tortuous bonds.

'Well, hurry up, man!' he called querulously from his corner. 'The other fellow will be back directly and then we'll all be in the soup!'

Maitland shot him a venomous glare. 'I've a damned good mind to leave you to whatever fate your lousy associates have in store for you!' he grated. 'After your diabolical behaviour this morning, you deserve to be well and truly whipped!'

'Now, steady on, Will, old man!' returned Fenton, looking only slightly abashed. 'I wasn't going to hurt Miss Venables—'

Georgianne, whose thoughts, until this point, had been entirely concerned with trying to come to terms with Maitland's hurtful rebuff, drew in an indignant breath. 'You were trying to force me to marry you!' she exclaimed resentfully. Then, turning towards Maitland, she went on, 'Your delightful cousin also spun Biggins out there and the other man, Hopkirk, some ridiculous tale about me being your uncle's long-lost heir—he apparently owes a large sum of money to somebody called Allardyce and managed to convince our captors that my supposed inheritance is going to pay off the debt!'

'Then it's a great pity that he didn't wait around long enough to discover that Melandra's child is, in fact, Stephanie Highsmith!' retorted Maitland, with a scornful laugh. 'By that lady's own admission, she and Fenton were set to elope this very evening! Hoist by his own petard, by God, and jolly well serves him right!'

Frowning slightly, Georgianne gave an indifferent shrug. 'Whilst I can't disagree with you there, might I suggest that any further discussion on the matter would be better left until a more convenient time? As your cousin has just pointed out, Hopkirk, along with who knows who else, may well be on his way here by now and I, for one, would prefer not to be here when he discovers what has happened to his colleague!'

'Miss Venables is quite right, Will!' cried Fenton, casting up an anguished look at his cousin. 'Be a good fellow and unfasten these cords—you can take me to task later.'

'You may be sure that I will, you snivelling coward!' grunted Maitland, as he leaned over to apply his penknife to his cousin's bonds. 'If your suspicions are correct, we had better make haste—we still have to harness the horses to your carriage.'

'Let's just hope that the blasted springs aren't completely jiggered!' exclaimed Fenton, screwing up his face in agony as the blood slowly seeped back into the veins at his wrists. 'Cost me a small fortune...' His words petered out as he became aware of the none-too-friendly expression on his cousin's face. 'Yes, well, I dare say we'd better get on!'

'Any idea what happened to your shoes?' Maitland asked Georgianne, as they made their way across the clearing to the stand of trees where Biggins had parked the carriage.

'I believe he tossed them into the bushes,' replied Georgianne, nodding to a nearby patch of gorse. 'I'll get them.'

She started to turn, but Maitland, with a determined shake of his head, put his hand on her arm to stay her. 'I'll go,' he said. 'Your hands would get scratched to pieces.'

But hardly had he taken two steps towards his objective before the sound of approaching horses reached their ears. With no time to ponder as to the possible identity of the oncoming riders, he grabbed Georgianne by the hand and hurriedly dragged her back into the shelter of the bothy.

'Stay here!' he commanded her as, whipping out his pistol, he hurriedly cocked it, ready for action. Then, turning to Fenton, who had followed them, he asked, 'Is your weapon still in its place under the driving-box?'

At his cousin's nod, Maitland, after telling Fenton to follow him, sped across the clearing and, reaching under the seat, drew out the leather pouch that held the pistol, along with the ramrod and several cartridges.

Thrusting the pouch into his cousin's hands, he hunkered himself down behind the body of the carriage and, after instructing Fenton to do likewise, said, 'You keep them loaded and leave the firing to me.'

Less than half a minute later, Hopkirk, accompanied by two other men, swept into the clearing where, as soon as his eyes alighted upon the prostrate form of his companion, he leapt angrily from his horse, yelling, 'What in the hell's been going on here?'

Georgianne, having tucked herself into one of the far corners of the bothy, found herself trembling with uneasiness, due mainly to the fact that she was unable to see what was happening outside. There was a great deal of cursing and shouting and rushing about; then came a shot, followed quickly by a second and then a third! Then, suddenly, the sounds of more riders crashing through the undergrowth came to her ears, followed by the crunch of booted footsteps as someone approached the bothy! Fearing the worst, she hunched herself back against the stone wall, her fingers pressed tightly to her lips and her eyes closed, waited in silent dread for the expected retribution.

At the touch of a hand on her arm, she let out a gasp of horror and her eyes flew open, only to witness a smiling Maitland standing in front of her.

'You can come out now,' he grinned, as he calmly handed

her her shoes. 'It's all over—Cat's arrived and he and his men are dealing with what's left of the scoundrels!'

Hot, sticky and decidedly dishevelled, Georgianne, who had never been more frightened in her life, was unable to make up her mind whether to burst into hysterics or simply to throw herself on the ground and howl her eyes out! Her wrists were hurting, her gown and stockings were smeared with mud and grass stains, her best Sunday bonnet was crushed beyond repair and most of her hair had come adrift from its pins! What she really wanted to do was to hurl herself at him and feel the comfort of his strong arms around her but, in view of his earlier rebuff, she realised that this was not an option. Struggling to hold back the tears that threatened, she endeavoured to pull herself together and forced herself to enquire as to the outcome of the confrontation.

She thrust her feet into her shoes saying, in as casual a tone as she could conjure up in the given circumstances, 'I heard shots being fired. Are Hopkirk and his men all dead?'

'Most certainly not!' came his cheery response. 'I just put them out of action for the foreseeable future—it would appear that abduction and blackmail don't go down very well in these parts! Are you ready to go home now?'

'Oh, yes, please!' she replied fervently. 'I feel an absolute wreck and I've had more than enough excitement for one day, thank you very much!'

Fighting back the desire to reach out and pull her into his arms for, now that he knew that she was safe at last, to him she had never looked more adorable, Maitland took a deep breath and merely nodded. Then, taking her by the hand, he led her over to the re-assembled carriage, beside which Fenton was standing and looking, as Georgianne could not help but remark, more than somewhat pleased with himself.

'What about that, then!' he chortled, as he stood back to

allow his cousin to hand her up into the seat. 'Went down like ninepins—each and every one of them, and all due to my impeccable reloading ability!'

Her eyes flew across to gauge Maitland's response to these high-flown and somewhat improbable claims. She was expecting him to give his cousin the set-down he so rightly deserved, but he merely shook his head and shrugged his shoulders, before striding off to confer with the viscount.

'I dare say you'll both be leaving soon,' she said, in a small voice, her eyes fixed firmly on Maitland's back. 'Now that you've solved your mystery you'll have no reason to stay.'

'Couldn't have worked out better, as far as I'm concerned,' responded Fenton, looking extraordinarily cheerful, as he climbed up beside her on the driver's seat. 'Amazing piece of luck, Stephanie turning out to be the missing heiress, wouldn't you say?'

Georgianne looked across at him in astonishment. 'You can't imagine that she'll welcome you back with open arms after this morning's little fiasco, surely!'

'Oh, she'll no doubt get on her high horse for a little while,' he returned, quite unabashed. 'But, given that she's very keen to get to London before her grandmother gets back, I dare say I'll soon manage to sweeten her up. After all, it was an easy mistake to make and you've not been harmed in any way, have you?'

'I doubt if my uncle will see the situation in quite that way!' retorted Georgianne, her eyes still on Maitland who, having waved Catford and his escort party on their way, was now heading off through the copse to retrieve his own mount.

Fenton's eyes clouded over. 'Yes, well, I'll face that bridge when I get to it,' he replied. 'His lordship has always struck me as a pretty reasonable fellow—I dare say he'll soon come round to my way of thinking!'

Knowing Lord Gresham as well as she did, Georgianne could not help thinking that Fenton was in for a rather nasty shock if he imagined that the earl was the sort of man who could be won over by a few flowery phrases. But since her mind was now fully occupied with her concern at Maitland's apparently having gone off without them, she refrained from answering. Less than a minute later, however, a huge surge of relief flowed through her as he re-appeared, leading his chestnut stallion behind him.

'Down you get,' he instructed his cousin tersely. 'I'm driving Miss Venables back—you can take Pegasus!'

'Steady on, Will!' cried Fenton, cringing back in dismay. 'You can't really expect me to ride that great brute of yours, surely?'

'I assure you that I can and I do,' replied Maitland. 'Now be a good fellow and hop down—this young lady has had more than enough of your company for one day!'

Chapter Twenty-Three

❧❧❧❧❧

As he guided the carriage out of the clearing, Maitland was still undecided as to how he might best bring up the subject that was closest to his heart. Whilst he had no doubt about the intensity of his own love for Georgianne, it had been impossible for him to convince himself that these feelings might be reciprocated. For, despite the fact that she had returned that stolen kiss with what, at the time, had seemed to him a good deal of enthusiasm, he had not yet been able to convince himself that the deep affinity that seemed to have developed between the two of them over these past couple of weeks was anything more than a figment of his own hopeful imaginings.

Added to which, it was difficult for him to put aside Catford's warning that she, in the mistaken belief that the unenviable stain of illegitimacy was sufficient reason for her to cling to her single status would, as likely as not, reject any offer that he might make her. And, whilst it was true that his friend's assurance that Georgianne was not entirely indifferent to him had gone a long way towards strengthening his resolve, he was still very conscious of the fact that he needed to tread very carefully, lest he made a complete hash of the whole proceedings.

Although Maitland's continuing silence had the effect of making Georgianne feel even more downhearted than ever, she ungrudgingly attributed his lack of conversation to the fact that having to steer a carriage along such a bumpy and rutted track must require a good deal of concentrated effort. But, when, at last, the carriage rolled off the heathland onto the turnpike's firmer surface and he still kept up his somewhat taciturn vigil, she could not help but feel that it must be she herself who was the cause of his pensive demeanour.

She could only assume that, after having had to disentangle himself from her somewhat impulsive embrace, he must feel that he had to keep his distance, lest she felt the need to throw herself at him again! Suddenly she was incensed by the thought that, whilst the male of the species seemed to consider it perfectly acceptable to grab hold of an unsuspecting young woman and kiss her whenever the fancy took him, the rules were, once again, quite different for his female counterpart. Not that she had objected to the kiss, as she was forced to remind herself. In fact, she had found the whole experience quite earth-shattering and, given half a chance, would more than welcome a repeat performance! But, if Maitland's recent conduct were anything to go by, the likelihood of that ever happening again was exceedingly remote. Nevertheless, and despite her present heartache, she drew some slight comfort from the knowledge that these past few days in his company had brought her so much pleasure and delight that, even if she lived until she were ninety, she knew that she would never be able to forget him.

As the carriage rolled up Gresham Hall's front drive, she shot him a quick sideways glance. Whilst she was sure that he would need to come into the house in order to acquaint her uncle with the details of all that had happened in the last few hours, she could only pray that he did not intend to leave without giving her the chance to thank him for his kindness. For, although he had made it painfully obvious that he did not regard her as anything more than the cousin of a friend, there was no reason not to want to wish him Godspeed in his future life.

As he watched Georgianne being ushered into the house by the highly relieved half-dozen or so of her relatives who had dashed down the front doorsteps the moment that the carriage wheels had been heard on the driveway, Maitland could not help a somewhat wry smile from appearing on his face. It was clear that any attempt on his part to try to snatch a few minutes alone with her, in order to confess his love, was going to prove not at all easy in these present circumstances.

Heaving a deep sigh, he realised that he was going to have to shelve that highly challenging issue until a more conducive moment presented itself, since there were, clearly, other more pressing matters that required his immediate attention. Driving round to the stableyard, he tossed the reins to a waiting groom, leapt out of the carriage to join his now rather more subdued cousin and together, the two men followed the waiting Catford into the house and thence across the marble-chequered hallway into the earl's study, to where they had been urgently summoned.

A little hurt and somewhat surprised not to see Stephanie amongst the excited group that had rushed out to meet her, Georgianne immediately enquired of her aunt where her friend might be.

'I had to send her to her room,' came Lady Letitia's regretful reply. 'Ever since Mr Maitland informed her of this ridiculous inheritance, she has been behaving in the most disgraceful manner. I was obliged to send one of the men off to Harrogate requesting Lady Highsmith's immediate return.'

Holding Georgianne away from her, she scrutinised her carefully. 'You look as if you could do with a good wash, you poor child. I will have some hot water sent up to your room directly, but I would ask you to keep well away from Stephanie, if you would—we had best leave it to her grandmother to deal with the silly girl's nonsense!'

'But we all know that Lady Highsmith isn't Stephanie's grandmother!' cried Georgianne, in protest, as she made for the stairs. 'I don't wonder at the poor girl behaving oddly— she's sure to be in the most terrible state of confusion! I know exactly how she feels! I must go to her at once!'

Hurriedly mounting the stairs to the second floor, and without waiting to knock, she threw open the door of Stephanie's bedroom and charged inside. There, to her utmost consternation, she found her friend complacently tossing her belongings into the large wicker trunk that had accompanied her on her arrival at Gresham Hall.

'Oh, no, Steffi!' cried Georgianne, rushing forwards and trying to stay the other girl's hands. 'You must not think of leaving! I could not bear it if you were to go too!'

'Well, I must say you do look a mess, Georgianne!' exclaimed Stephanie, who was totally unmoved by the expression of anguish on her friend's face. 'And, please don't be such a goose! You must know that it will be quite impossible for me to remain here now. Apart from the fact that everyone is set on giving me the cold shoulder, I need to get back to Highsmith House before my—that scheming old harridan, I should say—receives your aunt's summons!'

'But, how will your being there help matters?' asked the bewildered Georgianne, as she slumped down on her friend's bed.

'I should have thought it was perfectly obvious,' retorted Stephanie, still continuing to stuff her possessions into the already overflowing basket. 'I have to find the papers—the old dear is sure to have kept them—she's always been very meticulous about such things. According to your aunt, she adopted me soon after my mother died—some garbled tale or other about her own daughter dying in childbirth after the fellow she ran off with abandoned her—I really didn't pay that much attention!'

'Although, it does, perhaps, explain why Lady Highsmith was inclined to be so strict with you,' put in Georgianne gently.

'Possibly.' Stephanie shrugged. 'But it doesn't mean that I am obliged to stay with her now. From what I have been able to gather, once I get my hands on this Bellingham chap's inheritance, I'll be as rich as old Croesus and will be able to do whatever I please!'

'But, what *do* you intend to do?' enquired her friend, even more perplexed than she was before. 'You can't still be thinking of running off with Mr Fenton, surely?'

'Well, it's true that I may still have to make use of the silly noodle,' Stephanie was forced to concede. 'But I certainly don't intend to marry him, if that's what you're thinking! I shall have to get him to take me to see this solicitor chappie, of course, but, as soon as all the financial business is sorted out, I mean to set up my own establishment in one of those fancy London squares that we're always reading about, and have myself the best time ever!'

'But, you can't mean to live on your own, Steffi,' Georgianne pointed out in dismay. 'You would never be accepted into society if you even hinted at such a scandalous course of action!'

'Oh, I shall hire myself a highly respectable companion, of course,' returned her friend airily. 'It seems that my father was a count of some sort, so I suppose that makes me a countess and, with the amount of money that I shall have, I doubt that I will be short of company. Anyway, I don't have time to discuss the pros and cons of the thing right now. I have to go and find where my ex-grandmama has hidden my birth papers—I shan't be able to lay claim to the money without them!'

Thrusting on the lid of her now overflowing basket, she then endeavoured to close it but, after failing, at the third attempt, to fasten any of the leather straps, she sat back on her heels in disgust.

'I can't think how Madge ever got the stupid thing done up in the first place,' she wailed. 'There are exactly the same things in it as there were when I came!'

'It would seem that servants do have their uses, then,' observed Georgianne, hiding a smile. 'Perhaps, it would be better if you let Emily deal with your packing. I'll get Moffat to send the trunk over to Highsmith House as soon as it's done.' Pausing, she gave the other girl a searching glance, before adding, 'You've quite made up your mind to go, then?'

With a determined nod, Stephanie got to her feet and, coming over to join Georgianne on the bed, she put her arm around her friend's shoulders. 'Please don't begrudge me this marvellous opportunity, Georgianne,' she said, with a slight catch in her voice. 'This money will finally give me the chance to do what I have been wanting to do for years, and I promise you that I shan't let it spoil our friendship—once I am settled, I shall send for you and we can have the most amazing times together, you'll see!'

Biting back the tears that threatened, Georgianne gave her friend a weak smile. 'I shall miss you most dreadfully, Steffi, and Willowby won't be nearly as much fun without you. I do so hope that this new life you have chosen brings you the sort of happiness you crave.'

'You may be sure of that,' laughed her friend, as she

headed for the door. 'I'm just off to the stables to see if I can persuade one of the grooms to rustle up a carriage for me—I don't fancy walking four miles in this heat. Wish me luck!'

Having watched Stephanie skip down the stairs until she was out of sight, Georgianne started to make her way towards her own bedchamber. She knew that she ought to wash and change before putting in another appearance downstairs but was concerned that, if she stopped to do so, Maitland would be long gone before she had readied herself.

She came to a sudden standstill and, after rubbing her fingers across her mud-streaked cheeks and raking her fingers through her unkempt curls, she ran quickly down the stairs but, on reaching the empty hallway, she was forced to conclude that her uncle's interview with Maitland and his cousin must still be ongoing.

But, even as this thought crossed her mind, the door to Lord Gresham's study opened and a visibly crestfallen Fenton emerged, followed by Catford himself who, after closing the door behind him, limped hurriedly to her side.

'Oh, Georgie, my dearest girl!' he cried, as he wrapped his arms around her and hugged her to his chest. 'Thank God you weren't hurt! I'm so sorry I didn't get the chance to speak to you before we left but once I knew that you were in Will's safe hands, I just got on with what had to be done! Forgive me?'

'Of course I forgive you!' She smiled up at him. 'It wasn't really so dreadful and I'm just thankful that it's all over! May I ask what you did with those dreadful men?'

'We dropped them off at Sir Joseph's house,' replied the viscount. 'Dare say he'll send them off to the county jail, where they'll be held until the next assizes and then, if they manage to escape the hangman, they'll most likely be transported.'

As a little shudder ran through her, Georgianne, casting a quick glance at Fenton, who had thrown himself down on one of the Hall's plush-covered sofas, then whispered, 'What about Mr Fenton? He looks as though Uncle Charles has already given him a good dressing down!'

'No more than he deserves,' replied her cousin, shrugging indifferently. 'Maybe it will make him think twice before he goes round abducting any more helpless females!'

'Oh, come now, Cat!' she chuckled. 'I wasn't aware that you ever thought of me as helpless!'

'No, well, perhaps not,' he conceded, with a grin. 'But you know what I mean.'

Nodding absently, her eyes travelled to the still closed door of the study. 'Uncle Charles can't be finding fault with Mr Maitland's handling of the situation, surely?' she asked, doing her utmost to adopt the most casual of tones.

'Certainly not!' returned Catford, his eyes suddenly gleaming with suppressed amusement. 'Daresay he's just offering his thanks and congratulating him and all that.' Then, after eyeing her searchingly for a moment or two, he went on, 'If you don't mind me saying so, my pet, you're not looking at all the thing! Hadn't you better hop back to your room and tidy yourself up a bit? Er—how about if we meet in the lake pavilion in about twenty minutes?—there's something I need to speak to you about.'

'In the lake pavilion?' returned his cousin, somewhat bemused. 'But why all the secrecy? Surely you can tell me whatever it is right here and now?'

'Er, no, not really,' replied the viscount, casting a nervous glance towards his father's study. 'Wouldn't do for Pa to come out and see you looking such a mess, you know. Off you go now, there's a good girl!'

'Twenty minutes, then.' She laughed as she made for the stairs. 'And don't keep me waiting!'

'One moment, if you please, Miss Venables!'

Having seen that Georgianne was about to leave, Fenton had risen to his feet and was hurrying towards her. 'I wonder if you would mind asking Miss Highsmith if she could spare me a few minutes of her time?' he asked anxiously. 'I do need to speak to her rather urgently.'

Her foot already on the bottom step, Georgianne paused and turned. 'I'm afraid Stephanie has already left Gresham Hall, Mr Fenton,' she informed him. 'She took off for Highsmith House a good ten minutes ago—you'll need to hurry if you want to catch up with her.'

His face cleared. 'Oh, thank you—I'd best be on my way then!' He turned to go but then, as if something had just occurred to him, he turned and said, somewhat shamefacedly, 'Sorry about this morning's little fiasco, Miss Venables. I had no intention of harming you, I swear!'

Georgianne, who could not help but feel rather sorry for the man, especially in view of the rather dim prospects that she knew were in store for him, was quick to assure him that she bore him no ill will. Thanking her profusely, he made at once for the front entrance while she, with a quick wave at her cousin, turned and sped off up the stairs.

Scarcely fifteen minutes later, clad in one of her prettiest gowns, with her hair restored to its normal elegant coiffure, the much-refreshed Georgianne stepped down from the rear terrace and started to make her way down to the lake path. She could not imagine why Catford had chosen to arrange this somewhat clandestine meeting and could only suppose that he wanted to share something of his and Alice's future plans with her.

There was, however, no sign of her cousin when she stepped up into the summerhouse so, walking over to the opening that faced towards the lakeside, and gazing out at

the peaceful vista beyond, she found herself forlornly recalling her previous visit to the spot. Hardly more than a week
ago and so much had happened in that short space of time.
How she would be able to persuade herself to return to the
same dreary day-to-day existence that had been her lot until
Maitland had arrived and turned her life upside down, she
could not even begin to contemplate.

'Still studying the wildlife, I see,' came a voice behind her.

Her eyes widening and in total confusion, she spun round to
find herself face to face with the subject of her mournful reverie.

'I thought you had gone!' she gasped. 'Cat asked me to
meet him here!'

'So he told me,' observed Maitland, regarding her with a
certain amount of anxiety on his face. 'Would you prefer
that I left?'

'Oh, no! Please don't!' she hastened to reply. 'That is—
I—er—you are very welcome to stay and enjoy the view,
of course!'

'And a most enchanting view it is,' he returned softly, his
eyes never leaving her face.

At his words, a rosy blush covered Georgianne's cheeks
and, all at once, she felt quite breathless and was unable to
do anything other than gaze back into his eyes, her heart
almost grinding to a stop as she tried to make sense of the
unfathomable expression therein.

'I couldn't believe that you would leave without even
saying goodbye to me,' she managed eventually. 'I dare say
you must regard me as the most dreadful nuisance, but—'

Her words stuttered to a halt as Maitland, with a helpless
sigh, reached out and pulled her into his arms.

'M-Mr Maitland!' she squeaked in astonishment, as she
felt him bury his face into her hair. 'What are you doing?'

'I'm trying to tell you that I love you, you darling little

idiot!' he groaned impatiently. 'And, for pity's sake, do stop calling me Mr Maitland!'

Unable to believe her ears, Georgianne, who could only assume that Maitland must be set on playing some sort of hideous game with her, tried, without success, to extract herself from his hold.

'You're talking nonsense!' she protested. 'Please let me go!'

'Not until you let me kiss you!' he retorted, holding her even more closely.

Since the thought of being kissed by him once more was almost too much of a temptation to resist, Georgianne found herself hesitating momentarily, causing Maitland to hold his breath as, with an expectant gleam in his eyes, he stared down at her.

But, then, with a decided shake of her head, she recommenced her struggle saying, somewhat reluctantly, 'You're really not being at all sensible, Mr M—I mean—er, Will. Cat could appear at any minute!'

Maitland heaved an exasperated sigh. Despite Catford having advised him to take his cousin by surprise and meet any resistance head on, he was finding the going much tougher than he had expected. 'Do stop finding excuses, Georgianne,' he urged her. 'Catford has no intention of showing up, I promise you. It was merely a ploy to get you here so that you and I might have a few minutes alone together and, if you really don't want me to kiss you, you only have to say so!'

Biting her lip, she regarded him silently for a moment or two then, making up her mind, she said, 'Well, I dare say I would like it very much, but I really can't imagine why you should want to do so!'

'*Why I should—!*'

Suddenly incensed, he loosened his hold and, lifting his

hands to grip her by the shoulders, he began to shake her, roaring, 'Because I love you, *love* you, dammit! How many more times must I tell you? I love you and I'm trying to ask you to marry me!'

At this, her face went white and she tore herself from his grip. A stolen kiss before he left was one thing, but this was too much to bear. 'No, no!' she whispered, backing away from him. 'You can't love me—you mustn't—it's quite impossible!'

Having remembered that both Catford and the earl had told him that it would be far better to let Georgianne reveal the truth about her birth in her own way, rather than letting her find out that he had known about it all along, Maitland took a deep breath and, doing his best to control his impatience, said quietly, 'Oh, but I can and I must, Georgianne, and it is perfectly possible, I assure you!' He paused and an apprehensive frown sifted across his brow. 'Unless, of course, you can't find it in you to return my sentiments! Is that what this is all about, Georgianne? Are you trying to tell me that you don't love me?'

Startled at the sudden directness of the question, Georgianne could do no more than shake her head and sigh, 'No, Will, I'm not, because, as it happens, I love you with all my heart. Nevertheless, what you are asking of me is still impossible!'

Although his heart was filled with joy at her response, Maitland was almost at the end of his tether. 'Why is it impossible?' he pressed her.

'Because—because—' she began, but then, pausing, she shrugged her shoulders resignedly and went on, 'I suppose it's only fair that you should be given the true reason, Will and, since you won't want to marry me anyway, once you know, I might just as well tell you straight out.' Facing him squarely, she then said, 'The fact of the matter is that I can't marry anyone, Will, because I had the great misfortune to be born out of wedlock!'

For a moment, whilst inwardly applauding that she had finally found the courage to bring her fears out into the open, Maitland regarded her in absolute silence then, placing his hands back on her shoulders, he looked down into her eyes, now moist with unshed tears, and said gently, 'And you really believe that my knowing that is likely to make the slightest bit of difference to the way I feel about you, Georgianne?'

'It may not matter to you, Will,' she replied stubbornly, 'but you have a mother and sisters and—oh, I don't know—a host of other friends and relatives who would, I assure you, mind very much about such a thing!'

'I'm afraid my people don't move in such exalted circles as yours do, sweetheart,' he said, giving her a slightly rueful smile. 'They are merely run-of-the-mill country farmers and, I promise you, far too wrapped up in their own affairs to concern themselves over such trivialities.'

When Georgianne simply shook her head and made no response to these hearty assurances, Maitland, for once in his life, found himself at a complete loss as to how best to proceed. Although he was reasonably confident that pulling her into his arms and kissing her until she was too weak to argue any more might well achieve the desired effect, he was not entirely sure that this would do anything to help resolve the situation in the long term.

Realising that this was a decision that Georgianne would have to come to terms with in her own way, he stepped away from her and turning, walked towards the doorway and stared across the lake, racking his brains to try and come up with something that might persuade her to change her mind. His eyes drifted idly over the tranquil waters of the lake where they lit upon a group of swans making its stately and graceful way upstream. As he watched them, the vaguest germ of an idea began to form in his head and, drawing in a deep breath, he turned back to face Georgianne.

After he had moved from her side, she had waited, momentarily, for him to return but when, after several minutes, he gave no sign of coming back, she was not sure whether to go over and join him at the doorway or simply leave the building altogether. In the end, she did neither but went instead to the far side of the pavilion where she sat down on one of the curved stone benches and watched him as, with his arms folded across his chest, he leaned against the doorframe, seemingly engrossed in admiring the view.

As if it weren't bad enough that she had allowed herself to fall in love with the man, she thought, disconsolately fidgeting with the string of pearls at her neck. But then to discover that he returned her love and actually wanted to marry her was more than her heart could bear. Having been safely cloistered within the warmth and security of the Gresham family for so long, the thought of going out into a world where, at any time and on any day, the story of her dubious history might be made common currency, dragging both his name and her own into the public limelight, was too awful even to contemplate. Not that Venables was really her surname, as she quickly had to remind herself. For, even though she had always been known by her father's surname, the name actually written on her birth record was Georgianne Venables *Yardley*, which had been her mother's family name. Painfully aware that this would be the name that would be published in the newspapers, read out in the banns and printed on any marriage certificate, she found it hard to believe that Will could really be as light-heartedly dismissive about the matter as he had seemed to be. She felt sure that his mother would have something to say on the subject—it had, after all, been Viscount Tatler's mother who had insisted on Tatler withdrawing his offer and, although Will had referred to his family as country farmers, she was well aware that they were actually landed gentlefolk, whose social mores were hardly likely to be a great deal different from those of her own circle.

She was still pondering on the pros and cons of her dilemma when she heard Maitland crossing the floor to stand in front of her. She started to rise but, reaching out his hand, he pressed her back on to the bench and took a seat beside her.

'Do you recall that conversation we had about the various habits of swans and other creatures?' he asked as, swinging round to face her, his eyes captured hers.

Unable to tear her glance away, she gave a breathless nod, achingly conscious of the fact that her ability to think straight would be so much easier if he didn't always have this devastating effect upon her senses.

'Well, I seem to remember you remarking on the fact that it always seems to be the female's lot to stand on the sidelines awaiting her fate, whilst the various males of the species battle it out amongst themselves until a victor finally emerges. Do you remember?'

Not entirely sure where this odd conversation could be leading, Georgianne could only reply with another wordless nod.

'Then, if you would, I should like you to pay particular attention to what I am about to say to you.'

Without taking his eyes from hers, he reached across and grasped one of her hands and drew it towards him. 'Now, my love, the thing is this,' he went on, as he gently caressed her fingers, 'whilst I would be perfectly willing to take on any other fellow that you cared to name in order to win you over, I find that I just don't have the strength to keep pitting my wits against stubborn pride and blind prejudice. In one breath, you tell me that you love me and, in the next, that marriage to me is out of the question and, since I have pointed out a good many reasons why this simply isn't so, it would appear that, in this instance, I'm the one who is having to do the standing around and waiting!'

As Georgianne let out a gasp of protest, he put up his hand to still her.

'Just let me finish, my love,' he said. 'It isn't that I object to the waiting, as such, but I just need to know one thing. If you can honestly tell me that you would prefer to spend the rest of your life regretting what might have been, rather than face up to whatever fate or fortune may decide to throw at us in the future, then I will bow out of your life this very minute and never trouble you again. The question is this, sweetheart—do you really want me to admit defeat and give up now or do you love me enough to take the risk? You have to decide, Georgianne—this time the choice is yours!'

Letting go of her hand, he rose to his feet and, his lips tightly compressed, he stepped back, nervously awaiting her answer. There was nothing more he could do now. The rest was up to her.

As she stared up at his tight-lipped countenance, Georgianne found herself unable to think properly and, as the seconds ticked by one by one, she struggled to reach a decision. Then, finally, she gathered up her courage and asked, her voice a tremulous whisper, 'And you're really sure that you are prepared to face up to all the spiteful backbiting, Will?'

Hardly daring to breathe, lest he break the spell, Maitland gave a brief nod. 'Whatever happens, I promise that we'll weather it together,' he assured her, as he desperately fought back the urge to sweep her into his arms and soothe away her fears.

As the faintest glimmerings of hope began to stir in her

breast, huge tears welled up in Georgianne's eyes and she knew that, no matter what difficulties the future might hold in store for them, she loved him too much to let him go. Letting out a little sob, she jumped to her feet and flung herself into his eagerly waiting arms.

'Oh, Will,' she cried, as she felt the warmth of his love enfold her. 'I choose you—I choose you!'

'Thank God for that,' replied Maitland fervently, as he closed his eyes and offered up a silent prayer of gratitude. 'Now, for pity's sake, kiss me before I lose my mind entirely!'

* * * * *